Acclaim for
Flight of the Fox

"Flight of the Fox is an explosively paranoid thriller that pays homage to classics of the genre. Basnight delivers nonstop action and an everyman hero to root for."
— Joseph Finder, *New York Times*
bestselling author of *The Switch*

"Basnight's novel does double duty. It's both a fast-paced and furious thriller, and a thought-provoking commentary on a government gone wild. Read it."
— Reed Farrel Coleman, *New York Times*
bestselling author of *What You Break*

"Gray Basnight has written a clever, inventive, gripping, suspenseful tale that'll have you up nights until you reach the final page. Skillfully weaving fact with fiction, *Flight of the Fox* taps into our worst nightmares about the potential excesses of power."
— Charles Salzberg, author of the award-nominated Henry Swann mysteries and *Second Story Man*

"Flight of the Fox is a quick-paced story that puts you in the passenger seat of a thrilling adventure featuring, cyber and techno villains, and a fight for justice. Great action thriller!"
— Jerri Williams, retired FBI agent
and author of *Pay To Play*

FLIGHT OF THE FOX

ALSO BY GRAY BASNIGHT

The Cop with the Pink Pistol
Shadows in the Fire

GRAY BASNIGHT

FLIGHT OF THE FOX

Down & Out Books
3959 Van Dyke Rd, Ste. 265
Lutz, FL 33558
www.DownAndOutBooks.com

The characters and events in this book are fictitious. Any similarity to real persons, living or dead, is coincidental and not intended by the author.

Cover design by Zach McCain

ISBN: 1-946502-61-8
ISBN-13: 978-1-946502-61-2

"No wonder truth is stranger than fiction.
Fiction has to make sense."
—Mark Twain

"Kill a man's dog, break a man's rules."
—Sam Teagarden

CHAPTER ONE

Monday, June 13, 1938
FBI Headquarters, Washington, D.C.

Dear John,

This is to advise you of a new file entered to the bureau record, fully encrypted, and maintained *only* by me. It's because you are such a naughty boy. It's because of your habit of personally vetting all the strapping new talent that walks (or may be persuaded to confidentially walk) our enlightened side of the street.

This Sunday at Pimlico, I was off placing our bets on the fifth race while you arranged a tryst with that darling Great Dane you transferred in from L.A. Did you think I didn't know? Well I did, as any lover would. I also knew about the leggy Irish Wolf Hound at Belmont and that redheaded boy/man/god just graduated from Quantico with whom you decamped into the limo at Hialeah.

Why? For honor and career, naturally. Yes, my love, this is the bitter voice of mercenary cunning. It is my insurance against termination, transfer, or being dumped as your sweetheart.

Secondly, it shall be an angel to your darker nature, urging caution upon your fondness for risky plots which, though brilliant and always best for the nation, could imperil us all. Yes—*that*—is how devoted I am to you and our bureau.

Ah, love, do not despair. Tonight, we shall enjoy our cocktails in the cool air of the Florida porch while I assure you of my undying devotion.

Yours forever,
CAT

P.S. It shall be encrypted in annual chronological order via our favorite cipher. You recall our pet cipher, don't you, John?

CHAPTER TWO

Monday, March 30, 1981
Adams Morgan, Washington, D.C.

Word of the attempted assassination broke while Mark Trippler and his wife sipped sweet iced tea in their living room. From eleven o'clock that morning, the television was tuned to CBS for *The Price Is Right*, *The Young and the Restless*, and *As the World Turns*. It was during *Search for Tomorrow* that Dan Rather interrupted with news of gunshots fired at President Ronald Reagan. Two minutes later, when the phone rang, Trippler guessed who it was.

"Didja hear the news?"

"Yeah," Trippler sighed. He could tell that the caller was already drunk in mid-afternoon. "I'm watching now with my wife."

"Can you believe it? Twice in three months. First, that punk ponies up on goddamn John Lennon. And now this!"

"Yeah."

"The director was light years ahead of his time."

"Yeah," Trippler sighed again, bored beyond tolerance.

"Hey," the caller shouted, "you don't suppose—"

"Naw," Trippler yelled, cutting off the question he knew was coming. "Don't even think it. Operation Over Easy didn't do Lennon. And it didn't do this one. This is just another crazy-ass loner who's seen too many movies, took too many pills, or didn't take enough pills."

3

"Yeah, yeah, yeah," the drunk caller agreed. "But this sure as hell locks up history. Makes it look like loners did 'em all. That's good, ain't it? Puts us in the clear. Unless the rumor about that goddamn Dear John file is true. Hey, Trippler, you think there's any chance a file really—"

"No," Trippler interrupted again. "Forget it. There is no such file."

"I sure hope not." The caller changed the subject. "Hey, did you get your daughter a post at HQ yet?"

"Yep. They hired her straight out of law school. Give that girl a few years and she'll be promoted to the tenth floor. The sky's the limit for her."

"Fellow retiree?" his wife asked when he hung up.

"Yep. Slade Higgins. He's got every kind of cancer there is. Drinks all day long. From morning to morning. He'll be dead before Easter."

"Oh, too bad." Her eyes were glued to the console color Magnavox. "Well, I'm sorry, but I never liked that one much."

"Me neither. And I worked with him for thirty years."

Trippler was retired from the FBI, but didn't need to be on the job to know that the luckless Reagan shooter would have been a perfect recruit for Operation Over Easy. The poor bastard was an MP. Marginal personality. Capable of employment, marriage, paying the bills, yet brimming with all the schizo markers for being "managed," as the bureau called it. When handled effectively, an MP could be coerced into barbaric criminality. This particular shooter, however, crossed the nutbag barrier without manipulation. All that remained was to fill in the usual blanks: the school that booted him, the parents who cut him off, the job that fired him, the girlfriend who dumped him

"While you were on the phone, they said he was in surgery with a collapsed lung," his wife said. "I sure hope Ronnie's going to be okay."

"Yeah," Trippler said, "I sure hope so too."

CHAPTER THREE

Saturday, July 20, 2019
Sam Teagarden's House, Bethel, NY

Sam Teagarden mistook the tiny drone for a hummingbird.

Sitting on the sundeck near the bird feeder filled with sweet red liquid, he was accustomed to the motorized sounds of ruby-throated visitors. Yet there was something about the revved-up buzz of this particular bird that was not natural. Whatever it was, that unnatural—*something*—drew his attention from the unopened manila envelope at the top of the snail-mail pile he'd picked up at the rural post office an hour earlier. Glancing at the dangling feeder, he saw that the muted mechanical whirr was not coming from a hummingbird at all. It was a compact helicopter about the size of a baseball, hovering just beyond the railing.

His second mistake was to assume it was a toy.

"Well, hello there," Teagarden said. It held steady, as though watching him.

He leaned from the round table to peer through the gaps in the sundeck floorboards. He expected to see the shadowy outline of the boy who lived on the other side of the wooded lot.

"That you, Billy? You down there playing a trick on old Abe?"

Eleven-year-old Billy Carney enjoyed sneaking up, squirting a water pistol, and calling him "Old Abe," because he had a beard similar to President Lincoln.

5

"C'mon up here, Billy. Let's chat some more about the great mysteries of mathematics." But there was no answer. "Hey, Billy the Kid—you down there with your remote control?"

Still no response.

The glare of the afternoon sun made it difficult to see. He scanned the yard's edge and tree line of the adjacent undeveloped lot. No Billy there either.

His voice, however, did cause movement. It awakened Coconut, Teagarden's old and overweight yellow Lab who had the good sense to be lounging in the shade of the screened-in porch adjacent to the sundeck. Hearing his owner call Billy, and knowing perfectly well who Billy was, Coconut rose and lumbered to the screen door where he, too, took interest in the hovering device.

"Oarff." His tone held more idle curiosity than canine threat.

Beyond the railing, the drone appeared to hear Coconut's languid bark and reacted by climbing to a higher angle at the edge of the table's umbrella, shading Teagarden's papers and laptop. It was almost as though it were trying to gain a view without glare.

Teagarden watched it glide back and forth. He saw then that it couldn't possibly belong to Billy Carney because it was certainly no toy. It was a complex device, delicate but substantial, engineered with metal parts affixed by miniature rivets. As a mathematics professor and numerical analyst, he couldn't help admiring its perfect geometry. The body was little more than the open frame of a three-dimensional diamond, nearly like a lighter-than-air box kite. A camera lens hung in the geometric center that looked like a manic little techno-fetus as it feverishly spun 360 degrees. Short twin antennae protruded at the front and a trio of rotor blades held it aloft, each tilting independently to adjust for wind or, in this case, the afternoon sun.

"Oarff," the Labrador complained again, more forcefully

than before, his tail vigorously wagging.

"Don't ask me, Coco, I've got no idea what that thing is." Teagarden stroked his beard. "Some practical joker, I guess. Or maybe the news media are getting ready for the fiftieth anniversary of Woodstock. It's going to be particularly noisy around here with old hippies and eyewitness TV crews for the next few weeks. Reporters will probably want the usual interview with me as the Woodstock baby who was born while Country Joe was singing 'gimme an F, gimme a U, gimme a C, gimme a K.' And all the old hippies will be blasting Hendrix and Santana. So we might as well get used to it, just like I might as well get used to the idea of being half-a-century old."

Teagarden checked that the water bowl on the deck was full and within easy reach for the fifteen-year-old dog, who couldn't walk without severe pain. Unfortunately, for this sweet boy, the time had come. These were their final hours together. Teagarden had a vet appointment in two days from which he'd return home alone. He rubbed his own aching knees, still hurting since the auto accident the previous winter, then rose to open the screen door and admit his beefy dog onto the sundeck.

"C'mon, Coco. If that thing gets in the house it'll try to mate with the microwave. We may never get rid of it."

That's when the drone fired.

Phfft!

Teagarden couldn't know if Coconut jumped to protect his master, or only to smooch. Prior to suffering from crippling arthritis, it had always been the dog's nature to jump and smooch. Besides eating and sleeping, smooching was his favorite activity. When that big dog rose on his hind legs to brace his front paws on the chest of any willing human, he was nearly at face level with all but the tallest people, which allowed willing victims to engage in inter-species exchange of saliva. In this case, when Coconut jumped, it knocked Teagarden a step backward.

A moment later, the drone fired a second time.

Phfft!

And for a second time, without yet realizing it, Teagarden had his best friend to thank for saving his life. Despite his arthritic hips, the dog jumped higher, and took the second round in the back, loudly yelped, gasped for air and fell dead. Teagarden dropped to his knees to cradle his dog at the moment the third round was fired.

Phfft!

Instead of slamming his chest, it struck the cedar clapboard behind him, next to where the first round landed. Whatever type of projectile it was, it released a clear liquid that cauterized the timber, turning it white as it oozed down the wall.

CHAPTER FOUR

He stood in the safety of the main room, looking from the front window.

Coconut lay motionless on the sundeck. The dog's mouth gaped, his pink tongue hung beyond his black lips, the lids were halfway closed on his light gray irises. The entry point of the mini-dart was visible in the yellow fur of his back, near the withers. The poison, or whatever it was, had singed the blond coat with a small dark ring. Inside that ring, white bubbles foamed. As each bubble expanded and burst, it sent a thin mist into the air. Teagarden had never seen death consume a living being so quickly. He'd never heard of a poison capable of inflicting instantaneous termination of life.

In shock, hoping he was having a nightmare but knowing he wasn't, Teagarden stared at the drone that tried to kill him and did kill his dog. It still hovered just beyond the deck railing. The camera, the little techno-fetus inside the diamond frame held motionless, watching him.

Who would do this? More importantly—why?

He had no answers except that he'd been mistaken for someone else. Or it was a vicious crime committed by some sociopath intentionally targeting him.

Wait—that's the answer. It has to be.

It had to be because it was actually possible. Occam's razor, the very definition of logical frugality, says the hypothesis with the fewest assumptions is the correct hypothesis. Put another way, the simplest solution—*is*—the solution.

Teagarden had taught plenty of math prodigies over the years at Columbia University in New York City. Some were true geniuses and many went on to prestigious big ticket jobs with private science or government agencies. One, who was nowhere near the smartest, actually shared a Nobel.

There had been unstable geniuses as well, some of whom threatened him in the past. Therefore, following Occam's razor, it stood to reason that this was an act of revenge for failure to win referral to some government research project, or for his voting against a Ph.D. dissertation. The motive could be as simple as canceling a student's monthly stipend. He occasionally had to do those sorts of things when promising students fell behind or hit their own academic version of the Peter Principle and couldn't rise to the next level. Truth be told—*any*—of those former brilliant students could have evolved into the brilliant sociopath who engineered that devilish thing hovering just beyond the sundeck.

Thankfully, it had not fired a fourth round, which it had plenty of time to do before he escaped into the house. He guessed that meant it had only three rounds loaded into those tiny, forward-facing antennae, which were not antennae at all, but efficiently lethal weapons.

Still shocked at the sight of his dog sprawled dead on the sundeck, he began to catch his breath. Coconut must have sensed the danger. He was a smart boy. So smart, that he probably also knew that his next trip to the veterinarian would be his final outing, and that saving his master's life would be a more honorable exit than taking the doctor's needle.

"Sweet boy," Teagarden whispered. "You knew, didn't you? Maybe this is more honorable. Whatever—*this*—is."

Teagarden forced such thoughts from his mind. There was only one thing to do. He needed to call the police. In the small, though world-famous village of Bethel, that meant calling the sheriff. If he was lucky, a couple of state troopers might be available if they happened to be parked nearby on Route

17B, waiting to catch drivers exceeding the fifty-five limit. Keeping his eyes on the drone, he backed up to the kitchen island in the main room and picked up the old land line phone. When there was no dial tone, surging fear sent his pulse into orbit.

He returned to the front window. His cellphone was on the sundeck table, beside his laptop. But the drone was still there, waiting. Retrieving the phone meant testing his theory that it was incapable of firing another volley. Looking again at the body of his brave dog, he knew it was a theory he would not risk.

There were two additional options: the Toyota Camry in the front driveway and the shotgun in the basement.

Watching the techno-fetus, he backed to the front door on the opposite side of the main room. The drone held steady. The 360-degree eye pivoted within the geometric diamond to follow him. With his back to the front door, Teagarden felt for the knob and slowly opened it.

That's when the second drone fired.

Phfft! Phfft!

It was hovering twenty feet from the entrance, in a direct path between the front porch and the car. Just as he slammed the door, he saw the twin stains of white liquid dripping down the door's front panels at chest level.

That left him only one option.

CHAPTER FIVE

It had been many years since he fired the shotgun.

He'd never been a hunter. But he used to shoot skeet. While in undergraduate school at Chapel Hill, he failed to qualify for the U.S. team at the '92 Olympic Games in Barcelona. At the time, he suspected his age was a handicap because he'd skipped two years of high school and entered college at the age of sixteen. He did win the first backup spot, but there were no dropouts that year, so he never got the go-ahead phone call.

Fighting back fear and tears, he careened from room to room, flinging open doors so forcefully that doorknobs cracked the walls. In the cluttered basement he knew approximately where he'd stored the old shotgun.

The small workshop was illuminated by a single sixty-watt bulb with a pull chain. On first scan, he saw nothing. He pulled down the golf bag. Nothing. He knocked over an upright stack of lumber leaning in the corner. Nothing. He snatched a leather carpenter's apron from a wall hook.

And there it was.

The canvas harness holding the weapon stood upright, behind an old Packard Bell computer, which sat atop an older Kaypro II. He yanked the harness hard, toppling gallon-sized coffee cans filled with nails, screws and pieces of junky hardware, decades of impedimenta that accompanied everything from power tools to picture frames. The old gun looked fine. It was a Remington 1100, twelve-gauge, four-in-one auto-loader, the most popular shotgun in the history of the world. The stock had silly scrollwork fashionable in 1985 when his father bought it for him. The rust at the tip of the barrel had been there when he last fired it.

Now for the shells.

It may have been a crapped-up room, but he never considered it a room full of crap. Everything in it was perfectly useful. He now regretted that sentiment. The shotgun shells, wherever they were, would be easier to find if he'd cleaned out the shop years ago.

He pulled down more coffee cans filled with junk, flipped open boxes and unlatched portable tool chests.

Nothing.

He tugged the hard case that housed a chainsaw and stood on it to reach the upper shelves, frantically pulling at old math books and stacks of spiral notebooks filled with algorithm scribbles for decoding and deciphering, research for his master's degree at George Washington and Ph.D. studies at Columbia.

Still nothing.

His instincts nagged at him to settle down. The only way to find a solution was to be calm, turn inward and let the subconscious whisper the answer. That was the way all great solutions are born. It happens when people are in the shower, waking-up, falling asleep, mowing the grass, jogging. Only when the mind is empty of all competing nonsense, will the voice of atavistic clairvoyance speak loud enough to be heard by the conscious mind.

Teagarden cradled the twelve-gauge in both arms. He narrowed his eyes, trying to think back.

Where would an obsessively cautious man like me hide shotgun shells?

It seemed to take hours. In reality it took seconds. Shotguns shells are dangerous. They're especially dangerous chambered inside a shotgun. That's reason enough to never store them within easy reach of a firearm. Therefore, the safest place to store them in a house was—*nowhere*. They wouldn't be stored here at all. That meant they were outside, in the tiny garden shed with the gabled rooftop that made it look cute, like a gnome's home.

Teagarden hurried to the adjacent laundry room where there was a small window for venting the dryer under the screened-in porch. There wasn't a very good view of the side yard, but it was a better option than the front door. Using the clothes dryer as a foot hoist, he threaded the shotgun through the window, then squirmed out to the crawl space under the long porch where he terrified three chipmunks and a nest-sitting robin.

With the Remington cradled in the crooks of his elbows, he crouched between the wheelbarrow and lawnmower to lean forward and look about. The garden shed stood about forty yards to the left, against the rear fence in the shade of the big willow. The sundeck where Coconut lay dead was above and to the right, in the opposite direction.

From this perspective, nothing seemed out of the ordinary.

He listened intently for the low-pitched techno whirr. It came from above and to the right, the direction of the sundeck. There was no mistaking that sound. It was the same engineered hummingbird buzz of the drone that attacked him minutes earlier.

Then, he heard it again. The second buzz was also in the air above him. But that one came from the left. Then it came again, from the right. Then again, from the left.

As wary as a turtle hiding from sniffing coyotes, he poked his head past the lawnmower for a better look. The sight left no doubt.

There are four of them. Four! And they're circling the house.

CHAPTER SIX

Teagarden pulled his aching knees to his chest and listened to the pace of the orbiting buzz. It was rhythmic, like a musical refrain.

As with the much larger Predator drones that hurl Hellfire missiles, these were remotely controlled. It had to be the case. He wasn't ready to consider extraterrestrials. And it was apparent that when the first drone failed to kill him, the controller sent a back-up to the front door. When that too failed, the floodgate opened. Every hummingbird in the aviary had been released. He assumed that if his theory about firing capacity was correct, the first drone had since been re-armed. That meant a control vehicle was somewhere nearby.

The prickly lettuce and crabgrass weeds that sprouted around him held a vague odor of urine. He wondered if it was his own, but had no inclination to check. It was probably from Coconut's frequent visits under the porch, or the many chipmunks that used the space as a safe highway between their home nest and the bounteous ground under the bird feeder filled with sunflower seeds.

He calculated four drones because the first two were identical. The back-up pair was a little larger, the same design but the size of a softball. They all buzzed at the same steady clip, alternating in opposite directions like asteroids caught in the gravitational pull of a larger body. It meant that no part of the house was without surveillance for more than a second or two. He calculated their spacing. Each whirring sound rose, then faded to silence for perhaps two seconds, before the whirring of the next drone rose from the opposite direction and faded to silence for another two seconds. That didn't give a forty-nine-year-old math professor with bum knees much time to dash forty yards, open a garden shed, find shotgun shells, load at least four into a heavy old Remington twelve-gauge automatic, aim, fire, and—*hope*—he still had what it takes to hit four moving targets.

Moving targets—shit.

Teagarden recalibrated. Clay pigeons were moving targets. These targets were armed with a deadly poison and trying to kill him. They'd already taken out his best friend, now moldering in the afternoon heat on the sundeck.

The garden shed was dirty white with bright red eaves and matching red gables. One corner of the base sunk a little, the result of the latest flash flood, which gave it an antiquated, long-lived appearance. His wife, Kendra, built if from scrap lumber left over when the house was completed. She loved it, painted it, pronounced it a masterpiece, and named it "The Little House of Teagarden." Along with the color and enveloping shade of a nearby willow, the slightly sunken corner made it look more like an authentic gnome's abode than what it really was, a warehouse for rakes, shovels, birdseed—and shotgun shells.

None of it mattered now. There was no way he could make the dash to the shed and blast all four of the orbiting drones. Betting odds are based on numerical averages, and the numerical averages were overwhelming. A twenty-year-old Olympic sprinter couldn't do it. At his age, and with knees still hurting from the auto accident that broke his legs and killed his wife just eight months earlier, there was no way. He didn't stand a chance.

He thought of waiting them out. But that seemed pointless. He wasn't expecting visitors. And for all he knew, there were a dozen more of these things being mobilized by nearby controllers.

He again poked his head out, ever so slightly, from under the porch. He looked just far enough to see them circling, the weaponized antennae of each drone aimed at window level, ready to fire should the cameras detect movement. Teagarden listened for the timing again: clockwise whirr, two seconds; counter-clockwise whirr, two seconds; clockwise whirr, two seconds; then again, counter-clockwise whirr, two seconds.

What—is—happening? This was not on my day's agenda.

That morning had been occupied with his once-a-week summer math class at the local maximum security state pen. He enjoyed working with inmates struggling to earn a high school GED or college credits. It was rewarding work. Teaching math to students genuinely motivated to improve their lives was always rewarding, even if some were murderers. In some ways, it was better than his tenured job at Columbia University where he taught prodigies who planned on becoming the next Einstein so they could discover things like teleportation and molecular manipulation of antimatter.

On the way home from prison that day, he'd stopped at the Bethel Post Office to pick up his mail. The box was crammed, mostly with junk because he'd been in New York City for a few days, attending a math conference at the Marriott Marquis in Times Square. After tending to e-mail and paying bills, the afternoon was supposed to be occupied with baseball on TV and maybe a nap, to be followed by a phone conversation with his daughter at the Naval Air Station at Key West. She would pass the phone to his granddaughter, nicknamed Chopper, with whom he shared a birthday, and who always made him smile because it meant listening to her baby talk. She laughed when she recognized his voice and called out her pet name for him: "Da-Da Tea-Tea…Da-Da Tea-Tea." After that enjoyable afternoon, at some point during the evening, there would be dinner of some sort.

No. *This* wasn't anywhere on his "to do" list.

Crouching under his porch to hide from four buzzing drones

that spit deadly poison was definitely not a planned part of his day. Neither was being killed by one of these micro-monsters.

His knees ached. He leaned back to let his butt rest on the deck of the lawnmower. There was barely enough space to sit on his ankles, but then, he hadn't been able to do that since the accident. He wanted to weep for poor Coconut, yet dare not risk being heard by the circling drones, though he was uncertain if they had actual hearing. That first drone did seem to react when Coconut barked.

He scanned the underside of the screened-in porch. Old spider webs and wasp nests from previous years needed to be cleaned out. The support beams needed re-staining. The mama robin he scared away had built her home on a low cross-beam. From his crouching position, he could make out the rounded edges of three soft-blue eggs cradled inside the nest. The underside of the porch floor still held a rosy glow. It was redwood from Oregon. His wife designed the house based on a plan she saw in a magazine. She too had been a professor at Columbia. Kendra's subject was American history. Her book, *The Greatest American*, about Ben Franklin, had been a best-seller and short-listed for a Pulitzer, no surprise to anyone who knew her.

The drones droned, searching for their target. Right, left; right left. Right, left; right left.

Who put in an order for this? Some psycho genius who didn't get a full scholarship? Some pissed off candidate for the annual Randolph Honor who got passed over and blames me?

Whoever it was, he or she at that moment was most likely sitting nearby in a van looking at an array of video consoles with a game control. Probably a game control in each hand.

That's it—enough.

No more thinking about his dog, deceased wife, daughter, or granddaughter. And no more speculation about who was behind this, or why.

Focus. Focus!

Teagarden considered his options, but quickly realized he had none. Therefore, he had to create his own. The only way to do that was to invent a distraction, something that would draw all four orbiting drones from their circling vigil. In the movies, someone would simply toss a rock.

Yeah, right.

That's when he noticed the wire.

CHAPTER SEVEN

It was a newly strung coaxial television cable.

The cord was connected to a satellite dish loosely clipped to the sundeck railing. The installer left it rigged in a makeshift position the previous Monday, and departed with everything functioning. It allowed Teagarden to pick up his baseball games better than regular cable service and at a cheaper price, which was why he made the switch. The installer was supposed to return on Tuesday to scale the roof and secure the dish on the southern gable of the house. Afterward, he would tack down the wire along the eaves and bury the rest up to the point where it entered the house. Then came a call explaining he wouldn't be in the area again for a week.

That was routine.

The town of Bethel wasn't convenient to the sellers of goods and services requiring home delivery. It was off the beaten path for half-a-million hippies in 1969, and it was still isolated five decades later. The nearest shopping mall was sixty miles away, the local mini-hospital was more of an infirmary staffed by nurses, and there was one pharmacy in a twenty-mile radius. If there was a foot of snow, which was often, a delivery of heating oil required days of advance planning.

Teagarden looked back at the wire's entry point into the house. It was a caulked-up hole in the concrete directly under the laundry room window he'd just scampered from. Between that point and the satellite dish, the loose wire lay atop the ground. It stretched around the house, and draped limply over the deck railing to the dish.

That was it. It was his only way to create a diversion. If it worked, it might draw all four drones to the clamor. And that might buy him enough time to hustle in the opposite direction toward the garden shed.

All right, just get on with it. No point overthinking it.

Teagarden's knees creaked as he shifted to a squatting position. He gripped the loose cable with both hands and pulled gently, taking out as much play as he dared. Too much and he risked the drones noticing movement. Too little, and it could take too long to reel it in before dislodging the dish.

He waited.

He slowly tugged again to ease out a little more play in the line.

He waited.

He tugged again.

The quickly moving shadows of the drones passed by in the afternoon sun. Clockwise whirr, two seconds; counter-clock-wise whirr, two seconds. He tugged again. Clockwise whirr, two seconds; counter-clockwise whirr, two seconds. He tugged again.

Finally, the wire tightened to a point where he heard the distant sound of rubber pulling taught against the deck railing. That was it. He dare not pull any tighter.

Teagarden coiled the loose wire around his palms. He flexed his shoulders. Clockwise whirr, two seconds; counter-clockwise whirr…

"Urmph…"

In the next two seconds he yanked hard, hand-over-hand, fist-over-fist, hand-over-hand. It took more than two seconds. It may have taken five full seconds. However long it took, it worked. The dish dislodged with a noisy crash, first to the sundeck flooring, then it dragged up and over the railing before smashing to the bluestone boulders fifteen feet below.

Did it draw the attention of all four drones? He couldn't

be certain. If he looked out to investigate, it would eat up all the time he'd just created. So he bolted. He dashed from under the porch to the garden shed as fast as he could go, cradling the shotgun as he ran.

So far, so good. That much is obvious because I'm still alive.

The shed door creaked loudly when he yanked it open.

That's bad.

He quickly found the box. It was on a shelf, wedged between fertilizer stakes and carpenter ant poison.

Still no buzzing sounds from behind. That's good.

He one-handed the box, looking over his shoulder as he inserted first one, then two, then—he dropped the third.

Shit!

He grabbed a fourth shell and managed to insert it when the buzz of the first drone arrived. It came from the front of the house, immediately followed by the techno-whirr of a second drone zooming from the opposite side, past the screened-in porch on the same path he'd just run.

That was it. He was out of time.

The shotgun was loaded with three shells, but he still had to release the bolt to chamber the first shell before he could fire. The drones quickly found him and headed straight for the red and white gnome's home. Teagarden stood erect in the short doorway, he leaned slightly forward in a proper shooter's stance, released the bolt, aimed and fired—twice.

BLAM, BLAM!

He did it. Both drones shattered mid-trajectory. The way they blew apart was not unlike a clay pigeon, except there was no dust cloud. The drones exploded into hundreds of miniature pieces of metal. It looked phony, like a CGI special effect in the movies.

There was no time to celebrate. The other two drones were right behind the first two. Worse, he had only one shell remaining in the Remington. Teagarden pulled the shed door closed. He felt behind him for the box, and loaded one additional shell. His next move was instinctive, but from what instinct he had no idea. He leaned against a garden rake hanging upside down, the metal teeth poked him in the neck as he kicked the door open. The nearest drone immediately fired into the empty doorway.

Phfft! Phfft!

The twin smears hit the back wall of the shed, just above the carpenter ant poison. Teagarden stepped into the doorway, smoothly assumed a shooter's stance, and fired.

BLAM, BLAM!

And that was it. He'd done it. The second pair of drones exploded where they hovered between the house and the garden shed.

CHAPTER EIGHT

He stood next to his beloved Coconut.

"What do you mean, it'll take 'a while'? How long of 'a while' is a—*while*? That's bullshit," he shouted into his cellphone. "And stop telling me to calm down. They attacked my house!"

"Sir, our nearest trooper is handling a serious auto-accident with injuries. He's about fifteen miles from you. He has your address and will arrive soon."

He paused to take a breath. He shouldn't have been nasty with the dispatcher. She was only doing as she'd been trained. Dispatching a cop on an emergency basis for model helicopters was not in her playbook. A justifiable emergency involved real people, real injuries, a dead body, a man with a gun, shots fired, threat to life or property, or at the very least—trespassers. To her way of thinking, remote-controlled flying toys sounded like a nuisance complaint.

Standing on the sundeck, Teagarden forced himself to look at Coconut. The sadness of the image helped to calm his frantic state. He realized that he'd completely failed to convey the seriousness of his situation. He'd been so emotional with the dispatcher that he was nearly monosyllabic.

That was stupid. He had a Ph.D. in advanced mathematics. Yet all he'd told her was that his house was under attack by remote-controlled drones. No wonder. She had no idea what actually happened and understandably assumed he was nuts.

He was set to try again, including telling her that his dog

had been killed, when he saw the truck. It was small and boxy, moving slowly beyond the trees on a secondary road through the woods. The side panels bore wording he couldn't make out. He returned to the phone.

"Uh, now there's a truck on the road." The dispatcher paused to assimilate the information.

"A truck, sir?"

"Never mind. What about the sheriff's office?"

"Sheriff Klumm is unavailable right now," the dispatcher said. "Sir, Trooper Blaubach is the nearest law enforcement officer capable of responding. Please be patient. He'll be in transit shortly."

Teagarden watched the truck. It was barely moving just beyond the trees as though it were stalking something. It turned onto another secondary road.

"You know," he said, "when you kill a man's dog, you break a man's rules." He didn't know where that statement came from. It was as though someone else said it. The voice was flat and calm, a stark contrast to the way he'd spoken a moment before.

"Sir?" the dispatcher asked.

The truck glided past the house where Billy Carney lived on the other side of the wooded lot and came to a stop.

"Sir, please repeat that. Did you say your dog was killed by remote controlled airplanes?"

No one got out of the truck. It just sat there. It stopped where he could see it through an opening in the woods. It was the right-of-way for the power line, which cut through everything and crossed all highways from Buffalo to New York City. The truck was gray, about ten feet long, with big tires, and discreet white lettering on the side.

"Uh, helicopters," Teagarden said.

"Excuse me?"

"Not airplanes. Remote controlled helicopters. Very small. They killed my dog. I think he knew a final vet trip was close.

He jumped to save my life. I shot them down. Like skeet. Blam, blam. All four."

There was a pause before the dispatcher responded. He was speaking more calmly now, but he sensed he was still not rational.

"You fired at them, sir?"

"Uh-huh."

"So you are armed. Is that right, sir?"

Teagarden glanced at his old twelve-gauge Remington automatic where he left it, next to the laptop on the deck table. Before exiting the garden shed he'd reloaded it with four more shells just in case.

"Uh-huh."

He heard the dispatcher furiously typing. He could guess why. She was probably updating the previous communication with Trooper Blowback, or whatever his name was, to include the words, "proceed with caution, complainant is armed, emotionally unstable, possibly dangerous."

"All right. And what are the helicopters doing now, sir?"

"Can I ask you a question?"

"Yes, sir."

"Why would that truck stop in the only spot where he had a direct line-of-sight with my front deck?"

"Sir?"

Teagarden did not wait for her to respond. He dove to the floorboards, landing eyeball to eyeball with the dead Coconut, whose languid pink tongue was already turning gray from rigor mortis. The timing was close. He had dropped just as the whizzing bumble-bee whipped past, snapping a small hole in the window pane behind him. A microsecond later, sound caught up with speed, and he heard the muffled report. It was a type of underwater *burp* that came from the direction of the truck.

This time, there was no doubt about what happened. It was not mysterious. He knew he'd just been shot at by a real man, holding a real rifle, which fired a real bullet, which was intended to make him real dead.

Still gripping his cellphone, he dove onto the screened-in porch, then crashed through the screen and dropped onto the side yard. On the ground, he sprinted straight for the cover of the neighboring woods.

CHAPTER NINE

With his lousy knees, it was more of a labored than a true sprint, but fortunately he made it into the woods without being taken down by whoever wanted him dead.

He'd had enough. First it was drones, then an obtuse 9-1-1 dispatcher, and now a sniper. Never a big fan of cursing, once he was well within the tree line, he began a litany of profanity as he lurched through the undergrowth. With every surge of knee pain it was: "shit, shit, shit." Every turn of the ankle was: "goddammit, goddammit, goddammit." Every scraped arm on a tree branch was: "fuck, fuck, fuck." It went that way for several minutes. He crashed through the woods alternately kneeling, ducking, tripping and shouting: "shit, goddammit, fuck; shit, goddammit, fuck."

He was moving in a generally northern direction. That was fine because it was the opposite direction from the truck with the sniper. Other than that, he had no idea where he was going, where he'd emerge from the woods, or if he'd emerge at all. Nothing was certain. This was Sullivan County, where unexplored virgin forest and the Catskill Mountains go on for many scores of miles. It was nearly like the land beyond, beyond. Much of the terrain was impassable because bluestone slate erupted everywhere in slabs as large as houses. Every tree in the woods had to grow around it or push up under it, which posed a danger of precipitous drops, mini-cliffs coated with moss where the slightest stumble could result in broken bones. Having already survived a car crash that broke both legs at the knees, he did not care to repeat the experience. And at night—forget it. Not even hunters ventured through these woods after dusk, except four-legged predators. In the woods of Sullivan County, the coyotes owned the night.

He passed mostly aging poplar trees, young fir, and stout cherry. At a copse of tall pines, Teagarden stopped to rest in the soft needles. He sat down on an eruption of bluestone and checked his cellphone. Despite being in the wilderness where bird calls and his own exhausted panting were the only sounds, he still had a powerful cell signal. All five bars were solid.

Thank God for cell towers on hilltops.

During the run, he'd decided on his next move. While getting his breath, he looked up the name and pressed autodial.

"'Lo."

"Hey, Billy, it's Old Abe the math teacher from across the woods. How's my boy prodigy doing this afternoon?"

"'Kay. What's up, Old Abe?" Teagarden wondered how he could answer that question and decided it was best not to try.

"Hey, Billy, you still have those binoculars?"

"Sure. Used 'em to watch a red-tailed hawk this morning. He was perched on that big oak in the wooded lot. The other birds didn't want him there, so they teamed up, made a lot of noise, and ran him off. It was cool. Didja see it?"

"Afraid I missed it, Billy."

"'Kay. I'll call if he comes back."

"Sounds good. Listen, Billy, if you're not too busy, I've got a favor to ask."

"'Kay."

"I want you to take your binoculars and go up into your tree house where you can see my driveway and front yard. Watch what's going on for a few minutes. Then call me and tell what me you see."

"Sure. But I can do better than that. I got the new camera relay program. It's called 'lens-to-lens networking.' It turns my cellphone camera into a viewable remote. I can dial you in, then you can see on your phone whatever the camera on my phone is focused on."

"Billy, you're a regular techno wizard."

"Not really. I just pushed the download button. It's a new app."

"Well anyway it sounds like a good plan. But listen, Billy, don't go beyond your own yard and treehouse. Okay? There may be some nasty men at my house, former math students of mine who're super mad at me for flunking them out of school. So you just stay on your side of the wooded lot. Got it? Stay in your yard."

"'Kay. That's cool. I'll call ya back."

Teagarden hung up. He scanned a line of thick woods from his resting spot under the pines. Traipsing through them had been noisy. He guessed that if anyone followed him, he'd be able to hear them coming. At the moment, there was only silence. On any normal day, he'd consider that peaceful, and therefore enjoyable. But this was no ordinary day. And thanks to the last half-hour of his life, it was anything but peaceful.

He plotted the next few minutes. After Billy called back, he'd phone 9-1-1 again. Then he'd phone Sheriff Klumm. He didn't know the sheriff personally, but he and Kendra met him once at a local town council meeting. Besides being sheriff, his family owned the local Gas-n-Get station where they occasionally exchanged greetings. That was typical of most locals. If you weren't a retiree, a weekender from New York City, or Hasidim summering at one of the secluded Hasidic Jewish colonies, then you probably ran some sort of back-up business. There was no local industry to speak of. And in Bethel, the only notable attraction was the museum and amphitheater built on the site of the Woodstock Music Festival. But there was plenty of land. For most, the family back-up business was connected to the land. Sometimes it was lumber, sometimes hay, or harvesting bluestone, but most often it was pastureland for grazing cows. Cows were easy.

After explaining the situation to Sheriff Klumm, maybe he could return to his house. But only if they'd arrested a suspect. It would happen only if he could retrace his steps back through the woods. Otherwise, they'd have to triangulate his cellphone to find him and escort him out.

Billy's callback was prompt.

"Is your A/C broke?" he asked in a whisper.

"No."

"Your furnace?"

"Nope. That's not broken either."

"Well then, why is Harry at your house?"

"Who's Harry?"

"Dunno. But I guess he's the man who owns Harry's Heating and A/C Repair Service. That's what it says on the side of the truck parked at your house."

"A boxy, gray, ten-footer with big tires?"

"Yep. And funny thing about Harry."

"What's that?"

"He's more interested in your backyard than your furnace. What'd you do to it?"

"To my backyard? Nothing. Why?"

"Since when do heating repairmen need a leaf blower? Hey, wait a minute. Hold on, I'm going to put the phone down for a sec." Teagarden pictured Billy in his treehouse adjusting his binoculars. After a moment, he came back to the phone. "Oh, my mistake," he said, still whispering. "It's not a leaf blower. It's a vacuum cleaner. He's vacuuming your yard. Hang on. Okay, now he's going up to your front deck."

"Billy, what about that new app of yours?"

"Oh yeah. Hold on, I'll key you in. But the resolution won't be so hot. I've got my best tech people working on that."

Teagarden anxiously watched the cellphone cradled in his palm. After a moment, the bright green image of Billy Carney's name and phone number went dark. When the phone fluttered back to life, it had grainy, shaky video of his house and yard. It was like watching a distant ship at sea through a cheap telescope. He could make out a man descending the sundeck steps carrying what looked like his laptop and shot-gun. Whenever Billy's hand moved, the video broke up, turning it into digital cubism before settling back into the barely distin-guishable image of his split-level A-frame house in the woods.

"Billy, pan a little to the left, will you?"

"'Kay."

"That's it. Hold it steady, will you?"

"'Kay."

Billy was right. He could make out an industrial sized hose draping from the back of that truck with big tires.

Uh-oh.

Teagarden knew what that grainy video meant. Harry had vacuumed the splattered drones that left bits of broken metal all over the backyard. That's when he realized something else. Something bad.

"Uh, Billy?"

"What's up, Old Abe?"

"It just occurred to me. You can't see my backyard from your treehouse."

"Nope."

"Umm, Billy?"

"Yeah?"

"Where are you?"

"Well, Old Abe, it's like this, I circled around. I'm in the woods between your driveway and the road."

"And that's why you're whispering? Because if you spoke any louder, he might hear you?"

"Yep."

"Uh, Billy, that's really not good. I told you…"

"No worries," he interrupted. "This is fun. I like it."

Teagarden couldn't decide if he should tell Billy to quickly circle back and go home the same way he came, or just hunker down and stay hidden until the cops showed up. Before he could make a decision there came a series of odd noises that sounded like a football scuffle at the line of scrimmage.

"Billy? Billy is that you? You okay?"

"Uhh…uhh…uhh…Old Abe, I, uhh…uhh…"

Billy was trying to talk. But he seemed out of breath, as though he were running.

Uh-oh, that must be it. He was panting while running. Oh Jesus, he must have been spotted, so he took off.

"Yeah, Billy. I'm here," Teagarden shouted, sitting on the bluestone sofa. "Can you hear me? Billy, talk to me. Talk—no, no wait. On second thought, don't talk to me. Run. Run, Billy. Can you hear me? *Run!*"

"Uhh…uhh…uhh…"

BLAM, BLAM!

After a moment, another voice came on the line.

"Hello?"

"Yeah, hello," Teagarden said.

"Why did you do that?" It was a man's voice, calm and smug.

"Do what?" Teagarden demanded. "Who the hell is this?"

"You know what you did. Why did you do it?"

"Yeah, okay, asshole. Why don't you just tell me what it is I did? Then maybe we'll have a chat."

"You just blew away that kid while he was running through the woods," the voice said. "Two shots to the head with your shotgun. You killed him. Why did you do that?"

Teagarden let the cellphone fall away from his ear. He looked up beyond the pine trees as a red-tailed hawk flew over, its wings stretched wide to glide blissfully upon the warm summer air.

CHAPTER TEN

Saturday, July 20, 2019
Encrypted Field Communication
CoinTelSatOrbit53/NSA Apache Code Ofc Baltimore, MD

<apache code initiate>

TO: deep field cmdr
FROM: ice skater

SUBJECT: operation dear john

<secure field communication may begin>

ice skater to deep field cmdr: target escaped...4/pcs hardware down...total loss...clean-up complete...fox in woods...have advanced grant of supreme authority to make target publicly wanted murderer of local boy...pls coordin w/local auth on that...am in pursuit...

deep field cmdr to ice skater: acknowledged...will begin coordin w/local police...maintain supreme authority on target...and, your bill for 4/pcs of hardware now in mail...

ice skater to deep field cmdr: har-har...ice skater out...

CHAPTER ELEVEN

Sunday, July 21, 2019
The Woods of Sullivan County, NY

The balance of the afternoon was a prolonged walk on Queer Street.

Teagarden knew the voice on the phone had spoken truthfully. There was something about it that made him realize Billy Carney really was dead. He turned off his cellphone. Then, he turned himself off. He disconnected from himself. It was as though his mind uncoupled, leaving him without his personality, a boxer standing in the ring with no idea where he was, what he was doing, or why his opponent continued to throw punches.

It was partly because the death of his wife was still brutally fresh. Moments after the accident the previous November, he was barely conscious but he could see her body sitting next to him, behind the wheel, her head crushed. Now, an eleven-year-old boy was dead. For a man still healing both physically and emotionally, it was too much.

He sat on a large outcropping of bluestone for hours. At dusk, he stood and wandered about the evergreens. In the moonlight, their limbs appeared both sheltering and diabolic. And there were critters scurrying in the shadows: chipmunks, raccoons, groundhogs, the occasional black squirrel, and deer. The white-tailed deer always paused to watch, then ran as he approached. When exhaustion set in, he bedded down in a V-shaped alcove of bluestone slate held in place by cool earth. If he were a bear, it would be a perfect bed for the night.

Hours later, when he opened his eyes to the morning sun, he saw the opossum. It was perched six feet away on a fallen tree trunk, staring down at him. It studied him the way a sobered woman studies a stranger in her bed the next morning, trying to remember who he was. In the slanting glare, the creature's nostrils flared in and out. It reminded him of a sophomore he dated in Chapel Hill undergraduate school, whose rabbit nostrils always quivered. It made her appear suspicious of everything, even the choice of dinner vegetables in the cafeteria. At the other end of the opossum was that odd-looking tail, just as naked and pink as a human umbilical cord.

Teagarden's head gradually cleared while regarding the strange animal. He understood that he was back, that it was Sunday morning, and that his personality had re-assimilated from its fugue state.

He stood, stretched, rubbed his eyes, and scratched his mosquito bites. He couldn't remember much of the night, but he recollected everything about the previous day, right up to the moment the man's voice came through the phone. Then he pictured Billy Carney's dead body and he began to cry.

Who would want to harm that boy? And who would want a college mathematics professor dead so badly they'd kill an eleven-year-old boy just to get to him? It makes no sense that an embittered former student would be that demented with anger, that consumed with vengeance.

The opossum remained on the log, staring at the human intruder of his home. Teagarden turned his cellphone on. It quickly vibrated with an incoming call, yet the stubborn animal did not move. He pushed the connect button, but did not speak.

"Hello? Hello?" the voice said. "That you, Mr. Teagarden?"

Teagarden knew it was not the same voice that accused him of murdering Billy Carney. He would never forget the sound of that particular voice. Still, he did not speak.

"Okay, this is Sheriff Curt Klumm," the voice continued. "Listen, we've got a real mess out here. Now, you need to come on in Mr. Teagarden. There's no point in trying to get away after all this. As a college professor down there in the big city, you're smart enough to know that. Anybody as smart as you knows better than to play the odds on this thing."

The opossum shifted slightly. Its pink rat-like tail wrapped around its body in the way of a house cat when it settles down for prolonged surveillance. Teagarden remained silent. He cradled the phone in his neck for a two-handed scratch of his worst mosquito bites, including three large bumps on his neck.

"Talk to me, Mr. Teagarden. I'm ready to help you on this. But you do have to come in so we can figure this thing out. We've got a bad mess over here at your house."

"Are the men in the truck with you?" Teagarden said, breaking his silence.

"Truck?" Klumm asked. He paused to think. "Oh yeah, now look, Mr. Teagarden, I've heard your nine-one-one call. I understand you're not feeling too good. You need help, and we're going to get it for you. I promise you that."

"So the drone men are not with you?"

"Mr. Teagarden, I'm at my office up the road from your house in Bethel. I've got a couple of state troopers with me and my deputy. And when you come in, we'll take you down to the courthouse in Monticello. I'll have a doctor there waiting to help you. So you just tell me where you are, and I'll come on over."

The opossum's black eyes held steady. Teagarden looked beyond the creature, to the woods.

"I don't know where I am."

"I understand," Sheriff Klumm said. "Now that's not at all surprising. You just tell me what you see. Give me a street sign, a number, or a landmark. Whatever you've got, and we'll work with it."

"Opossum."

"How's that?"

"There's an opossum. That's what I'm looking at. A Virginia opossum. It's odd looking. Did you ever stop to think how strange looking the opossum really is? It's like a cross between a house cat and a rat."

He could hear Klumm muffling the phone in his hand to speak to someone in the room. He couldn't hear every word, but he did hear "...worse than...fuckin' brain snap...p-h-d.... helicopter drones...goddamn opossum..." He made a throat-clearing noise as he put the phone back to his ear.

"All right now, Mr. Teagarden. I just need to ask you to look around and give me a little more than that. Now, I know you can do it."

Suddenly, the opossum twitched defensively for no apparent reason. An instant later, it turned and scurried down the fallen tree trunk where it jumped into thick undergrowth and disappeared. Teagarden strained to see what had spooked the animal, but there was nothing. He listened. There were no crunching noises in the woods, nothing to indicate the approach of another animal, or of men.

"Hello?" Klumm's voice called out.

A moment later, Teagarden heard what panicked the opossum, though not from any direction in the woods. It was coming from the sky. There were two of them, and this time, they were not drones. They were helicopters. Real helicopters. They were flying low, just above the treetops. Teagarden put the phone back to his ear.

"Hey, Klumm."

"Yes, sir, Mr. Teagarden?"

"It's a setup. You hear me, Klumm? They killed Billy and they're trying to kill me, too. Some man named Harry."

"Now, Mr. Teagarden, I know you're not feeling very—"

But Teagarden did not wait to hear the Sheriff's response. He disconnected the call and turned off his phone. Afterward, he dropped back into the V-shaped alcove formed by blue-stone slate and watched as the helicopters, having lost his cell signal, wandered out of sight.

CHAPTER TWELVE

It made sense to wait, but not long.

He guessed he was on the phone with Sheriff Klumm long enough for them to ping only his general location. It meant that men would be canvasing the woods on foot, possibly with dogs.

After a few minutes, Teagarden left his cozy alcove, took a reading on the sun as best he could, and began hiking north. It was the direction he felt confident would eventually lead to Route 17, the main state highway that cut through the lower Catskill Mountains. If he got lucky, maybe he could hitch a ride out of the county.

The first of two favorable encounters along the way was a flowing stream filled with clean, ice-cold mountain water where he washed and drank. The second was a tractor path that led to a decaying apple orchard. Judging from the amount of deer and bear scat, and the visibly poor health of the trees, the orchard was long untended.

"Okay, let's go pick breakfast," he said, talking to himself for the comfort of hearing a friendly voice.

His casual brown shoes looked more like the dirty leather of a hobo, still he took care not to soil them further with animal dung. Finding one tree brimming with life, he pulled at the branches.

"You're a happy survivor of a dead New York State industry." He plucked two red apples that looked like passable McIntosh.

While eating the fruit, he returned to the wooded tractor path. It was overgrown, brimming with prickly bushes, but the bluestone had been bulldozed, which made for easier hiking. When the wooded path finally emerged at a road, the result was not a four-lane highway as hoped, but a short dirt road that dead-ended in one direction and T-boned at a narrow paved road about two hundred yards in the other direction.

He stepped from the tractor path, onto the dirt road. It was flanked on both sides by ramshackle huts hiding behind bushy undergrowth and dilapidated fencing. There were two signs nailed to the old fence. The first one read: Zabłudów Boulevard.

Teagarden took it to be someone's idea of a joke, probably a sentiment pertaining to the old country, either Poland or Russia, maybe Ukraine. A few feet beyond there was a second sign in Hebrew and English: שֶׁבֶט קיץ - Keep Out.

A third sign farther up was nailed to an arching birch tree: Camp Summer Shevat - Parking to Right.

That explained it. The wooden sheds were a summer getaway colony where Hasidic Jews vacationed. The Catskills were once known as the Borscht Belt, where the famous Jewish resorts were located. They're all gone now. Even that movie *Dirty Dancing*, about kids at a Sullivan County resort, had to be filmed in North Carolina. Many say the resorts were killed by television and affordable airfare to Miami and Vegas. But none of that stopped the ultra-Orthodox. They were coming to these small, privately owned religious camps in Sullivan County before anyone ever heard of Henny Youngman or Rodney Dangerfield. And they're still escaping to their homestead hideaways to beat the summer heat of Brooklyn. He'd never seen or heard of this particular camp, but that was no surprise. Neither had he ever been down this dead-end road, wherever it was.

He walked to the intersection at the opposite end, eyeing the late morning sky for more helicopters and the ramshackle bungalows for movement. There was nothing. Not a soul in sight. Except for noisy crows in the tree limbs, there wasn't a sound. The small parking area at one end of the bungalows held only a single vehicle, a rusting Toyota Sienna van with two flat tires.

"No. It can't be." He stood in the lonely intersection shaded by arching greenery. "It's not possible," he shouted.

What alarmed him loomed a half-mile in the distance. It was a giant parking lot. What's more, he knew it was just one of many giant parking lots linked by a circular road that looped farther in the distance. It meant he was only about a mile from the Bethel Woods Arts Center, where the amphitheater and museum now stood on the grounds of the old Woodstock Music Festival where he was born while Country Joe was on stage in 1969. And *that* meant he was only a half-mile from his own split-level A-frame house.

"*Very* odd," he said aloud.

Teagarden could practically see the hillside where he was prematurely born in a makeshift tent to a mother laying on her back in the muddy earth as if she were a member of an enormous tribe of hunter-gatherers. He was never certain of the precise spot. His mom could say only that it was halfway up the hill and to the right of the stage.

"But how?!"

There was only one explanation. It was the simplest, yet most complicated shape in all geometry—the circle. While semi-conscious the night before, he must have wandered south, not north. He sensed that he'd walked several hours in the dark. But however long or far, he'd basically retraced that same distance since sunrise.

Circles will do that. As simple as they are, they're the stuff of legendary mystery. The great mathematician Archimedes died while trying to understand them. When the Romans came to kill him, he pointed to his chalk etchings and told them, "Do not disturb my circles." A soldier accommodated the demand by running him through the gut with a sword.

"My own nighttime circle around my birthplace is going to be the end of me too, if I don't get off this road," he mumbled.

He rounded the fence and ducked into the bushes fronting the nearest bungalow. Being that close to his own house meant Sheriff Klumm and his men were nearby and possibly patrolling every wooded pathway. It likely also meant that Harry was nearby, doing the same.

Moments later, when two vehicles careened down the paved country road, he raced to the nearest bungalow, found the rickety main door unlocked, hurried inside and closed it behind him. Crouching behind a window, he watched with grim disappointment as neither vehicle drove on toward the huge museum parking lot. They both turned onto tiny Zabłudów Boulevard to enter the ramshackle compound of Camp Summer Shevat.

CHAPTER THIRTEEN

His luck, if it could be called luck, was holding out.

He watched from the window just long enough to see that it was not Sheriff Klumm with his state troopers who wanted to arrest him for the murder of eleven-year-old Billy Carney. Nor was it Harry in his truck with his drones and sniper rifle who wanted to kill him for reasons unknown and who *did* kill Billy Carney.

Oh Lord, why that sweet boy and not me?

Instead, the arrivals were residents of the camp, the actual owners of the bungalows. Between the two vans, there were seven or eight people, including at least one child, all dressed in traditional heavy black clothing of Hasidic Judaism. The men were carrying heavily laden bags from a shopping outing at Walmart and Home Depot.

Teagarden considered the risk. He guessed they were two, maybe three families. With twelve huts, six on each side of overgrown Zabłudów Boulevard, the odds were with him. There were three chances in twelve, or basically one in four that someone would enter the bungalow he'd chosen as a hide-away. That wasn't bad. Just the same, he tip-toed to the small second room to see if there was a backdoor.

There was not.

Now what? If they entered this particular bungalow he had only one choice: *Sorry, I guess I walked in the wrong cabin. No worries. I'll be on my way now. Mazel tov. Have a good day.*

That wouldn't work very well. Neither would asking for

their help if Sheriff Klumm had publicly made him a wanted fugitive.

He lingered in the doorway of the backroom, listening anxiously as the arrivals moved on to other bungalows. There was little talk, except one man who spoke irritably in Yiddish to someone who did not respond. As the families separated, there were subdued farewells, mostly among the women.

Okay, that too is good. They're not coming in here.

He turned again to the back room. There may not be a rear exit, but there was something else, something potentially helpful. It was an old Compaq computer sitting on the floor under a rickety corner table. He sat down and booted up the box and the ancient picture tube monitor.

He needed to risk logging on. While looking at the opossum and regretting his call to Billy Carney, he figured that whoever was trying to kill him with drones would try to communicate with him online. It meant they'd be monitoring his online address, hoping to pinpoint his whereabouts. Anyone with the sophistication to use deadly remote controlled drones smaller than a grapefruit and track his cell signal, must also be able to track his web usage. They'd probably try to stretch the communication by baiting him in some way.

The old desktop was not password protected.

Yet another break.

First he cruised news sites. There was nothing about him on the local or national news sites.

Nothing—*yet.*

That would change before the day was over. He knew because of what he found on the website of the local newspaper. It was little more than a blurb:

The Bethel Bugle has learned that Sheriff Curt O. Klumm is investigating the sudden death of 11-year-old William Carney, son of Terrence and Julia Carney, who work at Sullivan General Hospital in Monticello. No other details are known.

That said it all. He'd soon be a fugitive known to every law enforcement officer in the state.

Billy was a good kid. He wanted to cry again, but didn't. He needed to learn as much as he could, as fast as he could. It was now apparent that he was *not* up against a pissed-off former Ph.D. candidate who couldn't make the grade. Angry ex-students wouldn't feel obligated to create a complicated cover such as "Harry's Heating."

Okay, I've established who they aren't. That leaves me no idea who they actually are.

He stared at the dusty gray screen. It was about the size of the old black-and-white picture tube television his grandparents had through the '70s.

Then he did it.

He logged in to his e-mail. He had no idea if just logging on was enough to initiate a GPS trace, but assumed it was, so he resolved to make it quick, and depart.

There were six e-mails in his inbox.

Three of them were bill notices: the power company, the phone company, and the bridge and tunnel agency that automatically charged his credit card on file to upgrade his toll pass.

There was one e-mail from his daughter in Key West, with a time/date posting just an hour old. The subject line read: *Saying Hello.* That was good. She normally had Sundays off from the naval air station. It meant that she and his granddaughter were home and that both were fine.

Two messages were from friends, one new and one old. Cynthia Blair was the woman he'd dated a few times since spring. He last saw her the previous week while in the city for the math conference and had not been in contact since. She was a beautiful woman. A defense lawyer for an insurance company who'd recently separated from her husband. They hit it off well. They hit it off so well that it was unsettling for him. He was uncertain whether he was ready for another relationship.

The other message was from Bruce Kasarian, the colleague from Columbia who'd introduced him to Cynthia, thinking they'd be a good match.

He was right. They were a good match. He'd had dinner with Kasarian the night after last week's date. Kasarian wouldn't let it alone, he wanted to know if his matchmaking hunches were on target.

"Cynthia's nice, isn't she?" Kasarian kept asking. "Did you like her? Did you take her back to your apartment? Did you have sex?"

Oh brother, it was like being a frat boy all over again. Yes, Bruce, the answers are: yes, yes, no, and, yes. The one "no" answer was only because they hadn't gone to his uptown co-op apartment near the university. He'd spent no time there since Kendra's death. Besides, it was sublet to a student couple. Instead, he and Cynthia went to The Argonaut Hotel in Times Square where he stayed during the math conference.

He guessed what the e-mail messages were about. Cynthia wanted to say "hi" and thank him for an enjoyable evening last week.

Hint, hint.

Bruce Kasarian wanted to say "hi," and pass on some strictly confidential information that Cynthia was just as fond of him as he was of her.

Sorry, Bruce. Believe me, I'd like to see her again, but I've got more on my mind right now than praising your match-making skills.

There were fourteen messages in his Junk folder. He clicked on that file.

Six of them were sales pitches from online merchants. One was from Stuart Shelbourn, a former colleague who taught calculus at George Washington University. That one had an attachment. Six were from his students at the state pen where he taught every Saturday morning in the summer. That was routine. After each class, it was normal for inmates to stand in line to use one of three desktops in the prison library to work on their homework. Their e-mails were usually a pretense. What they really wanted was communication with someone on the outside. It was his practice to respond to them all, while ignoring relentless digressions upon subjects like "guilt vs. innocence," "trumped-up charges," "faith in God," "proof of a reformed heart," and "sex."

Sex, sex, sex.

Their favorite subject was the assertion that none of them belonged in prison. After that—it was sex.

Finally, there was this: *From: Harry's Heating and A/C Repair. Subject: Sam Teagarden.*

The subject line pumped a surge of icy cold up the center of his spine. He drew a breath and clicked. There were two short lines of type and a URL address to another website. The e-mail read: *thx, more fun this way, and btw, nothing personal.*

He clicked on the URL. The screen jumped to the image of a digital clock with the words, "I will find you in...." At that moment the clock began counting down: *10:00, 9:59, 9:58, 9:57...*

"Oh damn!"

The plastic mouse broke apart when it skidded off the tabletop; the cord yanked from the back of the clunky computer box.

Teagarden caught himself. The image of the clock spooked him badly and he cursed loud enough to be heard by occupants of other bungalows. He listened for the sounds of approaching footfall. Thankfully, there was nothing.

I will find you in 9:02...9:01...9:00...8:59...

So, he was correct that the killer would goad him. It was unquestionably a taunting e-mail. He watched the clock: *I will find you in 8:45...8:44...8:43...8:42...*

And this Harry man, whoever he was, was as nasty as they come. A real five-star sociopath. He leaned over to pick up the mouse to reassemble it and reconnect the cord to the computer box. In the time it took to do so, a new message appeared: *From: Harry's Heating and A/C Repair. Subject: Tick, tick, tick.*

Oh Lord have mercy. Who is this guy?

That message meant he was also correct about the sophistication of the surveillance. They were tracing his phone whenever it was on. Now he knew his e-mail log-on was also being monitored in real time.

He let Harry's second message go unopened. It was time to turn off the ancient machine and tip-toe from the bungalow when he noticed something odd about the message from his friend at GW University. First of all, it should not be in his Junk folder because they communicated all the time. And second, the return address was not gwu.edu.

It was from fbi.gov!

Hi Professor Teagarden,

Dad recommended you as someone who may shed light on the attached mystery. It's a series of encoded entries handwritten in an old spiral notebook that's been collecting dust in the FBI library, where I am archives librarian.

The file is titled CAT 38-CAT 72, though no one knows why, as that matches no proper coding system at the bureau. No one has ever deciphered it, and the bureau lost interest decades ago.

As a fellow math professor, Dad says you're a cryptologist who once worked for the CIA, and may want to take a look.

Regards,
Stuart Shelbourn, Jr.

P.S. I backed up with a hardcopy snail mailed to your summer address in Bethel, NY.

That explained why the message was in his junk box. It wasn't from Stuart Shelbourn, Sr. It was from his kid, Stuart Jr. Teagarden remembered that Shelbourn's son had degrees in criminal justice and library science.

Could it be?

He decided to take a chance. His instincts kicked in. Something about it dovetailed. He remembered now that when he picked up the contents of his P.O. Box the previous morning, there had been a thick manila package with a return address from Shelbourn. He was set to open it when that first demonic hummingbird drew his attention. It seemed reasonable that this e-mail had something to do with the sudden horror movie he was living, a horror movie where he had a starring role. If so, he needed to risk expending what valuable safe time remained in the bungalow before they zeroed in on him.

He turned on the nearby printer, watched it buzz to life, clicked open the attachment, and cued the computer to print one copy of all thirty-four pages. While they were slowly spitting into the plastic catch tray, he explored the rest of the small room.

There wasn't much. A small bedside table held a Torah. Beside it, the Spartan single bed was covered by a knitted throw blanket. A caftan lay at the foot of the bed, which Teagarden guessed was leisure wear for the bungalow owner. And judging from the nature of the two rooms, that owner was male, single, and elderly.

The only other furniture was an antiquated free-standing wardrobe cabinet. The door squeaked when he opened it.

Yes!

He knew the moment he saw the contents that he was going to be stealing more than thirty-four pages of paper and some printer ink.

He selected what he needed from the clothing rack. The outfit was too big for him. Whatever else the owner of this bungalow was, he was a little on the chubby side. But that worked. Teagarden simply pulled each part of the outfit over the top of his shirt and khaki slacks. It was the traditional garb of a Hasidic Jew: baggy black slacks, white shirt buttoned to the collar, tzitzit vest complete with dangling prayer strings, long black silk overcoat, and lastly, a wide hard-brimmed black hat.

When the slacks drooped, he transferred the belt from his khakis to the black slacks and tightened it. The only item that fit perfectly was the hat, what might be called a fedora, except that it wasn't. It was the easily recognized headgear of the Hasidim.

Inside the wardrobe door was a full-length mirror. Teagarden regarded his reflection. With his beard, he was nearly a natural, though he had no side curls. To make up for it, he mussed his beard to make it appear thicker and pulled his hair down his temples as far as it would go, then adjusted the hat to hold it firmly in place. Except for the tzitzit strings and incongruous brown shoes, he looked like a Wild West buffalo hunter, like some Wyatt Earp-type character. All he needed was a Winchester rifle to complete the appearance.

But there was something else. He also looked like a Hasid.

"Sir, I apologize to you," Teagarden said, speaking to the bungalow owner. "Whoever you are, wherever you are, if I can, I will repay you some day."

When the pages finished printing, he fished a black clip from a box of pens and rubber bands. He bound them together, folded them lengthwise, and inserted the packet into the inside breast pocket of his new coat. As he did so, the computer screen returned to his e-mail address. There was yet another message.

From: Harry's Heating and A/C Repair
Subject: You're welcome.

now it's even more fun…

Oh my God. It means Harry knows I just printed the file. How could he possibly know that?

At that moment, without being prompted, the computer jumped to the URL with the digital clock: *I will find you in 4:34...4:33...4:32...4:31...*

He had no idea if Harry really was less than four-and-a-half-minutes from Camp Summer Shevat. But he had no intention of waiting to find out. On a lark, he snatched up the Torah, tucked his chin into his neck, and departed the bungalow. At the lonely intersection in the woods, he turned and strode briskly toward the giant parking lot encircling Bethel Woods Arts Center.

CHAPTER FOURTEEN

It seemed the logical thing to do.

It was midday and he needed to avoid appearing like a loitering misfit. He entered the museum that paid homage to three days of peace, love, and rock music that took place on the adjacent hillside nearly fifty years earlier.

He idled about the lobby where he monitored the parking lot for Harry's truck, the sky for helicopters, the distant approach roads for patrol cars. Nothing was out of the ordinary. Fearing unwanted attention from museum guards, he took the only additional option. He stepped up to buy a museum ticket, which should have been simple. It wasn't.

Uh-oh.

"Sorry, ma'am. I appear to have misplaced my wallet. I'll be right back," he told the lady at the admissions counter.

That was stupid.

He'd forgotten to transfer his wallet from his khakis to the baggy black slacks covering his khakis. He could hardly stand there, undressing and looking like he was digging into his underwear to find money. Fixing the problem required a quick trip to the men's room. If the ticket lady thought it odd, she kept it to herself.

"Found it. I'll take one ticket please."

He did a quick tour of the crowded museum, pretending to look at the exhibits. A boisterous group of Japanese tourists did plenty of staring at the Hasid toting a Torah, but gave him wide birth. It was an odd experience that increased his paranoia.

The worst was confirmed when he finished reviewing galleries commemorating three days in the summer of 1969. Back in the lobby, he saw that the parking lot was loaded with cop cars. And the circular drive at the front door held two sheriff's vans.

Klumm is on the scene.

It meant that Harry was feeding his surveillance data to local law enforcement.

Could they be working together? Well—duh. They had to be.

He was paralyzed with fear until a small opportunity presented itself when all the Japanese tourists exited as a group. He fell in and departed with them for the short walk to their giant double-decker Kanagawa Nyūyōku tour bus, parked on the circular drive. Near the bus door, he peeled off to the parking lot, careful not to make eye contact with anyone. When he dared a single backward glance between parked cars, he saw it all. The lobby was filled with cops, troopers and deputies. One of them was talking to the ticket lady, who he feared was telling them about the odd man who had to go to the men's room to find his wallet. If so, she was describing his clothing as that of an ultra-Orthodox Hasid.

Stay calm. Don't panic.

Behind a row of parked tour buses, he veered toward the main approach road, walking casually as though praying, head down, Torah open, which was in Hebrew.

If they picked me up, it wouldn't take long to realize I can't read or speak the language.

"Minyan or Walmart?"

The deeply masculine voice came from the rear. Teagarden thought it was speaking to him, but wasn't certain. Not wanting to take the risk it was a law enforcement officer testing him, he ignored it and kept walking.

"Hello. Shalom aleichem," it called out. "אדוני, הלו?"

The mini-van pulled ahead of him and stopped so that Teagarden could no longer pretend not to see or hear. The man in the front passenger seat spoke in a third language which Teagarden guessed was Polish.

"Dzień dobry, proszę pana."

Teagarden stopped. The speaker was Hasidic, as were the driver and two passengers in the middle seat. They were all dressed, more or less, exactly like him.

"Minyan or Walmart?" the man asked again.

"Oh, sorry," Teagarden said. "I didn't hear you. I'm a little deaf."

"Yeah, okay. So do you want a prayer minyan or a lift to the Walmart?" He seemed irritated, or maybe suspicious that Teagarden wasn't what he appeared.

"Uh, Walmart."

"Get in."

One of the men in the middle seat opened the sliding door and Teagarden climbed in. As he squeezed past the other passengers, he awkwardly mumbled appreciation with the only Hebrew word he knew. Or was it Yiddish?

"Shalom, shalom," he said, without making eye contact. He plunked down in a rear seat, and opened the Torah. Only one of the four men in the van responded.

"Shalom," the skinny, young one responded in a bashful voice.

The driver gunned the engine, and they all snapped backward as the van jolted from a standstill. With four wide-brimmed black hats in front of him, he could barely see the road ahead, but knew it would lead to Route 17B, the two-lane highway that would take them to the nearest Walmart. About a mile away, they'd pass close enough for him to see his own home through the tree line, the split-level A-frame he'd built as a weekend house with his wife, and where he and Kendra intended to retire when the time came.

The van slowed for the stationary patrol car with blazing flashers as a warning to traffic. On the other side of the trees, cop cars were parked everywhere, including in his driveway. Uniformed officers walked the woods around his house and the undeveloped lot that separated his house from Billy Carney's. Their heads were down, as though looking for evidence in the underbrush.

Farther on, as the van stopped to enter 17B, Teagarden saw the truck again, the boxy gray, ten-footer with big tires. It was parked on the shoulder; the side lettering read *Harry's Heating and A/C Repair*. And there was a number: *555-FURNACE*. One man sat in the cab. Teagarden dared not crane his neck to steal a look, but did manage a brief sidelong glance under his hat brim. The man behind the wheel was about sixty-years-old, maybe older, with short brown hair and a receding hairline. His head was cast down as he looked intently into a glowing tablet or laptop. Though it was only a quick glance, Teagarden could see that he had a hideously thick scar on his upper lip. It could have been caused by botched surgical correction for a cleft palate, or a slipshod fix for a severe injury, possibly a bullet wound to the face.

That's Harry. Has to be.

In the Walmart parking lot, he mumbled more "shaloms" to the Hasidim, departed their company, and hurried to the store's lawn and garden entrance where a commuter bus was boarding. He guessed it was going either north or south.

"New York City or Binghamton?" he asked the driver.

"New York," the driver announced. "Port Authority Bus Terminal is two stops and two-hours down the road."

Teagarden paid the fare in cash and took an aisle seat in the middle. Watching the lower Catskills recede, he caught his breath and tried to pull his thoughts together. He realized he was essentially a fox running from two distinct groups. One was the law, which wanted him because of Billy Carney's murder. The other was still a mystery. The e-mail from Stuart Shelbourn Jr. may have something to do with it. He couldn't be certain, but he knew one thing—because he'd escaped both groups, he was either the smartest or the luckiest fugitive there ever was. Either way, he feared his luck was about to run out.

CHAPTER FIFTEEN

Sunday, July 21, 2019
Encrypted Field Communication
NSA Apache Code Ofc Baltimore, MD/Washington, DC/Coin
TelSatOrbit53/Bethel, NY

<apache code initiate>

TO: ice skater
FROM: deep field cmdr

SUBJECT: operation dear john

<secure field communication may begin>

deep field cmdr to ice skater: telsat sees evidence file has been downloaded...

ice skater to deep field cmdr: telsat evidence correct...can confirm...fox has hardcopy...

deep field cmdr to ice skater: um, why?...

ice skater to deep field cmdr: this fox is smart...as per bio, he once worked f/cia as cryptologist...

deep field cmdr to ice skater: i was told all e-mail erased...

ice skater to deep field cmdr: true...but he used primitive desktop...pre-cointelsat...not receptive to nsa viral code that erased recipient e-mail...pc was in private religious compound...

deep field cmdr to ice skater: u yanking me ice skater?...

ice skater to deep field cmdr: no sir...no offense, but i don't go that way...

deep field cmdr to ice skater: funnyman...no more f/u's...this knock-knock worrying eyes-only on 10th floor...u now have new job: make 10th floor stop worrying...get your fox now... and confiscate hardcopy...u on short leash...out.

CHAPTER SIXTEEN

Interstate 87, NY

He drifted in and out of uneasy slumber on the bus. During one nod, he relived the car crash. It flashed back with nearly as much intensity as when it actually happened, sending him lurching forward.

"Look out!" he shouted.

It was the final utterance he'd spoken to his wife of twenty-eight years. The driver of the on-coming van was speeding and had lost control on the same four-lane interstate they were traveling at that moment. For reasons never determined, the driver crossed the median, crashed the guardrail, became airborne, and, in the final few microseconds, flew straight into the left side of their car. It was a maroon convertible BMW Roadster that she adored. Police speculated that the van driver suffered a heart attack, though the autopsy couldn't verify it because there wasn't much left after he was tossed into high speed traffic. In the end, the best guess was routine law enforcement verbiage: "driver distraction and loss of control while traveling at an extremely high rate of speed."

"Sorry," he said to the passenger in the opposite aisle seat after shouting himself awake. She retrieved his hard-brimmed hat from the floor and handed it back to him.

"Thank you."

"Have a nightmare?" she asked. "You must be very hot in your outfit." Teagarden sensed she wanted to chat.

"I'm fine," he said with moderate curtness. He returned the hat to his head and looked away at the passing scenery of the New York State Thruway, the same scenery he passed that day with Kendra less than a year ago.

Yes, lady, it was a nightmare. That crash killed my wife and broke both my knees. That's what I'd call a nightmare.

CHAPTER SEVENTEEN

Ice Skater drove slowly toward New York City. He didn't want to get too far too fast in case Teagarden turned up somewhere in the woods of the Catskills. But he doubted that would happen. He sensed his prey had escaped him a second time. First at the house, now from the woods surrounding his house. Maybe he'd stolen a car or hitched a ride with an ally. Either way, he was confident that Teagarden was headed for the big city where it would be easier for a fugitive to hide.

He smiled at the idea. This was fun. It'd be more fun in New York City.

In a short period of time he'd likely receive another communication from the DFC in Washington on his target's whereabouts. When he did, he'd quickly be back on the trail. He'd eventually get this fox. But with this development, he'd get him *his* way. If it turned out that his way was not the bureau's way—well, tough. What were they going to do? Arrest him?

CHAPTER EIGHTEEN

The passing trees, cars, billboards, and guard rails had a hypnotic effect on Teagarden during the balance of the trip, allowing his intuition to kick in.

Just as when he'd awakened that morning in the bluestone alcove while looking at the opossum, a couple of insights bubbled to the surface. They came to him after a quick glance at the thirty-four photo-copied pages. They contained rows and columns of numbers, encrypted messages written in hand, first with a fountain pen, then a ball point over a period of years, maybe decades. Before getting his Ph.D. in advanced mathematics at Columbia he'd been an entry level code analyst with the CIA long enough to know encryption when he saw it. Cryptanalysis had been a lifelong sideline. Over the years, he'd padded his income quite nicely with private consultation to companies looking to better encrypt their corporate secrets in the era of fifteen-year-old computer whiz kids, not to mention presidential campaign hacking by Russia.

What's more, Stuart Shelbourn Jr. was right. With little more than gut instinct, Teagarden was confident he could decode the entire file. Those pages weren't ancient Egyptian hieroglyphics. Neither were they the Nazi Enigma machine. On the surface, they appeared complicated, but there was something about the sequences that looked familiar to him, even simple. To help his instincts advance to the next step, however, required peace of mind, and a computer. So it would have to wait.

As for the pursuers who wanted him dead, several possibilities came to mind. He was dealing with an organized intelligence group whose principal motivation was the encoded file tucked inside the pocket of his Hasidic overcoat. That's why they were at his house. They wanted the hardcopy snail-mailed to his P.O. Box. But if he was right, and they were as sophisticated as they seemed, he should not have been able to download the e-mailed copy. That message from Shelbourn should have been deleted as though it were the darkest secret of Beelzebub. He should have seen only utility bills in his inbox and unwanted sales pitches in his spam box. Whoever they were, they certainly had the capacity to delete e-mails with photo-copied attachments.

The fact that he did download it could mean there was a bureaucratic screw-up. Or maybe it was because someone had a beef with their higher-ups. Teagarden tilted toward the latter. He guessed that Harry was pissed about something, so he allowed the download to take place as an act of insubordination. His countdown clock reinforced it. It revealed something freakish about Harry's personality, which made Teagarden wonder if he could eventually make that "something" work to his benefit. If so, he might be able to make Harry become what people like him are typically called in news reports—"a disgruntled *former* employee."

There was plenty to think about during the bus trip. He'd left his house with only his wallet, cellphone and the clothes on his back. He needed things like cash, a change of clothing, food, a toothbrush, a laptop, a new cellphone, and pain medication for his knees. Hell, he needed a whole new identity. Worse, he couldn't pay for any of it with his MasterCard. Just one swipe with that magnetic strip at a clothing store, and police would likely be booking him for murder before he could get outside and hail a cab.

If that happened, he guessed that Harry would simply disappear. Teagarden's emotional call with the 9-1-1 dispatcher and the body of eleven-year-old Billy Carney was all it would take for them to label him a paranoid schizophrenic and put him away for years. They'd probably say the snap with reality was caused by the recent death of his wife.

It was almost as though he were peering into the future. *His* future. And he did not like what he saw.

The bus glided into Port Authority in the late afternoon. It ascended an internal helix and came to a smooth stop as though programmed by a higher power.

Knees aching, Torah in hand, Teagarden headed off on foot, looking like nothing unusual. Dressed as an ultra-Orthodox Jew, he was as common to the teeming streets of New York City as were people talking into dangling phone wires, women with spiders tattooed on their legs, and kids with the waistline of their jeans sagging to mid-buttocks.

His first order of business was simple. Like everyone else, he needed money, but in his case, it had to be old-fashioned cash.

CHAPTER NINETEEN

New York City

Teagarden couldn't remember why he knew about fox hunting.

A smart fox will run a zig-zag pattern to throw off the dogs. A dumb fox will simply bolt hard in a straight line. Dogs prefer a dumb fox because it makes them look better when they quickly catch the prey. Hunters prefer a smart fox because it's more fun.

He'd never been a hunter, and had no idea where this knowledge came from. Maybe he'd seen a documentary on PBS. But there was a flaw in the whole theory. It didn't take into account what the prey wished for—which was survival. Smart or not, the fox will always trust to his luck and hope that he's been paired with a pack of dogs as dumb as they come because it increases his odds of living another day.

That's what *he* was naturally hoping, to be a smart fox running from dumb hunters. Outsmarting Harry meant zig-zagging around New York City to get the things he needed, the basic creature comforts of life. Except for summers and weekends at their house in Bethel, he and Kendra called Manhattan home for two decades. He knew the city well and loved the wonderful, mad streets of America's biggest city.

He considered going uptown to their one-bedroom co-op near Columbia University which he still owned. He hadn't been back since shortly after Kendra was killed when he needed to retrieve her last will and testament. During that visit, he was only in the apartment ten minutes to avoid breaking into heavy sobbing. Besides, the apartment was now sublet to a pair of graduate students and it was certain to be under surveillance by whoever wanted him dead.

Forget it, the risk is too great. I have to figure another way without going uptown.

He walked north through Times Square, looking to make his first move. A giant sign on the façade of the Marriott Marquis Hotel portrayed Mick Jagger in neon and screamed details of an upcoming Rolling Stones concert at Madison Square Garden.

Wow, Jagger must be pushing eighty.

The first time he saw The Stones was at age six when his parents took him to the same venue. They were huge rock fans, which explained his birth on the final night of the Woodstock Music Festival. His parents loved The Stones and his wife loved them just as much. He first saw them with Kendra during the Steel Wheels tour in '89 when Jagger was forty-six, three years younger than Teagarden was now.

The year 1989—wow. Thirty years and a lifetime ago. How did I get to be this old? And yet I'm not really that old. It's more than a mystery of numbers. Mere numbers and the passage of time do not suffice as explanation. As a Ph.D. in advanced mathematics, I ought to know. But I don't. Neither did Einstein.

Between Times Square and Central Park, he selected a four-block stretch of Broadway that had a dozen storefront mini-banks. Keeping his wide-brimmed black hat pulled low to cover his eyes, he entered one after the other to pump cash from the ATMs. At each, he withdrew a thousand dollars, the maximum allowed per ATM, per branch, on his new Gold Customer card with Downstate Regional Bank of New York which had the best CD rates at a time when all rates were laughably poor.

While watching the slot spit money like playing cards, he

held cautious vigil in the security mirror over each ATM. The reflection of the convex lens made everything behind him appear distorted, like the past twenty-four hours of his life. Before departing each cash machine, he carefully folded the money and tucked it inside the breast pocket of his Hasidic coat where it lived with the thirty-four pages of coded numbers printed at Camp Summer Shevat.

He'd intentionally chosen a particular bank as the twelfth and last because it had an internal stairway to the IRT Subway line. Before entering the subway, he snapped his ATM card in half, then into quarters and dropped the pieces into the trash bin. He removed his MasterCard and did the same, letting the security camera see his hands as they made a showy display of it, like the hands of a magician performing a card trick.

That was the first zig. Now for the first zag.

He took a downtown subway to the trendy SoHo neighborhood and wandered until he found one of those large clothing store chains that occupy a big chunk of real estate at every mall in America. Typically, the men's clothing was stacked on tables to the right; women's clothing on tables to the left. There was no need to try on anything. His size hadn't changed in years. Besides, going into the dressing room to try on ordinary street clothes while dressed as a Hasid would draw unwanted curiosity. He selected one pair of jeans, one shirt, one pair of socks, one pair of boxers, and a plain army green baseball cap.

Everything went smoothly until he encountered the young lady at the checkout counter with a ridiculous tattoo of concentric black-and-white circles on her neck. The bull's eye of the target was halfway between her left earlobe and clavicle. Except for that, she was quite attractive. While ringing him up, she couldn't restrain her impulses.

"Why, Rabbi, you've made some way cool choices here," she said with a sexy smile. "My boyfriend couldn't have done better. You're not going undercover to do anything naughty are you?"

He was ready for her.

"Yes," he said. "I am."

"Ohh," she teased. "Well, I'll never tell. I hope it's something *really* fun for you."

Her eyes lit up with phony enthusiasm. Her breasts jiggled at him as she leaned over the counter to fold the jeans and shirt. He nodded appreciation of her innuendo and vigorously rubbed his beard.

Is this some kind of smarty-pants anti-Semitism?

He decided to play along.

"It's like this. I have tickets to see The Stones next month at Madison Square Garden. Do you have any idea how much trouble there would be if someone from my synagogue saw me there?"

"Oh well, in that case," she said, her voice shifting from sexy to sarcasm, "you'll need a pair of these." She reached into a cabinet on the counter and withdrew a pair of military style wrap-around sunglasses. "These will help conceal your secret identity while you're undercover watching those old guys trying to be hip."

Wow! Who's this twit to make fun of Mick's age? Okay, so she's not an anti-Semite. She's just a twenty-something, know-it-all.

"I'll take them," Teagarden said.

After paying, he put on his new sunglasses and took his bag filled with new clothing.

"By the way," he said to the lady with the bull's eye on her neck, "when I'm undercover watching The Stones, I'll still be a smart man doing God's work. You, on the other hand, will be a dumb shiksa with a dumb neck tattoo who works in a dumb store and spends all her spare time schtupping her equally dumb goyim boyfriend."

Tah-dah!

He departed the store to the sound of sniggers from customers standing behind him in the checkout line. He was immediately sorry. It meant they'd all remember him. But hell, sometimes you've just got to give it back when they deserve it. You especially have to give it back to the twenty-somethings who believe chatspeak is the height of Western civilization and constitutes all you need to know about anything.

He took a crosstown bus to a drugstore near the Lower East Side where he purchased a pack of disposable razors, shaving foam, aftershave, toothpaste and toothbrush, scissors, and a large container of the strongest over-the-counter NSAID medication he could find. From the back-to-school aisle, he selected a spiral notebook, pens, a Post-it pad and a backpack.

Once again, there was difficulty at the checkout counter. This time, it had to do with the populace of the Lower East Side. Though the neighborhood had morphed into mostly hipsters, the elderly man at the cash-register was a holdover from earlier times who wanted to converse in Yiddish. When Teagarden waved him off as though he were in a hurry or a bad mood, the old man became offended. Unfortunately, he too would remember his encounter with the oddly behaving Hasid. Teagarden was trying hard to be forgettable, if not invisible, but his disguise was working against him.

Next up, he needed an internet login, and a laptop.

He took the East Side subway back to Midtown. In a private stall in the men's room of the Midtown Manhattan Library, he popped two NSAID tablets for his knee pain, then shed the heavy outfit. Using the pen knife on his key chain, he removed the store tags and put on his new clothing. He stashed his cellphone, toiletries, newly purchased writing pads, and thirty-four-page document in the backpack. He ditched his old clothing and stolen Hasidic exterior in the bathroom trash bin, pushing the garments down so they sank below the soft topping of paper towels flooding the bin's edge.

Much changed in appearance, he patrolled the rows of publicly available computers, selecting one that had been abandoned while the latest user was still logged on. He inserted his

USB, also attached to his keychain, into a port on the back of the machine and began loading encryption software.

```
launch.txt
quicklaunch.txt
initiate webpass.exe/view/etext/extract
download files
start.exepass.ifile.password/zebra-override
start.exepass.ifile.password/selectfiles
start.exepass.ifile.password/usernames
start.exepass.ifile.password/logins
save as launch.bat
download to usb drive: port2
```

Being an independent consultant on computer encryption and decryption, he was competent on the ins and outs of basic software. It looks complicated, but the little-known secret was that it's not really very mysterious. Like a foreign language, once you get the basics, you know enough for elementary communication.

He extracted his USB from the port for later use.

Still using the active login left by the prior computer user, he researched tourist hostels in Manhattan where he hoped to secure a room without a credit card or proper identification. He found one that might work called Madison Park Euro Lodge in the Flatiron District, which seemed to be for tourists on a budget. He made a reservation online as Tom Samuels from North Carolina who'd be paying cash and printed the confirmation.

Now it was time to get a message to his daughter. The idea came to him during the bus ride to the city. Her favorite movie as a kid had been *Dogfight Girl*, about a female F/A-18 Hornet fighter pilot, which first made her want to go into the U.S. Navy. As a child, she was so smitten with the idea that he and Kendra nicknamed her Dogfight Daughter. She responded by enthusiastically naming her parents Dogfight Dad and Dog-fight Mom.

He typed the message.

To: Eva Ghent
Subject: Dogfight Girl Sequel/Advance Planning

Dear Major Ghent Tactical Combat Training Team, NAS Key West:
As assistant to the producers for the planned sequel to the movie, *Dogfight Girl*, I am contacting you to arrange future advice and assistance. The working title is *Still a Dogfighter Pilot.*
Do not be concerned with advance negative publicity.
Thank you, we look forward to your response.
Best Regards
Sr. Assistant Producer

He knew the e-mail would land in her Junk box. He knew too that she would open it because of the subject line. She would figure its true meaning when she saw her father's image splashed on national news. She would also understand that his reference to negative publicity meant his present dilemma.
Now for a new computer.
A block away, was a store informally known by New Yorkers as "The Big BM," the nickname for the brick-and-mortar outlet owned by the king of online retail. It was a huge open-floored space where customers sat at computer consoles to research, order, and buy just about anything that existed. The unique attraction of the brick-and-mortar version was that instead of waiting for delivery by snail-mail, your purchase was handled by robots, and delivered to your position in minutes—also by robots.
Computers, books, and clothing arrived from massive underground warehouses. When the item was stored at a warehouse

in Queens, high speed drones took to the air, landing on the roof of The Big BM building, which functioned as a landing strip. There, an army of robots received and unloaded the drone, swept the bar code, and sent the item flowing downward through the building to the position of the purchaser on the main sales floor.

Before ordering, Teagarden browsed what was available. Among the new showcased offerings was the much buzzed about "PC Packets," or "Flexi-Flats," as they were called in television ads. It was a package of ten sheets of thin plastic that could be adhered to any surface and, when activated, perform all the functions of a personal computer. Each square was about the size of a paper-towel, with the life-expectancy of six months. But at a price of twenty thousand dollars for a pack of four, most consumers stayed away.

Teagarden opted for a plain-old laptop on sale for seven hundred dollars. Thankfully there was nothing memorable about this purchase. He fed eight one-hundred-dollar bills into the machine at his console position and received his change. Seven minutes later, the robotic automation gently lowered an attaché-shaped cardboard box to the countertop where he waited while sipping a complimentary cup of hot tea.

Zig and zag complete.

CHAPTER TWENTY

Madison Park Euro Lodge

"I'm sorry, I simply don't have it. As I've explained, I lost my driver's license."

He spoke to the lady at the front desk of Madison Park Euro Lodge in a sticky sweet southern accent. It was the third time he had told her that he didn't have proper I.D., yet she never looked up from her computer screen. She continued typing and mouse clicking as though it were vastly more important. His irritation index was growing.

The reception area was small. Besides her work alcove, there was a two-seater couch and two folding chairs. A large, flat-panel TV on the wall opposite the couch was tuned to a quasi-news program about the forthcoming fiftieth anniversary of the Woodstock Music Festival. The opening ceremony was just over seven days away. Once begun, the celebration was scheduled to last a full month, ending on the day that happened to be his fiftieth birthday. So far, no one from the media had contacted him for an interview as one of the "Woodstock babies."

He decided on another tack.

"Actually, I didn't lose it," he said, drawing out the syllables with an oozing North Carolinian drawl. "They stole it. My bicycle, too."

"Uh-oh," she said, still not looking up from her screen. "Did they hurt you?"

He guessed she was about forty-seven or forty-eight. Judging from her appearance and accent, she was likely Eastern European, maybe from one of the Balkans, probably working the front desk at the hostel in exchange for free board. She wasn't bad looking, but neither was she attractive. Her body was relatively slender, the face unnaturally round and plump, her breasts disproportionately large. The most unattractive thing about her was her curt manner. Teagarden reminded himself that in a post-9/11 world, hotel clerks were required to ask for proper I.D.

"Could be worse," he said. He rubbed one side of his head. "They knocked me off my bike on the New Jersey Palisades before I crossed into the city on the GW Bridge. I was outnumbered. One of me, three of them. They took my bike and wallet. Lucky for me I always keep my money in a separate compartment. I learned to do that on my last biking trip through Arizona."

"I know that area up there. It is beautiful on those New Jersey cliffs above the Hudson River. I hear that some movie stars live there. But it is bad, too. There are many hidden places for the bad kids to hide."

"Yeah," he said. "I've learned that the hard way. I had dismounted to look at the view of the Manhattan skyline. That's when they came up from behind."

She nodded absently.

"Anyway," he continued, "I have your e-mail confirming my reservation. I booked it at the main library in Midtown. And I've requested a quick replacement of my driver's license from Raleigh. I gave this address. They promised emergency delivery in a couple of days. Hope that's okay." She nodded again. "So I'd like to pay for three nights in advance."

She glanced at the printed confirmation from Madison Park Euro Lodge and his handful of cash.

"Okay," she said. "You're okay." She keyed in his registration on the desktop. "Did you bike all the way from...

down there?"

"Down there?"

For the first time, she looked straight in his eyes.

"Is not Raleigh down there?" she asked. Her tone was defensive, as though he'd accused her of not knowing Raleigh's geographic whereabouts.

"Oh—*that*—down there," he said, trying to recover to a friendly footing. "Yes, yes," he said, thinking his accent must be working. Having attended undergraduate school in Chapel Hill, he knew it really was the way locals talk—down there.

"So, you are biking with a church group?"

"No. This trip is solo. My wife recently passed away. It's my way of getting out, remembering, honoring. You know, YOLO. I'm trying to be young again while I still have my health and the summer off. I'm a math teacher."

She was instantly bored with his story.

"Okay, okay" she said. "Just sign this card. Here is your key. Room 412. It has a little bit view of Madison Square Park. There is no air conditioner and no bathroom. The bathroom is down the hall. Please give respect and help us keep it clean. No smoking in the rooms or loud music. If you need something I am here at the front desk or in my room, number 413, which is next to yours."

CHAPTER TWENTY-ONE

Encrypted Field Communication
NSA Apache Code Ofc Baltimore, MD/Washington, DC/Coin
TelSatOrbit53/Bethel, NY

<apache code initiate>

TO: ice skater
FROM: deep field cmdr

SUBJECT: operation dear john

<secure field communication may begin>

deep field cmdr to ice skater: telsat alerted...fox's bank accts
tapped in nyc...

ice skater to deep field cmdr: great...just great...u told me all
cards were canceled...

deep field cmdr to ice skater: screw-up at cointelsat desk...
they killed mstcard...dri. lic...but missed cash bank card...
must be new acct...

ice skater to deep field cmdr: great...and u tell *me* no more
f/u's...let's fix probs on your end at hq...and release more
drones to me...what u say?

deep field to ice skater: regarding screw-ups…how'd your fox get to nyc?…

ice skater to deep field cmdr: seems he dressed as heb… slipped through…

deep field cmdr to ice skater: and u complain about screw-ups at telsat desk???…eyes only on 10th floor getting just as worried about u as your fox…get to nyc…now…pick-up one surveil. drone model f-89 at javits fed bldg.…canvas all hotels from the waldorf to fleabags…now…and get your fox…now…

ice skater to deep field cmdr: already on way…out

CHAPTER TWENTY-TWO

Madison Park Euro Lodge

As hotels and hostels go, it was one level above flophouse, yet it was in the trendy Flatiron District, which was more trendy than SoHo.

The tiny room had an old picture tube TV dating to the late twentieth century. Made of dirty white plastic and shaped like a loaf of bread, it was mounted to a turntable bolted to an oversized bureau. He turned it on. There was no cable or DSL, so the video didn't work, but it had a built-in radio that worked fine. He tuned-in the Yankee game.

The single bed was passably firm. Directly over the headboard hung a cheaply framed poster of *Guernica*, Picasso's gray, black, and white masterpiece of Spanish farmers and livestock in the Basque country being blown up by bombs. For a moment, he wondered if he should worry about bed bugs, but let it go.

If Kendra were with me, she'd tear the bedding apart and scour every inch of the linens and mattress with the flashlight she always carried when traveling.

He dumped the contents of his backpack on the bed, including sandwiches and a bottle of beer purchased at a deli on his way to the hostel. He took what he needed and walked to the bathroom, lugging his boxed-up laptop with him. The last thing he needed was to have his room robbed while he was down the hall shaving.

When he tugged on the bathroom doorknob, he got a soprano-pitched earful.

"It's occupied. Take it easy."

Other guests came and went from their rooms while he waited his turn. They were mostly young people who trucked noisily down the staircase, happy to be heading out for a night of clubbing in New York City. When the bathroom door opened, it was the same curtly unpleasant woman who'd checked him in.

"Oh, sorry," Teagarden said to the receptionist. "I must have checked in just as your shift was ending. I hope I didn't delay you."

"It is no problem," she said, "I had double-shift today. But my work is finally finished."

She regarded him with a different demeanor, no longer borderline hostile, though she still spoke with a psychologically flat affect. It made him wonder if she wasn't molded by something dreadful. If she was from the Balkans, she would have been a child or teenager during some of those war years in Bosnia and Kosovo where the list of nastiness included bombing, torture, rape, murder.

"Mr. Samuels, I was just going to have some wine in my room. If you would like to join me, you may be my guest. It is Sicilian red. Not bad." She made the invitation without a beat of hesitation.

Teagarden was taken completely off guard.

"Oh, thank you," he mumbled. "May I take a rain check?"

"Of course."

Unruffled, she turned and walked back to her room.

Whatever the details, he felt confident that her personal story was ugly, which made him feel sorry for her.

In the bathroom, Teagarden clipped his beard with his new scissors, tossing handfuls of whiskers into the toilet. He lathered and shaved with the disposable blue plastic razor. After rinsing, his skin stung mightily, making him glad for the Old

Spice aftershave.

He studied his face in the dirty mirror. It was the first time he'd been clean-shaven since he was a twenty-one-year-old graduate student at GW University. Having met his wife at Columbia where he got his Ph.D., she'd never seen him without facial hair. Near the end of her life, in teasing imitation of Billy Carney, she also took to calling him Old Abe. The thought of them both made him grieve all over again. It took all the strength he could summon to push off a double wave of sadness.

I don't look so old. I may be moving in on fifty, but without the beard, heck—I look closer to forty-nine.

Back in his room, while eating his turkey-cheddar sandwich and sipping beer, he unboxed his new computer, hooked the cord to an outlet, booted up and registered the machine with the manufacturer as Tom Samuels of Raleigh, North Carolina. As with all trendy neighborhoods in Manhattan, the Flatiron District had nearly universal Wi-Fi.

He inserted his USB, clicked on the USB icon, and downloaded the contents labeled "launch.bat" which he'd run on the public desktop in the Main Midtown Library. He initiated the file, which immediately launched a menu of six identities and passwords that users had foolishly allowed the library computer to remember.

It wasn't much. But Teagarden hoped it was enough. Odds were that none of them was overly tech savvy because they'd all left personal information on a public hard drive for anyone to steal. If he were interested, he could probably download bank account numbers and be transferring funds before the night was over. But all he wanted was a login ID that Harry, Sheriff Klumm and the New York State Police didn't know about.

The first was a military man. No, thanks.

Number two looked like a hormone bursting teenage male who was probably a video-gamer. That meant he knew about computers, and the fact that his ID was left on a public hard drive was suspicious. That made him a big nope. As a fugitive, Teagarden didn't need to be suckered into some other hacker's sticky trap.

Next up was Ms. O'Malley, possibly a tourist from mid-America, maybe checking-in on her driveway security camera. She ought to be good.

He continued down the list.

The next one was clearly a football fan from Denver. She'd be okay, too.

Then there's a lady from who-knows-where who either loves asparagus or hates asparagus.

Finally, Mr. Dan Jones with the password "yellow4submarine." A Beatles fan.

He's probably older than I am, and uses computers mostly for typing, so he ought to be safe, too.

Teagarden keyed in the SolarRay web browser, downloaded the Orange Circle e-mail provider and logged on as danjones.

Beauteous.

Mr. Jones' inbox was ordinary. Much like his own, it was loaded with bills. There were debt notices from a power company in Missouri; a national-based cellphone company; two credit cards from banks in Canton, Missouri; a nursing home in Quincy, Illinois; and an auto insurance company in St. Louis. There were several e-mails from Sandy, one with a subject line reading: "Oh Dan, please let us hear from you."

He couldn't resist. He opened it.

From: sandyjones@orangecircle.com
To: danjones@orangecircle.com

Dear Dan,

We are all so worried. What are you doing in that New York City. I am very worried for your safety.

There are too many Muslims there. It's a bad place.

Whatever I did, I am sorry. Please let me hear from you again, so we can talk about it.

Your mother sends her love. It was her 90th birthday yesterday and the nurses gave her a cupcake with a candle & sang happy birthday.

Please call.

Love,
Your wife, Sandy.

Perfect. This man is definitely not worrying about the integrity of his passwords.

How ironic was this? Here he was, stealing the ID of a man who was also on the run in New York City, though for vastly different reasons. Whoever Dan Jones was, he wasn't running *for* his life, more likely he was running *from* it. He was probably pissed, sick and tired, and, as they say, "just couldn't take it anymore." Maybe he got fired for the umpteenth time, or his sex life was lousy, or he just learned he had brain cancer. Whatever it was, Teagarden sensed that Dan Jones might be suicidal.

Hang in, Dan. My wife was killed on the New York State Thruway while sitting right next to me. My dog was killed. The neighbor's boy was murdered and the police think I did it. Plus, a team of sociopaths is stalking me, trying to kill me with high-powered sniper rifles and poison-shooting drones. If I can endure all that, you can certainly endure the lyrics to the country music song playing inside your head.

The Yankees lost. When the station went back to all-news, there was no mention of Billy Carney, but then, he was in New York City now. He guessed it would take a while longer for his fugitive status to go statewide, then national.

In bed, he stared at the sequences of numbers on the thirty-four pages. Every entry was brief and written by the same masculine hand that inked each small, meticulously noted number.

Teagarden had already guessed they were diary entries. He now saw from the uniform pressure of the pen that they were all written with attentive care, almost like a scribe from the Middle Ages.

Interestingly, each page was topped by a different eight-digit heading, and every passage under the page heading began with the same eight-number series. The heading on the first page was: 10906010.

It was followed by a dozen diary-type entries, all in numbers and each beginning with the same eight numbers: 44, 55, 11, 18, 99, 15, 77, 14.

He flipped forward. The eight digit heading on the second page was: 38124072.

It was followed by only half-a-dozen entries, each beginning with an identical paired number sequence, yet different from the previous page: 88, 51, 42, 17, 9, 5, 77, 91, 63.

The heading on the third page was followed by nearly two-dozen separate entries, each of them also began with a repetition of identical numbers.

It was a consistent pattern. There were repeated sequences within each page. Yet when comparing separate pages, the numbers were different.

Teagarden saw the meaning immediately. Each page was encoded with a different pre-set cipher. He was looking at thirty-four separate codes, each requiring its own formula for decryption. Though each page had a unique coding system, he sensed that all were drawn from a similar coding concept.

Too tired to begin transcribing numbers for letters, he speculated about what those repetitive headers might signify when decoded: attn staff, take note, desk memo, code name, eyes only.

Of course, it wasn't guaranteed that each number corresponded to its own particular letter. Each repetitive sequence could signify its own pre-set word, or pairs of letters, in which case the meaning could be: time sensitive, general order, undercover agent, field encrypted, begin communication.

He worked it until he drifted to sleep, his face staring into the illuminated screen of his new laptop, his head dreaming variously of his wife, Cynthia, Sheriff Klumm, Harry the bad man, Billy Carney, the Hasidim of Camp Summer Shevat, and Dan Jones. Each of them was surrounded by swarms of numbers that could spin, fly and hover. Amid the floating numbers, Coconut appeared sitting under a scripted banner flapping in the wind: "Kill a Man's Dog, Break a Man's Rules."

It was not a pleasant dream.

CHAPTER TWENTY-THREE

Monday, July 22, 2019

He was shaken awake by raucous commotion during the wee hours.

It seemed to be happening on two fronts, in both adjacent rooms. At first he thought he'd awakened in the middle of some Roman orgy. The sounds of orgasmic copulation raged all around him, banging the walls, rocking his bed.

Oh, brother.

Teagarden rubbed his eyes and sat up on the side of the single bed. His newly shaved face still felt odd to the touch. The radio was on, tuned to an all-news station. He shut it off. The digital read-out glared the time: 2:43 a.m. The room was partially illuminated by the shadowy glow from street lights.

He got up and sat by the window. The orgy in the room next door was making the cheaply framed poster of Picasso's *Guernica* vibrate.

Oh, brother.

Well, at least it's not Sheriff Klumm or Harry the furnace and A/C repairman breaking down the door to capture or kill him. Outside, the lamps of Madison Square Park reflected in a misty fog. It must have rained while he was sleeping. The fog made the park look romantic, like a picture postcard on a steamy summer night.

For a moment, he listened with envy to the Bacchanalian revelry. The idea of an orgy always seemed alluring, but listening to it took the fun out of the fantasy. It sounded like torture, like men and women suffering a violent fate. It was easy to imagine that the groans were actually coming from the famous image, the Basque civilians and livestock being slaughtered in northern Spain. For a moment, he imagined that he, Coconut, Billy Carney, and Kendra were in the painting, moaning with agony along with the tormented horse, the man on fire and the decapitated human head flying through the air.

This time, he didn't think it, he said it aloud.

"Oh, brother!" He rubbed again at the curious feel of his newly naked face.

It sounds like a whole platoon of people in there bumping and grinding. How many can even fit into these tiny rooms?

He'd had enough. He pulled on his jeans. In the corridor, he locked his door and trotted down the hallway past room 411, the orgy room that made *Guernica* vibrate. In the single bathroom he took his time, washing his face, showering, and studying his image without the beard he'd had for nearly three decades. On the return trip, the orgiastic racket in 411 had stopped, but noise still raged on the other side.

And—*that*—was room 413, where the abrupt receptionist lived.

Before unlocking his door, he leaned toward hers. There were a number of voices, but they were not the sounds of humans in the throes of sexual ecstasy. They were the sounds of humans being angry, arguing, whining, imploring. He recognized the Eastern European voice of the receptionist rising above the others, speaking in Russian, or what sounded like Russian, but could have been any of a dozen languages from that general region of the world.

He shouldn't have been surprised at the subject of argument. But he was.

Hearing only snippets of broken English, he made out the words: "Serpico...eight ball...Tuesday...snowbird...two kilos... Colombian nitro...Metro-North...seven hundred dollars...Tuesday…brown meth…two grand…Tuesday…daddy in Westport…forty-five thousand…Tuesday, Tuesday, Tuesday!"

Great.

There was an orgy happening in one adjacent room, and a noisy drug deal in the other. It meant the irritable Eastern European woman was making her way in America by earning more than a humble income as a receptionist in a tourist hostel. It was *her* voice repeating the word "Tuesday" over and over again.

He guessed she was telling her guests that Tuesday was to be her payday. Pay up on Tuesday, or no more dope, or no more free rooms, or no more protection from the Bureau of Immigration, or whatever it was she was brokering on their behalf.

Teagarden remembered that the NSAID container he bought at the pharmacy on the Lower East Side had a cotton ball stuffed into the top. He opened the lid and pulled the cotton into two parts, inserting one into each ear. He put two NSAID tablets on his tongue and washed them down with warm, stale beer from the bottom of the bottle.

Returning to the single bed, he curled his arms around his ears and pulled his knees into a fetal position. Behind his head in room 411, multiple male and female voices were again beginning the slow, rhythmic groans of sexual ecstasy.

CHAPTER TWENTY-FOUR

He was still in a fetal position when the antique white radio awakened him.

Apparently pre-set by the previous guest, it clicked to life with a local newscast at 6:00 a.m., startling Teagarden from a fitful sleep. Worse than being startled, he learned from the newscast that—*he*—was the lead story:

A massive manhunt is underway in our area this morning for a suspected murderer.

Columbia math professor Sam Teagarden is wanted in the shooting death of an eleven-year-old boy in the upstate town of Bethel, where he has a summer home.

Officials say he may have suffered an emotional breakdown linked to the recent death of his wife, Kendra Teagarden, the well-known author of the best-selling biography, "The Greatest American," about Ben Franklin. She was killed in a wrong way crash on the New York State Thruway that severely injured her husband, who is now a fugitive.

He's forty-nine, six-foot, a hundred and eighty pounds, and may or may not have facial hair.

He is believed to be armed and dangerous.

If you see Sam Teagarden, police urge you to call nine-one-one immediately.

The next story in the newscast was about the latest underground nuclear test conducted by Iran, and that nation's vow to destroy all of Europe, Israel and the United States in a single massive pre-meditated thermonuclear assault committed in the name of Allah.

"Oh, what an honor." He jumped to turn off the radio. "They've put me ahead of the end of Western civilization."

He leaned to the window providing an angled view of Madison Square Park, the Flatiron Building and surrounding streets. Nothing seemed out of the ordinary. Though trendy, it was an unusual part of town not known for much of anything, except the conversion of massive old office buildings into overpriced condo units. There was a pre-dawn lull just ahead of the morning crush of people and cars. No NYPD patrol cars could be seen. More importantly, there was nothing that looked like Harry's Heating and A/C Repair truck.

He had two choices. He could stay put in the house of orgies and druggies, which bore risk if they were somehow tracing his movement and purchases despite his zigging and zagging. Or he could strike out for new, safer digs. Now that a physical description had been issued, taking to the streets in pursuit of deeper cover seemed to carry greater risk than ever. Besides, staying put would allow him to research what may be his best weapon of defense—those thirty-four pages of encrypted data.

That settled it. He would stay put for the time being. With that resolved, he turned to two basic human needs: food and coffee.

Teagarden pulled his belongings together and shoved them all into his backpack. He put on his green army cap and military-style sunglasses and headed outside. This time, the receptionist who lived next door was nowhere to be seen. That was good. Now that he'd shaved his beard, it was best to avoid her. He'd read somewhere that in a post 9/11 world, hotel workers were trained to notice anyone who radically altered their appearance.

The person at the front desk was a drowsy overnight security guard who nodded politely as he passed through. Tea-garden nodded back.

And he was right. There were no police cars anywhere. He looked for Harry's truck. Nothing. He looked for black Ford vans with smoked windows parked at the curb. Again, nothing suspicious. As for the people, they were mostly dog-walkers, joggers and harried workers headed for the early shift. In the park, there was the usual assortment of the homeless and sleepless. But he knew that during the day, Madison Square Park was a magnet for all kinds, especially at lunchtime.

One great thing about New York City is that within a single block's walk, decent carryout can be had at any time of the day or night. He quickly found a bustling deli where he bought a large coffee and a sesame bagel, toasted with fried egg, ham, and butter.

Not worrying about calories may be the only good thing about being a wanted fugitive. Besides, I'm starving.

The shift change happened while he was out. The night watchman was gone and—*she*—was back. It was their third encounter, but their first with him clean-shaven.

"Good morning, Mr. Samuels," she said, recognizing him immediately without the beard and sounding far less curt.

"Morning," he said, with a sticky-sweet North Carolinian twang. He wondered if she was miffed because he turned down her invitation the previous evening.

Back in his room, he attacked the thirty-four pages. He logged onto his laptop using Dan Jones' I.D., and researched the words: spiral, code, decode, encryption, circles, rotate.

It immediately kicked back with a number of possibilities.

Caesar Cipher: simple method of substituting one letter or number for another to encode or decode secret messages. Named after Julius Caesar who communicated in code.

ROT13: variation of the Caesar cipher that replaces a letter with the letter that comes thirteen letters after it in the alphabet. Developed in Rome after Caesar.

Cipher Disk: invented in 1470 Italy, utilizing two round plates and marked with letters and numbers for the purpose of encoding and decoding messages.

The Jefferson Disk: cipher system utilizing multiples of disks, each marked with letters that are rotated to encode messages and turned back again by the same pre-determined number of rotations for decoding. Invented by Thomas Jefferson and used by the United States Army into the early twentieth century.

Enigma Machine: multiple series of mechanized rotor-ciphers for blind encryption by a typist, most notably used by Nazi Germany.

Of course, that's it!
Teagarden instinctively knew it was the solution. The pages held nothing more complicated than a simple number for letter substitution. It was some sort of disk rotation system. He should have seen it earlier. The history he'd just read was more fanciful truth than real truth. The story that Caesar invented rudimentary ciphering was probably encouraged by some Roman PR guy wearing wingtip sandals. Fact is, basic number substitution had probably been around since the ancient Sumerians. The infamous Enigma Machine used by the Nazis was nothing more than a simple letter-substitution system, but multiplied a thousand times over to make it more complicated and, presumably, more secure.

There was nothing secure about Enigma. Not really. It was ahead of its time, and very complicated. But complicated encryption equals complicated decryption, which the great Alan Turing proved. It really doesn't matter how many layers of letter-for-letter or number-for-letter encoding are packed on. Somebody will eventually figure it out. It wasn't until mainframe computers existed that real and virtually indecipherable code was possible—and that was only as strong as the weakest employee with a security clearance.

He looked at the first of the thirty-four pages: 10906010. Followed by: 44, 55, 11, 18, 99, 15, 77, 14.

If he could learn the code for those eight letters, he could apply them to the corresponding numbers within every entry on that particular page. Knowing eight of the twenty-six letters in the alphabet would be a giant leap forward.

He wished he could logon to one of the algorithm websites available to him at Columbia. It would make the job go a lot faster. The university's math and computer science departments had machines that helped crack the human genome, and had recently proved that the speed of light was not the ultimate speed limit of the universe. He knew better than to try those sites. The police and maybe Harry would surely find him in a matter of minutes if he did.

Instead, Teagarden tried three encryption programs available to the public. In this case, the public amounted to the unfortunate Dan Jones who was running away from home and hearth in Missouri. The programs were all mediocre. But he stayed with deepdecipher.com, which seemed the best of the lot. When he entered the first eight numbers—44, 55, 11, 18, 99, 15, 77, 14—the website kicked back with thousands of possibilities.

That was stupid. How many eight-letter words are there in the English language that do not repeat any letters? Answer: a lot.

He keyed-in the instruction to search for pairs of four-letter words without repeating letters and again it came back with too many options.

He modified the command to search for standard pairs of words known to be used in beginning formal communication or informal salutation. That didn't work. The computer seized-up and the webpage froze. It came back looking like an anagram game for idle entertainment.

```
D  L  U  G        Z  M  _  N
Q  E  _  _        B  _  H  V
P  C  A  _        F  O  X  Y
S  T  I  R        J  K  _  W
```

Well, that's no help.

The general consumer website was nowhere near sophisticated enough to figure pairs of four-letter words with specific meanings.

Teagarden was about to reboot the laptop when he looked closer. There were blanks in the jumbled pairs for a reason: the instruction asked for *no repeated letters.* There were thirty-two places, but only twenty-six shown, because there are twenty-six letters in the English alphabet.

He stared at the anagram.

I may be a fox on the run, but I've got no interest in "stir foxy," or "foxy stir."

Then he saw it.

```
D                        N
  E                    H
    A                O
      R        J
```

Teagarden stared at the frozen computer screen. That silly, rudimentary website had done it. It found the first, vital clue.

Every entry on every page began with the words: "Dear John."

Oh—my—God.

At that moment, there came a loud banging on his door.

"Open up!" the voice shouted. "Emergency. Open up!"

CHAPTER TWENTY-FIVE

Like the computer screen in front of him, Teagarden froze.

For a second time he felt an icy jolt shoot up the center of his spine.

What now?

He considered performing a control-alt-delete to unfreeze the laptop. Looking at his room door, he worried that whoever was on the other side was prepared to perform a similar function on him, except that would be more like a control-alt—*decease.*

Then it came again, working back from the other end of the corridor.

Bam-bam-bam!

"Open up!" the voice shouted. "Emergency!"

"Okay," Teagarden shouted back.

He quickly loaded his backpack with his three most important possessions—his cash, the laptop and the *Dear John* document. When he opened the door, there was no one in the corridor. No Harry. No Sheriff Klumm. He squinted toward the staircase. At the far end of the hallway there was a single firefighter and one other hostel guest standing in his open doorway. The firefighter was clad in a yellow-glow, fire-retardant uniform and helmet.

"Exit immediately," he shouted. "Everybody out."

Teagarden left his door open and hurried to the stairwell. The odor of smoke relieved his anxiety because it meant there was a real fire somewhere in the building. As he hurried through the small lobby he stopped beside the two-seater couch, dumb-struck at twin images being broadcast at that moment on the flat-panel television. It was a side-by-side wanted poster.

They were dual images of his own face.

One was his New York driver's license photo with a full beard. The other was the same photo, altered by computer program to display his face as clean-shaven.

Then it got worse. The words under the photos read *$50,000 Reward for Fugitive Wanted for Murder of New York Boy.*

Several firefighters noisily descended the steps behind him, their radios blaring with updates from other firefighters knocking on doors and ordering full evacuation. Teagarden pulled the brim of his cap over his eyes and stepped to the street. The Eastern European receptionist/drug dealer was standing at the front of the evacuated crowd. After seeing his image on television, he was uncertain if he should speak to her or simply hurry off as casually as he could manage.

"Westport, Connecticut," she said, stopping him.

"Sorry?"

"The rich boys from up there. They come down to city on commuter train. They book rooms, go out to party, buy drugs, come back here." She pursed her lips scornfully. "Co-caine, heroin, crack. They cook, they boil, they smoke, they snort, they mainline. Sometimes they pass out. And that's when their little candles start fires."

"Oh," Teagarden said. He couldn't help but admire her in-stincts for playing both sides of the street, enabling the drug-gies and blaming them too.

"Then we have this." She gestured at a front room on the second floor where the smoke was pouring from an open win-dow. "This group has been in that room since Friday. Today is Monday. So the fun-times weekend for them turns now to fire."

Teagarden wondered if the firefighters were going to break glass in the adjacent window of the same room.

"It looks bad," she said. "But it is really just a mattress. The repairman man will now come and clean, plaster, paint. Is always problem like this. Always big problem with the rich kids."

"Thank goodness it's not too serious. I suppose their parents will bail them out of jail."

"Jail? Hah! You think just because this is America it works like that? Perfect all the time? Maybe in your North Carolina. But let me tell you, when white boys make trouble here, they are not taken to gulag. This does not happen for them. Cops know these are not black kids. Look," she said. "Look around. Do you see police?"

"No."

"No. That is right. But firefighters come." She nodded with respect at them. "That is good. They come fast. In America, it is the fire department that works—*the best!*" She was genuinely appreciative.

"Well, I'm glad for that," Teagarden said, continuing with his southern drawl.

"Besides," she continued, "the druggies ran away already. And when police arrive, they find nobody. The druggies, you know, they don't give real name. None of them. They all have fake cards, fake license, fake this, fake that. Fake, fake, fake. But I hear them talk about their wonderful Connecticut. Westport, Bridgeport, Southport. All the ports up there." She sighed as she finished speaking, then turned to Teagarden, crossed her arms under her breasts which pushed them higher for his benefit. She gave him a searching look. "Mr. Samuels, like all men, you are better with clean shaved face."

He tried to say thank you, but only stuttered.

"I know what you are thinking," she said.

"You do?"

"Yes. You wonder why I am here." He nodded. "Mr. Samuels, I am manager of this tourist lodge for one year. With the money I make here, my children in Chechnya eat good breakfast every day."

I apologize for accurately guessing your story.

It was apparent that she had not seen his wanted poster on television. That is, not—*yet.* The news networks must have just begun airing it as the firefighters arrived. She didn't realize it, but by displaying her breasts for his consideration, and telling him about her personal situation, she was also telling him that he had to depart her company. Now. Immediately before she returned to the lobby. He knew that the moment she saw his broadcast wanted poster, she'd do everything possible to claim the $50,000 as her own and consider it a happy American-style jackpot.

"Well," he said, "we all do what we must for our families."

"In the name of God, this is true."

The gathering on the sidewalk grew in size as more guests evacuated. Most of them were young tourists. Teagarden assumed some were participants of the nighttime yodeling contest in room 411.

Some firefighters milled about, talking on two-way radios and looking up at the smoke that poured from the one window. The first police patrol car approached from a block away. Almost immediately, the second car appeared from the opposite direction.

Time for me to be going now.

"I think I'll go get something to eat while this mess gets fixed," Teagarden said. He turned to exit the gathering crowd. "Good luck."

"Call me Svetlana," she called out. "Talk to you later."

He did not look back, but only turned his head over his shoulder.

"Okay, Svetlana. Later."

Wow.

CHAPTER TWENTY-SIX

A shady part of Madison Square Park that lay catty-corner to the hotel seemed a reasonable spot to settle for the time being.

Only half-a-block wide but two blocks long, the park was teeming with humanity at that time of morning and offered a good opportunity for Teagarden to hide in plain sight. He could watch the front of Madison Park Euro Lodge from a park bench and still have plenty of escape points, including side streets and subway stations. On the way, he ditched his army green cap, and bought a blue hat with a short floppy brim from a sidewalk vendor.

Clean shaven and with his face concealed by no more than a hat and military style sunglasses, he felt exposed and vulnerable. He considered returning to the Midtown library on the off chance that the Hasidim outfit was still in the men's room trash bin. He quickly rejected the idea.

That would be stupid. On the other hand, everything else also seems stupid at this point.

He considered calling Sheriff Klumm and turning himself in, but rejected that, too. He would do that as the final move if nothing beneficial came from his decryption. He knew he'd be better off with Klumm than Harry. It was like when the Nazis considered surrendering, they preferred the Americans to the Soviets. And for good reason. The Soviets would kill them because of Stalingrad.

Teagarden watched Madison Park Euro Lodge from a distance as the patrol cars remained at the scene after the firefighters departed. That meant the mattress fire was extinguished, but he feared another type of fire was igniting in the lobby.

He entered the park's double-gated dog run and found a bench, hoping to look as mindless as the dog owners who were mostly on cellphones or had their noses tucked into tablets. There were three times as many dogs as people. Two elderly, overfed Alaskan Malamutes took to him immediately with slobbering affection.

He gave rubbies to the big Malamutes. He withdrew the thirty-four pages, picked up an abandoned newspaper and copied the numbers from a random entry onto the broadsheet. For simplicity, he picked a relatively short passage. The page heading read 10906010. The entry read:

24-21-11-15-36-76-26-64
76-64-84-26-31-41-66-76-94-21-66-99-24-11-99-31-64-
36-15-64-21-99-76-15-14-21-34-11-64-5-21-6-5-15-31-
84-41-21-64-84-16-76-5-76-96-21-5-11-84-31-76-64-76-
94-21-5-21-11-41-99-31-66-66-21-34-11-66-11-41-14-11-
84-26-84-15-14-34-31-64-15-41-21-24-88-76-14-21-31-
66-76-94-21-99-76-15-6-11-84
60/20/6010

He watched the sidewalk in front of the lodge. The police cars were departing. From the dog run he could see them muscle their way into traffic. One made an illegal U-turn and sped away. A few more minutes passed as the lumbering Malamutes bound with happiness from him to their owners to a bouncing tennis ball and back to him. Each time they came back to him for more petting, he obliged.

"Hey, boys. Hey, you two. What a pair of big ol' happy boys you are. You're just like my giant happy dog, Coconut."

After saying it, he realized it had been less than two full days since his dog was killed. It seemed more like two decades. He went back to his scribbled numbers. Above each one, he jotted the known letter code for the first eight:

D E   A R   J O H N
24 21 11 15 36 76 26 64

He eyed the front of Madison Park Euro Lodge. Everything was calm. He considered phoning Svetlana from a public phone, wondering if she might be more interested in him than in the $50,000 reward.

Yeah, right. What were the odds of that? With her situation, no way she'd prefer me over the money.

He turned back to his scribble on the newsprint and filled in all the numbers known to stand for the letters D-E-A-R-J-O-H-N where they repeated:

D-E-A-R-J-O-H-N
O-N-84-H-31-41-66-O-94-E-66-99-D-A-99-31-N-J-5-N-
E-99-O-5-14-E-34-A-N-R-E-6-R-5-31-84-41-E-N-84-16-
O-R-O-96-E-R-A-84-31-O-N-O-94-E-R-E-A-41-99-31-66-
66-E-34-A-66-A-41-14-A-84-H-84-5-14-34-31-64-5-41-E-
24-84-O-14-E-31-66-O-94-E-99-O-5-6-A-84
60/20/6010

No word separations jumped out, though he guessed the final set of numbers were a date. And it partially matched the numerical heading that governed all entries for that particular page, which meant the topline heading was also a date of some sort.

That works.

He should have seen it earlier. The final numerical entry was a date written as month, day, and year, each in two digits. That meant the page heading was the same year, but written only as four digits, which, in turn, meant that each page accounted for one full year. The thirty-four separate pages represented a total of thirty-four years.

Well, that's some progress.

He needed to feed his partial translation into deepdecipher.com to achieve complete decryption for at least that one entry. He again looked for the two big Malamutes, but something had happened. Instead of idle joyous bouncing in the dog run, they were at the opposite end, fixed at the gate, frantically angling for a better view of something in the direction of Madison Park Euro Lodge.

Teagarden strained to see what grabbed their attention.

The truck!

It was parked at the curb in front of the lodge, the same boxy, meanly efficient looking vehicle with overly big tires.

But it was worse than that.

The dogs were not fixed on the truck. They had seen, heard, and smelled something else. Three uniformed New York City police officers had entered the park at three different points. Each of them walked a police dog consumed with manic energy, barking and straining at their leashes like bloodhounds. It was as though they were all on the trail of a powerful scent.

His scent.

Oh crap!

Teagarden did the only thing that came to mind. He departed the dog run, intentionally leaving the double gates wide open.

CHAPTER TWENTY-SEVEN

What followed was canine bedlam.

Instead of the dogs of war, it was more like the dogs of wild abandon. The two large Malamutes ran straight into the park to intercept and befriend the approaching police dogs. They were followed by an army of yammering, tail-waggers ranging in size from rat to warthog.

Teagarden was viciously cursed by panicked dog owners who frantically chased their fleeing babies. Two animal owners, one man and one woman, actually chased *him* several paces, taking fist swings at his back before thinking better of it and turning to pursue their beloved pets. Having no time to apologize or explain how guilty he felt, he hurried to a side street where he quickly saw that he had not escaped.

The officers spotted him while straining to hold their K-9's. One of them pointed, yelled an order, and all three released their dogs.

That's when Teagarden ceased being a smart fox. In that moment he became a dumb fox. He could think of only one thing.

And that one thing was as dumb as they come.

Run!

He bolted as hard as his creaky knees could manage. The nearby presence of a subway entrance helped. Once underground, it was dumb luck that a train was entering the station at that moment.

Paying the fare never occurred to him, but getting over the

turnstile wasn't pretty. There was no way he was going to jump it like an ordinary fare beater. His lousy knees forced him to pause, hoist his weight to sit on the turnstile edge, pull up his legs, spin his butt, and delicately slide over to stand down on the opposite side.

The police dogs had no such limitations. All three were in the station and plowing under the turnstiles as the train doors opened. Their momentary confusion amid the waiting crowd gave Teagarden enough time to move down the platform by one car-length.

As he entered the train, he saw the K-9 trio casually stepping aboard the adjacent car as though it were their daily commute. In the crush of passengers, the conductor must not have noticed because he closed the doors and the train pulled from the station before the pursuing cops caught up.

Unbelievable. If anyone ever makes a movie about this, no one will think this scene remotely possible.

It was a downtown N-train. *N* as in nuts. *N* as in nasty.

The next stop was Union Square at 14th Street, a large meandering station with dozens of tunnels and exits. Surviving until the next stop was his only hope. He hastened forward, away from the car with the dogs. Despite the deafening noise, he could hear muffled screams of startled passengers in the adjacent dog car. Teagarden pictured the animals trotting up and down the aisle, sniffing everyone, searching for a scent that matched his.

He yanked the heavy sliding door to cross into the next car to put two car lengths between him and the dogs.

So far, so good.

He kept going, elbowing his way past everyone, desperately trying to put one more subway car between him and the K-9s.

How is this going to work when I do exit? The fox never escapes.

The N-Train. *N* as in never.

He stepped on an elderly man's foot.

"Hey, pal!"

He stiffly bumped the shoulder of a man blocking the aisle.

"Yo, watch ya ass, man."

He snagged a woman's purse, bumped a baby carriage, and swung wide around a beggar playing the accordion.

Keep them doggies movin'...

He crossed into the next car as the train pulled into Union Square station, putting him a total of three cars away from the K-9 team.

The steel wheels squealed as they ground to a halt. Behind the sliding doors, he stood directly opposite one of the many exit tunnels leading to more tunnels and other subway connections.

Okay, just cross the platform. Four simple strides. That's all I have to do.

Before the doors opened, he realized the dogs were not his biggest problem. In anticipating the fugitive's flight path, the N-platform at Union Square Station was swarming with police.

Keep it together.

When the doors swung open, he raced across the platform to the next tunnel, nearly brushing shoulders with two uniformed cops who failed to see him because their attention was diverted by the sudden clamor. Three cars away, the three dogs did a simultaneous bolt from the train. Once on the platform, they furiously sniffed the odor-filled air, checking billions of floating scent molecules. They had probably learned his scent from his pillow at Madison Park Euro Lodge. Now, their powerful nostrils needed only a single atom that belonged to forty-nine-year-old math professor Sam Teagarden, Ph.D., Columbia University, to let them know they detrained at the proper station.

But dogs do not belong on subway platforms.

As they inspected the crowd, the passengers noisily fled and cowered, giving each K-9 a wide berth. The chorus of passenger fear was predictable: "Oh my God," "Dogs, there's mad dogs here," "Look out," "Yo, who let the dogs out?" "Help, I'm afraid of dogs…"

It was a good diversion. He didn't make it happen the way he had at the dog run, but it was just as useful.

As cops rushed to take control of the free-roving K-9 team, Teagarden made his getaway. He strode through the first exit tunnel, turned and strode through another, down a staircase, up another staircase, around the corner, and up to the surface. Guessing his blue floppy hat was key to his description of the moment, he ditched it in a trash bin.

At an exit on the west side of Union Square Park, he slowly ascended the steps to the shaded urban green. He pretended to be looking at his cellphone, which had been turned off since Sunday morning. With downward cast eyes, he peripherally scanned his immediate surroundings on the surface. Grass, benches, pedestrians, traffic. It all gradually came into view.

He almost sensed it before he saw it. The truck with big tires. It was cruising the eastern border of the park, not fifty feet from where he stood in his blue hat with the floppy rim. Teagarden gave a quick glance at the driver. It was the same man, about sixty years old, tall, receding hairline, thick surgery scar on his upper lip.

Teagarden knew it was micro-seconds before he'd be spotted. As casually as he could, he turned and descended back into Union Square Station where he caught an uptown train to 34th Street.

Thirty-fourth Street. That's appropriate, because I really do need a miracle.

CHAPTER TWENTY-EIGHT

He avoided Macy's Department Store with its security staff and array of Big Brother cameras. Instead, he visited several smaller stores across 34th Street, with lurid neon signs and dirty windows.

In a discount cosmetics shop, he bought hair coloring and cotton balls. From the eyeglass vendor he purchased reading glasses that sat on the middle of his nose and hung by an idiot chain. His last stop was Galaxy Sport and Apparel World, so crammed with racks and jammed stacks of clothing that shoppers could barely maneuver. In such a store, he figured the owner wouldn't care if he cut the tags off the clothes he purchased to wear them out. Nor would anyone care if he applied spray dye to his hair in the changing room. Wouldn't care, that is, so long as he didn't steal anything and paid in cash.

So that's what he did.

He bought a pair of off-the-rack gray dress slacks, blue dress shirt, red tie, navy sports coat and black leather shoes. In the changing room he ditched everything except underwear and changed into his new clothes. He tinted his hair and eyebrows with gray-colored dye and stuffed cotton into his cheeks to make his face plump. The reading glasses rounded out the effect.

From 34th Street, he walked north to one of the best kept secrets in Times Square.

The Argonaut was the only hotel in the famed area to retain an air of old-world New York City cheesiness. The new hotels were overpriced, high-rise monstrosities. In the last forty years, the older ones that hadn't been torn down had been remade bigger, and then bigger yet again. It was all done to maintain appeal for a new generation of tourist that injected millions of dollars each day into the New York economy while visiting the Disneyfied crossroads of the world. It had to be done. In the old days, Times Square had tilted so far in the wrong direction, that it violated everyone's comfort zone except muggers and workers in the porn industry.

Yet some businesses still clung to the old ways. The Argonaut was one of them. Managed by a close-knit family that stubbornly resisted change, it was small, reasonably clean and rich with throwback character reaching well beyond the wild and wooly days of the 1970s. It was the same hotel lobby where a Sicilian mobster was shot dead by another mobster in the 1950s, where soldiers were bivouacked in the 1940s while awaiting the ship that would take them to European battlefields, and where Broadway glitterati gathered in the corner bar in the 1930s to celebrate or skewer the latest stage premiere. It was the same hotel where he had stayed the previous week during the math conference at the nearby Marriott Marquis and where he spent one wonderful evening with Cynthia.

The lobby smelled of mothballs. There were two musty old plush sofas and an ancient mirror so faded with age that it returned only fuzzy reflections. The men's room had a lengthy trough-style urinal so stained and chipped it could have been a hand-me-down from ancient Greece. Next to the brown shellacked coat room was a bank of ancient landline payphones, each requiring four quarters before yielding a dial tone.

Confident of his new business-style appearance, Teagarden stepped to the last phone stall, picked up the receiver, and deposited the coins.

"Madison Park Euro Lodge," the voice said. He let the pause speak for itself. "Madison Park Euro Lodge," she said again.

"Hello, Svetlana. This is Sam Teagarden." This time, the pause was hers, which told him she recognized his real name.

"Oh."

"How are you, Svetlana?"

"Fine."

"That's good. Listen, I was wondering. May I swing by this evening for a glass of wine in your room?" Another pause. "Svetlana? Are you there?"

"Yes. I am here. Please do come by. I work only one shift today. How about six o'clock in room 413. Or if you prefer—"

"How long would it take, Svetlana?"

"What do you mean?"

"What do I mean? Well, I don't mean how long would it take for me to arrive. I don't mean how long would it take for us to get acquainted. I don't mean how long would it take for us to copulate. What I mean is, how long would it take for you to collect the fifty thousand after I got arrested?"

Another pause.

"How long do you think, Svetlana?"

"Mr. Samuels..."

"It's Teagarden. You know my real name. However, you should continue calling me Samuels on this phone call because it's safer for both of us."

"I am sorry, Mr. Samuels," she said, "but you know that I am a guest in this country, and..."

"And if the police knew you were helping druggies from Connecticut, they'd deport you? Is that what you mean?"

The pause in her flat affect was longer this time.

"I don't know what you talk about."

"Well allow me to help you, Svetlana. Let me tell you what I'm talking about. I'm talking about the fact that the kids from Westport, and Southport, and Bridgeport, and Eastport, and all the other ports are safe at Madison Park Euro Lodge because you make them safe. How much do you charge them? Do you actually supply their dope, Svetlana? Are you their dealer? Or just their den-momma and watchdog?"

"I had to tell them it was you," she said. "I am on temporary visa. I do not want to be deported. I need to stay in America, and I want to—"

"Svetlana, as soon as one of those kids gets busted, I'm going to see to it that they finger you. Fugitive or not, I can still make that happen. And when those kids get around to telling their full stories, you will do prison time. Only after you spend a decade in maximum lockup with the other ladies will you have to worry about deportation. Those ladies on the cellblock and exercise yard will be fun for you Svetlana."

"What do you want, Mr. Samuels?"

"Video."

"Video?"

"Yes, video. From the lobby security camera. Of the older man. No uniform. He's tall. Receding hairline. Has a thick scar on his upper lip."

"Yes, I saw that one," she said. "But I did not speak with him."

"So you know who I'm talking about? He's on your security video?"

"Yes. He stood in the reception area. So I have some video of that one."

"Well that's good, Svetlana. Because if that—one—as you call him, suspected that you had spoken to me again, includeing this phone call right now, your life would be in serious danger. Do not doubt me on that, Svetlana."

"All right. I do not doubt."

"Good. So, I ask you again, do you think they're listening now?"

Another pause.

"No."

"Svetlana, I'm not fooling around here. That man is a bad man. If you had any business with him, or if he suspected you of having any contact with me, other than checking me in last night, you *will* be in danger. Do you hear me?"

"Yes. I hear."

"And if you are lying to me, frankly, it would be best for you to head straight to JFK and get on the next flight to Chechnya."

"Mr. Samuels, I did not talk to him. He took no interest in me. But I heard one man refer to him as FBI. And I heard him being called by his name. They called him Mr. McCanliss and Special Agent McCanliss."

"McCanliss. Okay, that's good Svetlana. Now here's the deal. You download a chunk of video that includes his image and send it to me. You do that, and I'll let you carry on with your job that allows you to buy a healthy breakfast every day for your children in Chechnya."

The pause was brief.

"Where do you want me to send the video?"

"The Argonaut Hotel in Times Square. Put the disc in an envelope, address it to Tom Samuels, and send it by way of bicycle messenger. Now. Have it dropped off at the front desk at The Argonaut Hotel."

"I can e-mail it to you."

"No. I need the old-fashioned DVD, Svetlana."

"Very well."

"Right now, Svetlana. Don't wait."

"I will not wait. I am starting now, while we talk."

He could hear the sound of her typing and mouse-clicking.

"Bicycle messenger. Front desk at The Argonaut. Got it?"

"Sure. I have got that," she said. After a moment, she said, "Mr. Samuels?"

"Yes?"

"My offer of wine…it…well, if you are still…"

"Thanks, Svetlana. Maybe some other time."

After he hung up, he considered calling his daughter. She'd know by now that he was in trouble and would be desperately worried. But it would have to wait. Any call to her conch house on Key West or to her office at Boca Chica Key, which housed the Naval Air Station, would not only be traced instantly, but would risk drawing her into this mess. That was something to be avoided at all costs.

No matter what happens to me, I need to keep my daughter and granddaughter out of this—what do I call it? A surrealistic mess? A clusterfuck? A surrealistic clusterfuck? Yeah, that's what it is.

He departed the hotel and crossed the intersection. He bought coffee from a sidewalk vendor and stood at the nearest subway entrance to observe the hotel's front door. After twenty minutes, a bicycle messenger arrived, parked, locked his bike to a pole, and entered the lobby with his shoulder bag. One minute later, he emerged, unlocked his bike, mounted up and rode off.

Teagarden let another hour go by. Nothing more happened. That meant Svetlana believed him. She had done what he told her.

He picked up the package being held for Tom Samuels. When the receptionist hesitated, he mentioned that he'd been a resident at The Argonaut the previous week for the math conference at the Marriott. That, and a twenty-dollar bill got the package handed over without further question.

What was the name Svetlana overheard in the commotion of her small lobby? Was it McCanliss? That's it. What kind of a name was McCanliss? It didn't seem like a killer's name. He had no idea what a killer's name sounded like. Moriarty, maybe. Mr. Hyde, Ahab, or Adolf. But McCanliss? Is sounded so—not evil.

CHAPTER TWENTY-NINE

He took two NSAID tablets.

Needing a place to work, and confident now that it was temporarily safe, Teagarden returned to The Argonaut lobby and settled onto one of the musty sofas that reeked from decades of stale cigarette smoke. In the middle of the new Times Square Theatre District, it really was the hotel that time forgot.

I wish my knee-joints could be the bones that time forgot.

He selected a spot angled toward the back wall near an emergency fire exit. From there, visitors could not see his face, but he could still observe the center of the room. He inserted the DVD into the CD/DVD-ROM slot of his laptop and cued it up. The video was only seventeen seconds long. But that was enough. Uniformed police and firefighters milled about the small reception area at Madison Park Euro Lodge, as did the man with the pronounced lip scar.

And there was someone else in the video. Directly behind the man Svetlana called McCanliss, was the big, flat-screen TV. At that moment, the all-news station was again airing the wanted poster of him—Sam Teagarden. It was the same side-by-side images: him with facial hair, and photoshopped rendering of him without it. The screen was directly behind the same man he saw in the boxy truck with big tires as he departed Bethel on his way to Walmart in a van with the Hasidim.

He was in his early sixties, tall, perhaps six-three. His lower jaw was sharply recessed, probably because of an overbite. The lip scar was thick and wide, indicating an imperfect surgical correction of what must have been an extreme cleft palate. The hairline was receding, but he had plenty of hair elsewhere on his head, though it was so closely cut that he looked balder than he really was.

Teagarden copied the video to his hard drive and watched it again.

He saw, too, that McCanliss had a strong body and long, powerful arms. He wore casual clothing, including some sort of over shirt on top of a basic pullover. The over shirt likely covered a firearm cradled on his waist or in an armpit.

Teagarden moved to his next task. He clicked the SolarRay browser, logged onto Orange Circle as Dan Jones, and typed the password "yellow4submarine."

Once again, he couldn't resist. He opened the string between Dan and his family in Missouri.

From: sandyjones@orangecircle.com
To: danjones@orangecircle.com

Dear Dan,

If you won't call, please keep e-mailing so at least we will know that you are alive.

We are desperately worried. And you are not dishonest. Why do you imply that you are?

Your mom, of course, doesn't understand, but your daughter misses and needs you. I lie and tell her you are working in that city.

Please come home.

Love,
Your wife, Sandy.

From: danjones@orangecircle.com
To: sandyjones@orangecircle.com

I like it here. The people are honest, even the scumbags are honest because they don't pretend to be anything else, unlike me.

From: sandyjones@orangecircle.com
To: danjones@orangecircle.com

Dear Dan,
We are all so worried. What are you doing in that New York City. I am very worried for your safety.
There are too many Muslims there. It's a bad place....

He stopped reading when he came to the message he'd seen already.

Wow, Dan. You're having a major mid-lifer. My heart goes out to you, my friend. I hope you're not headed for the George Washington Bridge or the Empire State Building.

Then he remembered that a barrier was installed long ago on the Empire State's eighty-sixth floor observatory. He'd have to climb it before making the big leap and Dan didn't sound like the type for that. But there was no such barrier on the bridge.

He logged off Dan's e-mail and logged onto deepdecipher.com where he entered his first partial decryption of the pages. After he submitted it, the screen turned into a series of moving arrows indicating that the website was processing the request.

Teagarden hadn't realized it, but the lobby was actually a cocktail lounge. When the waiter approached, he ordered lunch: a pint of beer and a sandwich. Thankfully, few others were about. At this time of day, all tourists were off visiting the Statue of Liberty, Wall Street, Bloomingdale's and Strawberry Fields. He knew about the hotel because it was known to students for being clean and less pricey. He had first stayed there as a precocious nineteen-year-old undergraduate senior from Chapel Hill looking to see more of America and the wider world. In those days, Times Square wasn't for the suburban minded. With Cynthia the previous week, she remarked how easy it was to imagine wanted fugitives using The Argonaut as a getaway. Little did she know how close to home that statement would hit just a week later.

Their encounter in room 306 that night brought a surge of new experiences, emotional and carnal. She was his first sexual partner since losing his wife, and his first in nearly three decades with anyone other than his wife. It could have been horribly awkward. For most, it probably would have been, yet it wasn't because of her intelligence and kindness. She somehow understood the corners of the box he was living in, the fragile sadness that haunted his waking each morning. That awareness allowed their love making to alternate between tenderness and a passion of the flesh that united and finally enveloped them in comforting embrace.

When the sandwich and beer arrived, he removed the cotton balls from inside his cheeks. The website finished while he was eating. He clicked on the results. The web program filled-in only the letter *I*.

That was the best he was going to get from a general public decoding website. As every Scrabble player knows, the vowels are easy. It's what comes after the vowels where things get dicey.

He turned off the laptop and stared at the numbers, seeing a couple of possibilities worth playing with. He opened the paper napkin that came with his sandwich and bore the words *The Argonaut, a Taste of Old New York*. Jotting down letters, he worked on the puzzle the old-fashioned way, transcribing the numbers by hand just as he'd done in the park opposite Madison Park Euro Lodge before he let slip the dogs of chaos.

This time, he wrote in the letter possibilities, turning the number 84 into the letter *T*, and number 41 into the letter *S*.

Starting with the last letter in the first line, it seemed reasonable to turn D A 99 I N J 15 N E into DAY IN JUNE.

That allowed him to enter the letters *Y* and *U* throughout the message.

D-E-A-R-J-O-H-N
O-N-T-H-I-S-66-O-94-E-66-Y-D-A-Y-I-N-J-U-N-E-Y-O-U
14-E-34-A-N-R-E-6-R-U-I-T-41-E-N-T-16-O-R-O-96-E-R-
A-T-I-O-N-O-94-E-R-E-A-S-Y-I-66-66-E-34-A-66-A-S-14-
A-T-H-T-U-14-34-I-N-U-S-E--24-T-O-14-E-I-66-O-94-E-
Y-O-U-6-A-T
60/20/6010

That opened up a line of intuitive, logical guesses. The letter *P* seemed to work for 96, *B* for 14, and *L* for 66.

He spaced the words and letters for legibility.

He didn't bother with the other numbers. No need to spin the wheel to buy another vowel. He was ready to solve the puzzle, including punctuation.

Dear John,
On this lovely day in June, you began recruitment for operation over-easy, illegal as bathtub gin used to be.
I love you,
CAT
60/20/6010

Not bad for a solo working lunch.
Now he only needed to determine the date at the end. Better yet, knowing this one passage would make decoding other entries on that same page much easier. Unfortunately, it didn't explain the purpose of Operation Over Easy, or identify the author. The person who wrote this file was someone named,

code-named, or nicknamed "CAT." And he still faced the task of analyzing all other pages, each of them encrypted in their own unique code. A simple one-number-for-one-letter substitution required time, something he didn't have a lot of. The job would go much quicker if he could nail the original translation source.

Still, he'd made moderate progress, which he celebrated with a long gulp of beer.

CHAPTER THIRTY

Being a teacher, his professorial instincts kicked in.

It was time for a test. Nothing major. Not a mid-term, just a pop-quiz to see if everyone was doing their homework. In this case, his test needed to pose a little pushback on Mr. Harry McCanliss. In return, he might learn if his personality assessment of the bad man with the ugly lip scar was correct.

Teagarden withdrew his cellphone and turned it on for the first time since Sunday morning in the woods when he spoke with Sheriff Klumm while staring bleary-eyed at the opossum. The device buzzed to life.

First he logged onto his e-mail, ignoring every entry except one in his spam folder.

To: Sam Teagarden
From: movieinthemail.com

Received your complaint about an unplayable version of "Dogfight Girl."

A replacement is now in the mail.

Please let us know if there is anything further we can do.

Well, the return address wasn't from movieinthemail.com. But neither was it directly from her personal e-mail address. She'd sent it from some unrecognizable third-party address at the Naval air station: naskeywestpublicrelations@usnavy.mil.

Good.

That meant she received the previous day's message and fully understood. He logged off e-mail and tapped to open an incoming text message.

From: Harry's Heating and A/C Repair
found your crossword puzzle in progress.
nice work w/dogs.

No surprise there. He figured the sociopath McCanliss would again taunt him about escaping a third time.

He clicked reply and typed.

finished that partic. puzzle.
will leave proof f/u'r enjoyment at present location.
me? i'm gonna tell the world about operation over easy.
ha-ha

He tapped send. Half-a-minute later, he walked through The Argonaut's main revolving door as the response arrived.

From: Harry's Heating and A/C Repair
u r fun.
i like this.
i like u 2.

Gee, thanks, Harry. I'm just wild about you, too.

There it was again. Imperious macho. He sensed it had to be this man's Achilles heel. The problem was in figuring how to capitalize on the knowledge.

He turned off the phone and returned the moist cotton balls to the inside of his cheeks. He crossed Eighth Avenue where he partially descended the steps at the subway entrance, leaving only his head above sidewalk level. From that safe distance, he again kept watch on the hotel like a fox poking from the burrow's entrance to monitor for trouble.

A few seconds later, when trouble arrived, it wasn't a matter of who, but—*what*. And this time, there was no mistaking it.

It buzzed west from Times Square. Unlike the minichoppers that attacked him in his yard, this drone had a traditional fixed-wing design. Unable to hover, it overflew the hotel entrance and climbed sharply to gain altitude so it could turn and make a second approach. Teagarden descended a few more steps. On the machine's return buzz, he saw with a quick glance from deeper in his concrete burrow that it was an older, cheaper model. The 360-degree bottom-mounted camera spun frantically, scanning every face on the street. Accustomed to the routine patrol of traffic drones, drivers and pedestrians took little notice. Teagarden turned away from the camera as it passed overhead.

After two low-level flyovers of The Argonaut's front door, it continued east. He guessed the remote-control pilot would have it circle the surrounding blocks to scan the more heavily populated Times Square. It was natural to assume he was hiding in that bustling tourist crowd, instead of one block west on Eighth Avenue.

He counted the minutes. The drone had arrived in less than two. The first NYPD patrol car screeched to a halt less than a minute after the drone and was followed almost immediately by two more. It took the truck a little longer, about three minutes more to get to the site in Midtown. He could see the driver where he double-parked at the corner and stepped outside.

It was McCanliss—the same man he'd seen in Bethel and sitting in traffic at Union Square. The same man in the video sent by Svetlana.

And he'd been correct about the height. During his walk from the truck to the hotel entrance, Teagarden saw that Harry was about six-three and built like a boxer with long, draping arms, giving him a reach that would rival Muhammad Ali.

It was a scenario similar to the one at Madison Park Euro Lodge. Harry would linger in the background, looking and listening, while the police pressed the man at the front desk for information on the fugitive and showed photos. Teagarden had intentionally left the Argonaut lunch napkin he'd used to decode the entry under his beer bottle, knowing it would end up in Harry's possession.

He waited as a red double-decker tour bus stopped at the curb. He turned his phone on again and quickly keyed in the text message: "only a 2nd rate fixed-wing drone! how come? btw, how'd I manage to dwnld complete hardcopy of file? was that your mistake? does main ofc know about "op over easy?""

He pushed the send button and dropped his cellphone into the rear stairwell of the tour bus as it pulled from the curb. It would rest there until at least the next stop, about ten blocks north at the entrance to Central Park.

He stepped back into his concrete subway burrow and watched the new round of action unfold.

First, the air filled with the squeal of police sirens, followed by more cop cars. That was followed by the same old fixed-wing drone buzzing up Eighth Avenue as it locked-on to his cellphone signal. And that was followed by McCanliss racing back to the truck from The Argonaut lobby.

Beautiful. If McCanliss really is FBI, why am I outsmarting him and all of his high-tech toys? There's no longer any mystery as to how nineteen Arabic men got away with living in the U.S. while some learned to fly a commercial airliner without bothering to -learn how to take off, or land, a commercial airliner.

He descended to the platform and caught an uptown train. Despite being a nationally wanted fugitive, he was ignored by everyone with their heads tucked into cellphones. He sat on the bench, balancing his backpack on his lap. The office costume was working better than the Hasidic outfit because it drew zero attention. The reading glasses perched on the end of his nose completed the charade. He looked like every corporate businessman on his way to or from the office. After all, the business of America *is* business.

The test had worked. He'd determined that, yes, they were on top of him with a swift and coordinated response. Plus, he'd taken a poke at Harry in a way he hoped would snag his swaggering testosterone. If the home office was monitoring all communications, Teagarden had just made it obvious to them that this McCanliss fellow was *their* problem, too. Further, he'd just demonstrated that he was in the process of breaking a rudimentary code where each entry began with the words "Dear John"—a code that, for reasons he did not yet understand, they did—*not*—want decoded and released.

Oh brother, are you guys really descendants of the G-Men who whupped John Dillinger and Al Capone?

He shook his head at the flashing shades of tunnel darkness as they whipped past the train windows.

Dark, darker. Dark, darker. Dark, darker.

I'm pressing my luck. If I keep this up, they're going to corner the fox. It's only a matter of time. I need to disappear. I need to get completely off the grid.

CHAPTER THIRTY-ONE

The FBI Building, Washington, D.C.

"Mr. Natujay, I assure you the Deep Field Command is on solid legal ground here."

It was the third time she had said it and he heard it each time. It wasn't that he didn't believe her. Yet, to him, it sounded like a shopworn advertising slogan. He looked at the ceiling of the DFC's conference room. *His* conference room in *his* corner of the basement in the FBI Building on Pennsylvania Avenue. He wanted more than slogans. But he didn't want a fight. Not with her. Her father had worked with Director Hoover and helped run Operation Over Easy, which later formed the DFC. Anyone who worked for Director Hoover was company royalty. And anyone descended from first generation royalty, was second generation royalty.

"What if the legality is challenged?" he ventured. She glanced at the cubicles outside of the conference room.

"Mr. Natujay, you oversee the DFC of the FBI. Its very existence is a complete secret. Therefore, who would challenge it? For it to be challenged, the challenger must be made aware of it."

"What about Congress?"

"What about it?"

"They get reports. They're informed about clandestine activities."

She wanted to laugh. The idea of *this* Congress challenging anything the FBI does in the name of national security was ludicrous.

"Mr. Natujay, if any elected official or government appointee poses a problem regarding this matter, it will be done only in the court of Homeland surveillance. That bench is in camera. The only people watching are the participants, and they're all sworn to secrecy, not to mention sworn to upholding the security interests of the United States."

"And you're comfortable with that?" he asked her.

"I am perfectly comfortable with arguing before that confidential bench that safeguarding the image of the bureau is, in this historic and vital instance, nothing less than ensuring the safety of the United States itself. As far as we are concerned, it is one and the same."

"What about the press?"

She leaned back in her chair, balancing one elbow on the narrow armrest. For her, there was nothing overtly wrong with this Walter Natujay fellow. He'd been a loyal public servant in the field of national security. Still, she never liked him. He was black. Not African-American, but black nonetheless. Black is still black. What was he? East Indian, Pakistani, Bangladeshi? It was all the same to her. She had no idea if he was Muslim. Moreover, he'd been promoted to DFC commander under a previous president, and not just any previous president, but—*that*—president.

Thankfully, he was due to retire soon. Good thing. That was the only reason be hadn't already been transferred to inventory control. When a government lifer is breathing on a pension, the system has a built-in hands-off policy. When they've put in their time, they're allowed to coast. But for her, the sooner Natujay applied for his government pension, the better.

Outside, a faint mist of afternoon rain was just beginning. She hoped it would cool things off. The weather on the East Coast had not been horrible, but it was stifling in D.C. Nothing unusual about that. The father of the country made the call some 230 years ago. He told them to stop arguing and start building the city on a clump of swampy Potomac wetlands. Consequently, when it's merely hot in Baltimore or Richmond, it's stifling in D.C.

"Mr. Natujay, how many deep field agents do you have currently under management?"

Here it comes. He had hoped to avoid confrontation. As deputy director, she works on the tenth floor, has the ear of the director, and is in line to be the president's National Security Advisor. Being a hostile blip on her radar was the last thing he wanted, mostly because she had the authority to turn him into road kill.

"Ms. Trippler, right now there are eleven active agents. As you know, Operation Dear John is presently assigned two of them, one code-named Ice Skater and another code-named Copper Miner. Of those two, only Ice Skater has been granted supreme authority to take life when and where necessary."

"Right. Ice Skater is the fuck-up in New York that the tenth floor is worried about." It wasn't a question, but he answered her as though it were.

"Yes, ma'am. He is."

"Then, Mr. Natujay, I suggest you grant Copper Miner supreme authority as well. Let Copper Miner complete the job here in D.C. and Virginia, the part that I am telling you is perfectly legit. It needs to be done. The tenth floor wants it done. As chief legal counsel to the FBI, I am telling you there is nothing to be concerned about. So get it done. After that, if Ice Skater still has not accomplished the desired result with this Teagarden character, then you must team Copper Miner with Ice Skater. Maybe the two of them can successfully perform the task as a unit."

"Very well, Ms. Trippler. If that is what the tenth floor wants, that is what I will order."

"And, Mr. Natujay?"

"Yes, Deputy Director?"

"As for the press?"

"Yes?"

"The press and the public are the reasons why Operation Dear John was formed last week as a mission within the DFC. Preventing that file from being decoded and released is the reason why two of your agents are now granted supreme authority for domestic kills. Do you understand? It is—*the*—reason. Do you understand? The press is—*the*—reason why I am here talking to you at this present time."

"Yes. I understand."

"The bureau is a family, Mr. Natujay. Our family. My family. *Some* of us were born into it. And when I say some of us, I mean—*me*, Mr. Natujay. My father served under Director Hoover. On his order, my father founded Operation Over Easy, the predecessor of the DFC. And we need to put this risk behind us so we can get on with our good work protecting the American people."

"Will do, Deputy Director Trippler."

CHAPTER THIRTY-TWO

Encrypted Field Communication
NSA Apache Code Ofc Baltimore, MD/Washington, DC/Coin
TelSatOrbit53/Arlington, VA

<apache code initiate>

TO: copper miner
FROM: deep field cmdr

SUBJECT: operation dear john

<secure field communication may begin>

deep field cmdr to copper miner: u now have supreme authority...proceed immediately with dbl job you've been researching in dc and va...10th flr prefers concurrent...

copper miner to deep field cmdr: k...btw, have been researching weather...heavy rain later today...did you ever drive on
shirley hwy in northern va. during heavy rain?...

deep field cmdr to copper miner: never mind...just do it...
more instructions to follow...

CHAPTER THIRTY-THREE

Shirley Highway, Arlington, VA

"Look at this rain!" the driver complained. "You can't see anything through this fog except taillights."

"Yeah," his passenger agreed. "But when it's like this, I always admire these Virginia commuters. They're real pros."

"Why do you say that?"

"Look at them. They're driving safely. Every car out here has their four-way flashers turned on. Nobody's weaving in and out as though the road were their own private NASCAR track." The young driver grunted agreement, and turned up the speed on his wiper blades. "Not that I don't appreciate my son picking me up in the city for your mom's birthday dinner."

"Sure."

"But in this weather, the Metro would have been quicker."

"I had to drive myself anyway. And I have another motive. I need to talk, Dad. I didn't want to do it online, on the phone, or around mom. That's the real reason why I wanted to pick you up at G.W."

"Uh-oh. Job life or personal life?"

"Job."

"Well, you're the spook, I'm only a humble math professor. But go ahead."

"That's the problem, Dad. I'm not a spook. I'm not a cop. And I'm not a fed. I'm only a research librarian with a discipline in criminology. But somebody's got it out for me. Weird things are going on."

"Like what?"

"Like, I'm suddenly being watched. A new security camera was installed in the ceiling last week, with a lens trained straight at my desk. My computer's been tampered with. And somebody put a new SCD on my main keyboard."

"What the hell is an SCD?"

"Stroke Counter Device. It records everything you type and separately stores it forever as backup, just in case the files get erased. I never had one until last week."

"Maybe you're up for a promotion and they need you to pass one final clearance before the boss makes the announcement. That's the way spooks do it."

"At my apartment on P Street?"

"What about your apartment?"

"Guys are watching it. Around the clock, in shifts. I see them getting in and out of a truck parked at the curb. They go to the Starbucks at DuPont Circle. They use the public restroom, buy coffee, then they get back in this panel truck with lettering that says 'Durgan's Lawn & Garden Service.' It's like they don't care if I see them. Plus, my snail mail is being tampered with. Why would they want to look at all those junk catalogs in my mailbox? It's mysterious."

"Well, they're welcome to come get my junk catalogs. You'd think that in the year 2019 we'd be rid of all that oil-based crap."

"Besides, I'm not up for one."

"One what?"

"Promotion. I'm not up for a promotion."

"Oh."

The driver was about to speak again, to tell his father about the static on his phone line and the sudden aloofness of his boss. Then there was the Asian woman who raced up beside him with a camera and snapped a close-up shot while he jogged in Rock Creek Park. She didn't really want a photo.

She only wanted to jar his nerves. She wanted him to *know* that he was under surveillance.

Traffic prevented him from saying any of it to his father. There was an opening in the jam of cars which he used to turn onto the high-speed ramp and ascended to the triple deck of Shirley Highway. The collision happened when he picked up speed on the rain-slicked, elevated straightaway.

First, the drone hovered directly over the hood of his car.

"Hey, those things are supposed to help prevent accidents." His father spoke just as the drone fired a high-pressure jolt of concentrated air that made a sound like *vah-WOOSH-tah,* shattering the main windshield.

"Jesus," the driver shouted, as his wheels turned into a broadside skid.

The car gained speed and rolled a total of five times before hitting the concrete barrier where it was immediately smashed by two additional vehicles. The third pounding came from an SUV the size of a tank that forced the concrete retaining wall to give way. The impact sandwiched the first and second cars, sending them tumbling to the main highway three levels below.

In the end, a dozen vehicles crashed, six people were injured, three seriously, and five were killed. Two of those five were Professor Stuart Shelbourn, Sr. of George Washington University, and his son Stuart Shelbourn Jr. a librarian with the Federal Bureau of Investigation.

The Virginia State Police called the accident "weather related."

CHAPTER THIRTY-FOUR

Monday Night, July 22, 2019
Encrypted Field Communication
NSA Apache Code Ofc Baltimore, MD/Washington, DC/Coin
TelSatOrbit53/Wilmington, DE

<apache code initiate>

TO: copper miner
FROM: deep field cmdr

SUBJECT: operation dear john

<secure field communication may begin>

deep field cmdr to copper miner: good work...very tidy...
where u?...

copper miner to deep field cmdr: thx...am on i95...near wil-
mington...on way north to nyc...

deep field cmdr to copper miner: good...

copper miner to deep field cmdr: where is ice skater?...& does
he know i am coming?...

deep field cmdr to copper miner: ice skater is at safe house near Central Park Zoo...his fox gone silent...he's working theory that fox is shacked up...haven't told him u are now his partner...u tell him...*carefully*...

copper miner to deep field cmdr: understood, say no more....

CHAPTER THIRTY-FIVE

Madison Square Euro Lodge

She felt safe there.

It wasn't much, but Svetlana Gelayeva thought of room 413 at Madison Park Euro Lodge as more secure than anywhere she'd ever known. After enduring the war years in Chechnya, it felt like true shelter. The Russian soldiers killed her father, raped her mother and frequently raped her, too, even as a child.

The months that followed were better, but still not good. She survived with factory work, cleaning homes, stealing, and occasionally selling her body to Chechen rebels and Russian soldiers. When the men were young, they were less of a threat, and she could be in charge. And sometimes, when they were sweet about it, it made her feel—well, helpful.

Now, at the age of thirty-three, she looked much older. Her two children were being raised by an aunt on a small potato farm near Grozy while she worked as a drug dealer in America. It was the most financially productive period of her life. Ironically, it was also the safest.

When the knock came at the door, she had no reason to worry about her safety.

"Ms. Gelayeva?" he asked.

He knew her name, so she cracked the door. It was late and she did not recognize him in the semi-light of the corridor.

"Yes?"

"Ms. Svetlana Gelayeva?"

"I am the manager. How can I help you? What room are you in?"

"I'm with the FBI." He flashed his shield. "May I come in?" He didn't like the delay in her response. He particularly didn't like that her eyes betrayed no fear. They nearly always show fear, no matter if they are guilty of something or innocent of everything. But she betrayed no trace of fear. He put two fingers on the door and slowly pushed it wide enough to enter. "I'm sorry," he said. "I don't mean to frighten you." He closed the door behind him. "But it is of vital importance. I need to know what Sam Teagarden told you. It is very important that you tell me."

It was only after he was inside her room that she recognized him in the full illumination of her bedside lamp. He was the same man who arrived with the police after her 9-1-1 call to claim the $50,000 reward for a wanted fugitive. The same man who stood quietly in the reception area, observing everything. The same man whose image she had downloaded to DVD and sent by bicycle messenger to The Argonaut Hotel. The same man Teagarden had warned her to be careful of or "your life would be in danger."

She stood her ground with the tall man with the long arms and thick scar on his upper lip.

"It is all right, you do not frighten me," Svetlana Gelayeva said. "He told me nothing. He checked into this lodge where I am manager. He used the name Tom Samuels."

"Have you spoken since he departed?"

"No. But while here, he shaved his beard. I recognized him from the TV as the man who killed that little boy."

"Yes?"

"Yes. So I do right thing. I call police. I tell police he changed the way he looked by shaving beard. It was right thing. So, when you catch him, the $50,000 is mine. No?"

"Yes. But that's not what I wish to speak about."

"Well then, what? My visa is good. I am a legal resident. I work very hard in America."

"I don't care about immigration. My interest is in the phone call Sam Teagarden made to you this afternoon. The one from The Argonaut Hotel."

For the first time her eyes flashed something other than flat disregard, though he couldn't be certain it was fear.

"I, uh…"

"What did he say, Svetlana? What did he ask you? What did he tell you?"

"He asked me for a date."

"So you have spoken since he departed?"

Svetlana knew it was mistake. Still, she held her ground without betraying fear.

"It was personal."

"Personal?"

"Yes."

She spoke with as much casual disregard as she could muster. Her eyes gave him a small something. It was not an old school come-hither flutter, but nonetheless, it was the same idea. In the few seconds that passed since he entered her room, she came to understand that neither arrest nor deportation were the threats. Having been in serious danger many times before, she knew to show indifference, to work the problem while on total emotional shutdown. She glanced behind her at the double bed and window unit air conditioner.

"This room is the best," she said. "And I will turn the a/c up high, if you like. It will be very private." She gave him another discreet, small something with her eyes.

He glanced contemptuously at her bed.

"Did he sleep here last evening?"

"No."

"Did you take up his offer of a date when he phoned?"

"No."

"Well then, we're back where we started, aren't we?"

"I do not understand these questions. I saw on TV that he is fugitive. I call police." She mustered all the casual lack of concern she could manage. "That is all. There is nothing else, Mr. McCanliss. So, do you understand now?"

"I didn't tell you my name, Svetlana. Did you tell *him* my name?"

Another mistake. This time, she knew it was bad, and there was no undoing it. But what was he going to do? Rape her? She'd been raped before.

"No," she said. "I heard your name this morning during fire emergency, but I did not tell him."

"Did he mention the file?"

"The what?"

"The file, Svetlana. Did he tell you about the file while you were fucking him, here in the best room?"

She leered, pretending to be offended.

"We did not—"

His right hand shot to her trachea like a serpent. He did not grip her entire throat in the way of a mad man, but used only a powerful thick thumb and forefinger. He squeezed her larynx so forcefully he could feel her vocal cords smashing under his fingertips. With only that two-digit grasp, he hoisted her entire body until her face rose level with his own so he could watch her die. As she suffocated, her bulging eyes betrayed no fear. When she was gone, his fingertips had nearly pierced the skin of her neck as though making the universal hand gesture signifying "A-Okay."

CHAPTER THIRTY-SIX

The Boathouse, Sparta Township, NJ

Perhaps it was because she was a lawyer that she instinctively sensed the path of least danger for him.

Teagarden did not spend the night in Cynthia's home on her side of the lake in Sparta, New Jersey, nor in the home of her ex-husband on the opposite side of the lake, where she took him to water the plants.

Her ex-husband's house was a large three-story colonial, lavishly furnished with an elevator, spectacular view of the lake and sloping backyard that led to a narrow pier with a boat ramp. Technically, it was still half hers because they bought it while married and had not yet settled the deed. It was the one remaining piece of business holding back full resolution of their divorce. She was the home's caretaker for the summer, while he was a visiting scientist at the Large Hadron Collider near Geneva.

"He's over there studying what happens when particles collide, while I water his plants twice a week," she said, "but I don't mind much."

"You mentioned last week that you're still on good terms. It's better that way."

"Yes. I agree."

She led him to the master bedroom, ridiculously huge with four skylights over the king-sized bed. A flat-panel TV as large as a movie screen hung opposite the bed, on a wall that held recessed bureau drawers. She took a pair of nearly new jeans and two pullover shirts from the top drawer.

"Here," she said. "You'll be more comfortable when you get out of that silly sports coat. The fit won't be perfect. He's a little taller. But you can turn up the cuffs. And you can take the cotton out of your cheeks now. Who was it who did that in the movies? Was it Brando in one of those Godfather movies that airs twice a week on cable?"

"I believe so."

They walked downstairs to the large glass-enclosed porch, where he watched as she watered the plants.

"Do you see that small building in the woods next door at the lake's edge?"

"Sure. Is that yours, too?"

"No. It belongs to a co-op of fishermen who come in the winter when the lake is iced over. I don't understand why they fish only when you need to saw a hole before dropping the bait. But they love it."

"Is your husband part of that crew?"

"Absolutely not." She gave an incredulous laugh. "The only fish Ernest ever wanted to see was on his dinner plate. The idea of scaling and gutting a freshly caught flounder would make him retch."

"Oh."

"Anyway, as a good neighbor, I still keep a key to the boathouse for those guys, just in case. I think that's the best place for you to stay for the next few days."

When she finished watering the plants they walked through the woods to the small building. It was basically a studio apartment, rustic, but with all the comforts of home: daybed, tiny bathroom, galley kitchen, old-style cable TV hook-up plus an active Wi-Fi router. There was one small closet with flimsy louvered doors and a storage loft that covered one-third of the ceiling, with a narrow ladder that leaned to one side. Fishing gear hung from wall hooks, bookshelves were stuffed with reels and fish line instead of books. Old rods were stacked in a corner under two freshwater trout, preserved and mounted on facing walls, their mouths arching toward each other as though straining toward an unrequited kiss.

Being directly at the water's edge, the boathouse had a straight-on view of Lake Mohawk, a large body of water around which the settlement of Sparta was built.

"I can't thank you enough," he said. An awkward moment passed between them. It was a moment he knew would happen where the subject of their previous intimacy would be addressed. Instead of bringing it up, he skirted the subject.

"You didn't mention last week. If you're comfortable talking about it, tell me what happened to your marriage?"

She paused, then said, "Well, it's like this, after twenty-three years of marriage and one wonderful son later, Ernest realized he was gay."

He must have looked shocked, because she laughed at his reaction.

"What's so funny?" he asked. "That doesn't sound like a pleasant experience at all."

She laughed again.

"I suppose you're right. It wasn't pleasant. But sometimes life is just so absurd that you have to laugh. Besides, Ernest is such a sweet man, it's nearly impossible to dislike him."

"If he's gay, doesn't he have someone other than you to water his plants? A partner?"

Another laugh.

"That's the joke," she said. "The man who broke up our marriage, dumped Ernest last winter and ran off to Paris with a ballet dancer."

This time, they both laughed. It felt good. It was the first time he'd experienced the relief of laughter since before the drones arrived at his house in Bethel. He realized she was right, life can be so absurd you just have to laugh. If you can.

There was no laughing earlier that afternoon when he first

approached her on the sidewalk outside her high-rise office building near Lincoln Center in New York. She was not at all frightened. In fact, she was genuinely pleased to see him. After a walk around Lincoln Center while he told her the story, she readily agreed to help.

"Sam, I want to tell you something," she said, addressing the awkwardness of the moment he was avoiding. "I didn't stay with you at The Argonaut last week just for the fun of it, although it was fun. I did so because I wanted to be with you. You're a good man, and I like you. I knew that before I slept with you. And I knew the moment I saw the news that there was no way you could have done that horrible thing."

"Lawyer's instinct?"

"Hush. Well, okay, some lawyer's instinct was involved. As for knowing you're a good man—that's all womanly instinct."

"Thank you."

"Stop thanking me. Besides," she said, gesturing at the interior of the boathouse, "now that I've brought you here, we're in this thing together. By the way, your friend Bruce Kasarian at Columbia tells me that nobody there believes you did it, either. He says people in the math and science departments are considering a public petition to the governor."

"What good would that do?"

"None. I don't practice criminal law, but I'm familiar with the system. No offense, Sam, but your colleagues are academics, and academics don't get this sort of thing. A petition urging local police or the FBI to stand down on a fugitive wanted for murder is wasted effort."

He sat on the daybed and sighed.

"Sam, you're exhausted. Let's not delay your rest any longer. You can stay here in the boathouse as long as you feel it's safe. I'm in a Manhattan courtroom all day tomorrow. But I'll visit tomorrow night."

"What if it's not safe? The police and the assassin-squad

may eventually connect you to me as...as..."

He considered saying "as an acquaintance," which sounded so clinical he feared it would be insulting. On the other hand, calling her a "lover," though they had been lovers, seemed presumptuous.

They both sensed an enhanced conversation about their relationship would take place soon enough. But the timing wasn't right, so it would have to wait.

"Good point," she said, covering for his discomfort. "Come over here. You see that small chalet directly across the lake, surrounded by clumps of forsythia? It's partially illuminated by lights from a huge mansion next door, the one with the circular stone driveway."

"Yes, I see it."

"That's my rental. It's what I call home until the situation with the big colonial next door gets resolved." She put a hand on his arm. "Sam, let's make a plan. I don't mean to treat this lightly, like some silly spy movie. Although it does remind me of playing secret agent with my son. We had wonderful games of intrigue that would sometimes go on for days."

"You must have been a fun mom."

"Actually, it was Ernest's idea. He wanted Alex to know that imaginative alternatives to video games really exist and can be even more fun."

"Smart," he said, impressed. "So what do you have in mind?"

She stepped to the sliding glass doors.

"If I think it's unsafe, I'll put a cactus in my bathroom window. It's in a bright blue pot. You'll be able to see it with the binoculars, which are there on the counter."

"Fine."

"You do the same. If there's something iffy going on, take this empty wine bottle with the candle stuck in it, and put it on the railing of the little porch out there beyond the sliding doors. No need to light the candle. I'll see it fine with my own binoculars. And by the way, everyone in this town has either binoculars or a high-powered telescope. It's de rigueur for life on the lake in Sparta. So if you're inspired to try skinny-dipping, be advised that you will be observed, videotaped and probably uploaded to YouTube."

"I'll be careful," he said, knowing that compared with the last two-and-a-half days of his life, this was going to be a holiday.

Before she left, they kissed briefly in the boathouse doorway.

CHAPTER THIRTY-SEVEN

Tuesday, July 23, 2019
Central Park Zoo, New York City

The California sea lions have always been the box office stars of the Central Park Zoo.

The two men stood behind a happy gaggle of day campers watching the seals romp and perform in the rocky pool. The children and their counselors wore orange T-shirts emblazoned with the words, "New Hope Cathedral Day Camp, Easton, Pa."

McCanliss, aka Ice Skater, was the older and taller of the two. The younger, shorter man, Durgan Donnursk, aka Copper Miner, had the figure of someone diligent about exercise and calorie intake.

"So you've heard nothing?" Donnursk asked.

"Nothing since yesterday near The Argonaut Hotel."

"Is he shacked up?"

"Unknown. I'm looking into that possibility," McCanliss said. "I've got one lead in northwest Jersey. I plan to hit that tomorrow morning. State and local Boy Scouts will join in. You can come along if you like."

"Oh, I will come along," Donnursk said. "You can be certain of that."

McCanliss didn't like his tone.

"Look, Durgan, you're here for Q-and-A so you can file a report about Bethel to the coat-and-tie assholes on the home shop's tenth floor. So do me a favor. Could you just do your job without getting up in my grill? What do you say?"

Two angelic campers turned to look at the older man using foul language. A camp counselor enveloped them in his right arm, discreetly returning their attention to the sea lions.

Donnursk ignored the insult. "I heard he's broken the Dear John code. Your screw-up in Bethel allowed him to download it. Now he's actually *broken* it? I mean, *Jesus*, Harry."

"Let me ask you something, Durgan, since you're so plugged into the tenth floor. Is there any truth to the rumor that the file is named 'QB69'? As in Queen Bitches?" McCanliss was set to break into sarcastic laughter.

"Harry, just answer the question. I'm not here for jokes."

McCanliss sighed. "Yeah, yeah, yeah. He broke the code. Well, he's broken one entry that I know of. But that single entry happens to mention Op Over Easy."

Donnursk was stunned.

"Goddamn, Harry. Do you know how much damage that can do?"

This time, several campers heard the younger, shorter man swearing. They glanced with discomfort at one another. Their counselor turned to stare daggers at the two men, who ignored him and casually stepped away from the frenetic huddle of kids cheering the performing sea lions.

"Aw c'mon, Durgan," McCanliss said. "It can't be that bad."

"Well, the tenth floor thinks it's that bad. They're crapping footballs over this."

"Look, neither of us knows for certain what Op Over Easy really was. Technically, it's all rumor. Even at our level. So if it gets out in the press, they can just deny it. Like always. They can just call it nonsense like the Air Force does for all the assholes who think Martians landed at Area 51."

"Harry, this is not some Area 51 bullshit. This is Operation Over Easy. We know what it was. It was the 1960s program that became the DFC. And the DFC is now you and me. It's our job. It's who we are. It's the reason we do what we do for our country."

"Yeah, yeah," McCanliss said with an eye roll.

"Goddammit, Harry, wise up. This is your granddaddy's syphilis popping out in our bloodstream two generations later."

"Okay, all right already. I'll nail Teagarden and put a stop to it. That's what my grant of supreme authority allows. I will nail him."

"No, Harry—*we*—will nail Teagarden. We are now a team working with approval for dual supreme authority. You fucked up in Bethel, so no more solo. The tenth floor is making us a duo. That's what I'm here to tell you. We're a unit."

This time it was McCanliss who was stunned. His nostrils flared around the thick scar under his nose. Donnursk liked seeing that. It made him feel he had the upper hand.

"That's right, Harry. I'm not here for a mere Q-and-A to file a report to the tenth floor. We are officially a squad of two—yoked. *Partners.* And let's hope I'm not too late, because if he's decoded the entire Dear John File, learned about Operation Over Easy and everything that involves, then goes public, well then—*we*—*are*—*all*—*fucked.* You understand? American history in the second half of the last century will be revealed to be a total lie. Our enemies will love it, and our international allies will totally bail on us for being a historic fraud. Do you understand? *That* is how serious this is."

He stopped talking as they strolled deeper into the zoo. They entered the penguin's house and emerged on the other side.

"And there's something else, Harry. Who the hell is Svetlana Gelayeva and why is she dead?"

"Look, Durgan, I'm operating with supreme authority here. That was my call. There was reason to believe she knew about your precious Dear John File. So it was a preemptive kill. Therefore, it was justifiable. Doesn't that tell you *and* the tenth floor that I'm on the job? That I'm on top of it? That I've got their back? That I'm covering for them?"

"Was it clean? Can it be traced back to you? Because if it can be traced to you, that's going to complicate this partnership."

"Of course it was clean. That upstate Boy Scout sheriff thinks Teagarden killed the kid in Bethel and now the NYPD thinks he killed *her* too. It's perfect. There's no way to connect me to that kiddieland sex-and-drug parlor in the Flatiron District. It's that simple. And do me a favor, don't call this a 'partnership.' We may have to work together for a couple of days, but we are *not* partners."

"That kill better be clean," Donnursk said.

"Besides, didn't you just conduct a pre-emptive double assassination on Shirley Highway in Northern Virginia?"

"I did. And it was as clean as they come. The tenth floor was impressed with it. Unfortunately, the tenth floor is not happy with you. The bosses up there are worried about kickback from this Svetlana Gelayeva incident."

"Jesus, Durgan, lay off. I'm telling you it was clean. Formula 409 clean. Nobody can place me as being in that tourist hostel. Besides, is there anything the tenth floor isn't worried about these days?"

"Harry, I'll tell you something they *are* worried about—they *are* worried about *you*. Why do you think I now have supreme authority and have been assigned as your partner? It's because he escaped you in Bethel and downloaded the file. Then you let him get away in New York City, resulting in the manager of some fleabag flophouse getting eighty-sixed. If I were DFC commander, I'd be worried about you too."

McCanliss was uncharacteristically subdued.

"Well they can stop worrying," he said, almost apologetic.

"Let me ask you, how'd he happen to land on that particular Over Easy entry in the 'Dear John File'?" Donnursk asked.

"Looks like dumb luck. Just like every other thing about this arithmetic teacher. He's got spunk. That's all."

Donnursk craned his neck to look up at the taller man. He glared with impatience.

"Harry, the man shot down four top-of-the line K-32 drones like they were clay pigeons. Do you know how difficult it is to take out one K-32 set to kill with epipoxilene? And he did it—*four*—times."

"Relax, Durgan. That was just more dumb luck. This guy is not Stasi, KGB, or Gestapo. He's not Al-Qaeda. He's not an ISIS sleeper. And he's certainly not Jason Bourne. He's a teacher. A Ph.D. in arithmetic. A forty-nine-year-old math professor at Columbia Liberal University. His parents were hippies. He was born at the Woodstock Music Festival for Crissakes. His name is personified milquetoast—*Tea-gar-den*. And I am telling you: *I...will...get...him!*"

Durgan held his upward gaze of contempt, straight into Harry's eyes.

"Your analysis is missing some key elements," he said. "As a young man, this fox spent a year in the decryption department at the CIA. He moonlights as an expert cryptologist for private industry. He's eluded you and every cop in the state of New York. Now he's decoding the Dear John File while disappearing from bureau radar. And you call all that 'spunk' and 'dumb luck'?"

"Actually, it was only two of the newest K-32s. The other two were older, slightly bigger K-32 test models."

"Harry, that's not funny. This is no joke here. He's got the file. I repeat, is that what you call dumb luck?"

"Well, what do you want to call it, Durgan? He sure as hell doesn't have foreign assistance. This is not an international case. He's domestic. Totally solo. No training. And that was a junior-level gig he had at the CIA. He was a kid back then."

Donnursk continued staring with the repugnance that

every new generation holds for its predecessor when the disease of elderly weakness is in the air.

"I repeat, what do you call it?" McCanliss demanded.

The sea lions barked and clapped on a rock-island in the middle of the pool where a zoo worker tossed fish as a reward for making the church group from Pennsylvania laugh with delight.

"Never mind what I call it," Donnursk said. "I'll tell you what the tenth floor calls it. They call it 'disaster.' And like I said, they're scared shitless. They think you've been outsmarted, and that's not all they're worried about where you're concerned. So what do—*you*—think of that, Harry?"

"I'll tell you what I think, Durgan. I think you're a goddamn genius. Isn't that the way it is? You're the hotshot who nailed that simpleminded retarded kid who stole everybody's password at LAX."

"That's right, that was me, and there was evidence that kid had Chinese backing." He paused, then said, "So?"

"So—*what?*"

"So is that it?" Donnursk asked. "You've got nothing else except that you don't like me?"

"Yeah. I got something else," McCanliss said. "Can you tell me how that encoded file came to be delivered to Teagarden in the first place?"

The question finally compelled Donnursk to back off. He glanced at the sea lions performing for their lunch. The animal on the highest rock ducked jealously whenever the food-fish was tossed to another on a lower rock. The worker teased the complainer with a fish of its own, then tossed it to another. The church campers laughed and applauded at the frustration of the top seal.

Donnursk sighed.

"All right, Harry," he said, "I'll tell you. I have not been told, as they say, for the record, but I tend to be more plugged in than you. There was a report that a blackmail file existed after Director Hoover died in 1972. His secretary, Miss Helen Gandy, issued a confidential warning, but no evidence was ever found so it was assumed to be no more than a rumor. There was a lot of gossip in those years. Turns out, it did exist. It was collecting dust in the FBI library for decades. The tenth floor only found out about it last week when the security software coughed-up an in-house warning on the words 'CAT 38-72,' as in 1938 to 1972. It was spotted when the assistant librarian snail-mailed a photocopy of the original to Teagarden. Nothing is confirmed, but office chatter indicates it was mailed in total innocence. Poor guy went through channels to ask if anyone cared. No one did. Then he sent it out for private analysis. The clerk thought he was doing his job."

"And this librarian patsy was one of your two pre-emptive hits on Shirley Highway?"

"Yes."

"Great. All because the tenth floor failed to clean up their own house forty-seven years ago." Donnursk shrugged with apathy. "So tell me something else, Donnursk, how do you come to know all this?"

"Let's just say I'm ambitious."

"Okay, Mr. Ambition, how soon did they act on this e-mailed message after the librarian pushed the send button?"

Donnursk swallowed and looked away. It was his first sign of weakness since they entered the zoo and began a verbal brawl that at times could be easily overhead by anyone nearby.

"Not until the software monkeys noticed a warning in the back-up system, which was three days later," Donnursk said. "That's when they notified the tenth floor, which called you in and sent you to Bethel with supreme authority. You retrieved the hard copy just fine, but you let him download the e-file in that Hasid shack like some cat playing with a mouse."

The older man clasped his hands together, tossed back his head and laughed in a spasm of delight. For a moment, he looked and sounded like one of the sea lions performing for lunch.

"That's terrific," McCanliss said, spluttering the words past his laughter. "That's just terrific. It took them three days to figure out their own mistake. And the tenth floor geniuses are worried about—*me?*"

He leaned back and laughed louder.

In the background, the sea lion on the top rock was finally tossed a fish of its own, prompting loud applause and laughter from the church group.

CHAPTER THIRTY-EIGHT

The Boathouse, Sparta Township, NJ

Teagarden slept poorly Monday night.

He spent most of Tuesday watching the lake and enjoying the creature comforts of the boathouse, particularly the shower, which had plenty of hot water. He continued to play it safe by logging-on as Dan Jones, hoping to get more decoding assistance on the internet, but there was nothing more to be had. The best mainstream website was useless, leaving him to play a silly combination of crossword puzzle and word jumble with a ballpoint pen.

As for poor Dan, he was hanging tough.

From: danjones@orangecircle.com
To: sandyjones@orangecircle.com

I say I am dishonest, because I am. 45 years in Canton is enough. I saw a crazy woman talking to a squirrel in Central Park yesterday as she fed it popcorn. You know what she was saying? She was saying—I love you, I love you and respect you like my brother. Sure, she was crazy. She was also honest. Maybe you need to think about that.

Whoa.

Teagarden felt a tug of sympathy for Dan from Canton, Missouri, and hoped he had the good sense to stay out of

151

Central Park after dark.

The bathroom window across the lake didn't display the cactus in a blue pot in the morning. That night, his hostess arrived with a supply of food for the fridge, plus chicken teriyaki carry-out and a bottle of good Bordeaux. She was in a particularly good mood because she'd just won a personal injury trial that saved her insurance company millions. A drunk construction worker fell from a scaffold and seriously hurt his back. His lawsuit claimed the scaffold was faulty, which it was, yet she prevailed.

"We had a common sense jury that concluded if he hadn't consumed a pitcher of screwdrivers for lunch, he wouldn't have been hurt by faulty scaffolding," she said. "Common sense juries are hard to come by. So when you get one, it's darn refreshing."

"Makes sense to me," he said.

They ate together while he related more details the previous day near her west side law office. He started with the four drones, Coconut, and Billy Carney. He went on to tell her about the rude woman in the SoHo store, his narrow escape from the dog run, using the "yellow4submarine" password of a stranger named Dan Jones from Canton, Missouri, and the surveillance disc he received from Svetlana. He explained that he had to have a DVD because the only way he could receive it electronically was via the Dan Jones e-mail account, which would have blown his cover.

She thoughtfully listened to every detail. Afterward, she assured him that once he was proven innocent of murder, the other crimes related to being a fugitive would be dismissed.

"That's good," he said. "Now I only need to prove my innocence as a nationally wanted child killer. I'm going to need a good common sense jury like you had today."

"Meantime, you must stay underground."

"What if I go public with the security video from the Madison Park Euro Lodge? Maybe I could hold a secret press conference, or seek exile in Moscow like that man who leaked all that NSA information a bunch of years ago when Obama was in office?"

"Too risky."

"Why?"

"Sam," she said, "believe me when I say this—the law will not protect you. The police will be happy to kill you, but only if circumstances require it. On the other hand, this other mysterious man is hunting you for precisely that purpose—to kill you. Unlike the police, it's his job. It's as simple and ugly as that. Unfortunately, if you're killed by either team, proving your innocence will be nearly impossible. So you need to stay alive. And the way you do that is by staying underground."

He sighed deeply. "You are so right."

She poured more wine.

"Why did you receive this document in the first place?"

He thought before he answered. The red liquid swirled in his wine glass. He never saw Billy Carney's body, but could picture him lying in the woods, his youthful limbs bloodied by two rounds of twelve-gauge buckshot. He did see Kendra's body. When he regained consciousness, she was sitting next to him as though resting, the front of her head a deflated basketball.

"Years ago," he began, "I worked for the CIA in the encryption/decryption department. It was one of the most boring jobs I ever had. I mostly just watched the clock for eight hours."

"Sounds like your typical government job."

"It was. And the cafeteria food was worse than college. Of course, I was in my twenties, so I thought the job made me cool. You know, a spy. It helped me meet girls, which was the only thing I had on my mind at that age. Later at Columbia, because of that boring government job, I did my Ph.D. dissertation on the Morley Dilemma, which I first learned about at Langley. It's a theory that rising complexity diminishes contrary complications."

"Never heard of it," she said with a small laugh. "What in the world does that even mean?"

"It's more theory than real mathematic formula. It means that sometimes, for *some* problems, the more complex you make it, the simpler it can become. Emphasis on the word 'some.' Conversely, the simpler you make something, the more complicated it can become for a certain subset of people if they presume it to actually be complex. It's ironic, but it does happen, largely because of the human factor. And the Morley Dilemma applies very nicely to issues of encryption and decryption."

She held a sip of wine in her mouth while looking at him, then swallowed.

"Okay, so I repeat my question. How did you come to possess the document that seems to be at the root of all this?"

"Oh, right." He took a breath and sighed again. "A long-time friend named Stu Shelbourn who teaches math at GW in D.C. has a son who's some sort of archives clerk at the FBI. It was the *son* who sent me the document. It's a series of en-crypted passages in an old spiral notebook that he said had been lying around for decades and that nobody was interested in. He invited me to see if I could break it. Apparently he felt it would be fun to figure out its meaning. I'm guessing he thought it might be something he could put in a before-and-after library display case. You know, Cold War relics and all that. If I'm right, he made the offer to me as a lark, totally innocent."

"Oops. Your Federal Bureau of Incompetence at work."

"Cynthia, I just want to make certain of one thing: I can't have my daughter and granddaughter get caught up in this. That's the bottom line for me."

She didn't have much to say about the mathematics of de-cryption, but she was ready for that subject.

"I understand. Sam, if they do get caught up, I doubt they'd be at risk of personal harm. Hurting them would only make your story look more credible, which is the last thing they want, and I say that entirely as a lawyer. But you should know they might ask your daughter to issue a plea for your surrender."

"That could be indelicate. Did I tell you what my daughter does for a living?"

"No. What?"

"Navy aviator. Stationed at the Naval Air Station near Key West. It's on the adjacent island called Boca Chica, but she's not working on a very popular program. She flies the new pilotless X-47 for Operation FIDROPRO. It stands for 'Fighter-Drone Program.' The navy temporarily mothballed the plan. But she still teaches trained pilots how to play a video game with a real bomber tooling around in the sky."

The information sent Cynthia deep into thought. He could tell that she found it interesting, or significant, or potentially troubling, but she said nothing more about it.

He changed the subject.

"Here, maybe you can help with this." He wrote out his one fully decoded entry for her. She sipped more wine while taking a prolonged period to study the words.

Dear John,
On this lovely day in June, you began recruitment
For operation over-easy, illegal as bathtub gin used to be.
I love you,
CAT

He could see her mind working. It was the mind of a lawyer, which in some ways was like the mind of a mathematician. Numbers cut. They bore right through deceit. Galileo discovered numbers that bore through deceit of the church. And that's what lawyers are trained to do. If they're good, they too instinctively know how to cut through deceit.

"Well," she said after her examination, "I don't have any

substantial interpretation of the meaning, but I can tell you two things. First, these pages are definitely the reason they're hunting you. And second, you need to decode this entire file. Only then will we know the best way to move forward."

Yes!

It made him feel better. It was independent affirmation of what he'd been feeling these past long days. Now, at least, he had someone to help. That meant a great deal. When the alternative is going it alone, having at least one ally is as good as having an entire army.

Come to think of it, that's what marriage is—a partnership that unites two people into an army. That's the way it was with Kendra. We had each other's back.

Still chewing his dinner, he picked another entry at random, and hastily wrote above the numbers known to stand for the letters D-E-A-R-J-O-H-N. He passed it to her.

"Let's take a shot at this one together," he said.

"Okay. Well, the first letters of the line under 'Dear John,' might form the word 'today.' If so, that means eighty stands for T, and fifty-nine for Y."

She passed it back to him.

Teagarden thought the word "infiltration" could be formed at the end of the second line and beginning of the third. He filled it in.

"Good," she said. "And the word 'arrest' is in the fifth line. Plus seventy-six must stand for the letter U in the word 'your.'"

She wrote them in.

"Of course. The ending is the same as the other one," he said. "It's 'I love you, cat.'"

"Very good," she said. "I think we're close."

"Try to read what we've got so far."

"Okay. It says, 'Dear John, today your infiltration of the something society resulted in the arrest of a founding somebody. You something, something. You are such...' Ah! '...you are such a nasty—BITCH.' Sam, that's it. It says, 'you are such a nasty bitch.' And it's signed, 'I love you, CAT.' Who calls someone a bitch, then professes their love?"

"I hate to say it, but married people do that."

"Come to think of it, I said that to Ernest just last month," she said. "But then he deserved it. He really can be a bitch, though he's a sweet man most of the time."

Having finished dinner, he leaned over and kissed her. They put their crossword-jumble aside and embraced.

During the night, they made love twice, once on the small porch where they could observe the surface of the lake, and once in the boathouse daybed. She opened the sliding-glass door so they could hear the sounds of the night wind on the lake while her forty-five-year-old body loved his forty-nine-year-old body with kindness and passion. He reciprocated with gratitude and passion.

She departed in the pre-dawn darkness for her chalet on the opposite side of the lake.

"Not bad for a guy about to become a half-century old," she said, leaning down to kiss him goodbye.

"Mmm," he groaned. "More courtroom action today?"

"Always," she said. "People trying to get even are my bread and butter." She kissed him again. "I'll see you tonight. And keep the curtains drawn. The one thing we know for certain is that your hound dogs have the resources to chase down every trail."

CHAPTER THIRTY-NINE

Wednesday, July 24, 2019

It was total happenstance.

Teagarden didn't intend to check her rented chalet across the lake that morning. He'd naturally monitor her bathroom window later in the evening, after she arrived home from work. He was making coffee and staring at the sunrise when he saw, or thought he saw, distant movement in the chalet window. He picked up the binoculars and focused on the bathroom window.

And there it was. The bright blue pot holding a stout green cactus was perched on the windowsill. On the other side of the chalet was a bumper-to-bumper jam of black, unmarked cars and several New Jersey State Police patrol cars. Because of the lack of space, two vehicles were parked in the circular driveway of the mansion next door. Near them was Harry's boxy truck with big tires and lettering that read "Harry's Heating and A/C Repair." Teagarden's brain immediately landed on the only possible explanation.

Bruce! It had to be Bruce Kasarian, his colleague at Columbia.

He again blamed himself for not thinking of it earlier. Of course. They'd grilled everyone who knew him at Columbia. When questioning his fellow math professor, they learned that he had set up the introduction to Cynthia. It could only be Kasarian who would drag her into the mess.

Oh, Bruce, please say you didn't tell them we slept together at The Argonaut Hotel. I should never have told you that, but you were such a relentless snoop.

Whether Kasarian gave up all details or not, it was a natural that once they learned about her, they'd show up unannounced. She must have excused herself to use the bathroom to put the cactus in the window. It was a good thing she left the boathouse when she did. Otherwise, they'd want to know where she'd been and why she was just getting home at that hour.

What am I supposed to do now? There aren't any crowded city parks or subway stations in affluent, suburban New Jersey.

He pulled the drapes tight on the sliding glass doors so no one could see him spying on the chalet in case they were training their own binoculars on the lake and its surroundings.

He quickly tried to fit the pieces together. They probably had a search warrant for her rented chalet, and if they knew about her they certainly knew about her estranged husband, which meant they had a warrant for the big colonial next door. He went to the rear window of the boathouse to check the road behind the colonial.

It was not a welcome sight.

There were unmarked fed cars and more state troopers vying for parking on the narrow road. But there was something else. It was another truck. The same model, the same efficient-looking boxy design with big tires.

Now there are two of them?

He trained the binoculars on the truck: Durgan's Lawn & Garden Service, 555-GARDENS.

He went back to the drapes covering the sliding glass door and turned the field glasses on the other truck: Harry's Heating and A/C Repair, 555-FURNACE.

It appeared these dark-ops people were hard pressed for inventive cover. Then again, he guessed the truck façades must be effective because who would suspect them of being anything other than what they claim.

There was nowhere to run. He'd be shot in three seconds if he made a break for woods or water. Seeing no exterior opportunity, he took the only interior option that came to mind. He cleaned all evidence of boathouse habitation. The job went quickly because there wasn't much. He stuffed his sports coat and laptop into the backpack and straightened the daybed. He poured out the coffee, wiped down the small counter and tightly bagged the garbage from last night's dinner.

If there were dogs, the garbage would be a problem. They'd smell it from outside the boathouse. But they'd smell him and her and their lovemaking too. So what difference did some garbage make?

Peeking through a narrow crack in the shades, he could see them inside the colonial. They milled about in the glass-enclosed porch where he'd stood with Cynthia the night before last while she watered her husband's plants. He guessed they were impressed by the extravagance, the built-in bureau, skylight, huge TV, and particularly the elevator.

Two minutes later, state troopers and plain-clothed cops were in the backyard inspecting the sloping yard and boat launch at the end of the narrow pier. They too had binoculars, which they used to scan the lake shore in all directions. The only good news was that he didn't see any dogs. If they brought dogs, his minutes were numbered.

He could hear the troopers yelling as they moved about the adjacent property.

"What about the boat down there?"

"Just a rowboat and a canoe. Empty."

"The lake?"

"We're working it."

"There's an island over there."

"We're working it."

"The woods?"

"We're working that too."

Teagarden stepped closer to the side window. Uniformed police were filtering back to the house. Plainclothes men hung at the lake's edge, eyeing the water with interest and suspicion. One of them waved a signal to another. A few sailboats on the lake were big enough to have lower berth compartments. He guessed they'd all be summoned to the shore for inspection before the police were satisfied.

The vulnerability of his position was obvious. They'd naturally be drawn to the little building in the woods next to the big colonial. The boathouse probably wasn't on their list of properties, and they probably didn't have a search warrant because it wasn't linked to the names of Cynthia or Ernest Blair. She sensed that was best. Now it didn't matter. That quaint little building would naturally lure anyone in the crowd who knew how to see what they were looking at.

Teagarden gave the backyard one final glimpse through the side window. And there he was.

Standing right there.

It's him.

McCanliss, the tenacious sociopath, tall, balding, with the long arms of an orangutan, and that grossly disfiguring lip scar, was standing in the middle of the sloping backyard. He looked like a statue. He wasn't giving orders or participating in the search. Instead, he was staring at the boathouse. For a terrifying moment, Teagarden thought McCanliss was staring— *directly at him.*

He backed away from the window shade. Though still suffering the after-effects of two broken knees, he scaled the ladder to the storage loft with the alacrity of a gymnast, hauling his backpack and plastic garbage bag with him. He silently pulled up the narrow ladder, scooted from the loft's edge, and crawled behind two large, corrugated storage boxes, bumping one as he went. The cardboard was so fragile with age that it burst a seam, sending out a flood of musty old magazines.

But wait, McCanliss's truck was on the other side of the lake near Cynthia's rental. Yet he was here in Ernest Blair's backyard. Maybe he got a lift in a patrol car because of the parking jam in the mansion's circular drive. Or maybe it was something more strategic, like wanting the truck to be seen in one location, while he staked out another. Thinking about that possibility was interrupted by knuckles rapping three times on the yard-side door of the boathouse.

Bam, bam, bam.

Seconds later, the same loud rattling came against the sliding glass door on the lakeside.

Bam, bam, bam.

"Hello. Hello."

"Anything?" a second voice called from a distance.

"Don't seem to be," came the response. "Locked up. Looks unoccupied."

"It's not on the manifest. You think they want me to call in a warrant?"

"The king shit feds will tell you if they want it. It's their show. But they can't search every house on the lake. If the psycho-punk who killed that kid is in this town, my money says he's out there in one of those boats."

"Yeah, guess so. Trooper Sunderman is putting in the speedboat at the town launch. He'll be all over the sailboats in a couple of minutes. And they'll check the island. I bet the son of a bitch is on that island."

"Well, if he's around here, he sure as hell ain't got no-where to hide. Besides Jersey troopers, we got county deputies from two states, Sparta cops, and a whole regiment of feds poking behind every bush."

"Yeah. It's a big show, that's for sure."

Teagarden figured he was listening to the voices of New Jersey State Troopers, and that McCanliss was a silent observer of the whole operation, just as he'd been at Madison Park Euro Lodge. After their brief inspection of the boathouse windows, they rejoined the main group and all voices faded to indistinct shouts and curses. He wondered if McCanliss was still standing in the sloping yard, still staring at the boathouse, still seeming to understand the importance of what he was seeing.

Hours later, after all voices and hubbub concluded, Teagarden stayed where he was. For the balance of the day, he remained concealed in the loft behind a ladder, a plastic bag of garbage and two ancient, ruptured cardboard boxes. It was hot and cramped, but manageable. To pass the time, he read old magazine articles in the slanting light. He read about things he hadn't studied since high school. Things like race riots, the Cold War, the space race, and Vietnam. When the articles weren't of much interest, he flipped the pages, looking at the advertisements that seemed from another world. Many promised astonishing health benefits from smoking cigarettes. A woman was orgasmic over her new "heavy duty, electric powered, upright, vacuum cleaner with space age suction." And a brand new 1957 Chevy Bel Air could be had for $1,850.

It was late afternoon when an ad for a toy in a boy's magazine from the mid-twentieth century allowed Teagarden to guess the basis for the master code of the entire Dear John File.

CHAPTER FORTY

FBI/CIA Safe House, East 64th Street, New York City

It was a crash pad for federal agents.

The FBI safe house near the Central Park Zoo was not exclusive to the FBI. Field agents from the CIA, Secret Service, and NSA frequently passed through. There was even the occasional veteran from Interpol and Britain's MI6. The cost of New York City hotels and the expense of maintaining a perpetual nationwide state of hyper-security required all agencies to pinch pennies wherever savings could be found.

There was nothing special about it, except the address. East Sixty-Fourth Street just off Fifth Avenue is about as exclusive as it gets in New York City. The company apartment, as it was called, occupied the entire second floor of a former private mansion, converted to a sitting room, small kitchen, two baths, and six tiny bedrooms. The first floor was occupied by two privately owned apartments; the basement housed medical offices belonging to a dentist and a dermatologist.

Office talk was discouraged in the apartment, so working agents walked around the block to discuss business. Many preferred to visit the nearby Central Park Zoo to compare notes and speak in confidence. "The seals don't talk" as one expression put it. "Let's go walk among the civilized" was another, which cynically placed caged animals on a higher moral ground than humans.

The younger and shorter of the two FBI agents returned to

his room after spending all day in Sparta Township. He'd expected to see his older colleague, but McCanliss wasn't in his room or the common area. He'd departed Sparta Township that morning without sending a message to the DFC in Washington and without speaking to anyone at the scene, which was a blinking red-light violation of protocol. A call was placed to the office at the Javits Federal Building in lower Manhattan. McCanliss was a no-show there as well.

Donnursk really didn't want to speak to either of the two CIA men watching baseball in the main sitting room. He knew them to be sullen and arrogant. But he had no choice. They were lounging on the couch like bored lovers, their ankles overlapping on the ottoman, quart bottles of beer cradled between their thighs.

"Gentlemen, anyone seen Harry McCanliss since morning?"

One of them ignored him. The other gave a begrudging response without turning from the large, flat-screen TV.

"Fuck no!" he barked.

Well, that went about as well as he'd expected.

Donnursk knocked on the door of Thomas Rose, another FBI agent in the DFC whose code name was Box Cutter. He was the company stud, the golden boy with Hollywood good looks, believed to be on the job principally because his cocksmanship put him there. Every office has one. Among this one's romantic interests was Paula Trippler, chief FBI legal counsel, who had an office on the mysterious tenth floor of the main building in Washington. Because of her influence, or so it was believed, he was working the cushiest job in the DFC, a mission designed to force the bankruptcy and eventual shutdown of *The New York Times*.

"Come in."

"Hey, Thomas, have you seen McCanliss since morning?"

"Sorry, Durgan, I haven't seen Ice Skater since earlier this week. But then I've been so busy I've spent very little time in the apartment." He was reclining in the rumpled bed, smoking. A semi-naked woman sat on the opposite edge, her back to him. She'd already put on her panties, and was working bra straps around her shoulders as Rose spoke. "I've been racking up overtime. Maybe that's another reason my gig is called Operation Killtime." He reached to help his companion connect the strap between her shoulder blades.

"Okay, thanks," Donnursk said.

The woman turned to glance at him before he closed the bedroom door. He recognized her as a frequent guest named Ursula. It was against the rules, but in her case, everyone looked the other way. She charged a hundred dollars per half-hour. That was her "company discount."

He went back to his own tiny room and closed the door. After opening his laptop and logging on, there came a knock.

"Come in."

"Hi, Agent Donnursk." It was Ursula. "How are you?"

"Fine, Ursula."

"Would you like some company?" she asked.

He closed his laptop.

"Sure, Ursula, come on in."

CHAPTER FORTY-ONE

The Boathouse, Sparta Township, NJ

It was a true eureka moment thanks to a chance discovery buried in a seventy-year-old boy's magazine. The ad was for a toy decoder ring offered by a children's radio show that ran from 1947 to 1953 called "Captain Tom Daggers." He already had a sense that the code for the thirty-four pages was simple. Seeing that advertisement, he intuitively grasped exactly how simple.

He was so absorbed with the discovery that he remained in the cramped loft. He worked all morning while half-a-dozen law enforcement agencies hunted for him in the nearby yards, on the lake and in the woods of the lake's island. By midday, the noisy action was more nautical in nature with boat horns, loud engines that gunned through choppy lake waters, and distant protestations from boaters being ordered to "heave to." By late afternoon it had completely ceased. There were no more men rapping at the doors or leaning to peek into the boathouse windows.

That meant Cynthia had been right. Though curious, they had no way to connect the little building in the woods to her or her husband. Consequently, they did not seek a warrant.

Bless you, Cynthia. You really sensed the safest path in a worst-case scenario.

It grew miserably hot in the storage space, but he had no choice except to endure it. Using the large storage boxes to block the laptop's illumination, he searched the internet to confirm his idea and found proof in seconds. The "Captain Tom Daggers" ring didn't match any page. There were also decoder rings offered by a chocolate milk company, a popcorn-candy company and a dime novel series about Indian fighters, spies and secret agents. But it was a decoder ring offered by the UWHECO cereal company where Teagarden nailed it.

It issued a new toy every year from 1899 through 1942. That's when UWHECO, which stood for Union Wheat Company, was defeated by the competition, went bankrupt, folded and was never heard from again. Every January during their years in business, the back of UWHECO's "Big Wheat Flakes" cereal box printed a cutout application to be filled-in and mailed to receive the toy "absolutely free." Customers were urged to "collect them all" and to "hurry, while limited supplies last." Beginning in January 1933, the back of the box warned, "don't be left out, but don't overdo it, only one per customer."

Teagarden clicked on the image of the first ring issued in 1899.

Sweet.

He clicked on the image of the final one issued in 1942. It was larger in diameter and more substantial looking, but basically the same.

Beautiful.

He flipped through web pages showing each year's unique "come-on" pitched to kids. In 1899, it was about foiling Spanish spies "on precious American soil," and told boys, "Now you can charge up San Juan Hill with Teddy Roosevelt." In 1917, it was "Secret messages to help sink German U-boats." In 1921, it promised "The secret to prevent thugs and gamblers from ever again fixing the World Series." There was no surprise about the theme of the final toy in 1942. It was about the Nazis: "Now you can help defeat Hitler by sending super-secret messages to undercover American agents in Berlin and Munich."

Each ring had an outer circle of letters, with an inner circle of matching numbers so that each letter in the alphabet could be encoded with its own designated number. That was it. UWHECO offered a completely new rudimentary Caesar Cipher to kids every January.

In later years, the rings became a little fancier. Instead of two static circles, an inner knob could be turned until the desired number appeared in a little window to reveal the designated letter for encoding or decoding. But the simplicity of the concept remained unchanged. It meant he'd been correct in mentioning the Morley Dilemma. This thing was simple, so simple everyone believed it to be complex. That explained why the hard copy had gone un-deciphered for the past six decades. They took a look and assumed it was either utter nonsense, or simply—*too*—complex, or both. Then, it was forgotten.

Well, almost forgotten.

Teagarden took his first decoded entry from the thirty-four pages and breezed through the website. He looked at enlarged images of each ring until he found one where the numbers and letters matched. The year was 1921. Every letter matched perfectly.

Even better, with that ring he finally had a date to attach to the bottom of the entry:

Dear John,
On this lovely day in June, you began recruitment
For operation over easy, illegal as bathtub gin used to be.
I love you,
CAT
June, 1961

He took the entry he and Cynthia worked on the night before. The ring issued in 1912 seemed to work. He quickly finished decoding the message and added the date at the end:

Dear John,
Today your infiltration of the Mattachine Society resulted
in the arrest of a founding member. You set him up of course.
You are such a nasty bitch.
I love you, CAT
January, 1952

He researched the Mattachine Society and learned it was one of the first organizations in the nation to promote equality for homosexuals in the face of medieval intolerance. One website complained of a policy where FBI agents "secretly grilled neighbors of job applicants to ensure that no federal employee was, or ever would be, homosexual." That site called it a "cruel hypocrisy drawn from the Gestapo playbook, especially since the two top agents in the FBI were closet queens."

Teagarden researched those two top agents. From 1935 to his death in 1972, J. Edgar Hoover was the top man. His number two during that entire time was a man suspected of being his lifelong lover, Clyde Anderson Tolson.

For the third time since Sunday, a jet of ice-water shot up the middle of his spinal column.

Oh…my…God.

There it was, on the computer screen. The stark black and white letters jumped out as though they were Times Square neon. Tolson's initials. *He* was the diary keeper. The pages Teagarden had been carrying belonged to the FBI's long-serving second-ranking agent—Clyde Anderson Tolson. He was CAT, the author of every encoded entry on every page. And the "J" in J. Edgar Hoover stood for John. The man's full name was *John* Edgar Hoover.

Teagarden not only saw it, but understood what he was looking at. He understood it with unequivocal certainty. The thirty-four pages was Tolson's life insurance policy against being dumped as a lover or demoted from his lifelong spot as number two at the FBI. Once every entry was decoded, those pages would likely reveal much more than their personal sexual orientation. They'd also likely reveal how ugly things got in the twentieth century during the Hoover years. It was obvious. The FBI wasn't certain the pages existed, but when it was learned the document really did exist—they took action. They tried to kill him because if the document were published, it would prove nothing less than institutionalized treason.

Teagarden hadn't been running only for his own life. He'd been running for something bigger and more important. He was running because the FBI wanted to prevent publication of the wretchedly ugly story of its own crimes.

Oh…my…God.

CHAPTER FORTY-TWO

Thursday, July 25, 2019
FBI/CIA Safe House, East 64th Street, New York City

He'd waited long enough, maybe too long.

The next morning, long after Ursula departed, Donnursk resumed his plan, now delayed by nearly twelve hours. He wanted supreme authority on McCanliss as well as Teagarden. That meant betraying his partner.

So what?

The man was simply too old and too cynical. He had little respect for the job, and—*no*—respect for tenth-floor authority.

He searched the company apartment, again asking if anyone had seen Ice Skater.

No one had.

He poured coffee and made toast in the galley kitchen. He buttered both slices, then took his coffee and breakfast back to his bedroom, opened his laptop and logged on.

CHAPTER FORTY-THREE

Encrypted Field Communication
NSA Apache Code Ofc Baltimore, MD/Washington, DC/Coin
TelSatOrbit53/New York, NY

<apache code initiate>

TO: deep field cmdr
FROM: copper miner

SUBJECT: operation dear john

<secure field communication may begin>

copper miner to deep field cmdr: u heard from ice skater? he's mia since wed morning in sparta, nj.

deep field cmdr to copper miner: no word here at main ofc... nothing on shack-up theory?

copper miner to deep field cmdr: nothing...she's connected lawyer...i played it by book...still got her under e-surveill...if she's lying we'll soon know.

deep field cmdr to copper miner: ok...catch-up w/ice skater and get teagarden...

copper miner to deep field cmdr: be advised...ice skater refused to work with me...appears he may have gone solo...off the radar...

deep field cmdr to copper miner: that is bad. if ice skater does not turn-up by tonight, you have supreme authority on both teagarden...and ice skater...understood?

copper miner to deep field cmdr: understood...

CHAPTER FORTY-FOUR

The Boathouse, Sparta Township, NJ

It had to happen.

He needed a bathroom and his aching knees were killing him. They had to be stretched and exercised. He felt as though he'd sweated away five pounds in the overheated loft, worsened by the constant use of his laptop.

Teagarden lowered the ladder before dawn. On the floor, he limbered stiff muscles and limbs in the dark by stretching to the ceiling and bending to touch his toes. He put the heel of each foot on the daybed and leaned into his knees like a ballet dancer warming up at the practice bar. It didn't stop the pain. But it helped.

At the small refrigerator in the galley kitchen, he retrieved two pieces of fruit left by Cynthia to take back to the crawl-space, an apple and a pear. He gulped over-the-counter pain-killers and washed them down with tap water.

Rest break concluded, he returned to the storage loft, and pulled the ladder up behind him. When the sun came up Thursday morning, he didn't dare risk being seen by anyone left behind to monitor the scene. He decided to wait for indication from Cynthia that it was safe to move about, guessing that it would come with the eventual removal of the cactus from her bathroom window.

If runaway slaves could do it, I can do it too.

Besides, he had his work cut out for him, and he could do

it just as easily while in hiding. All he needed was his laptop, the thirty-four pages and a ballpoint pen. There was one problem, however. When the computer battery died, he had to drape an electric cord to a wall outlet below the loft. Should anyone return to peek in the windows, the sight might arouse curiosity. But he had to chance it.

Instead of decoding from beginning to end, he jumped around. In the course of doing that, he made another discovery. The first page was composed in the year 1938, the final page was written in 1972, the year John Edgar Hoover died. That totaled thirty-four years—one page for each of thirty-four years.

He verified that the UWHECO decoder ring he used to decode the first page was the first ring issued in 1899. The ring he needed to work on the final page for the year 1972 was issued in 1932. That also totaled thirty-four. Clyde Anderson Tolson, aka CAT, was not very creative when it came to numbers. He selected the simplest possible cipher based on an antiquated mail-order toy. Then he began at the beginning and went forward in a straight line, year after year, toy ring after sequential toy ring, until the Grim Reaper knocked at his lover's door.

Few people realize that numbers, in one form or another, make up the beating heart of the universe. Without mathematics, there would be no food, shelter, and clothing. Numbers are the lifeblood of all that is animate and inanimate, too: Earth, stars, music, faith in God, life itself. They are all composed of and grounded in numbers.

The apple and pear were refreshing and welcome.

Now that he knew how simple the code was, he was confident that he would have eventually deciphered the entire Dear John File on his own. But because he saw a breakfast cereal advertisement in an old boy's magazine, he'd get the job done in a few hours. Instead of slow and laborious decryption, it would be quick, clerical labor. That was eerie. Peculiar mysteries were happening to him, but so were peculiar answers to the mysteries. When this was over, provided he survived, he planned to think long and hard about what it all meant. Maybe it meant he was being guided by an unseen hand. If so—why him? Was he chosen for the job?

He forced such thinking from his mind.

That's foolish indulgence. There's nothing special about me.

Teagarden opened the laptop and settled down to learn what the thirty-four pages had to say about events during the reign of the FBI's first, and longest serving director.

Lying on his back in the cramped space, he dropped the leftover fruit cores into the garbage bag. He wiped his sticky hands on Ernest Blair's borrowed blue jeans, picked up his ballpoint pen, and went to work.

DEAR JOHN…

CHAPTER FORTY-FIVE

Encrypted Field Communication
NSA Apache Code Ofc Baltimore, MD/Washington, DC/Coin
TelSatOrbit53/New York, NY

<apache code initiate>

TO: ice skater
FROM: deep field cmdr

SUBJECT: operation dear john

<secure field communication may begin>

deep field cmdr to ice skater: where u?...report...

deep field cmdr to ice skater: respond...convey status...

deep field cmdr to ice skater: 10th floor now beyond tolerance...be advised, u r on report...

deep field cmdr to ice skater: last chance...snap out of it...

deep field cmdr to ice skater: ok...have it u'r way...

CHAPTER FORTY-SIX

Central Park Zoo, New York City

It was feeding time.

McCanliss saw the latest communication from the DFC commander. He ignored it, turned off his company-issued cell-phone, and plopped it into his half-full coffee cup, destroying it. He replaced the lid and dropped the cup into the public waste barrel next to his favorite bench in the Central Park Zoo.

Fuck 'em all.

He knew something they didn't know.

He knew that Teagarden was hiding in that boathouse. He knew it without confirmation. He could smell it. They, how-ever, were too stupid to see what he saw with clarity. Now that the tenth floor has sent Donnursk to be his partner, why should he tell them anything?

He had no intention of handing Teagarden over to Don-nursk. If he did, Donnursk would get the credit. Instead, he planned to get Teagarden his own way. More importantly, he'd get Teagarden—*on his own.*

He turned back to the snow leopards that had just received their first meal in three days. The twin shanks of meat had the contoured shape of sheep legs, each of them capped with a ragged meaty top, still shaggy with tufts of unshorn wool. Instead of attacking the flesh with gluttonous appetite, the leopards laid beside their meal, stroking it with their tongues.

It made McCanliss smile.

CHAPTER FORTY-SEVEN

The Boathouse, Sparta Township, NJ

Teagarden continued decoding and reading the results of his decryption, skipping from dated entry to dated entry.

Dear John,
    You are gone only two weeks and I am in deep mourning for you, my love. This is the final message in my diary. One of your operation over easy psychos ponied-up on that ass from Alabama yesterday. No one will ever suspect clever you of setting up the hit on that corn pone governor by that patsy. Lord, what a screwball that Bremer was. He makes Oswald look sane. I now see that you knew all along that no one would ever connect the dots. God, I do desperately miss you.
    I love you,
    CAT,
    May, 1972
    P.S. you would love the cherry blossoms this year, they are magnificent.

Dear John,
    Ha! You nasty boy. I am always happy to cover for you. But now I hear that your date with Dorothy Lamour was an all-nighter at the Willard Hotel. Does she, John? Did she? Or didn't she? Well, the p.r. dept is pleased with the society page press speculating that you have a movie star girlfriend. You

are such a naughty boy.
I love you,
CAT
March, 1940

Dear John,
I have just reviewed the JFK files. Dear God! That man makes Casanova look like a cherubic choir boy. And the photos reveal he's not even well endowed. Ha! Poor Irishman. If he's elected, I think we shall keep our jobs for many years thanks to your new file on his, ahem, personal habits!
I love you,
CAT
June, 1960

Dear John,
So, you finally had your way with that new agent, the darling golden haired god you met at the Fontainebleau Hotel. Was he your winning stake at the poolside poker table? Is that how you landed him? Was he hung like a quarter horse? You are such as hussy.
I love you,
CAT
February, 1955

Dear John,
Chasing commies is one thing. But you must be careful with Roy Cohn and Joe McCarthy. I don't want you infected with their buggery bugs. They are vicious, dirty beasts. Best you stay with us good "clean" boys at justice. After all, we know what a bar of soap is—really—for.
I love you,
CAT
June, 1953

Dear John,

I fear you shall be undone with this Operation Over Easy business. It's just too much. Doctors/agents/mobsters (and you) secretly managing six recruits? All diagnosed as marginal, anti-social and/or schizophrenic: two career criminals, a catatonic, a Christian-Palestinian, an ex-marine now living in the S.Union, and a scummy low-level Dallas mobster. All managed by you, senior agent Mark Trippler, and a few other semi-stable agents including that schizo Slade Higgins. To what end, John? I am worried about you. Oh John, please be careful with this one.

I love you,
CAT
April, 1962

Dear John,

Today your surveill of King's subversive march in Selma was quite a success. Our men got top notch mug shots of every one of those no good trouble-makers from "The National Association for the Almighty Colored People." Good intel for future.

I love you,
CAT
P.S., you were right to approve Efrem Zimbalist Jr. for the TV show. He is such a darling.
March, 1965

Dear John,

Oh John, oh John.

What has your Operation Over Easy done this time? I am worried for you. So what if JFK had no interest in Vietnam. And so what if he fired you after his re-election. We would have simply retired to Hialeah as great American heroes on fine government pensions. Now what? What if they trace these schizo/nut-cases back to you, Agent Mark Trippler, Slade Higgins, the headshrinkers, freelancers and ex-mobsters managing Oswald? They—too—are a bunch of marginal personalities and patsies just as he was a patsy. I hope for your sake no one ever connects those dots.

I love you,
CAT
November, 1963

Dear John,

I hope you will now completely disband Operation Over Easy. That subversive S.O.B. King was one thing. But, oh Lord, RFK? Well, of course I know why. It's because he'd have withdrawn from Vietnam. Plus, he'd have fired us both, where Nixon will keep the war going and allow—us—to go on forever, as well we should. But John, oh John, oh John.

I love you,
CAT
June, 1968

Dear John,

You were such a darling at the party last night, dancing a jig in celebration of Truman bombing all those dirty little nips. Of course, only I know that you were really dancing because you met your weight loss goal. Just imagine—twenty pounds lighter! And you look wonderful, my darling. Congratulations!

I love you,
CAT
August, 1945

Dear John,

I totally agree that it's high time to order full battle stations on all those Italian greaseballs. After last year's meeting in Apalachin, NY—you had no choice. They pushed you too far. And don't worry about what they know about us. They shoot blanks when it comes to us. Besides, it'll be just like the good old days when you cornered all those bank robbing hillbillies. And with Purvis long gone this time around, busting the mafia will be all your show.

I love you,
CAT
January, 1958

Dear John,

Happy birthday, lover! Just think, you are half a century today! I hope you like my present.

I love you,
CAT
January, 1945

CHAPTER FORTY-EIGHT

Central Park Zoo, New York City

"It's four-thirty. The zoo is closing now, sir. Please make your way to the exit."

McCanliss ignored the attendant. He preferred to stay and watch the snow leopards. He wanted to reach in and give his longtime friends a goodbye pet where they lay next to the lamb shanks. After many years, and hundreds of walks through the Central Park Zoo for business and pleasure, he knew this would be his last.

He was done.

Over the years, his favorite animal had been Gus, the polar bear who was ultimately euthanized. Ah God, he was a powerful, charming creature. He had a wonderful mix of wild brutality and childish curiosity. Of course, Gus was thoroughly ill in his mind. Living in a cage, no matter how natural, will do that. You could see it in his behavior—alternately obsessive, manic, depressed, despondent, happy, violent. Sleep was his only true freedom.

McCanliss often wondered what Gus the polar bear dreamed of. Female polar bears? The open sky? Deep waters? Infinite ice? Unfettered freedoms? Or maybe Gus simply dreamed of eating the California sea lions for lunch. After all, he smelled them every day of his life as they frolicked in the fishy waters of the adjacent compound where they performed for tourists.

Whatever that bear dreamed, whatever he wished, he existed at the edge of life. That's why the polar bear was his favorite. Gus reminded McCanliss of himself, of his own life. They both had what the psychiatrists call "marginal personalities." Their impulses needed to be kept in check. They appeared whole, yet were actually fractured. And they were so dangerous they needed to be caged in their own respective ways.

But for McCanliss—no more cages. He was done.

"The park is closing, sir." It was another attendant sweeping the zoo of visitors, this time a young lady. She wore the standard zoo uniform of khaki slacks and a pullover bearing the message *Be a Zoo Lover*. "Please make your way to the exit," she said.

After Gus the polar bear was euthanized, McCanliss learned to enjoy the snow leopards, Zoe and Askai, so adroit on their feet. And he loved the penguins, so animated and genuinely happy about life. The penguins reminded him of puppies, too young to know anything of the pain that life will deal them. As for the sea lions, they were the least of all the animals because they surrendered to the rules. As long as they performed and clapped and bayed and barked and obeyed the attendants, they got the fish. Getting the fish meant survival. It meant winning. And more than that, as long as they obeyed, they were loved.

It also meant they surrendered.

In was ironic. McCanliss saw himself in each species. He'd been a human version of Gus the polar bear, yet felt as though he'd behaved like a California sea lion.

No more. Gus the polar bear was gone. And soon, he'd be gone too. Never again would he beg like a sea lion.

No more.

He'd heard of the Dear John File early on. Every agent had. There were always rumors. Some said it was coded-named QB69, speculated to stand for "Queen Bitch." As for the "69," it was understood with a smug wink to be a sexual reference. No one really believed it existed. If anyone did, they kept silent. Personally, he never cared one way or another. Why should he care if there was a secret file verifying that the founding director of the FBI walked the other side of the street? He never met the man. But he knew the real problem amounted to much more that sexual orientation. It was all the *other* stuff rumored to be in the Dear John File that worried the tenth floor. They were panicked about release of operation details from the 1960s, all of it before his time. They were illegal actions taken in the name of saving and keeping America as the great place it was believed to be. On that subject, it was more important that company members stay silent. Better to suggest the founding director was merely gay than to suggest he had anything do with murdering the Reverend Dr. Martin Luther King Jr.

That would be bad.

For them.

It's a routine flowchart: if this happens, then that happens. Problem is, management never seems to read any flowchart of their own making.

If this, then that.

Well, he could read his own flowchart. It was bad for him as a kid living on a U.S. airbase in Italy, the same base where the local surgeon botched his cleft palate surgery, leaving him with a lifelong and uncorrectable scar. He was born on that base at Aviano. In some ways, he died there, too. He was there when he learned his father had been killed in Vietnam, the only war the U.S. lost. But it wasn't lost because of foreign armies. It was lost because of internal armies: hippies, liberals, Democrats, students, professors, protestors, movie stars.

Idiots, all of them.

He felt he could do more for his country and more to avenge his father's death by domestically policing the U.S., than any contribution he might have made following his father's path to the Air Force. That's why he went into the FBI. It wasn't until 9/11 that he began to change his way of thinking. 9/11 was caused by rank incompetence, followed by a shamefully bureaucratic cover-up. The direct consequence was two perfectly avoidable wars.

If this, then that.

In 2004, there came another flowchart: he lost his son in Iraq. Captain Winston McCanliss was a troop transport pilot with the 10th Mountain Division out of Fort Drum, New York. His death changed everything all over again. It changed him, his life, his family, his outlook. His wife divorced him. It made him go from routine law-abiding FBI agent to zealot for the cause, a warrior, a black ops performing sea lion for the agency. His son's death made him double-down on his father's death. That's when he was inducted into the DFC. Whatever they wanted from him, they got it. If they wanted the rules broken, he broke the rules. If they wanted someone dead, he killed them. Disappear? He made them go away. And if they wanted an amateur fox to become a wanted murderer, then he murdered an eleven-year-old boy to make it happen.

But no more.

Once again, they couldn't read their own flow charts: if this happens, then that happens.

It had been fifteen years since Winston's transport crashed in Iraq. In that time, thanks to the granting of supreme authority, he had plunged into the dark side for the bureau. And now, just because he'd lost four K-32 model drones, and one (and only one) fox had slipped through his fingers, they were worried about him?

That didn't fit.

In all those years, this had been his only slip-up.

Sure, he deliberately left a copy of the encoded file in Teagarden's inbox. So what? He didn't think it would be downloaded by him or anyone else. Why bother with clerical details? He was a DFC agent operating with a grant of supreme authority. He was going to kill the target. Zap him with a K-32 programmed to kill with epipoxilene—instant heart attack without any chemical trace.

Nothing to it.

Then this Teagarden managed to take out all four K-32s, both the older and newer versions. That intrigued him. For the first time in years his skills were challenged. It made his job fun.

Until now.

And because of this one screw-up on a case involving the Dear John File, they're doubling down on him? They're granting supreme authority to someone else on the same case? And not just someone else—but Durgan Donnursk. He was a weight-lifting, vitamin-popping, punk kid. Hell, he probably watched CNN, too.

When Donnursk was coming up in the bureau, his nickname was Special Agent Dunno. And if he's reading this thing correctly, they're telling Donnursk to consider him, McCanliss, as the *co-fox?* They're telling Donnursk to hit Teagarden— *and*—hit him?

Screw that.

If his time was up, he was going to spend his last minutes giving them what they deserved. Besides, the Dear John File was a screw-up of *their* doing. Not his. They failed to clean their own house nearly fifty years ago. Once again, just like 9/11, they want to prevent their dumb-doing from becoming their *UN*-doing. And they wanted him to be the UN-doer.

No more. He was finished. It was their doing. Let it be their own undoing.

They don't understand their own flowcharts.

If this, then that.

"Sir, it's now four-forty-five. Make your way to the exit, please." It was the same male staffer who'd spoken to him fifteen minutes earlier. But this time, he did not continue walking. He stood beside McCanliss where he sat on the bench watching the snow leopards, waiting for him to stand and exit.

"Time to go, sir."

McCanliss looked up. He could kill this annoying man with one blow. He'd become a cadaver in a matter of microseconds, his brain squeezed to mush. He could do it with a hand to the throat, a fist to the temple, a foot to the neck. It would be so easy.

"All right," McCanliss said to the man.

He rose and slowly made his way toward the exit. He wondered what the zoo attendant would have done if Gus the polar bear had escaped his cage and roamed into Central Park.

"Please come again, sir. The park reopens tomorrow at ten o'clock."

On Fifth Avenue, instead of walking to the safe house on East Sixty-Fourth Street, he walked deeper into Central Park amid the bikers and joggers. He knew the tenth floor would soon be buzzing as if he really were Gus the polar bear who'd just escaped and was really strolling about, unfettered, with all his power and wild brutality.

If this happens, then that happens.

The—*this*—part of the equation had already happened. Now the—*that*—part of the equation was about to happen. But for the first time, it was going to happen his way. He was no longer working for the tenth floor.

No more behaving like a California sea lion. Instead, Special Agent Harry McCanliss would be more like Gus the polar bear. Or more like Zoe and Askai, the snow leopards.

Now, he was working for himself.

And best of all, he knew where the fox was going next.

CHAPTER FORTY-NINE

The Boathouse, Sparta Township, NJ

It was a tedious chore made less tolerable by the stifling heat and cramped space of the boathouse loft.

Yet Teagarden stayed with it most of the day and was almost finished with all thirty-four pages by early evening. He lowered the ladder and descended to the boathouse floor, taking care to stay clear of the windows. Using the binoculars, he looked for any evidence that Ernest Blair's big colonial was still under surveillance. He saw none. The windows showed no movement. The truck and all trooper cars were gone from the narrow street. Across the lake, the cactus in the blue pot was still in the bathroom window of Cynthia's rental. He assumed she left it there after going to work, but he wasn't going to risk the possibility that Harry the furnace repairman, or Durgan the lawn and garden man, or some other agent was lurking about. He would wait for word from her before making his next move.

Moments later, back in the loft, he received that word. He logged onto Dan Jones' e-mail, whose name and password she had cleverly remembered when he regaled her with every detail of his story.

From: danjones@orangecircle.com
To: sandyjones@orangecircle.com
it's not from me. you should know by now that I am done

191

playing games. maybe it's from someone you need to tell me about who's using my i.d.

From: sandyjones@orangecircle.com
To: danjones@orangecircle.com
Dan, please tell what this "pox on both houses" means. I will meet you anywhere, but I need to understand.
Please don't tell me you are drinking and smoking too.
And I certainly hope you are not toying with my emotions.
I still love you,
Sandy

From: danjones@orangecircle.com
To: sandyjones@orangecircle.com
a pox remains on both houses...take canoe at pier's end, paddle toward town ctr...meet me @ 10 pm under boardwalk at German beerhall called Östreicher Haus. i will guide with cig. lighter.

From: sandyjones@orangecircle.com
To: danjones@orangecircle.com
Oh Dan,
You are a good man.
Please remember that and only that is what I will always think of you and nothing else ever for all time.
I love you,
Sandy

From: danjones@orangecircle.com
To: sandyjones@orangecircle.com
I say I am dishonest, because I am.
Forty-five years in Canton is enough.
I saw a crazy woman talking to a squirrel in Central Park yesterday as she fed it popcorn. You know what she was saying? She was saying, "I love you, I love you and respect you

like my brother."

Sure, she was crazy.

She was also honest.

Maybe you need to think about that.

Once again, that's where I came in.

Sorry, Dan. I'll try to make this up to you somehow, but please don't make it any worse for yourself than you already have. You can take it from me, your wife certainly does not have any secret lovers to confess, and frankly, my sympathies are starting to lean toward her.

He logged off. The messages made him feel renewed appreciation for having Cynthia as an ally.

And what an ally. She's as smart as they come, well adjusted, willing to risk everything to help him, and all of it in one very attractive package. That reminded him of the back of the box verbiage he'd been reading for each year's new decoder ring: "just for you, new and improved to avoid secret dangers lurking around every corner, a very sweet deal, an all-in-one powerful device."

Then he came to his senses.

She said both houses are still at risk. He didn't own an all-in-one powerful device to help him avoid secret dangers which, in his case, really did lurk around every corner.

After gulping more NSAID, he spent the next few hours napping as best as he could manage in the heat of the storage loft. He needed to rest while he could.

CHAPTER FIFTY

FBI/CIA Safe House, East 64th Street, New York City

Donnursk felt good about himself.

He lay on the bed in his room at the safe house. He remembered how good he felt when he graduated from the FBI Academy at Quantico.

His first assignment had been tailing a low-level courier for an arms smuggler. It meant covertly flashing his badge at the TSA security guy at Reagan National Airport so he could pass through the gate with his weapon still cradled in his left armpit. That felt good.

His first arrest had been a computer hacker in Richmond who stole bank account passwords and sold them for drug money. The perp was a pimply faced punk who got off with six-months' probation. Still, it felt good.

He'd been a member of the DFC for only a few months. Yet he'd handled his first assignment sanctioned by supreme authority with flying colors last Monday night on Shirley Highway. The DFC loved him for it. That meant the entire tenth floor loved him. And that meant he was golden.

The last few days had been the best of his career thus far. He'd been assigned two simultaneous jobs protected by supreme authority. He wasn't certain if that had ever happened before, but guessed it had never happened for anyone as quickly as this. It seemed like the bureau equivalent of winning MVP in your rookie year. Because of it, he was now their top "go to" agent.

Now, job number one was—kill Sam Teagarden.

Job number two was—kill McCanliss, aka Ice Skater.

The first job he would complete for the agency, his country, his sworn duty.

The second job was much more. He'd complete it because he'd enjoy it. McCanliss was one of the last old timers from the 9/11 era. He was a part of the team that failed to connect the dots. Of course, they were all responsible. They—*all*—failed to detect nineteen Arabic foreign nationals living in the U.S. while learning to fly commercial airliners without bothering to learn how to take off or land a commercial airliner.

To his way of thinking, anyone with the bureau at that time shared responsibility, but not one of them took responsibility.

Not a single one.

Now it was time to hold one of those old timers accountable. The DFC commander's instruction was "if ice skater does not turn-up by tonight, you have supreme authority on both the fox…and on ice skater."

Well "tonight" had arrived and Ice Skater still had not turned up.

Time to go to work.

CHAPTER FIFTY-ONE

The Boathouse, Sparta Township, NJ

It was steaming hot, a perfect night for a naked swim in the lake with Cynthia. Maybe someday they'd be able to do that, providing he survived the murder charge and the whole FBI mess.

From the windows, the thick woods around the boathouse blocked a full view of the sky, but Teagarden had a good straight-on view of the lake through the sliding glass doors. There was no moonlight reflecting on the lake. The water surface and shadows of the distant shore seemed laden with the full weight of muggy summer darkness. He didn't know if there was a new moon in the sky and considered going online to check the lunar phase, then decided against it.

Whether the moon was dark or the sky merely cloudy, it wasn't like he had a choice. In a few minutes, he'd be out there paddling toward his only ally. Though he did hope for a dark sky.

The last thing I need is to get on that lake in a canoe and have the clouds open up to cast a full moon spotlight on me. If that happened I'd be—well, I'd be a sitting duck. Cynthia warned that locals have binoculars and telescopes. Even if the police and FBI had stopped monitoring the lake, the locals would spot me and call 9-1-1.

He pulled together his few possessions, taking care to wrap the thirty-four pages, now almost completely decoded, into a

196

protective plastic bag taken from the galley kitchen. It seemed a reasonable precaution since he was about to go canoeing in the dark.

He knew the pages would be historic if made public. It would be a mean revelation that many would prefer to leave hidden, to keep the past cloaked in beguiling innocence.

He opened the sliding glass door just wide enough to slip out. Once outside, he stooped low and pushed it closed with a foot.

Crouching low, there was a strong smell of freshly cut grass and chemical fertilizer. He moved slowly, going as easy on his still-healing knees as he could while maneuvering down the embankment of the neighboring yard, Ernest Blair's yard. He paused every few feet, cocking his head, first to one side, then the other, listening for any sound that might be out of place with the night. The most prominent noise was the lapping of tiny waves at the shore's edge caused by a light breeze. Beyond that, the night was still.

He army-crawled down the narrow pier where the lights of many houses lining the waterfront came into view. Some were glamorous mansions that basked in their own spotlights; others were older and smaller with only a humble jelly jar porch light to illuminate the door. To the right, the island stood out as a large shadow.

It was here that he could see the moon phase. It was a waning crescent, showing itself only briefly behind what looked like high altitude altostratus coverage.

He slowly rose above the pier planking to look left where he could see the town center about a mile away with the lights of stores, streets, and traffic signals just beyond a short bridge. He remembered passing over that bridge when Cynthia drove through town Monday night. Was it possible that was only three days ago? He didn't remember seeing a German beer hall, but knew it would be there, just as she said.

He was about to scoot the full length of the narrow pier

when a dark movement on the lake caught his eye. It was a mere shade cast against a darker shade at the water's middle, closer to his girlfriend's small chalet.

Teagarden froze. Squinting in the dark, he tried to focus on the spot where he detected movement. He considered what natural phenomenon could have caused it. A log or tree branch? The lake had no current except the wake when fast boats roared past, so it was possible for a log to remain perfectly immobile. But this seemed too large for a log. And it was certainly no fish, unless the lake had dolphins.

The water made faint slapping sounds at the pier supports below him. For the first time, he heard animal life. Birds perched somewhere on the water's surface, probably ducks, maybe geese. Their distant vocalizations carried to him as soft murmurs by the unique acoustics of the overcast night and contours of the shore.

Then it moved again.

With another quick flicker of moonlight, Teagarden caught the outline of a man sitting in a stationary rowboat. In the dark and from a distance, he could see that it was not a movement of alarm. He wasn't fishing in the dark. Therefore, he had to be law enforcement. Teagarden wondered: FBI (Harry or Durgan), state trooper, local police, sheriff, sheriff's deputy?

Whoever he was, he'd drawn the short straw for solitary night surveillance on the lake, in a direct line between Cynthia's small chalet and her ex-husband's large colonial. And he was bored. That shadowy movement in the dark was a shifting of his weight to stretch. Having just endured thirty-six hours in a cramped storage loft, Teagarden easily recognized that for what it was.

Now what do I do?

If they posted a night watch on the lake, it was a certainty they'd be monitoring the fronts of both houses. That was Cynthia's "pox on both houses" warning. She likely had no idea that there was also someone on the lake, probably watching the island. Cops were worried about the island because it was large and wooded and not heavily populated, creating plenty of hiding places in the darkness. After a thorough search, they probably still had concerns and wanted to know if any boats might slip away from it during the night.

I carry on—that's what now. There's no alternative. Cynthia's canoe plan is the best hope, though it means risk of being seen by this night watchman on the lake.

He silently crawled the remaining length of the planking which occasionally creaked with mild objection the way old wood and loose nails often do. At the end, he saw the outlines of two vessels floating in the water just off the pylons, a small canoe and a rowboat, each secured by short ropes.

The idea came to him in a flash. It meant going all the way back to the yard, but he saw no alternative. Teagarden turned and army-crawled back to the yard's edge, where he felt along the ground for a good sized rock. He selected two that nicely fit in his hand, each about the size of a tennis ball, and tucked them into the backpack.

After returning to the pier's end, he eased over the side using ladder rungs nailed to the pylons to slip into the water. Poised on the bottom rung to prevent his laptop from getting wet, he pulled the canoe close. He lowered the backpack into it, unzipped the main compartment and removed the sports coat. He felt for the oar, and placed it beside the backpack where he could easily find it again in the dark when the time came, which he hoped would be soon. He let go of the moored canoe and fully slipped into the water. At that proximity to the shore, it was chest deep. The water was warm and felt good.

Getting wet isn't that bad in muggy weather. Under better circumstances, it would actually be enjoyable.

Standing between canoe and rowboat, he felt inside the rowboat for the oars. It was an old aluminum boat that he knew would make a great clattering noise should it bump anything. He carefully raised each of the two oars, crisscrossed them, and stood them at the back of the boat, propped against the rear bench. For the next part, he had to pull the rowboat toward the pier's rungs so he could work above the water line. There, he unfolded and draped his sports coat over the upright oars so that each shoulder of the coat hung perfectly on the crisscrossing paddles. He reached to the jacket front and managed to secure one button to hold it in place.

It was eerie how well it looked. From just a few feet away, it was a headless man, a ghostly boater, adrift on a black lake under a starless sky.

Now he could only hope the officer on the nightshift would see it, and think the same when the moment was right.

He reached up to the pylons above the pier planking and undid the two ropes securing the rowboat and canoe before again slipping into the water. He turned the rowboat to the right, toward the large island, and pushed it has hard as he dared.

His next task was to force the distraction.

He dug into the backpack for one of the rocks. Before the shadowy outline of the drifting rowboat disappeared in the darkness, he held the rock in a knuckle ball grip and lobbed it at the headless oarsman.

It landed squarely in the hull and rattled about on the aluminum flooring, making a startling ruckus in the otherwise quite night.

Perfect. Just call me Mariano Rivera.

Teagarden didn't wait to see if it accomplished the desired results. He leaned into the canoe, gave himself a hearty leg thrust from the pier, and paddled as hard and quietly as he could.

First right, then left. Right, left. Right, left.

He was easily fifty feet in the opposite direction when the first floodlight beamed to life, followed by the squawk of a two-way radio. It was the watchman on the lake.

"Boat...boat...southwest of island...toward main boat

ramp...two hundred yards."

"Roger. Copy that," came the audible response on the two-way. The second and third beams of light shot across the lake's surface, one from each shore. It wasn't difficult to know when the lights found the target.

"There it is...rowboat...single occupant...stop...heave to."

The watchman on the water cranked his boat engine and motored toward Teagarden's contrivance.

"Stop or I'll shoot...stop...heave to...last warning...stop or I *will* shoot you."

Teagarden continued paddling toward the town, using rapid strokes, away from the noisy action.

Right, left. Right, left.

Blam! Kah-chuck. Blam! Kah-chuck. Blam! Kah-chuck. Blam! Kah-chuck.

He knew what that was. It was a pump action shotgun, probably twelve-gauge. The engine of a second motorboat roared to life along with a second voice.

"Klumm anything? Am on way. Hold those light beams steady."

Blam! Kah-chuck. Blam! Kah-chuck. Blam! Kah-chuck. Blam! Kah-chuck.

Momentary silence followed the second round of shotgun blasts. The lights held on the rowboat, never sweeping toward him. He kept paddling.

Right, left. Right, left.

When the ruse was discovered, the distant voices sounded like echoes from a deep canyon.

"Shit!"

"What is it? Klumm, you okay?"

"Deception!"

"What?"

"Goddammit, Blaubach, listen to me. It's a deception. There's nothing in this boat except an empty coat."

The two-way radio again squawked to life, sounding like

an electronic duck. "This is Klumm. He's broken through. All points, abandon lake surveillance. He's on foot. Initiate road blocks. And pick up that lawyer woman. I told those feds. They didn't believe me. Now this *proves* she's involved. Pick her up for aiding and abetting."

Teagarden stole a quick glance to the rear. There were three small boats, the middle one was the aluminum rowboat. The other two held one man each. They were training a powerful light onto the surrounding waters, sweeping the immediate surface between them and the colonial in search of evidence.

Teagarden kept paddling.

So, it wasn't the FBI. It wasn't Harry or Durgan. It was Sheriff Klumm from Bethel, New York, and he'd brought along at least one New York State Trooper across state lines to New Jersey.

Is that even legal?

The man named Blaubach was the trooper the 9-1-1 dispatcher promised would soon be on his way to the original crime scene at his house.

That's interesting. The FBI was here and backed off, but Klumm stuck around. That sheriff is smart, and his heart is in the right place; he thinks he's after a child killer, while the FBI thinks they're after a whistle-blower that'll embarrass the crap out of them.

Right, left. Right, left.

He paddled under the short traffic bridge bordering the town center and veered left under the boardwalk near a controlled waterfall that fed the lake. The flickering signal he was looking for came from a platform above a rocky embankment on the right, near a concrete flood wall. He hoisted his backpack, stepped from the canoe and gave it a push back on the water. He worked his way up the rocky embankment as rapidly as his knees would permit. Near the top, he saw that the flickering signal was not being made by a cigarette lighter, but a foot-long device used to ignite charcoal briquettes.

"Sounded like trouble," she said.

"It was, and there's more to come."

"You don't know the half of it. Let's go."

They walked behind the flood wall and across the top of a narrow dam that controlled the slow-flowing waterfall he'd seen a moment before. On the other side of the dam, they stepped over a banister onto a shallow balcony and walked through French doors leading to an empty party room in the basement of the beer hall, Östreicher Haus. The triangular bar in the corner looked as if it hadn't been used in years. She set her purse on the billiards table and withdrew a windbreaker bearing the logo for the fiftieth anniversary of the Woodstock festival and a matching cap.

"Put this on," she said. "Pull the cap down over your eyes, but don't be too obvious about it. We're going upstairs. Walk past the bathrooms on the first landing, then continue up another flight, through the pub, and out the front door to the sidewalk. Don't stop for anything. Any questions?"

"What happens outside?"

"We get into a silver Jeep Cherokee that belongs to my son's girlfriend."

"Right," he said. "Let's go."

CHAPTER FIFTY-TWO

Interstate 95, New Jersey, Delaware, Maryland

"Where's the girlfriend?"

"I said it belonged to my son's girlfriend. I didn't say she was driving it."

Before reaching the New Jersey Turnpike, they could see the drones hovering at the main interchange in the distance. They hovered and busily spun about like a disturbed nest of large, angry hornets as they checked license plates on passing vehicles.

"I figured on them," she said. "It's why I borrowed a car with no connection to me. They're probably using facial recognition. They didn't know I was involved until tonight. So I'm hoping they haven't programed my image yet. You, however, better climb over and hide on the floor in the back," she said.

"Right. I'm accustomed to hiding in tight spaces by now. And I hit the Dear John jackpot while hiding in the boathouse loft."

"Tell me about it."

There was a blanket on the back seat. He rolled to the floor and curled up where he could see the outlines of her feet under the driver's seat.

"Cynthia," he said, "that file, I can't believe it, it's—well, I can't tell you how important it is. If it's ever published it'll be the American version of Martin Luther's Ninety-Five Theses. It'll transform the way Americans see their country, maybe even transform America itself. It proves the FBI did things like…"

"I know," she interrupted, "organized libel, mass disinformation, spying on the private sex lives of national figures, blackmailing presidents, smearing political candidates as homosexual, and—yes—assassination. Some suspected it all along. Your file proves it."

It was a strange pause. He wasn't certain he'd heard correctly.

"But how…"

"Sam, I know we spoke about my darling ex-husband who is now openly gay and happily spending the summer in Switzerland, but did I tell you about my son? Did I say what he does for a living?"

"I don't believe you did."

"Lawyer. Like me"

"Okay. So?"

"So he works for Justice. He's a junior defense attorney in the NSD, National Security Division. Boring as hell and pays no money. He works on lawsuits and complaints related to the old Patriot Act. His office is actually in the Justice Building on Pennsylvania Avenue, directly across from the J. Edgar Hoover FBI building. By the way, Congress has funded a new FBI building to be constructed in the burbs."

"Okay, so how—"

"So he tells me there's a long-lived rumor within the FBI and Justice Department about something called the Dear John File. Been an underground joke for decades. They've nicknamed it 'QB69,' as in Queen Bitches. You know, two old closet queens leaving nasty clues about each other's libido, and threatening to go public on each other. All that old-school George and Martha stuff. He says it's ancient legend, like ghosts in the White House, secret messages concealed in the Declaration, and space aliens at Area 51. No reasonable person believes it. At least, if anyone in Justice really does believe it, they tend to keep their mouth shut."

"I believe it," he said from the rear floor.

"Me, too," she agreed.

Careful to maintain a proper speed, she drove south on the New Jersey Turnpike where more drones hovered at every toll gate. On her advice, he pulled the blanket tight around his body.

Teagarden added this experience onto the growing coincidences allowing him to survive and, he hoped, eventually prevail. Had Bruce Kaserian introduced him to anyone other than Cynthia, had he not had that one-night encounter with her at The Argonaut Hotel, things would be different. And now there is the coincidence that her son works at Justice— and that he has actually *heard* of the Dear John File.

More and more I'm wondering if somehow I wasn't handpicked for this job by some higher power. Once this is over, if I survive, I will look into finding a church and a minister to speak with.

Looking at her feet, he related details of the last three days in the boathouse. He included Wednesday morning's search, hiding in the loft for hours, discovering the code-breaker while glancing through cereal ads in an antiquated boy's magazine, and researching each decoder ring online to nearly complete translation of the entire file.

She did the same for her side of the story, which took longer because there was more to tell. The agents knocked at the door of her chalet just minutes after she arrived home Wednesday morning from their night of lovemaking in the boathouse. They thought she was lying during the Q-and-A, which led them to a full search of the entire area, including the lake.

"They read me like a book," she said. "The search boss was a wimpy guy in an oversized FBI windbreaker who stood in a corner and stared at me while others lobbed questions. When I said I had to go to the bathroom, he practically sprouted antennae. He wagged a finger at a female agent to go with me."

"Sounds unpleasant."

She shook her head in the darkness of the Jeep Cherokee as she approached the Delaware Memorial Bridge.

"It was unpleasant. And there are a lot more drones up ahead. Zooming all over."

He rose just enough to peek into the distance. They were larger than the ones that attacked him in Bethel. Each one was about the size of a basketball and equipped with light beams that scanned the interior of passing vehicles. Seeing that, he quickly ducked back down and tightened the blanket edges.

"Can you imagine?" she continued. "In my own home! Just because they have a search warrant, I can't go to the bathroom by myself."

"What'd you do?"

"I let the lady agent walk with me. At the bathroom door, I told her to wait outside."

"Did she?"

"Of course. How do you think I got the cactus in the window?"

She told him about her phone conversation with Bruce Kasarian later in the day, who was profusely apologetic for telling FBI agents about their one night together.

"That's how they knew about me," she said.

"Yeah. I figured that one out. But why'd he tell them? He's been such a good friend for years. Why'd Bruce do that to me? And to you?"

"Oh, Sam, don't blame him. They grilled the poor guy for three hours, right there in his office at Columbia. It's what they do. It's what they know how to do best. They intimidate people. I'm telling you, it was so upsetting having them in my house, firing questions at me. I'm sorry to tell you, I considered confessing everything just to make it stop. And I'm a courtroom lawyer. I know how to play the game. It was spooky to be on the receiving end. No lie."

"I'm sorry," he said from beneath the blanket in the back. "I should never have gotten you into this."

"Never mind that sort of talk." She took a deep breath, preparing to pass on two additional developments. "I've consulted a couple of fellow lawyers about this. One in New York and one in D.C. They're top notch brains, criminal law, constitutional law, and trustworthy."

"And?"

"And they're working for us now, making calls, trying to work something out—but in the meantime, they're concerned about your daughter."

"They wouldn't dare hurt her. Federal agents can't do that."

"I know and I agree. But the lawyers see a problem. It's like this: these men we're dealing with are what the security industry calls 'in the black,' or 'deep shadow.' Their budget isn't public; Congress doesn't officially know they exist. They don't operate by the rules. They make accidents happen, including heart attacks. You were supposed to be one of their accidents. Instead you've become more of an 'uh-oh.'"

"I get that part, but why involve Eva? My daughter has nothing to do with any of this."

She took another deep breath. "I'm sorry to say this, but the lawyers think there's reason to fear the sociopaths will now be happy to smoke you out anyway they can. It's because you're outsmarting them. They might decide that using your family is an option."

"Oh God, Cynthia!"

"I know, Sam," she said. "Don't get too worried yet. You've had contact with her so you know she's okay. And this particular aspect of the overall problem does not apply to your sheriff, who tried to shotgun you in a rowboat."

"And he came damn close to nailing me. That man is smart. He makes the feds look like amateurs."

"Right. So here's my suggestion regarding the FBI. If we get separated, you need to figure a way to team with your daughter. Or at the very least, you need to let her know to be extra careful about her safety and the safety of her own daughter."

"That makes sense. But how could I possibly get to Key West? I can't exactly board a flight at Reagan National."

"We'll figure something out. Meanwhile, these two lawyer friends of mine are working an angle on your behalf, but they have to work their way through the ranks. It'll take a few days for them to get to the people who issue orders in the dark."

"So my job is to stay alive until somebody applies the brakes."

She took another deep breath and swallowed.

"Listen, Sam, there's something else. How plugged into the news have you been?"

"Not much. I read a little online news in the boathouse. Iran is threatening to blow up the world. And I know I'm a wanted man. That's enough news for me. Why?"

"I'm afraid I have some bad news about your math professor friend at George Washington University—Stuart Shelbourn."

Teagarden threw off the blanket and bolted upright before catching himself and lying back down.

"Oh no!" he groaned.

"I'm afraid so. His son, too. They're both dead. Kasarian mentioned it to me and I found it online. Traffic accident in northern Virginia. At least, that's what the Virginia State Police call it. There was a torrential downpour at the time."

"Oh God…"

"And there's more. The woman at that tourist hostel in Manhattan where you stayed."

"Svetlana?"

"Yes. She was found strangled yesterday morning. There's some media speculation you did it."

He curled tighter on the floor of the car's backseat. First Billy Carney, then Stu Shelbourn and his son, and Svetlana, too. Though she was a drug dealer, she didn't deserve to be murdered. And all those deaths were because of a dusty old folder encrypted with a century-old toy decoder ring that was innocently mailed to him. It was more than his stressed emotions could process. For the balance of the drive down I-95, all the way to Fort McHenry Tunnel at Baltimore Harbor—he wept.

CHAPTER FIFTY-THREE

Friday, July 26, 2019
Key West Airport

It was an intriguing sight.

McCanliss stepped aside from the crowd on the tarmac to admire the old twin-prop airplane parked in the distance. He raised his hand to shield his eyes from the sun's glare. As a boy, he'd dreamed of being a pilot because of that airplane. It had been his father's favorite. "Everything before it was a vestige of the Wright brothers," his father said of the model, "and everything after it was modern aviation." That was in 1970 when he was a child and the plane was already ancient. Now, it was rare to even see one. Yet there it was—a Douglas DC-3 sitting stationary at the end of the taxiway at Key West International Airport. He considered it a positive omen, a blessing upon the decision he'd made in the Central Park Zoo while watching the snow leopards.

He stepped back into the crowd and entered the small terminal where he collected his checked bag that concealed his two securely locked firearms: a Glock 22 and a Savage Arms 220 bolt-action sniper rifle.

"Welcome to E-Y-W," the woman's voice barked as she grabbed the suitcase from him and hurried toward the parking lot. "Holy crap!" she shouted. "What the frig have you got stashed in this thing? Lead?"

His eyes sizzled with anger. He was a micro-second from

injurious violence when he realized what had happened. She was a Key West cabdriver and this was her way of snagging a fare. For her, it was like spear fishing. You spot your fish, and when it passes, you strike.

He took a breath and decided to go with it.

"Gold," he said. "I carry my pirate treasure with me."

"Fricking great. Most New Yorkers come to the Keys hoping to *find* sunken treasure," she said. "You're the first to bring it back. Hey, listen, if you're planning on dumping it in the ocean, let me help you with it. I won't steal any. I promise."

She was tall and big boned, with an old-style shag haircut and skin banded by so much sunburn it would rival a diamondback rattlesnake. Her husky voice and boisterous personality matched her lumbering body. She looked to be about fifty-years-old, but because of her skin, it was difficult to tell. She could have been as young as thirty.

"I spotted you on the tarmac," she said. "You were eye-balling the DC-3."

"Yes, I was."

"Belongs to a good old Conch nicknamed Pangolin. He takes it up a couple of times a week for tourists. It'll cost ya, but I hear it's worth it. He's known to buzz Cuban airspace just for fun. Apparently he likes risking World War Three."

"Thanks, I'll remember that. What was it you called Key West?" he asked.

"E-Y-W. That's our airport designation. It's right there on your bag check."

He looked down. The tag on the case holding his firepower read "EYW."

"Stupid, ain't it?" she said. "Seems like it ought to be K-E-Y, or at least K-Y-W. But people who make those decisions don't ask me how things ought to get done." She gave a rowdy, barking-dog laugh at her own comment as they entered the parking lot. "That's their loss."

"Well, by one commercial aviation coding system it actually

is K-E-Y-W," he said. "It all depends on which system is being used."

"No shit. I only know our bag tag system. So you in the airline business?"

"No. I just know about that sort of thing."

"Okay. So where you staying?"

"No reservation yet."

"Well, you've got the perfect Key West cabbie for that. So tell me, which one of our three reasons for visiting are you: boats-and-water, peace-and-quiet, or fun-and-party?"

"Something quiet in the Old Town area."

"Right. The Poor House Inn on Poor House Lane. It's right next to the cemetery. Dead people tend to be real quiet." She hacked out another dog laugh. "Except when drunk college kids jump the fence at night to party among the graves. They love our cemetery where some tombstones are engraved with amusing messages, or eulogies, or whatever you call 'em. Course, Yankee snowbirds can overdo it some- times too. But the frat boys from up north, holy crap, they're the worst."

Her cab was a twenty-year-old Buick painted yellow and sounded like a washing machine when she cranked it. He took her business card. It read "The Queen of Haul." When she wasn't working her old Buick as a taxi, she was hauling landfill and trash in her dump truck.

"How'd you know I'm a New Yorker?" he asked.

"When you been doing it this long, you just know. Besides, I'm from Jersey. Jersey can spot New York in the dark, know what I mean? It's been twenty years now. Bayonne don't miss me, and I don't fricking miss Bayonne."

Yet another dog laugh.

He paid the fare, tipped her, thanked her, and told her he might call her sometime just to see how she handled the pick- up line. It didn't seem to faze her one way or another. After he got out, the big Buick lumbered up onto the curb and sidewalk to make a noisy U-turn, presumably heading head back to E-Y-W for another fare.

In his room, he showered, changed clothes, and returned his Glock to the small of his back. Using binoculars, he gave the neighborhood a careful sweep from the window. It was a sleepy, residential area that had no similarity to the frat party atmosphere that hammered 24/7 on the other side of the island. The gates to the cemetery were open, but only one lone cyclist in a Hawaiian shirt peddled slowly through.

McCanliss withdrew the components of his sniper rifle from his luggage. He snapped the stock to the barrel and trigger mechanism, mounted the telescopic sight to the free-floating barrel, and looked through the range finder reticle designed to adjust for distance and bullet drop. All was good. He loaded a magazine box containing five .338 magnum bullets. Setting the full assembly on the table by the window, he turned the dials to delicately adjust the butt plate and cheek rest. Every-thing was fine. He broke the rifle into its two main units and locked them securely in his luggage.

The tall bronze-skinned cabdriver couldn't have known how perfect The Poor House Inn was for his purposes. After asking for a room on the second floor in front, he found he had a good view of the property he'd come to Key West to monitor. It was exactly half-a-block away on Olivia Street, the house where Navy Aviator Captain Eva Ghent, née Tea-garden, lived with her baby daughter.

CHAPTER FIFTY-FOUR

Washington, D.C.

He scarfed more NSAIDs in the dark.

It was still night when they circled the city on the Beltway and entered Washington, D.C., from the east, through Anacostia. They drove west on Pennsylvania Avenue, past the Capitol, Smithsonian, FBI Building and Justice Department.

"Pass up your Woodstock cap," she said as they passed Federal Triangle.

From his hiding place on the backseat floor, he could see the flashing lights of the drones. Again about the size of basketballs, they were thickest where Pennsylvania Avenue doglegs around the Treasury Building and the White House. Teagarden knew they were routine security drones. Still, they'd probably been programmed with his and Cynthia's images by now. It didn't take IT people long to key in new facial recognition entries that could be shared by all of Washington's security forces.

"Stay down," she said. "As we used to say when I went to Georgetown Law, 'this town's got more bacon than the Smithfield Ham Company.' We wouldn't want to get nabbed when we're this close to our appointment."

Having attended GW for graduate school, he too knew Washington. "We're near Justice. Are you going to park and wait for your son to arrive at his office?"

"No. I'm not getting my son involved in this. He's the best thing that ever happened to me—way too precious."

The question had been thoughtless. She was right, of course. It was the same way he felt about his daughter and granddaughter. He didn't want them involved either.

"Besides, my son's not in the office today. Or tomorrow. Or the next day. He's at the World Court in The Hague defending the U.S. in litigation involving international torture. How ironic is that? Those Patriot Act cases are going to linger in the system for decades."

"Well, he ought to be safe there."

"He is. I've arranged to hear from him three times a day through his girlfriend."

He recognized the façade of the Willard Hotel, then felt the pull of inertia as the car turned right on Fourteenth Street. In that direction, they'd soon be circling Lafayette Park and the White House.

"So tell me, why have we come to D.C. and driven past the very office building where John Edgar did his nastiness? Who's the appointment with?"

"Sam, we need protection. And there's no better protection than the House Speaker."

"You've got an appointment with *him!?*" he shouted, throwing off his blanket with disbelief.

"No. That would be a little beyond the range of my contacts. But it's close. We've got an early appointment with Danford Shackton."

"Okay. Who's Danford Shackton?" He tried not to sound deflated.

"Attorney. I went to Georgetown with him. After law school, he went into government service, while I went for the money. We've both succeeded rather well in our chosen fields."

"Okay. So how's he going to help us?"

"He's the chief lawyer for a big-time House committee, called Homeland Security Subcommittee on Cybersecurity, Infrastructure and Security Technologies."

"That's a bureaucratic mouthful."

"I know. The speaker of the House is a member and keeps a tight watch on it."

"Okay," he said again.

"Danford Shackton has the ear of the House speaker, and the House speaker has the ear of everybody on the Hill. Now all we have to do is fill him in on everything. Get him a copy of the Dear John File, and wait."

"What will we be waiting for after we do all that?"

"First, we wait for the most important thing of all—for you to be cleared. Then, we wait for everything else: news reports, arrests, investigations, congressional hearings, mass firings, lawsuits, presidential pardons. But hey, let the chips fall where they may."

It sounded like a good plan, though time-consuming. Teagarden wanted to ask where he would live while waiting for all those falling chips. But he didn't.

"Where's his office?" he asked.

"Capitol Hill."

"That's the opposite direction."

"We're not going there."

"Okay. So, may I know where we're going to meet this Mr. Shackton?"

"His private residence. An apartment in Foggy Bottom."

"Great. Under better circumstances, we could visit my old apartment. When I was a grad student in this town, I lived in Columbia Plaza. It's near the Watergate. There's a terrific pub nearby called The Red Lion."

"That's where he lives," she said. "He has an apartment in the Watergate."

Teagarden flopped back to the floor and pulled the blanket over his head.

"Do you see any irony here?" he mumbled. "The Watergate. What an appropriate place to report a government crime spree from the last century."

CHAPTER FIFTY-FIVE

The sun was just beginning to rise as Donnursk entered Washington via Wisconsin Avenue and drove south through Georgetown. In Foggy Bottom he cruised past The Kennedy Center and parked in a space within view of The Watergate Hotel. He left the front cab, walked around and entered the rear door of the truck labeled "Durgan's Lawn & Garden."

He was proud of the truck, proud that it had his name on the side. The FBI had only a dozen agents, give or take, in the DFC, and within the DFC it had only three satellite trucks: his, Ice Skater's, and Street Cleaner's Carpentry and Home Repair truck, stationed in Los Angeles. Each was a status symbol capable of turning the occupant into the controller of a clandestine fleet of mini-drones with enough firepower to qualify as a medium-sized air force.

Inside, he flipped dozens of switches and pressed a dozen more buttons to boot up every electronic device, including an AWAC box that connected directly to the DFC's own satellite. He put on a headset and checked to make certain every member of the surveillance team he'd requested was in place and ready.

"Truck one, in place. All units respond."

The response squawked in his ear, one by one:

"Watergate Hotel lobby. All set."
"Virginia Avenue east of Watergate Hotel. All set."
"Virginia Avenue west of Watergate Hotel. I'm set too."

"Watergate, sixth floor of hotel. I'm here."
"Watergate Hotel, north front, on foot. Ready."
"Watergate Hotel, main parking garage. I'm in place."

Fine. Everyone was where they should be. Donnursk leaned back in the chair and waited.

CHAPTER FIFTY-SIX

So far, so good.

Sam Teagarden breathed deep relief when they parked the Jeep Cherokee in the basement garage and rode the Watergate elevator without challenge.

Danford Shackton's apartment was elegantly decorated in a 1930's Art Deco style, with a balcony view of a GW University dormitory across Virginia Avenue that was once a Howard Johnson's Hotel. In its hotel days, it played a key role in the scandal more than two generations earlier that exposed extraordinary foolishness and paranoia in American government. It's where the CIA lookout man for the Watergate burglary team was stationed with binoculars. Teagarden had come to believe that Watergate and Vietnam were a fulcrum in American history that ended all public naïveté. Before Watergate and Vietnam, people believed in their government; afterward, they didn't. It was that simple.

And here he was, trying to tell people they had no idea just how bad those years really were. The Dear John File would only add to that era's crimes and hypocrisy by re-opening old wounds and making them hemorrhage all over again. The idea worried him. Would people really want to know, or would they prefer to just turn the page? Maybe no one would care, or worse, they'd blame the messenger.

Though it was pre-dawn, Shackton was prepared for his guests. He was dressed in a dark suit and had a full pot of coffee ready in the kitchen. He was a slender man, with an old world charm brimming with formal courtesy. Teagarden noticed that his hands had unusually long fingers, which made him wonder if Shackton played the piano. He learned the answer when they walked from the kitchen with their coffee mugs to the living room where a baby grand prominently occupied one corner.

They thanked him for taking the risk of admitting two fugitives into his home, one of whom was wanted for child murder. Shackton assured them in a professionally courteous voice that he did have concerns, but that his respect for Cynthia was his reason for allowing the meeting.

Teagarden let her do the talking. She related the full story to her friend. At the part about the decoded file, Teagarden handed over the thirty-four pages for Danford Shackton's examination. His host took his time flipping through them, carefully reading every deciphered entry. He was quick, yet it seemed to take ages. Afterward, the stress factor increased when Shackton took more time to look off into empty space.

"If this document is authentic," he said finally, "it's rather like the Rosetta Stone in reverse."

"How so?" Cynthia asked.

"Well, it's like this," Shackton said. "When the Frenchman, Mr. Champollion, deciphered the Rosetta Stone, he presented the human race with a historic treasure. It was a wonderful insight into a once-great civilization. We could finally understand the people of ancient Egypt. They could speak to us some two-thousand years later."

He turned to gaze into Teagarden's eyes. Teagarden held still, fearing that Shackton was set to give voice to the very thing he'd been worrying about. He was afraid that if no one wanted to know this truth, he'd be abandoned to face phony murder charges.

"Yes?" Cynthia said. "And...?"

"And—instead of a blessing, this is more of a cursèd insight into a civilization that may not be as great as we thought."

"Dan, are you saying what I think you're saying?" Irritation bleeding into her voice.

Shackton thumbed the pages as his thoughts turned inward. He looked into their eyes. Cynthia first, then Teagarden. He thumbed the pages again. An antique clock ticked noisily somewhere down the hall.

"No," he said finally. "No, I'm not saying what you think I'm saying. My mind is made up. The very thing that makes this country great is the will to allow truths to be told. All truths. Including truths that reflect back at us with toxic radiation."

Teagarden heard himself exhale with relief.

"Mr. Teagarden, I have a home office down the hall, and in that office I have a copier. I would like to take these pages there. I would like to scan them and simultaneously fax them to my staff and the full House committee, together with a memo detailing the story behind them. But I want something in return."

Teagarden looked at Cynthia. He guessed what was coming.

"And what's that?" she asked.

"I want you to surrender. Not to the FBI or the D.C. Metropolitan Police, but to another investigative agency. Then, if this is proven valid, as I believe it will be, you will be totally exonerated." He thumbed the pages again. "Given the extraordinary nature of this document, you may become something of a heroic figure, though, of course, you'll be reviled in many circles, which will be difficult for you."

It was Cynthia who again broke the silence.

"Dan, it's an interesting proposition. Of course, Sam cannot, that is, *we* cannot stay on the run forever. But—"

"The committee I manage for the House has an investigative arm," he interrupted. "We hold witnesses in camera all the time. The CIA and FBI are not the only federal agencies whose budgets pay for safe houses. The difference is that, in my safe house, no one drowns you in a bathtub and calls it water-boarding. We just house and feed you until it comes time to testify before Congress."

"No offense, Dan, but there are different forms of torture. Can you give us a heads-up on the general location and conditions?"

"Suburban Maryland. It's not the high life, but it does have all the comforts of home, including a fully stocked kitchen."

"I can't speak for Sam, but a kitchen is not a strong attraction for me," she said, with a note of sarcasm.

"I apologize," Shackton said. "I didn't mean that the way it sounded. Here are the facts. The groceries are bought for you but you do your own food prep. You will have full use of the house, patio, and private backyard. Any reasonable need or basic necessity will be met, including medical. The fact of your confinement will be made public but not your location. As for police and reporters, I personally will see to it that they are—*not*—informed of your whereabouts."

"You have the authority to defy an FBI subpoena?" she asked.

"Oh, most certainly I do. My committee's purpose enjoys clandestine protection of national security at the highest level. That ranks far above any fugitive warrant, FBI or otherwise. In fact, I doubt they would bother to challenge me in court." He waved the thirty-four pages in the air as he spoke. "But if they did, I would have so much fun embarrassing them with this, they'd fast give it up."

Teagarden and Cynthia exchanged glances that betrayed mixed feelings. His shoulders had a vague slump, her head nodded ever so slightly as she regarded him. They knew that their run from black-ops feds, police, and sheriffs had to end, and they knew that this was as good a deal as they could possibly hope to receive under the circumstances. But neither of them wanted to say it out loud to the other.

Teagarden made the call.

"Yes, you certainly may," he said.

"May what?" Shackton asked.

"You asked if you may scan and fax the pages and send a memo. My answer is yes. Yes, you may. And you called me 'Mr. Teagarden.' No more of that, please call me Sam." He looked at Cynthia. "And as to the rest of your offer—I accept."

She exhaled relief.

"So do I," she said.

The three of them walked past the mahogany wainscoted corridor to his home office where the window had a view of the Watergate's interior courtyard. The computer and printer were already turned on. Shackton fed the pages into the top of the printer and mouse-clicked instructions to print and simultaneously scan a copy of each image into a new file that he called "The DJF." He quickly typed his memo as the pages chugged forward.

From the doorway, Teagarden tried to suppress his agitation as he watched the pages feed into the scanner. The beeping and whirring of that electronic device were vital to ending his nightmare. He glanced nervously toward the front door, paranoid that police, or federal agents would storm the apartment at that moment, smash the fax machine, throw it to the floor, then make them all disappear.

Watching each page getting pulled into the whirring mechanics and spit out into the feeder tray felt like religious redemption. It was as though he'd been on an arduous pilgrimage that challenged faith and finally reached the objective, the cathedral of truth where he was blessed and freed from his sins with divine sanctuary.

Thank you, Mr. Danford Shackton. Thank you, Ms. Cynthia Blair. Thank you, Homeland Security Subcommittee on Cybersecurity, Infrastructure and Security Technologies.

And finally...

Thank you, God.

Sensing that his gratitude verged on spilling into heavy grief, Teagarden walked back to the living room to be alone. He opened the sliding glass door, stepped onto the balcony, and broke down sobbing as the sun rose over the nation's capital. He wept for eleven-year-old Billy Carney, for his friend Stu Shelbourn, Stu's son, and for Svetlana. And he wept for the victims of Operation Over Easy: President John F. Kennedy, civil rights leader Reverend Dr. Martin Luther King Jr., and Senator Robert F. Kennedy, not to mention the 58,000 who died serving their country in Southeast Asia. They, too, were victims of heinous deception.

Shackton was right. This file really was a Rosetta Stone in reverse. It proved the existence of a program that recruited young men with marginal personalities, borderline schizophrenics raised in brutal homes who knew only lies, psychological abuse, and violence. They were probably assigned managers who regularly called and visited them over the years, sent them on bogus training excursions, told them they were being groomed for important missions, and were on track to become secret agents or undercover spies with a license to kill. One was actually sent through back-channels to the USSR to pose, emphasis on the word *pose*—as a Soviet enthusiast while believing himself to be an actual undercover American spy. It was now apparent that his Soviet trip was a setup that, when the time came, would make him look like the marginal cuckoo he actually was. A second of the young men would, after he committed assassination, try to persuade anyone who'd listen that he was managed and financed by a mysterious controller named Raul. And then there was the Christian Palestinian.

Teagarden couldn't help but wonder why the people of the twentieth century didn't fit the pieces together. Whatever the reason, they didn't. They believed the relentless story being fed to them: Communist grudge case, racist loner with a rifle,

Palestinian psycho with an Israeli beef.

Teagarden wiped streaming tears from his cheeks; his tongue tasted the liquid bitterness of salt. To the east, the Washington Monument rose against the glare of the sun. To the west, early morning joggers maneuvered in and out on the trails of Rock Creek Park where they were getting a cardio workout ahead of their day at the office. Below on Virginia Avenue, traffic was still thin at that early hour.

That's when he saw the truck.

The next few moments stretched into a millennium and compressed into a microsecond. The world stopped as it spun out of control; he was paralyzed with shock.

The truck—parked a block away on the other side of Virginia Avenue—advertised Durgan's Lawn & Garden Service. Then his brain took in the whole scene: man directly below—running...on cellphone...man on roof of dormitory...rifle...man on street frantically pointing...sniper on dormitory roof...man shouting...rifle...cellphone...sniper...Washington Monument...joggers...rifle...sniper...rifle...sniper...rifle...

"Here are the originals," Shackton said, stepping onto the balcony. Cynthia stood behind him, smiling with confidence that they had made the right decision.

Teagarden snapped from his trance. He gripped Shackton by the shoulders and yanked him hard into the living room, simultaneously knocking Cynthia down and away from the balcony. They fell together like graceless children in a game of roughhousing gone wrong.

That's when the sniper fired.

CHAPTER FIFTY-SEVEN

Key West, FL

He had some play time.

McCanliss knew it would take a day or two before Donnursk realized that Key West was Teagarden's last option. Of course, there was always a chance that "Dunno" Durgan would corner and kill the fox somewhere between New Jersey and South Florida. But this particular fox had successfully eluded everyone, including him. That was a first. For that, he respected Teagarden as the only consequential failure of his career. The odds were on his side. He was gambling that an amateur like Donnursk wouldn't get close to a man as smart as Teagarden—or as lucky.

But it would take a while before he could move the truck that far south, so he took some leisure time. He arranged to have this Pangolin hippie take him up in the DC-3 the next day. A one-hour flight in the classic aircraft while sitting in the co-pilot's seat would cost him seven hundred bucks. But what did he care? His days on Earth were numbered. So, why not? It would be fun. He deserved at least that much. He deserved to have at least one last pleasurable moment.

After breakfast, he casually strode the quiet streets of Old Town. The weather was warm, but not unbearable. He walked through the cemetery, glancing at tombstones and above-ground burial vaults. Many were works of sculpted art, eroded by the ages. It was the final resting place of many victims of the Battleship Maine, which contributed to the start of the Spanish-American War. There was Ernest Hemingway's favorite bartender, and a local waitress whose tombstone read *I told you I was sick.*

"Cute."

He imagined what his own tombstone might read. If he were buried in this cemetery, he'd probably get only the basics:

Harry McCanliss
1956-2019

Or maybe:

Here Lies Harry McCanliss
1956-2019
He Was Sick Too

It didn't matter. He wouldn't have a stake in the wording. Neither did he care. He didn't believe in God. Life was temporary; death was permanent. A dead body was a cadaver. It's not resting in peace. When a body dies, no spirit pops out to fly like Tinker Bell to heaven, nirvana, Valhalla or any other fantasy paradise. Those were the facts. Everything else was total delusion of the flock whose sole job it was to be shorn by the shepherd when their turn with the shears arrived.

South of the cemetery on Olivia Street, he walked past the house just as she arrived pushing a baby stroller. That could mean several things. She's off duty on Fridays, works a late shift, or had been placed on leave pending resolution of her father's situation. He guessed it was the latter. The U.S. Navy was not known for letting anyone facing troublesome controversy get anywhere near a four-hundred-million-dollar fighter jet or a five-billion-dollar aircraft carrier.

She was young, in excellent physical condition with broad-shoulders, high cheekbones, an aquiline nose and brown, deep-set eyes. Her hair was short and tight, nearly like a man's.

"Pardon me, is the public beach in this direction?"

"Walk down Grinnell Street," she said with a nod and speaking in a tone neither friendly nor curt.

"Thank you. You have a cute baby."

"Thank you," she said.

CHAPTER FIFTY-EIGHT

Washington, D.C.

The first shot struck Danford Shackton in the chest, slightly off-center.

He fell to the floor on his back, gasping for air. The gaping wound to the left of his sternum alternated between gurgling and sucking. A great volume of blood seemed to be everywhere in an instant as though a plasma-filled piñata had burst.

Teagarden and Cynthia dragged him from the open window. Two seconds after they began pulling, a mere four seconds after they collectively fell to the floor, the light went out of Shackton's eyes.

The second shot hit Cynthia as she was still kneeling, still clinging to Shackton's left arm. It pierced her left calf and continued on an angled trajectory into the dark oaken flooring where it burrowed a shallow tunnel that sent up a flight of splinters stretching five feet across the room. She fell backward, clutching her leg, her own crimson blood flowing into Shackton's.

Teagarden threw his arms in the air as though surrendering. He stepped back one baby step, then another, and another until he bumped the wall beside the baby grand piano on the opposite side of the living room.

The third shot puffed into the couch upholstery.

The fourth slammed the wall, six inches from Teagarden's head, slightly rattling a Tiffany sconce.

The fifth opened a small hole in the back wall, continuing into the kitchen where it concluded with a dull metallic thud, probably in the stainless steel refrigerator.

Oddly, no one cried out. Except for the sucking flow of blood in Shackton's chest, and whizzing sounds, the assault happened in complete silence.

Then the mute button was released.

Her piercing shriek was so loud that it snapped him from his own paralysis. He dove behind the couch and crawled to her. Not knowing if it was the best thing to do under the circumstances, but unable to make any other decision, he forced his straining knees to kneel. He picked her up, cradled her in his arms, and hurried to the front door as one more shot popped into the wall behind him. The elevator was still there, waiting for them. Inside, the button for the parking garage level was so low on the panel, he could barely lean down to push it while holding her.

And the pages!

The thirty-four pages, now splattered with blood, were still in his hand. Shackton had returned them to him just before he was felled by the first bullet. Despite his pain and awkward position, Teagarden managed to fold them into the hip pocket of Ernest Blair's blue jeans while hoisting Cynthia higher into his arms so he could lean down and push the button.

In the basement parking garage, she tried to talk as he carried her back to the Jeep Cherokee.

"I can't," she mumbled. "I can't. You go. Leave the car. Leave me. Just go. But remember the plan."

He laid her down beside a rear wheel of the Jeep where they were concealed. He removed his pullover shirt, ripped it lengthwise and tied a tourniquet above the wound in her calf. Then he tied a second one at mid-thigh.

"Leave me," she said between gasps. "Sam, he e-mailed the pages. He sent them. I saw it. The House committee has the whole thing now. That pushes the start button. You have to go. If they get you now, it'll all be for nothing. Remember, what you said? You need to stay alive until somebody applies the brakes."

He pulled his backpack from the Jeep, withdrew the water bottle and gave her a sip. He splashed water on her leg, his arms and chest and used the remainder of the ripped shirt to wipe the blood. From the backpack, he withdrew the second pullover she'd given him from her ex-husband's bureau and pulled it on.

"I remember," he said. "But I can't leave you. If the sniper finds you alone he'll kill you and say I did it. It'll be the same as the others."

"You have to. It's the only way. Sam, the medics will take me to GW Hospital. It's only a couple of blocks from here. I'll work my end from there until it's safe for you to come back."

He dug in his backpack and withdrew the DVD Svetlana had delivered by messenger to The Argonaut Hotel. He slipped it into her hip pocket.

"I should have given this to you earlier. It's the video I told you about. It contains the image of McCanliss at Madison Park Euro Lodge in Manhattan."

It could only have been the continuing surge of adrenaline that allowed him to pick her up again. Instead of going back to the elevator, he walked with her cradled in his arms in a low crouch between parked cars, toward the vehicle exit ramp. Though writhing in pain during the short trek, she struggled to put one hand on the side of his face.

"I hope you realize that I am madly in love with you," she whispered into his ear as audibly as she could manage.

At the toll gate, he gently laid her on the raised exit ramp near the garage attendant, who raced from his booth.

"Call the police and an ambulance," Teagarden said, still kneeling beside Cynthia. "She's hurt bad. I tied a tourniquet on her leg, but she needs to get to the emergency room fast.

"Right," the attendant said, running back to his booth to

make the call.

Teagarden kissed her goodbye.

"For God's sake, Sam, be careful," she called out in a loud whisper. "I don't want to lose another good man. And remember what I said about teaming with your next partner. She'll help keep you safe now."

Teagarden turned away and walked up the ramp. He exited on the backside of the Watergate Building where the huge off-white façade of the nearby Kennedy Center loomed like an ancient Roman temple.

CHAPTER FIFTY-NINE

It looked like a giant dirty-white Kleenex box.

For many, there was something Soviet-like in its unwieldy appearance. For better or worse, the Kennedy Center was a massive, look-at-me, national performing arts center.

He had nowhere else to go, so why not walk toward that big, white monster of a building? Once inside, he might be able to disappear somewhere within its network of corridors and theatres.

He set his bearings and strode as casually as he could manage while sirens wailed behind him. He bordered on another spell of amnesia. Unlike his blackout in the wilderness of Sullivan County where he first lost track of time, he knew he wouldn't be allowed to wander the streets of Washington very long. He was only seconds away from being approached by law enforcement officers.

Just keep moving as casually as possible.

He fought against the tendency to sit on the curb and weep with exhaustion and fear. He wiped streams of sweat coursing down his face and neck, a giveaway if they saw it.

Cynthia was right when she said "this town's got more bacon than the Smithfield Ham Company." Hoping it would help him concentrate and prevent another blackout, he ticked them off in his head like a word game:

Let's see, there's DCPD, FBI, Secret Service, Capitol Hill Police, White House Guard, CIA, campus police at George Washington University. Even the U.S. Park Police carry guns in this town.

That's a lot of cops. And if they're not all looking for him, they all will be very soon.

It was still early in the morning, yet there were a dozen buses in front of the Kennedy Center, ready to begin the day picking up and dropping off school groups. Their drivers stood nearby, chatting in small gatherings on the sidewalk. Three buses owned by a company called "Easy Excursion" were already taking on passengers.

Teagarden cruised them to check the roll signs above each windshield. The first read *Atlantic City, Taj Mahal*; the second was headed for *Gettysburg Battlefield*; the third said *Virginia Beach*. The first two were going in the wrong direction. The last one wouldn't get him far, but he was in no position to argue and had no time to look for something better. It worked at the Walmart in Monticello. He could only hope the same lucky lightning would strike twice.

"Room for one more?"

"Yes, sir," came the driver's response. "Like the TV ad says, 'sand and fun in the sun just two hours away.'"

He paid the cash fare to the driver, took a seat in the rear, and within minutes was riding to Virginia Beach on a bus three-quarters filled with sleepy teenagers. They'd turn rowdy soon enough, but for now, the hour was too early for them to animate.

The bus looped into traffic ahead of an invasion of police cars fanning out from the Watergate. At the Lincoln Memorial, a score of cops on foot waded into the early morning crowd and across the Memorial Bridge looking for him. They eyeballed tourists, joggers, and morning dog walkers, stopping anyone that fit the description of white male, six feet tall, late forties.

Once again he counted his blessings. It seemed the whole world was looking for him, yet he had again avoided the net. He dodged them in Bethel, New York City, Sparta Township, and now Washington, D.C.

Either I'm really good at this, or they really are bad at it. Imagine if I were actually armed and dangerous. That would be unpleasant for everyone.

The bus maneuvered through Arlington to the Shirley Highway where it took a steep ramp up to the triple level for HOV vehicles. At the top, there was a gaping hole in the guard wall temporarily covered by mobile concrete barricades. It was obviously the site of some horrible accident. Teagarden leaned into the window for a better look at the asphalt three levels below where it appeared stained with the darkness of crashed metal, fire, and blood.

CHAPTER SIXTY

Old Town Alexandria, Virginia

It was breakfast time.

Speaker of the House Henry Wayne Alderman, a Louisiana Democrat, had a mouthful of buttered whole wheat toast when he opened the e-mail from Danford Shackton on his Nook.

It was his obsessive breakfast routine to eat two slices of toast each morning, one whole wheat and one rye. The first always received only butter; the second slice got a thin, perfectly spread layer of jam, artfully spooned to the precise edges of the square. It was usually peach but sometimes strawberry, occasionally grape, and much less often, cherry.

After breakfast, he habitually stood at the kitchen sink to gargle a mixture of milk, honey, whiskey, and three drops of tincture of iodine for one full minute before expectorating the daily ablution. He had never been sick a day in his life and swore that it was due to his homemade morning gargle concoction. In his home district of Lawson Parish the mixture was famously known as the A.G.D., the Alderman Gullet Douche. In the late 1980s, a local pharmacist marketed the idea as a health tonic, but it never caught on, not even in Lawson Parish.

Outside of his rented townhouse on Old Town Alexandria's Rupert Alley, the driver of the black Ford Town Car waited for him to finish breakfast so he could be chauffeured to his office inside the Capitol Building. Another ten minutes and he'd have finished with breakfast, gargled, phoned his wife back home in Louisiana and head off to work on Capitol Hill.

But none of it happened because on this particular morning, he did not finish the toast, get to the gargle, or phone his wife.

The e-mail read:

Mr. Speaker,

I am forwarding the attached file to every member of Home Sub-CIST. Please open and read IMMEDIATELY. I believe it to be a matter of extreme (and delicate) urgency pertaining to national security. More backstory to follow when I get into the office.

See you in a couple of hours,
Dan Shackton

Home Sub-CIST was an acronym for The Homeland Security Subcommittee on Cybersecurity, Infrastructure and Security Technologies. Since 9/11, two foreign wars, the NSA leaks of 2013, and Russian hacking that helped elect a president in 2016, it had become the most important and most watched committee on Capitol Hill. The President was known to keep up with the committee's docket, regularly phoning to learn legislative views so as to balance the CIA's hand-wringing on the south side of the Potomac.

The House speaker trusted Danford Shackton. He knew him to be a freakishly smart lawyer who understood more about navigating the halls of Congress and the wider federal government than most members of Congress. That Shackton was openly gay never deterred Alderman from appreciating the man's talents. Why would it? He had been a longtime supporter of LGBT issues. He voted in favor of every gay rights bill he encountered as a state and now federal legislator. Privately, especially back home in his bayou district, which some-times seemed to have more alligators than people, he let every-one know his way of thinking on the subject. After the Su-preme Court upheld the right to same-sex marriage, they stuck to the old school way of thinking. And when they gave voice to those opinions, Alderman sometimes weighed in with his favorite, albeit peculiar and somewhat vulgar rant on the subject: "What do I care what a man does with his pecker, after all, it's *his* pecker. Why hell, if a man can't do what he wants with his own pecker then what kind of country is this, anyway?!"

His constituents didn't like it, but they voted for him any-way, mostly because of his position on other issues, including his championing the right of every victim of Hurricane Katrina to sue the federal government and win unprecedented sums in out-of-court settlements. They were still doing it fourteen years later, and that was all it took for them to overlook his liberal views on homosexuality.

Toast in hand, he did as Shackton instructed and opened the attached file. It was the Dear John File, fully decoded by nationally wanted fugitive Sam Teagarden in obsessively neat handwriting. What he read very nearly caused him to choke on his buttered whole wheat. He focused particularly on pas-sages dated to the winter of 1963 and the spring of 1968.

"I will be goddamned," he whispered to himself. "This fucker is the holy wrath of God the Father Almighty, Maker of Heaven and Earth." He read further. "Holy Mother of Christ, this thing is the electronic burning bush."

His cellphone rang before he could speed-read half the file. The voice at the other end was his press spokesman, a former reporter from New Orleans named Willy Baaktau.

"I'm glad I got you first, Mr. Speaker," said the bass bari-tone voice with the French-Southern accent.

"Go ahead, Baaktau. Wattchu got for me this Friday morning?"

"Brace yourself, Mr. Speaker. This news is bad. Danford Shackton is dead. He's been shot in his apartment at the Watergate. This Teagarden fugitive who's wanted in New York for child murder may be involved, but initial press reports say the FBI is citing a spurned gay lover as a probable motive."

"I will be goddamned," Alderman said, looking at his Nook where the Dear John File was still open.

CHAPTER SIXTY-ONE

From: danjones@orangecircle.com
To: naskeywestpublicrelations@usnavy.mil
Subject: Dogfight Sequel
Attn: Captain Eva Ghent

Thank you again for your willingness to provide technical ad-vice for the planned sequel to the movie *Dogfight Girl.*

We are now filming B-Roll and would like to make an appointment to meet at your convenience.

Best Regards
Dan Jones,
Sr. Assistant Producer

CHAPTER SIXTY-TWO

To: danjones@orangecircle.com
From: naskeywestpublicrelations@usnavy.mil
Subject: Dogfight Girl Sequel

Will be happy to meet at Navy Air Station on Boca Chica Key regarding movie sequel.

Please phone the P.R. Ofc. at N.A.S. Key West at your convenience.

Ask for Raymond Bakerfield.

Best Regards

Public Relations Office

CHAPTER SIXTY-THREE

Washington, D.C.

"What in the name of heaven…"

Congressman Toddman Lee Gaynor, a Kentucky Republican, sat at his desk consuming the printed pages of the Dear John File, which his staff had named as the day's "top priority."

At ninety-two, he was the oldest serving member of Congress, as well as the longest serving U.S. representative in American history. Thanks to good hard-working Kentuckians, he'd been on the job for fifty-nine years, and still did the job the old-fashioned way—with voluminous use of paper. His office was the least ecology minded in all the federal government. He'd never used a computer in his life, at least not through direct, intentional contact, which was widely known as key to his politics and faith. During campaigns, he was known to hold up a ballpoint pen and call it "the best thing God ever allowed mankind to invent for conveying information." He publicly pronounced himself an "anti-computer crusader," and a "robot fighter for Jesus."

It paid off nicely.

In the last twenty-five years, he'd been advised by campaign staffers and statistical researchers that his old-fashioned face-to-face habits combined effectively with his Christian principles to help him win elections. They labeled his views on the computerization of everything as "a lovable image" that thoroughly endeared him to the people of his 7th District in the Bluegrass State.

"The Lord hath spake," he told voters. "It just goes to show I have a direct line with the good Lord. If He wanted me to interact with computers, He wouldn't have made me—*a man*—if ya know what I mean."

Such language was his conservative-minded idea of a wink-eyed joke brimming with socially acceptable sexual innuendo. Every time he referred to himself as "a *man*," the staff demurred, laughing politely while making perfunctory "tch-tch" noises with pursed lips to indicate requisite disapproval at what, for him, was bawdy.

At that moment, no one was laughing.

His staff knew what was in the attachment forwarded by Danford Shackton. They downloaded it on the office's one computer concealed in the back room. They printed a hardcopy and read it in its entirety before the Congressman arrived at his office in the penthouse of the Rayburn House Building. Shortly afterward, they heard news of Danford Shackton's murder, which apparently happened just moments after he sent the file to every member of Congressman Gaynor's House Sub-CIST Committee. For nearly twenty years he'd been chairman of a congressional panel whose sole purpose for existence was, ironically, about electronic communications via computers. It was something the pundits only occasionally objected to and which his fellow Republicans never mentioned as a contradiction of good sense.

The staff advised their boss of the Shackton killing after he arrived and sat him down with the document.

"Oh my Lord," he said softly while reading. "Oh good Lord in Heaven, what...in...the...world." He gulped. "What...in...the...name...of...heaven...is...this?"

CHAPTER SIXTY-FOUR

Encrypted Field Communication
NSA Apache Code Ofc Baltimore, MD/Washington, DC/Coin
TelSatOrbit53/Washington, DC

<apache code initiate>

TO: copper miner
FROM: deep field cmdr

SUBJECT: opdearjohn

<secure field communication may begin>

deep field cmdr to copper miner: i drop gift in your lap after telsat tap learns of shackton d.c. meeting and u can't deliver?...explain...

copper miner to deep field cmdr: u said watergate hotel...

deep field cmdr to copper miner: correct...watergate hotel... still waiting f/ explanation...

copper miner to deep field cmdr: there are two watergates... one is hotel...one is residence apt bldg...we were airtight on hotel because u said hotel...

deep field cmdr to copper miner: so how did clusterfuck happen if u were surveilling wrong bldg?...

copper miner to deep field cmdr: street team spotted target on balcony in adjacent apt bldg.... i confirmed w/visual i.d.... gave shooter green light...shots missed...they were gone before we could shift from hotel to apt. bldg...

deep field cmdr to copper miner: now we've got a dead congressional lawyer...woman in dcpd custody at gw e r... teagarden escaped again...misinformation dept working overtime to explain to press...house speaker doubting us...and 10th flr going nuclear...

copper miner to deep field cmdr: k...now what?...

deep field cmdr to copper miner: our only option...double down...get to key west...monitor daughter...teagarden likely headed there...get him...and get ice skater...

copper miner to deep field cmdr: will do...my word, no more f-ups...

CHAPTER SIXTY-FIVE

Washington, D.C.

Traffic was light in the early morning heat.

House Speaker Henry Wayne Alderman did not bother going to his office in the Capitol. Instead, he had his driver take him straight to the Rayburn Building directly across Independence Avenue. It was late July, and Congress was about to go on summer recess for August. If he was going to do something, he knew he had to get the ball rolling quickly and in person.

"Good morning, Mr. Speaker," the main security guard said, admitting him to the elevator bank. Alderman ignored him. He pushed the button for the top floor, where the office of Congressman Toddman Gaynor was known on the grapevine as "God's Penthouse," and "Methuselah's Cold-Water Flat."

He knew the file threatened a national crisis centering on the rights of the people to know the truth, which for him was the essence of true democracy. America had endured enough secrecy. After the last two wars and years of domestic snooping on every man, woman, and child—he'd had enough. And he wanted it to stop. He wanted the file to be formally investigated, and if found legitimate, released to the public.

"Jesus, what a shit storm that will create," he said to himself, standing in the elevator, consumed with manic, racing thoughts. If it were to happen, he knew it would require the blessing of the man serving his thirtieth term in Congress. He understood the moment he saw the file, that his ideological opposite, the extremely conservative ninety-two-year-old Republican from Kentucky, would be the fulcrum of any decision on this bewildering discovery. It was simple: either the facts would go public or they'd be dismissed as the maniacal workings of a man with a gun, a computer and a sick mind—the consequence of the recent death of his wife.

"It's just shy of a fucking nuclear bomb," he said aloud.

People in the elevator heard him talking to himself and exchanged glances. The two congressional staffers, one building janitor, and three cafeteria workers all recognized him as the Speaker of the House, the third in line to be president of the United States. Though curious, they said nothing.

CHAPTER SIXTY-SIX

"This can't be good," Walter Natujay mumbled after hanging up the phone.

He'd been summoned to an immediate appearance on the tenth floor. His previous meeting with Paula Trippler had been in his own basement office where all covert program offices were located, including his own. In nearly forty years with the bureau, he'd set foot on the tenth only once. That was when they tolerated him being there just long enough to promote him to become the first black man to head the DFC.

Both the tenth and eleventh were smaller than all others by about two-thirds, right-angled and cantilevered over the front, giving them an architectural quality of exclusivity. It was known that the tenth housed personnel working internal affairs and covert oversight, the bureau within the bureau. But God knows what the eleventh floor housed. As far as Natujay knew, no one had any definite idea. Construction on the building began while Director Hoover was chief, but wasn't completed until after his death. In the early years, various imaginative rumors about the eleventh floor circulated on the grapevine. Among them: party room, gay bar, torture chamber, secret lab for cryogenic freezing where Walt Disney, Hoover, Hoover's mother, Clyde Tolson and Senator Joe McCarthy were all preserved.

Two agents met him when he stepped from the elevator to the tenth floor lobby and escorted him to the large conference room where one wall was lined with mirrors which Natujay presumed were two-way viewing panes. The table was a traditional oval; the chairs were old-style barrel backs with aged leather seats. Besides himself and Paula Trippler, two others were in the room, a stenographer and the director of personnel, Ronald Wheeler, who'd been with the bureau nearly as long as Walter Natujay.

"Mr. Natujay, do you know why you've been called to the tenth floor for this meeting, which is being taken down by a stenographer and recording equipment?"

"This morning at the Watergate?"

"That would be correct, Mr. Natujay."

"It was a miscommunication. Copper Miner was confused. A simple mistake, unfortunately."

"Really?" She crossed her legs under the conference table. "Has Copper Miner become *un*confused?"

Her tone and piercing stare were murderous. Not wanting her to see his Adam's apple bobbing, he tried to suppress swallowing, without success.

"Yes," he said. "I have moved to correct the error. Durgan Donnursk, that is—Copper Miner—is now en route to Key West where Teagarden is likely headed to rendezvous with his daughter, who has been under a loose, 'hands off' surveillance order. He has been told to double down. He will take out both Teagarden and Ice Skater."

"We are aware of that, Mr. Natujay. The tenth floor tends to monitor your communications rather closely. We especially tend to monitor communications that threaten to burn down our own house."

Sensing what was coming, he looked past her, focusing on a spot on the wall where a chair back had scraped the beige paint.

"I will clean this up, Ms. Trippler."

"Really?"

"Yes, ma'am."

"Whose idea was it to suggest to the media that Shackton

was killed by a jealous gay lover?"

"Ma'am, I do not know. Shackton's sexual orientation is public knowledge. He's made no secret of that. I did tell the bureau press officer that we are not ruling anything out. The rest is rumor and innuendo."

"Are you certain you made no reference to the file itself? No reference to details within the file that we wish to prevent going public?"

"Ms. Trippler, I am certain that no one in the DFC made any such reference to a spurned gay lover.' That sort of thing seems to take on a life of its own in the media. Some reporter at some liberal mainstream media outlet likely decided that 'not ruling anything out' gave tacit permission to make such a reference."

She didn't like his answer, primarily because it smacked of the truth, which meant he'd made no inappropriate public statements. That irritated her. She wanted him to be guilty of as many screw-ups as possible.

"And where is Ice Skater's satellite truck, Mr. Natujay?"

"At the company garage in lower Manhattan."

"And where is Ice Skater, Mr. Natujay?"

"Unknown, but I am confident that Copper Miner will eventually encounter him at Key West where the daughter lives. And when he does, as I've said, he has supreme authority to get the job done on Ice Skater, as well as Teagarden."

"What is Ice Skater's state of mind?"

"Unknown."

"What are his intentions?"

"Unknown."

"What is the status of Teagarden's daughter?"

"She's adhering to her routine. As I said, I have her under a Class-1 covert surveillance. Her whereabouts and all her communications are being monitored. She can't leave Key West without our knowledge."

"She's a Navy pilot. Are you monitoring every airplane the

Navy owns?"

"She's currently a robo-pilot only, in charge of teaching Navy pilots how to make the transition from cockpit to remote piloting. The principal aircraft is the X-47, which is presently mothballed. But she cannot board a plane and depart her base."

"And the media? Are they on her doorstep?"

"No. It seems they haven't learned of her existence, and she's not contacting them. As I said, she's keeping her head down. That's to our advantage. When Copper Miner arrives, he'll bump her to a Class-2—*overt*—stakeout with all the consequence of full in-your-face psychological surveillance. At that point, she will panic, which will of course expose Teagarden and probably flush Ice Skater as well. Unfortunately, it could also result in her going public, which risks a full-blown media gangbang. That would bear mixed result."

"Mixed result? Mr. Natujay, you're telling me that if we have a media circus on the Dear John File, it would be a— 'mixed result'?"

His sphincter muscle tightened. He had not meant media circus regarding the DJF, but only regarding the daughter. He was trying to hold his own, but she was looking for anything she could get. The interview was not going well and there was no way for him to make it better, except to be as honest as possible. He cleared his throat and looked away from her to help maintain his composure.

"Copper Miner knows how to execute his double grant of supreme authority on Teagarden and Ice Skater, then exit immediately, leaving the liberal media in the dust. Once done, the press will be easier to manipulate when and if they do get involved."

"And if Copper Miner is not as surgical as you hope?"

He'd had enough. He wanted to push back, but wasn't certain he could summon the courage. He resorted to boilerplate DFC language: "Ms. Trippler, all members of the DFC are trained to be as surgical as possible when working any case granted supreme authority. If they fail, if things get messy, we address that on an as needed basis. But until that happens, the nature of the mess and the nature of our response remains unknown."

She glanced briefly at the stenographer and director of personnel before returning to him.

"Do you think this meeting has any purpose, other than to discuss your calamity this morning at the Watergate?"

"I do not know, Ms. Trippler."

"Well, Mr. Natujay, let me fill you in." She slowly tapped a stylus on her netbook, reversing it end-over-end. "You have too many unknowns." He moved to interrupt her, but her right hand shot up. "Following your mess at the Watergate Hotel, and because of too many unknowns, you will be offered a choice. You may retire or you may stay on the job. If you stay, you will face departmental charges of rank incompetence, which may ultimately translate into formal criminal charges of treason, sabotage and violation of American national security. Not to mention termination of pension."

She stopped tapping her stylus and stared contemptuously at the black man who'd been with the bureau nearly forty years. She realized again that he actually wasn't that much older than she. As a recruit, he'd once worked with her father, Agent Mark Trippler, a founding manager of the original Operation Over Easy. Nonetheless, there seemed to be a schism she couldn't shake. To her, Natujay was, and always would be, old school.

Natujay glanced at Ronald Wheeler, the director of personnel, whose facial expression seemed to be trying to tell him something. He hoped it was something along the lines of, "this too, shall pass." He turned back to Trippler.

"I'll take retirement," Natujay said with a sigh.

"A wise choice, Mr. Natujay." She clipped the pen to the inside of the legal pad holding her netbook and closed the folder. "Mr. Wheeler will take you down to personnel on the second floor where you will complete the appropriate papers. Then you will leave the building immediately. A small commemorative party may be held for you among your office colleagues at a later time, but not before next month."

The stenographer stopped writing.

Walter Natujay rose and followed Personnel Director Wheeler from the tenth floor conference room.

CHAPTER SIXTY-SEVEN

"C'mon, Todd, this is damn important."

"Speaker Alderman, please watch your language. We do not speak that way in this office."

"I apologize, Todd. You know, I grew up on the bayous of my state and, well, that's just the way we talk down there in God's country."

"This entire country is God's country, my friend."

"Yes, of course. Tell you what, I'll pretend I'm in church. That way I'm guaranteed to behave myself by not swearing."

He considered his next move while looking at the nearby wall. It was decorated with individual framed photos of Congressman Toddman Lee Gaynor next to Presidents Kennedy, Johnson, Nixon, Ford, Carter, Reagan, Bush, Clinton, Bush and Obama. Curiously, there was no photo of him standing with the present occupant of the Oval Office. There were two prominent crucifixes, a display of the Ten Commandments and a blue-eyed Jesus glancing skyward.

The elder statesman smiled appreciatively at Alderman's agreement to cease using four-letter words and to consider his office as good as church. He returned to using first names.

"Well, it's like this, if you're right, and this file is a light shone upon dark chapters of America's hidden misdeeds of the last century, then it shall be like a plague upon the lives of our countrymen. It's as simple as that. We're not here to create the plague, Henry."

"Todd, we're here to serve the people."

"Au contraire," the Republican said, raising his voice and speaking in a harsh tone for the first time. "Listen to me, my good French-American friend from the bayous of Louisiana and from the opposite side of the aisle. We are charged with the job of making improvements, of building-up, of making people feel good, letting them know tomorrow is going to be as good as or better than yesterday. We must never worsen, tear down or make Americans feel badly about the history of this wonderful, God-fearing, Christian country."

The Speaker of the House tried to force his racing thoughts to settle. He knew that swaying the most senior member of congress meant showing deference to his ego. Doing that meant arriving in person, first thing in the morning. It was the only way. The man was thoroughly self-absorbed in his own righteousness, not to mention also being the vainest man on the Hill. A phone call simply would not have had the same impact, especially not on a matter this important.

Like most political insiders, he knew the real reason Gaynor hated computers. It was because they removed the human dimension, what most people call face-to-face communication. If the human dimension was removed, so was the spiritual dimension, what Gaynor called *fellowship*. For him, removing fellowship was the same as removing God. Gaynor deeply feared that the continuing tilt toward an electronic society was a dangerously sloping road toward total godlessness. In the 1960s, the Bible Belt labeled it a *push-button society*. In the 1980s, the religious right began calling it liberal media. Now, many among the evangelical masses called it the *World Wide Evil* and the *iDevil*.

That's why Alderman was there unannounced, sitting at that moment in Gaynor's penthouse. Yet he knew it was only a first step. He needed to reach the old man on a level that would have real meaning, which probably meant drawing on some biblical reference, preferably a lesson taken straight from a street-preaching rabbi in Jerusalem. Being himself a lapsed

Catholic, and in a frantically worried state of mind, Alderman could think of nothing.

"Todd, did you see the entries from December 1963?" he asked, stalling for time, trying to think of the best way to appeal to Gaynor's religion and simultaneously to his vanity.

"Which in particular, Henry?"

"Any of them. Pick one and read it to me."

"All right, my friend."

While searching, he gave a clumsy shuffle of the papers with fingers so pale, thin and bent with arthritis they resembled broken cigarettes. An aide stepped forward to help.

"May I select a document for you, Congressman?"

"Thank you."

He began reading the page handed to him by the aide: "Tuesday, December 24, 1963. Well what do you know, Henry, I just happened to land on Christmas Eve. That's a good omen." He adjusted his glasses and continued, "Dear John, thank God no one is questioning you or your Operation Over Easy. If they were, well, I just can't contemplate it. Your motive, of course, is wholly selfless because the bureau learned through covert means that he would—*not*—occupy Vietnam after the '64 election. And America simply cannot afford to be soft on Communism. I agree with you on that. We must defend the little, far off places.

"But assassination? And then assassination of the assassin?

"Oh, John. On one level it was a brilliantly executed plot worthy of Napoleon and exemplary of your astonishing mind and even more astonishing powers. But oh, my love, I fear that all you have done is make Robert, that little s-h-i-t brother of his, a shoe-in for the job four years from now."

Gaynor paused and wiped spittle from his mouth. He turned to his staff.

"I beg everyone's pardon," he said. "I spelled out that bad word; I should simply have omitted it. Please forgive me." He turned back to Alderman. "Henry, it's signed I love you,

CAT, December, 1963."

After a moment, Alderman broke the silence. "JFK was before my time, but you first came into office with President Kennedy. Todd, you were a part of that whole, feel-good youth movement back in the day."

Congressman Gaynor squinted to look at the wall of artfully framed photos. Not far from the image of him with President Kennedy was another photo of him standing between J. Edgar Hoover and Clyde Tolson.

"It's true, Henry," Gaynor said. "I was a Democrat for eight years. Then I had a change of heart for the '68 election, and I've now served this great nation as a Republican for fifty-one years. It's not always easy, but I'm proud of my record."

CHAPTER SIXTY-EIGHT

Encrypted Field Communication
NSA Apache Code Ofc Baltimore, MD/Washington, DC/Coin
TelSatOrbit53/All Points

\<apache code initiate\>

TO: all deep field operations
FROM: deep field cmdr

SUBJECT: personnel change

\<secure field communication may begin\>

...attn all covert operatives: be advised, deep field cmdr natujay has retired effective immediately...as deep field legal counsel, i will be the new—*interim*—cmdr & will manage all existing ops until a full-time cmdr is appointed...farewell gathering for outgoing cmdr tbd...

...that is all...

...p. trippler

\<apache encrypted communication terminated\>

CHAPTER SIXTY-NINE

Washington, D.C.

Finally, he had a brainstorm.

Democratic House Speaker Henry Wayne Alderman remembered the parable of the ten virgins. It popped from his subconscious, thanks to his days with the nuns at Benedictine in Lawson Parrish. When it became apparent that the committee chairman would not publicly recognize the importance of the truth, he decided it was worth a try.

"Todd, will you hand me a Bible, please?"

"With pleasure, Henry. Here you go. I carry this with me everywhere I go."

It was a well-worn copy of the King James Version. Alderman turned to Matthew 25. This particular version substituted the word "maiden" for the word "virgin." He began reading. "The Kingdom of heaven shall be compared to ten maidens who took their lamps and went to meet the bridegroom. Five were foolish and five were wise. For when the foolish took their lamps, they brought no oil; but the wise brought flasks of oil.

"When the bridegroom was delayed, they all slumbered.

"But at midnight there was a cry, 'Behold, the bridegroom comes!' Then all those maidens rose and trimmed their lamps. And the foolish said to the wise, 'Give us some of your oil, for our lamps are going out.' But the wise replied, 'Perhaps there will not be enough for us and for you; go to the dealers and buy for yourselves.'

"And while they went to buy, the bridegroom came, and those who were ready went in with him to the marriage feast and the door was shut.

"Afterward, the other maidens came also saying, 'Lord, Lord, open to us.' But the Lord replied, 'Truly, I say to you, I do not know you. Watch therefore, for you know neither the day nor the hour.'"

Ninety-two-year-old Congressman Toddman Lee Gaynor leaned back in his desk chair and smiled as he listened. It was one of his favorite parables about faith and being prepared for the moment when the moment arrives. He was flattered by the early, in-person visit from his Catholic colleague from across the aisle, and by the sly effort to use Holy Scripture to persuade him. But he would not be budged.

"That was mighty fine, Henry. You have a powerful, God-given voice for Gospel reading. I thoroughly enjoyed it. I certainly did."

Alderman closed the Bible.

"Todd, nothing like this has ever happened in the history of the United States. The hour is nigh, my friend. We must do the right thing for our country."

"Why do you say that?"

"Because it's the right thing to do."

Gaynor wiped his mouth again, adjusted his glasses, and leaned forward.

"Henry, I'm not saying it's true, but if J. Edgar really was what is called gay, and Clyde Anderson Tolson really was what is called gay, and Danford Shackton really is, er, *was* gay, too—then I ask you, how do we know these pages aren't just some of the unholy tricks that gay people enjoy playing on each other?" He thumb-flipped the edges of the DJF pages with contempt. "You know, these people are prone to some rather disturbing behavior."

Alderman thought briefly of reciting his line about 'a man's pecker is his to do with as he pleases. When he glanced at the angelic faces of Gaynor's staff, he knew the idea would backfire miserably.

"Well, my response is this: What if those pages are the real thing?—which I believe they are. And furthermore, I believe they will be validated as such."

The Republican reached to retrieve his Bible and protectively placed it on his desk.

"I appreciate that, I really do," the Republican said. "But if these pages are the truth as you say, then we must destroy them. The last thing we need to do to the American people is tell them their nation was an appalling fraud during the second half of the twentieth century."

"And the parable of being ready for the moment?" Alderman asked.

"Henry, my friend, you can believe me when I tell you— I've got plenty of oil in my lamp."

CHAPTER SEVENTY

I-95, Rocky Mount, NC

Donnursk was astonished at the confidential text message glowing on his cellphone.

He stood at the gas pump in Tarboro, North Carolina, refueling the truck while looking at the communication from Paula Trippler.

"Sweet," he crooned. "This thing just keeps getting better and better."

It was a perfect opportunity. All he had to do now was get to Key West and execute his double grant of supreme authority, which would neatly conclude Operation Dear John. Indeed, it would wrap the whole mess in a tidy ribbon for the tenth floor.

Then he'd head back to D.C., where he'd be received like a golden boy for neutralizing both Teagarden and McCanliss, not to mention saving everyone's collective fat from the Dear John fire. Then he'd let it be known that he's interested in filling the vacancy temporarily occupied by Paula Trippler. He felt good about his prospects. He was young, smart, motivate-ed and very talented. Not a significant screw up on his record until the embarrassment earlier that morning at the Water-gate. And it looked as if Natujay was getting hammered for that, which he deserved.

Donnursk capped off the truck's gas tank at nineteen gallons.

He wasn't quite halfway to Key West. It had been a long and weary drive on Interstate-95, but this news would make the second half of the drive go easier, because now he had something to look forward to.

After this mission, if he played every angle perfectly, he wouldn't be assigned any more missions from the DFC commander. Instead, he would be doing the assigning.

CHAPTER SEVENTY-ONE

Encrypted Field Communication
NSA Apache Code Ofc Baltimore, MD/Washington, DC/Coin
TelSatOrbit53/New York, NY

<apache code initiate>

TO: box cutter
FROM: interim deep field cmdr

SUBJECT: operation dear john

ATTACHMENT: Op. Dear John File

<secure field communication may begin>

interim deep field cmdr to box cutter: effective immediately, you are pulled off operation killtime...i am temporarily re-assigning u to opdearjohn...p/u ice skater's truck at company garage in nyc...drive to rendezvous with copper miner in key west asap...

box cutter to interim deep field cmdr:...but am making good progress on killtime...that newspaper is bleeding $$$...and am working angle w/right wing media that mexican int'l bailout will be found suspicious by commerce, trade and state... thus force total newspaper shutdown...

interim deep field cmdr to box cutter: understood...now that i'm in charge of deep field...i need my OWN man on dear john...you have supreme authority on ice skater and on the initial target named teagarden, see attached file for back ground...moreover, if copper miner gets in way, you have supreme authority on him too...then u will be back on operation killtime...

box cutter to interim deep field cmdr:...wow, my first grant of supreme authority (3x over!)...ok, will do...note: do not sign secure field communications with real name as u did a few mins ago...no worries this one time, tho.

interim deep field cmdr to box cutter:...thanks for the tip...good luck, and see you at my house in adams morgan, d.c., asap!...

CHAPTER SEVENTY-TWO

Key West, FL

He was the only passenger during a glorious flight on the classic DC-3.

The nose of the fuselage was stenciled with the nickname *Pangolin's Pastime.* The pilot had long gray hair twisted into a pony tail that draped to his shoulder blades. Like the Amazon woman cabdriver, he too was deeply bronzed. Unlike her, he was vigorously fit and classically good looking in a Holly-wood, gun-slinging sort of way. Because of the engine noise, they had to wear headsets with microphones to hear each other speak.

"The ceiling is high and the water is calm today," Pangolin said as the twin blades cranked. The noise of their engines quickly hit falsetto, then slid down the tonal scale to settle into a steady tenor. "It's a great morning for flying."

They flew east, then north to tag along the archipelago that stretches from Key West to Key Largo just below Miami.

"I had to swing wide to get around Boca Chica Key before cruising the Overseas Highway," Pangolin explained. Even with the headset intercom, he still had to shout to be heard over the propellers. "The Navy is on Boca Chica, and they don't like it when I buzz 'em. Tends to make 'em nervous. Maybe they're afraid I'll see inside one of their precious X-47 fighter drones. It's a plane designed to make all pilots will be a thing of the past, like cobblers or swordsmiths."

Halfway to Miami, he turned west and then south. A short time later they cruised low over the Dry Tortugas.

At first, Pangolin didn't care much for this man who paid extra to be the only passenger. He conveyed little personality and even less communication. Pangolin had an unpleasant sense that his face and body barely controlled a hidden rage, which worried him. But once they were airborne, the passenger's eyes softened and an inner bliss seemed to come over him. He even began to speak without being prompted for every grunt.

"That's where they imprisoned Dr. Mudd," Pangolin shouted. "You know, the man who helped John Wilkes Booth by setting his broken leg after he killed Honest Abe." McCanliss nodded. "You a pilot?"

"No. Both my father and son were pilots," McCanliss said. "My Baby Boomer generation got skipped."

"Commercial or military?"

"Air Force. My father was killed when his F-105 was shot down in Vietnam. My son was killed when his C-17 crashed in Iraq. My dad always told me the DC-3 was the greatest aircraft ever designed. He called it the lynchpin of aviation, the fulcrum between the Wright brothers and modern aviation. That's why I booked you. I've always wanted to fly in one."

When Pangolin heard that, he decided to give this passenger more than a routine tour. He took his classic airplane low, cruising just fifty feet above the water. He cracked the side windows to let air and ocean spray blow into the cockpit. Then he closed the windows and put the DC-3 into a steep climb directly over Key West, making the island recede in the window the way Earth recedes from the porthole of a rocket's capsule. After banking sharply to the south, he flew hard at a top speed of nearly two hundred miles per hour.

"Uh-oh," the pilot said, after a few minutes. "You see that island?"

"Yeah, sure."

"That's Cuba. And you see those two aircraft climbing to meet us?"

"Yes."

"That's the Cuban Air Force. MiG-21s. Made by the former Soviet Union. They don't like it when I buzz them any more than the Naval Air Station at Boca Chica likes it when I buzz their X-47 robo-fighters. They'll be on top of us in two seconds."

He banked sharply to make a U-turn and hightail it back to Key West. He was right about the timing. Within seconds, the antique propeller plane was flanked by two menacing fighter jets. McCanliss could see the pilot in the MiG on his starboard side of the DC-3 wagging a finger in reprimand. Pangolin wagged his wings, as if to apologize. A moment later the two fighter-jets withdrew.

"I'll never understand it," Pangolin shouted.

"What?"

"China, that's what."

"That's Cuba back there. So what about China?"

"Well, China is this huge commie nation that is the biggest economic whorehouse in the history of the world. And the U.S. is the biggest paying John who visits that whorehouse. It's where all the American companies go to shaft the Chinese workers who get paid slave wages, which is, of course, the reason we do so much business with 'em. Yet we had sixty years of hard-ass embargo against that island back there just because it's commie."

McCanliss wasn't sure whether he liked or disliked the pilot's comments. His father died fighting communism in Vietnam. His son died fighting religious fascism in Iraq. But he said nothing because he truly loved the ride. A flight on a DC-3 had been on his bucket list a long time. It made him re-member his father, and think fondly of his son. It wasn't much, but he wanted to hold on to it. Arguing with some old hippie pilot about China would only ruin the final pleasurable experience of his life.

Before landing back at Key West, Pangolin received a radio call from air traffic. McCanliss could hear every word through the co-pilot's headset.

"You got a request here from a captain with the Navy air station. Wants to know, can that old tub of yours make it all the way to Virginia Beach?"

"Sure," he said. "But why me? Did the Navy run out of airplanes?"

"Beats the hell out of me. It'll be one passenger up and two passengers back."

"When does this passenger want to go?"

"Well, as they say in Spanish, *inmediatamente*. When translated, I believe that means right now, you long-haired dummy."

"You got a name?"

"Hang on. She gave me her card."

"She?"

"Yeah," came the response. "And a rather handsome— *she*—she is. Okay, here it is. Captain Eva Ghent, U.S. Navy."

The name gave him pause. He more than knew her. He knew her well. He knew her before she married American Airlines pilot and former navy aviator John Ghent. That was when her name was Captain Eva Teagarden. The all-news TV networks were hound-dogging the Teagarden story as though it were the Holy Grail. He'd been following it closely. And with a name like Teagarden, he figured the man on the run in New York State and Washington, D.C., be her father. He thought of contacting her, but decided to leave it alone. Pangolin figured she needed to be left alone more than she needed to receive another incoming phone call, even if it was a friendly voice from the past. Besides, there had been no mention in the media of a daughter on Key West.

"Okay, I'm on approach now," Pangolin said to the controller. "I've got to fill up the tank. Then I'll park and meet her in the terminal."

"Nope," came the response from the air traffic control officer.

"Where then?"

"She wants you to taxi to the west end of the runway. She's waiting beyond the swamp inlet at that old vacant hanger, which ain't vacant no more."

"What's in it?"

"Not much. Just a little old hundred-fifty-million-dollar airplane known as the X-47B."

And that particular model aircraft was the reason he originally met Captain Ghent. If he'd stayed in the Navy, he'd have been switched from F-14s to the UAV X-47 program. She would have taught him how to fly that jet-propelled triangle while sitting in front of a computer screen. Problem was, he wouldn't be flying anything. The computer—*was*—the pilot. All he'd have done was make occasional keyboard inputs and watch the monitor. UAV stands for Unmanned Aerial Vehicle. It simply wasn't for him. He'd been flying since he was fourteen-years old, so getting transferred to Ghent's new UAV program on Boca Chica was not his idea of being a pilot. When he learned about his transfer, he made a down payment on the DC-3, and quit the Navy the following week.

"Okay," Pangolin said. "Tell her I'll be out at the swamp hanger shortly."

CHAPTER SEVENTY-THREE

I-95, Lumberton, NC

Thomas Rose, aka Box Cutter, was bleary-eyed and exhausted.

It seemed like he'd been behind the wheel for a solid week. In fact, he'd been on I-95 for twelve straight hours and was only nearing the South Carolina border. He had another ponderous twelve hours to go before arriving in Key West.

He pushed the pedal harder. The truck had a terrifically powerful engine but it was heavy and not easy to drive. It was so laden with communications/satellite surveillance equipment and firepower that it was like driving a tank. He watched the speedometer edge toward eighty. He'd already been pulled over for speeding near Petersburg, Virginia. No problem. A federal badge always helps with that sort of thing. And for him, it was an ego bump to see the state trooper's face go from snarky to suck-up after getting a look at his FBI shield.

Now, he was exhausted beyond caring. All he wanted was sleep. This was not his type of gig. He hated guns. He'd never been the storm trooper type, and never wanted to be. He was more of an "in house" agent. That's why Paula Trippler assigned him to Operation Killtime. Working a clandestine plot to force *The New York Times* into bankruptcy and ultimately out of existence was a cushy gig that required his accounting and business skills. Better still, it earned a higher him pay grade than all that "show me your hands" crap.

Of course, there was another reason she maneuvered to give him the best gig in the DFC with nearly limitless perks. Paula Trippler was his guardian angel. Whenever he was in D.C., they secretly rendezvoused at the house she inherited from her parents in the Adams Morgan section. She gave him the code name Box Cutter, which meant nothing but sounded menacing, especially when compared with the other DFC operatives: Ice Skater, Copper Miner, Road Manager, Utility Coach, Eagle Eye, Street Cleaner.

This, however, was a problem.

It was the first bump in the road wrought by his own willingness to lead her along as a lover in exchange for corporate protection and career growth. Because she trusted him, she wanted him to go to Key West and clean up this mess that had caused them all to get their collective tit stuck in the wringer. *Him.* He could hardly say no.

Rose rubbed his bleary eyes and tried to reason it out. All he had to do was get to Key West and help Donnursk kill a math professor and a renegade agent named McCanliss. The problem was, he had to do it without getting hurt, which was *not* guaranteed. And if he pulled it off, there would be follow-up problems. Interim Director Trippler would make certain he received all credit. But then she'd arrange a promotion and transfer him to D.C., where they'd be closer.

It was a fine example of an office entanglement backfiring. She was nearly two decades older than he, yet was such a fool that she actually believed he loved her.

CHAPTER SEVENTY-FOUR

I-95, Savannah, GA

I-95 can be a mean challenge to a driver's endurance.

Donnursk pulled over again near Savannah. He filled the tank and checked for any new communications from Trippler.

Nothing.

He bought a sandwich and soda. Back in the truck, before eating, he withdrew a foil packet of company supplied amphetamine. This particular packet held two thirty-milligram Adderall tablets. He pushed them from the aluminum backing, put them in his mouth and washed them down with soda. Then he cranked the truck's engine and headed back onto I-95.

CHAPTER SEVENTY-FIVE

Key West, FL

It was just the break he needed.

The news on the co-pilot's headset clued him in on the looming schedule, letting McCanliss know he still had time for one last night in the saloon.

It also allowed him to catch up on the facts of his own six-day-old case. While perched at the end of a bar in the Bahama Village section of the island, he watched news on the overhead TV. A shooting in Washington was the latest development. The math professor's attorney girlfriend had been shot in the leg and was speaking to the media from her hospital bed at George Washington University Hospital.

But there was something else, something unprecedented.

Something not good.

A liberal congressman and a big-name lawyer from New York City were yammering about increasing doubts that Teagarden had killed Billy Carney and about whether he had any role at all in the death of somebody named Danford Shackton. They blabbered endlessly about the possibility that Teagarden was actually a whistle-blower, a potential national hero on the run from "dark forces."

And there was more.

Also not good.

During the report, there was a quick flash of video showing Svetlana, who the newscaster said "May or may not have been murdered by Sam Teagarden." And in the background of that video—*was his own image!*

McCanliss couldn't believe his eyes. It meant his preemptive kill of Svetlana was—*not*—clean, as he had assured Donnursk in the Central Park Zoo. That little piece of video on the mainstream media would send Donnursk and the entire tenth floor straight over the edge.

"Jesus," he mumbled.

With this development, the situation had advanced from clusterfuck to intergalactic fucking among the heavenly bodies. Whole new stars would be born in the Milky Way because of this husbanding of Big Bang imbecility on the part of just about everyone within the Justice Department. Including him.

"Unbelievable," he said to the television mounted over the bar.

It verified his estimation that Teagarden really was smart enough to slip the geniuses on the tenth floor, not to mention the D.C. Metro Police. And why not? Teagarden ducked him in Bethel. It stood to reason that everybody else would lose him, too. Now he knew he was right. This guy had managed to reach Virginia Beach where his daughter was arranging to pick him up in a DC-3 and get him into hiding on Key West.

Smart. Hell, it was more than smart. It was brilliant. The man was a natural Jason Bourne, but without a gun or a black belt. Still, what was it to him? At this point it was a "so what?" He was done. He'd already made his plans. All he had to do was carry them out. He finished his drink and barked an order to the bartender, "Change the goddamn channel."

The TV was switched to a billiards competition without comment from the bartender.

McCanliss contemplated the time. Because he'd overheard Pangolin's planned trip to Virginia Beach, he knew he had at least until morning. He withdrew the card from his wallet given to him by the bronzed cabdriver and borrowed the bartender's cellphone to see if she was available.

She was.

CHAPTER SEVENTY-SIX

Southeast Coast, 20,000 Feet Altitude

During the flight north to Virginia, Eva sat in the co-pilot's seat of the DC-3.

"Would you like to talk about it?" Pangolin asked.

She was in no frame of mind to recount everything, but she was glad to see him. They used sportscaster style headsets with attached microphones to converse over the noise.

"Oh, Pang, what a horrible week this has been."

"I can imagine."

"If you watch the news, there's nothing much else to tell, unless you think he did it. I know he didn't."

"He didn't do it," Pangolin said. "I never thought so for a moment. In fact—"

"Of course he didn't," she interrupted. "My dad could no more harm a little boy than he could fly this airplane."

"And we're not the only ones who believe that. I saw a survey on one of the ridiculous news networks. Fifty-eight percent believe he's being set up. And sixty-eight percent believe he's some sort of whistleblower trying to reveal some wildly dark government secret from America's past."

"I saw that, too. Where do they get this stuff?"

"Your dad is now more of a national celebrity than a fugitive from justice."

"But, Pang, that same stupid survey said seventy-four percent believe he's motivated by stardom on reality TV, selling a book or some entertainment deal for a big paycheck."

"I intentionally left that out," Pangolin said. "There's other news that some New York lawyer is petitioning a congressional committee to offer amnesty in exchange for whatever information he's got."

The problem is, people are still trying to kill him. So how does he negotiate amnesty when hitmen are on his trail?"

"It does complicate things. At least he's turning a corner in the court of public opinion. Plus, Congress is considering an unprecedented offer."

"Congress moves too slowly," she said.

"Has Washington called you at all?"

"No."

"Are you being watched?"

"I think so. I'm pretty sure my phone and e-mail are monitored because things are sluggish and my landline phone is staticky. Plus, there's one creepy guy. It's not constant, but I've seen him a couple of times loitering around the house. But there are no uniformed police or anything like that, thank God."

"What about the media?"

"They don't seem to know I exist."

"That's bad," Pangolin said.

"Why? I thought it was good."

"It's bad because whoever's tailing your father and trying to kill him doesn't want a crowd around you. That would make you more difficult to get to and put the killers at risk of being spotted on somebody's security video. Spooks don't like cameras. Neither do cops."

"How come the media people haven't found me on their own?"

"Maybe because they're all anchors and no reporters, or maybe because the reporters don't know what shoe leather is for."

Holding control of the DC-3 with one hand, he reached to massage her neck with the other. She was pleased. It had been a long time, and she'd been racking her brain for a way to reconnect.

"I've got an idea," he said after a few moments. "After we pick up your dad, any chance the Navy will let me land at Boca Chica? Maybe he could claim sanctuary inside the naval air station. You know, like Esméralda did inside the cathedral in *The Hunchback of Notre Dame.*"

"Not a chance. They'd lock us both up. Besides, I've got to play out this phony drama I've concocted about an emergency landing at Key West. That's why my X-47 is parked in that civilian hanger by the swamp at EYW. Engineers, designers, and grease-monkeys will be on it all weekend."

"Are they going to find a problem?"

"Yes, I made certain of that."

They flew in silence at a low altitude over most of South Carolina, past Hilton Head and Charleston. She leaned toward him so he would again massage her neck. At the Outer Banks, air traffic control made him bank right, to stay east of Morehead City and Beaufort. When they were flying over Kitty Hawk, she spoke again.

"Do you like your new life, Pang?"

"Yes," he said. "Except for the part where you're not in it." She sighed with appreciation. "The good part is that I own this bird outright. The cost of gas and upkeep is a killer, but I enjoy it. I live on my sailboat. It's different."

"Anyone know that you were once Captain Kasey Landrew, the most feared fighter pilot in the U.S. Navy?"

"Nope. People know me only as Pangolin, the long-haired hippie who lets passengers sit in the cockpit of a classic DC-3. They always want to buy me drinks afterward. Don't know why. I guess it's something about the romance of old-world aviation. Too bad my drinking days are over."

"I'm glad for you, Pang."

"Which part—liking my life or my drinking days being over?"

"Both," she said, giving him the first smile since boarding the plane.

"Speaking of flying, that's Kitty Hawk directly below," he said.

They strained to look down at the lights illuminating the narrow strip of an outer bank off the coast of North Carolina. There wasn't much else to see.

"All it took was a hundred and sixteen years," he said. "From the Wright Brothers, to completely retooling for robots. Just a hundred and sixteen years. Jesus, Eva, what are computers going to take over next? Doctors? Maybe they'll put lawyers and politicians out of business. At least *that* would be good."

"I'm sorry," Eva said.

"Don't be. You didn't cause this."

"Listen, I'm not telling you I'm sorry about the program. I believe in FIDROPRO. Sure, it's a mothballed program, but it'll be back. Fighter-drones are not the future, they're the present, and they're here to stay. What I'm telling you is that I'm sorry I married John Ghent instead of Kasey Landrew. It was the biggest mistake of my life."

"May I ask something? Did you rebound to him because I'm twenty years older than you?"

Without answering, she looked down at the lights of Kitty Hawk, where the first airplane left the earth and flew for twelve seconds. They did not speak for the balance of the trip to Virginia Beach.

CHAPTER SEVENTY-SEVEN

"Mom would be proud."

"I don't know," Teagarden said to his daughter. "Honey, I'm freaked. It's been a nightmare. Hard to believe it's only been one week. Eva, people have been killed. And if your mom hadn't been taken from us, don't you think she'd be freaked, too?"

"She'd be worried for your safety, just as I've been. She'd also be proud of you."

Pangolin stopped the engines just long enough to refuel. The tiny airport at Virginia Beach was private, out of the way, and virtually unknown to commercial aviation, making it perfect for secrecy. It had a grass landing strip that Captain Eva Ghent, U.S. Navy, knew would be manageable for a DC-3.

"Dad, I can't tell you how good it is to see you for real. Let me tell you, I've been watching little video snippets of you all week on the news channels. It's been a dysfunctional travelogue of the East Coast: you dressed as a rabbi in the Woodstock museum, walking through the Walmart parking lot, New York City streets, the garage and elevator in the Watergate building. Did you know they've been airing security camera video of you using an old payphone in that Times Square hotel?"

"The Argonaut?"

"Yep."

"Did the camera pick up the numbers I dialed?"

"They fuzzed-out the part that shows your fingers pushing

the buttons, so, I guess—yes. They could probably make out the number you dialed on the original video."

Oh God! That's why Svetlana was murdered. They read the numbers and knew I'd phoned her. And I thought I was being so clever by outsmarting McCanliss at The Argonaut. Instead, I only caused another murder with my foolish guile.

He felt the approach of another wave of heavy emotion, which he struggled to fight off.

"Dad? Are you okay? What is it?"

"I'll tell you later, hon. It's complicated." He took a deep breath, trying to steady his voice and ward off emotional collapse. "First, tell me, are *you* being watched or followed?"

"I think so. That's why I wanted you to call the P.R. office at the air station. I've got a friend there helping me. I figured it was best not to take chances."

"Raymond Bakerfield?"

"No, Petty Officer First Class Joanna Manolo. There is no Raymond Bakerfield. When you asked for him, she passed you to me. It was our code."

"Your mom raised a smart daughter."

"My dad gets some credit, too."

The wave of emotion grew closer. Knowing he couldn't fight it much longer, he spoke in carefully measured words.

"If you're not taking any chances, how'd this plane get out of Key West with you on it?"

"Simple. I landed my remote bird at Key West International instead of Boca Chica. They may be watching my house, car, and telephone, but it's kind of hard for them to watch my X-47."

"What about the Navy? Won't they be annoyed that you landed at the wrong airport?"

"Not if you have a Mayday emergency called 'leak in the fuel line,' which I made certain I had. The Navy loves it when you save a hundred-fifty-million-dollar airplane from crashing in the Atlantic. When they're done fixing it, I'll sit at the video-game console on Boca and hop it back where it belongs, then get a nice round of 'atta-girl' from everybody."

"Allow me to be the first," he said. "Atta-girl!"

"Thanks, Dad. And by the way, that Dan Jones thing was a clever ruse. How'd you think of it? Dad, what..."

The wave of emotion finally arrived and slammed full force. He wanted to answer her, tell her that Dan Jones was just another man running from his life, but what emerged was an involuntary full-blown breakdown.

Sitting next to him in the back of the aircraft, Navy Captain Eva Ghent wrapped an arm around her father's shoulders, pulled him to her and held him. Below, the lights of Carolina's Outer Banks flashed past in the night on their way south to Key West.

"Don't worry, Dad," she whispered. "We're going to get through this."

CHAPTER SEVENTY-EIGHT

When his tears stopped flowing, he showed her the thirty-four pages of the fully transcribed Dear John file, still stained with the blood of Dan Shackton and Cynthia Blair.

She turned on the overhead reading light and adjusted the neck of the antique telescopic lamp to focus on the pages, reading random passages out of chronological order while he slept.

Dear John,

So, your Op. Over Easy patsy is back from the Soviet Union. Did Mr. Oswald learn anything worthwhile about that crazy commie, Nikita Khrushchev? Did he, John? Or are you just setting him up for something to come? Why are you keeping this operation in the dark? From the rest of the bureau— ok. But you are keeping it even from me? Me—John? Why do you trust Agent Mark Trippler more than me on this?

It worries me. One slip up on this thing—and we are walking in waist deep doo-doo.

I love you,
CAT
June, 1962

Dear John,

In the limo at Hialeah? Really? The limo, John? You haven't done that (to my knowledge) since 1938. I'm the first to admit that the new asst. director you posted to the Miami office is a statue of Italian marble straight from the Roman Em-

pire, not to mention luscious. But practicing the Roman arts in the limo while parked within view of the Hialeah race-track?

You are taking too many risks. I will punish you tonight, my darling.

I love you,
CAT
February, 1958

Dear John,

Do you remember how upset I was about your rendezvous with the asst. director at Miami? Well this is worse, John.

A recruit? A mere recruit at the house on 30th Place? Making him pay his taxes to Caesar in the middle of the day? And while I was in the office making excuses for you?

You are so very lucky I love you so much and am willing to cover for all your naughtiness.

With all my (angry) love,
CAT
June, 1958

Dear John,

I totally agree with your plan to pursue certain alliances with the president, especially as regards that loud-mouthed hippie John Lennon and that national scourge Jane Fonda.

But frankly, I think Nixon's enemies list goes too far. Please do not sign onto his political motives. As the head-shrinks diagnosed during his veep years, that man is afflicted with extreme paranoid personality disorder. He's a walking Shakespearean tragedy.

That said, by all means, we must preserve American integrity when it comes to our eventual victory in Vietnam. Thus, class-2 overt surveillance of Lennon and Fonda to scare the crap out of them, just like you did with that Fidel loving Hemingway, is the right move. Of course, you helped make Hemingway blow the top of his head off, but as the French say, "c'est la vie."

Tally ho in the hunt for commie lovers!
I love you,
CAT
March, 1972

Dear John,

Ha! I never knew LBJ had it in him.

And his cock! Oh Lord, John. The photo of that lunatic Texan taken through the two-way mirror at that hotel in Austin—the one with him fully aroused with that dowdy hill-billy woman.

Let's put it this way, I haven't seen one that long since we shared footlong hotdogs at the Maryland State Fair in 1936!

It makes JFK's look like your little pinky finger!
I love you,
CAT
September, 1965

Dear John,

I am informed that the Warren Commission is going to be released in the fall. Therefore, I encourage you to demand an advance copy for complete vetting by the bureau's legal counsel.

And, naturally, you (we) must make certain there is no hint of suggestion as to the existence or purpose of Op. Over Easy. If those words are ever leaked to the press—oh Lord, John— there will simply be no end to it. The fact that you had that maniac mobster Ruby hush-up the marginal personality patsy that you've so cleverly manipulated all this time is bad (and risky) enough.

Much love,
CAT
June, 1964

Dear John,

I totally agree. That natty Eleanor Roosevelt is most likely a communist, even if she is widow to a president.

And I agree that she is perfectly queer (tee-hee). About as big a lesbian as ever came out of a Texas convent. But more importantly, even if she isn't, it's perfectly fine to paint her as such because she is such a natty old softee on communism who loves the coloreds. I swear, she just loves them. If she ever gets her way, we'll be overrun with coloreds trying to worm their way into everything: business, schools, housing—or, mercy-me, even the FBI!

Go get her my love!
CAT
July, 1944

Dear John,

I am so glad you are finally phasing out Op. Over Easy. And your plan to evolve that program into a secret rapid response team called "deep field command" is ingenious. The bureau has needed a secret license-to-kill team (like the Brits) for decades. But we must be careful who we recruit. Their personality marginality must be minimal, or thoroughly masked so they pose no risk to our own corporate security. That—my love—is the true risk.

On another note, I love the blueprints for the latest revision of the new office building where management of that secret team shall be stationed on the 10th floor.

We are going to enjoy watching your beautiful building as it slowly rises directly across our avenue.

Dinner at the Mayflower tonight, my darling? I hope so. I only had a lousy salad for lunch in the company cafeteria. Oh, John, can't we do something about that place? The food is perfectly horrid. The FBI deserves a much better cafeteria than that.

I love you,
January, 1972

CHAPTER SEVENTY-NINE

Key West, FL

Her other nickname was Chispa, Spanish for Sparky.

"Never mind my real name. I am Chispa, the Key West Queen of Haul. I own a houseboat, a taxicab and a dump truck. That's all you need to know. People don't need real names in this town. They come here to get away from real names."

He didn't like her much. She had a snotty attitude about pretty much everything. It made him want to give her a hard pop in the mouth. At the same time, he enjoyed her company. He'd always been strange about women in that way. His wife was no exception. She nailed it during their final argument before divorcing: "You love only what you despise," she told him. "And that's as twisted as it gets."

"Okay," he said to Chispa, "nicknames work for me."

"You stay here long enough, we'll find you a Key West nickname."

"Already have one."

"I'm listening."

"Ice Skater."

She considered it, then shrugged and said, "Okay, Ice Skater it is. But you won't be doing much of that in the Keys."

They drank boilermakers: beer mugs with shots of whiskey. She downed her whiskey in one straight gulp before swallowing half her draft pint as a chaser. He praised her for her method, but preferred to pour his shot of whiskey into the beer and consume it more slowly, or, as he said, "respectfully," wondering if the word meant anything to her.

They got better acquainted during a pub crawl that lasted well into the evening. After brief stops at Sloppy Joe's and the Bull and Whistle, she recommended smaller, less touristy places frequented by veteran Conchs. She let him pay all tabs.

"You're the one who totes around your gold," she snapped. "So pay the bartender, Mr. Ice Skater Man, and let's move on."

At the Green Parrot bar, he decided to needle her on what he guessed would be a sensitive subject.

"And Bayonne?" he asked.

"What about Bayonne?"

"You said at Sloppy Joe's that people come here to get away from real names. In your case, you came here to get away from real names—*and* from Bayonne."

"That's right, so don't ask me anything about Bayonne. And don't bother asking me what I left behind in Bayonne either."

"No worries," he said. "Besides, I got a couple of secrets myself."

"Yeah, I know."

"What do you know?"

"I know you've got secrets, Ice Skater Man."

"Oh?"

"Fucking-A," she said. "For one, you carry your gold around with you. For two, you know about airlines, but you're not in the airline business. For three, you want to stay in the quiet part of town, but here you are in the party part of town. Number four, you got a crazy nickname that sounds like some CIA bullshit. And finally, there's that bulge in your lower back."

"What about it?"

"Nothing about it," she said. "It's your business. That's all. Just like this is my business."

Without regard for who might be watching, she dug into her shoulder bag and withdrew a nickel-plated .22 semi-automatic that looked cheap as dirt, like it would break apart in your hand if you fired a single shot. It banged her empty shot glass when she plopped it to the bar counter.

"And before you ask, the answer is yeah, it's legal. In fact, it may be the only thing in my life that is totally legit."

"That's a cute little piece of business," he said.

"You need it in my line of work," she said.

"Hauling garbage?"

"My other business, smart-ass. Chauffeur. Make that—*female*—chauffeur. You were in my cab. Sometimes the stranger in the backseat gets ideas about the woman behind the wheel. Know what I mean?"

He doubted she'd ever had that kind of trouble with kids on spring break. Everyone under twenty-five at this island get-away for snowbirds already had more sex in their lives than they could handle. As for older men—who comes all the way to Key West to bother with a leather skinned cab driver with a crusty New Jersey personality?

Nobody. Except maybe him.

"I do know what you mean," he said. "I've had some trouble with the guy in the backseat a time or two myself. But not the kind of trouble you mean." She slipped the silver gun back into her shoulder bag before it drew unwanted attention. "And I hope whatever trouble you encounter is only with midgets or little old ladies," he said, "because that .22 has about as much stopping power as bad words."

She held her beer with one hand as though offering a toast and patted the weapon in her purse with the other. "It holds ten pills. Each one is the size of my daily vitamin tablet. If the bad guy is still standing after swallowing all ten of 'em, well then, I guess he deserves a gladiator's thumbs-up from the emperor."

"I'll drink to that," he said.

They spent the night on her boat, docked on a polluted inlet near the airport. Her brown rusted dump truck sat nearby, more ancient looking than her taxi. It had a large pair of articulated metal forearms protruding at the front, used for locking onto a plow blade or some sort of bulldozer bucket. But the bucket was missing, which made the truck look like a fossilized museum display of reassembled behemoth bones with powerful tusks.

After sex, or what resembled sex, and before falling asleep, he contemplated his own imminent death. Of the three of them—his father, his son, and now himself—he wondered which sacrifice provided the greatest contribution to his country.

Probably his own, he decided.

CHAPTER EIGHTY

Gustav Crossroads, Lawson Parish, LA

Democratic House Speaker Henry Wayne Alderman flew home for the weekend.

After a late dinner with his wife, they retired to the back porch, sipped red wine and admired their two acres of perfectly manicured lawn. The summer heat cooled on the bayou during the evening, creating a low-hanging fog that seemed to make the dogwood and Mayhaw trees glow in the darkness, though they had long since lost their magnificent spring bloom. The yardman had mowed that day and placed fresh topsoil treated with hog manure at the base of each tree. Along with the cry of a hundred cicadas, the rich smells of freshly tended earth and cut grass filled the night air.

"Maybe it's best to just let it go," his wife said. "Hank, I love you and I'm sorry, but it's so dark. Oh Lord, it's so dark it's painful to contemplate." She almost laughed with disbelief at her own statement. "God, Hank, it's the sort thing that will make people feel violated."

"I know, sweetheart. That's basically what the Lord's Apostle from Kentucky said to me this morning in his office."

"Well, I hate to say it, but maybe he's right. Some will become so confused they'll just buy more guns for self-defense."

"Against whom will they be defending themselves?" he asked.

"That's the problem, Hank—there's no one. It's just the

mean truth. It's so alarming that some will have a nervous breakdown. They'll go postal blaming the wrong people. This isn't the wolf knocking at the door. They'll feel like it is. But it's not. It's only the nasty truth doing the knocking. And Lord have mercy, how do you tell people that a horrible badness from the past is actually good news just because it's the truth? People will feel so assaulted they'll want the National Guard posted on every street corner."

He sighed.

"I know, I know. Lord have mercy on our souls either way this thing goes," he said, looking into the night at the dogwoods glowing in the fog. "It's like having to choose between colon cancer and getting disemboweled."

His wife seriously disapproved of the expression, though she privately agreed with the mean irony of it. They sipped a second glass of wine while listening to the rhythm of the cicadas. When his cellphone rang, she volunteered to retrieve it from the kitchen. Seeing that it was from her husband's press spokesman, Willy Baaktau, she answered and exchanged polite talk with him while walking the phone back to the porch.

"It's Willy," she said, handing the phone to her husband.

Congressman Alderman knew it was important. Willy Baaktau knew the rules. Weekend calls were off limits, except during campaigns, and this was not campaign season.

"Watchu got for me this Friday evening, Mr. Baaktau?" Alderman crooned.

"Brace yourself again, Mr. Speaker. Congressman Todd Gaynor is dead. Apparent heart attack."

Alderman was dumbfounded. "Jayzuss," he said with an audible gasp.

"That's not all," Baaktau said. "When I heard the details, it just about made me jump right out o'my drawers. Sir, it happened in the Capitol about an hour ago. He collapsed right there in the House chamber."

"What in hell was he doing there at this hour?"

Hearing Baaktau take a breath on the other end, Alderman braced for more dramatic news.

"Mr. Speaker, I tell you the truth, this thing is nearly like somebody put a voodoo spell on that man. Word is, he spent all day in his office in a wildly irritable mood. This afternoon he apparently fell into an incoherent state. His staffers aren't talking, but I'm guessing it was more like a mental breakdown than a physical attack."

"Did his staff call a doctor?"

"They tried, but he wouldn't let 'em. He got mad and sent 'em home. Then tonight, he left his office and took the under-ground trolley to the Capitol where he was seen wandering the corridors, talking to himself, weeping, praying. The security guards say he was actually cussing. Can you imagine? Of all men—*him*, cussing inside the U.S. Capitol?"

"I will be goddamned."

"He went to the House chamber where he stood at the main podium and began ranting about the evils of homosexuality and godless computers. The night security guys said he seemed to think President Kennedy was sitting in the chamber, listening to him. Kept saying things like, 'Please forgive me, Jack,' 'I loved you, President Kennedy,' 'Please forgive me, Lord,' 'Jesus, won't you put more oil in my lamp.' Really crazy shit. When the EMTs arrived, they prepared a tranquilizer hypo. But he collapsed and died before they could get the needle into his butt."

Alderman knew his visit to Gaynor's office that morning had sparked these strange events. He absorbed the facts in silence.

"Mr. Speaker," Baaktau continued. "I know this is not what you had planned for your weekend at home with your family. But, sir, I think you need to scoot-on-out of Cajun country and come back here to D.C. on the first morning flight. Given what we're dealing with in the White House, they're all going to be looking to you for guidance on this one."

"Okay," Alderman sighed in agreement. "I'll get my gargling done early, then call to let you know when to meet me at Ronald Reagan." After he hung up, he turned to his wife.

"Time to call the National Guard?" she asked.

"I'm afraid so," he said.

CHAPTER EIGHTY-ONE

Saturday, July 27, 2019
Key West, FL

At dawn, the DC-3 glided over the calm, emerald waters of its home base.

On the ground at Key West, Pangolin maneuvered his plane close to the airport terminal so that Eva could depart and scope out the waiting area ahead of her father. He'd become such a well-known fugitive that following his suspected whereabouts had become a national preoccupation. So they needed to be smart.

The latest news reports theorized he was still on foot somewhere in the D.C. area. One ex-FBI agent who'd been a constant staple of speculation on one of the stomp-and-shout so-called all-news networks guessed he was holed-up in a motel no more than fifty miles from the Watergate building. On another network, a female prosecutor who'd been relentlessly outraged over the murder of Billy Carney, wondered if Teagarden wasn't prowling the nearest McDonald's, selecting his next little boy to sodomize and murder. Another channel had an expert in something called "geospatial profiling," which analyzed locational patterns of victims to determine the whereabouts of a suspected killer. That expert was the closest. He predicted that Teagarden was on a southern trajectory and forecast him to be somewhere on an axis that included Richmond, Raleigh, and Atlanta.

Eva slowly walked to the public restroom in the old terminal. The waiting area appeared normal. It was Saturday morning, and the full flow of air traffic had not yet begun. When it did pick up, it would be mostly inbound. Only a few early bird outbound passengers were waiting, mostly bored-looking middle-aged women. She knew from appearance that they were locals heading for a day of 3M: Miami, malls, and men. Not that the Keys didn't have shopping and plenty of men, but from West Palm down to South Beach, there was much more variety, especially when it came to reasonably attractive, middle-aged persons of the masculine gender and heterosexual persuasion.

When she saw him standing near the main entrance, she pretended not to notice and ducked into the ladies' room. He was relatively young, a little on the short side, buff, with short cropped hair and no suntan. Perhaps most telling, his face and eyes looked exhausted, but his engorged pupils were keenly alert. When she emerged from the restroom a minute later, he was gone.

Back on the DC-3, she described the mystery man to her father and Pangolin.

"It's doesn't sound like Sheriff Klumm and it's definitely not McCanliss, but that doesn't mean much," Teagarden said. "Well, there are more than two people looking for me."

"More than two!?" Pangolin said, incredulous. "My friend, you've got a whole nation looking for you. Right now, you're bigger than Tom Cruise." Teagarden and his daughter exchanged nervous glances. "Look, why don't I just fly the two of you to Nassau or Freeport?"

"Can't," Eva objected. "My toddler is in my Conch House with the nanny, and my robot bird is parked in the civilian hanger right over there by the swamp." She leaned into a window of the DC-3. Two men armed with M4 carbines stood guard at the distant hanger. She could tell from their posture that they were bored. "My crew is out there now working on the leaky fuel line."

"Is there another way out of the airport?" Teagarden asked.

"Sure," Pangolin said, "but not without risking unwanted attention. Key West does have a police force of its own, you know."

"Well here's my suggestion," Teagarden began, "Eva, you and Pangolin exit the plane as though you're the only two on it. It'll look better if you're seen together. Walk to the parking lot as a couple and pull your car to the front curb. I'll join you there five minutes later."

The words "together" and "couple" made Pangolin and Eva glance knowingly at each other. Teagarden had no idea they actually had been a couple not so very long ago.

"Sounds like a plan, Dad."

"Works for me," Pangolin said. "And if you would, please, Mr. Teagarden, pull the door of the aircraft shut when you deplane."

"Will do," Teagarden said.

CHAPTER EIGHTY-TWO

Donnursk made a snap decision.

He'd already spotted her pick-up truck in the airport parking lot. Confirming it was hers was easy for an FBI agent. The first commercial flight arrival of the day was still several minutes off.

Yet there she was.

She was stalking the terminal waiting area after arriving on a privately owned DC-3. He decided to lay back. It was what the training manual called "manifest evidence of aiding and abetting." Maybe it was because of the Adderall tablets that he couldn't recite chapter-and-verse from the textbook as he normally could. His mind was simply working too fast, overriding all natural impulses to sleep—but that was okay. He could still remember the basics from his Quantico training: "wait...be patient...surveil...observe...photograph and identify any and all collaborators."

The tenth floor would be impressed if he got more than just Teagarden and his daughter. Killing Teagarden would be easy enough, but it would be far better if he could kill Teagarden, his daughter—*and*—Ice Skater all in one quick, and very quiet piece of work.

If that happened, the tenth floor would practically anoint him as the chosen one to replace Paula Trippler.

He had no use for McCanliss, but the man was a seasoned veteran of the game. That he'd been so soundly tricked by this arithmetic teacher surely meant that Teagarden had help, including generous financial help at the international level. If he could prove that assistance came from Beijing or Moscow, or better yet—Tehran—he'd be a shoe-in for the top job once they dumped Paula Trippler the same way she'd dumped Walter Natujay.

In the parking lot, Donnursk attached a magnetic GPS tracer inside the wheel-well of Eva's truck. He returned to his own truck, departed airport grounds and parked on a side road, where he turned off the engine, turned on the GPS tracer, and waited.

CHAPTER EIGHTY-THREE

McCanliss snapped awake at dawn.

On the morning of his final day, he was awakened by the close buzz of the first airplane bringing more tourists to the southernmost point of the continental United States. Chispa lay next to him on the cramped captain's bed. She was on her stomach, head turned to one side, her lips contorted into a moist coil of pink. The back of her throat emitted a rhythmic cricket snore as the boat rocked gently where it was moored in stagnant swampy waters of the inner harbor. Her body had two color tones, deep bronze and alabaster white. The latter was perfectly contained within her bikini lines and looked sickly by contrast with the sunbaked brown.

He rose and pulled on his clothes. The Glock lay on the side bureau, next to her silver .22. When he laid his gun there while getting undressed, she laid hers next to it, saying, "Maybe they'll fuck during the night."

"Cute," he mumbled at the time, thinking again how much she disgusted him. "I hope they don't go off."

He verified that his weapon was loaded, checked the safety and tucked it where it had always lived, in his belt at the small of his back. Chispa barely shifted when his Glock made clicking noises. The whiteness of her buttocks was padded with fat and cratered with a subdural cottage cheese effect. McCanliss watched, wondering if she would waken. She did not.

Her bureau was a small laminated component built into a recess beside the captain's bed. He slid open the top drawer:

socks. He pushed it back and slid open the second drawer: underwear. He pushed it back and slid open the third: more underwear. It jammed when he pushed it back, making a squeaking noise. Still, she did not wake. He opened the final drawer: two boxes of .22 caliber bullets, an electric vibrator with a bright blue rubbery cap shaped like a medium sized penis, and a toilet kit with a broken zipper that bulged with money.

He couldn't be certain from that distance and in the faint light, but after thirty years on the job, he'd developed a sense about these things. He snatched a hundred-dollar bill and held it to the morning sun beaming through the small window.

Yep. His instincts had been dead right.

Okay, so she's got a toilet kit full of funny money. He seriously doubted she was a counterfeiter. That meant that whatever she was doing, she was being double-crossed. They were paying her in bogus bills. It was probably illegal aliens. She probably went out at night in this old boat, maybe thirty miles offshore, picked up a dozen Cubans, then ferried them back and turned them loose on South Florida's restaurants to compete for busboy jobs. Maybe she double-dipped by driving them all the way to Miami or Lauderdale. If so, that's probably what the dump truck was for. It would carry a lot more wetbacks than her taxicab.

The question was, did she know she was being paid in phony Franklins? He doubted it. Anybody on the run from Bayonne was too dumb to know if she was being cheated. If you're going to work the drug trade, smuggle illegal immigrants, cheat the welfare office or run a credit card hustle and end up hiding in South Florida to avoid a grab bag full of outstanding warrants filed by the Bayonne P.D., then you're definitely scraping the bottom of the barrel. He ought to know, he lived next door in Jersey City where his walk-up apartment had a view of the Holland Tunnel tollgate. It was ugly, but he liked it.

It took only a few steps in his bare feet to exit the cabin.

From the rear deck he could see what he had not seen in a drunken stupor the night before. Like her taxicab and dump truck, her boat was an aging hulk. Perhaps forty feet long, it was made of wood and probably dated to the late 1950s. The whole thing consisted of two tiny rooms below the pilot's cabin, a small sundeck up top, and a compact fishing deck at the rear.

He tip-toed around the narrow edge and scaled the ladder to the sundeck. It was just large enough for a pair of bamboo lounges and a clay pot filled with drooping red gladiolus.

He braced his hands on his hips and leaned back to stretch his spine as the belly of a gray fuselage glided directly overhead on approach to EYW in the morning light. It was a Bombardier Dash 8 turboprop. The noise of the propellers was like a voice from the past. There may or may not be a pilot on board. Aviation had become the perfect nexus of past and future in a single industry with old planes retooled so that software did the flying. The same was happening with fighter jets and trains. Cars and trucks were next. After that, it was anyone's guess which business would be revolutionized, or what occupation would be rendered obsolete by automation.

They'll never invent a computer to replace me. There will always be a need for black-ops hitmen.

McCanliss watched the plane's path from east to west as the computer made a smooth landing, cut the engines and rolled toward the small terminal. He stopped watching when it cruised past the DC-3, parked where he first saw it at the end of the Key West taxiway. And just behind that was the nose of the triangular X-47 poking from the old hanger beyond the swamp.

The presence of the DC-3 meant Pangolin was back from Virginia Beach. Which meant the fox was in Key West to meet with his daughter. Which meant that Durgan—"Dunno"—Donnursk was either in town or close to arriving. And all that, in turn, meant he had to go back to work.

"Time to turn in my retirement papers," he said. He gave

another greedy glimpse at the sky before returning to the inner cabin where he sat on the edge of the bed. Chispa was still asleep. The sharp contrast between bronze and alabaster turned his stomach. Now that he was awake and nearly sober, he questioned his judgment. Was—*she*—really going to be his last?

Why hadn't he taken up Svetlana on her offer before he killed her. She would have been more enjoyable. But then, his judgment with women had never been good. As his ex-wife said, "you only love what you despise." And he certainly despised this woman.

McCanliss withdrew the Glock from the small of his back and tapped the barrel at the base of her spine, the sacrum bone just above the intergluteal cleft. It woke her up. She roused, wiped her face and rolled over. She saw the Glock in his right hand and smiled.

"Well, good morning to you, too!"

He tapped the barrel on her other inverted triangle, the web of deeply black hair that pointed down, toward the delicate labia.

"Hey, you getting kinky on me, Mr. Ice Skater man?" she asked, adjusting her torso, pushing up pillows to support her neck and head. "What the hell's has come over you?"

He shrugged.

"Maybe you need a boilermaker to get your engine started? I'm out of whiskey. I'll restock later. Meantime, maybe you need some chow. There's a Cuban diner a couple of blocks away that makes a mean plate of ham and eggs. Serves potatoes and cornbread with plenty of melted butter. You want to get breakfast?"

"No, thank you," he said. "I'm watching my calories." He again tapped the barrel of the Glock on the delicate flesh of her pubis. "You need to do the same."

"Hey, buddy, you didn't have any complaints last night."

He tugged a pillow from what had been his half of the

captain's bed and covered her abdomen with it. He pulled up the sides of the pillow and cradled the Glock in the fold.

"I guess you could say, I've become the troublesome guy in the back of the taxi. You see, Chispa, this is my last day on Earth." Her eyes narrowed down like a camera lens. "Yours too," he said.

"Listen...."

The pillow muffled the noise. It sounded more like a dog's guttural bark than a gunshot. The bullet pierced her gut and shattered her spine, but did not kill her. He knew she had only another minute to live. Maybe two. Not wanting to risk the noise of a second shot, he did not fire a coup de grace to the head. Instead, he took the keys to her taxi and tossed her cellphone overboard.

From the pier, he noticed the boat's name painted on the bow in peeling yellow lettering: *Beyond Bayonne*. He turned one last time to admire the sunrise over the Atlantic.

CHAPTER EIGHTY-FOUR

Rose was weary with fatigue.

He sat in his truck parked near the cemetery where he watched the house on Olivia Street one block away. His eyes were so heavy it was difficult to focus.

Pushing through, he plugged in his laptop to send an encrypted message to Paula Trippler. She'd want to know he was in place after driving I-95 all day and all night in Ice Skater's truck. He intended to tell her he'd practically broken the sound barrier. If done straight, the drive from New York required a minimum of twenty-four hours. He'd done it in a nearly unbelievable eighteen.

He intended to reassure her that he was ready to complete his first supreme authority mission. He would kill Teagarden, McCanliss, and Donnursk. Her last encrypted communication said Donnursk should be killed—*if he gets in the way.* That meant he should go ahead and do it. It meant she wanted Donnursk gone because he and Natujay owned the screw-up at the Watergate that had provoked the Metro D.C. Police to question Teagarden's involvement. Consequently, the tenth floor was frantically trying to figure out how to explain the sniper-shot killing of a congressional lawyer.

Additionally, he needed to reassure her that he'd soon be back with her in the Pennsylvania Avenue headquarters building and her house in Adams Morgan. But he didn't. He didn't pass on any information to his boss and lover because he didn't send the encrypted communication. He didn't send it because while sitting in the truck and booting up his laptop, he fell into a deep sleep.

CHAPTER EIGHTY-FIVE

"Oh gosh, Eva," Teagarden complained as he climbed into her pickup.

"Hush, Dad. Just get in, and duck down in the back." From the front passenger seat, Pangolin reached over and draped a blanket over him.

"My daughter makes a living zooming through the sky in a sexy spaceship, but she drives a rusty old pickup. There's a psychology at work there. I'm not sure I want to know what it is."

"I don't do the zooming, Dad. I only operate the remote. Besides, I have to get around in something. And this old truck is convenient for storing all of Marnie's stroller gear."

He was only teasing. He'd been in her truck during previous visits and never lost an opportunity to kid her about it. In the age of expanding solar and battery-powered vehicles, it was a relic of big machinery: a rusting four-door, two-tone green, 1999 Ford F250 Super Duty with a corroding camper shell on the back. She bought it after her divorce when she needed wheels. John Ghent kept his remodeled '68 Porsche, which was all he wanted in the split. The reason for their divorce was about what he did not want. He did not want a child. Eva did. And that was that.

When the final divorce papers were signed, he kept his classic sports car, his pilot's job at American Air, and, as they later learned, his girlfriend in Miami. Eva kept the pregnancy and the Conch House beside the Key West cemetery. Marnie would turn three-years-old the same day in late August that Teagarden turned fifty. She had earned the nickname Chopper because of her habit of running in a type of whirligig while spinning her arms, which made her look like an out-of-control helicopter.

"Your mother thought that nickname was too masculine," he said, adjusting the blanket in the truck's back seat, as he'd done in the Jeep belonging to the girlfriend of Cynthia's son. "She preferred you call her grandbaby 'Princess,' or 'Cutie-Pie,' or something appropriately feminine like that."

"Dad, we've got a lot more to worry about than mom's sensitivity to nicknames. Besides, when we first started calling her 'Chopper,' Mom agreed that it was perfect."

They drove for a while in silence with the truck windows down. Teagarden inhaled the aroma of salty ocean air carried by the rushing wind. It felt good, but it made him sad because it was exactly what his dog Coconut had loved to do when the windows of his own car were down.

It had been warm in the Northeast where the summer heat hung over the Catskills. He expected it to be much hotter in Key West, where it actually felt about the same, maybe even a little cooler. That must be one of those mysterious climate phenomena caused by the waters of the Gulf and Caribbean. He liked mysterious things, but not mysterious meteorology. Numbers were his thing, and at that moment, the numbers were scary. The most applicable math formula to his current situation was known as the law of diminishing returns. Put too many people on the job and the eventual result is total failure. They simply get in each other's way. That was the case with Cynthia. Her involvement in his ordeal bore ugly consequences: Danford Shackton was dead and she was in the hospital with a bullet wound to the leg. He suddenly feared that seeking his daughter's help would cause similar results. In a flash, he realized the ugly truth of his mistake. He should never have come to Key West.

"Where are we going?" he asked.

"My house." He bolted upright.

"Eva, that's no good. Your house is being watched. Let's go to some hotel or something."

"Hey, lay back down! I don't want to lose you before we get squared away. As you know, I have an attached garage. We'll be able to enter the house privately. Just stay away from windows and don't use the phone."

"Eva, it's no good. People are trying to kill me, and people around me tend to get killed. I can't take that kind of risk with you and Marnie."

"Dad, this works for now. We need to let the Washington angle play out. News reports say there are more members of Congress moving into your corner. They're on one of those Homeland committees, the one about domestic surveillance."

"You're welcome to hide out on my sailboat," Pangolin volunteered. "It's just a little twenty-foot sloop, but has all the comforts of home."

Teagarden knew the idea caught Eva's attention. He couldn't see her, but he could feel her looking with interest at the passenger in the front seat. He too liked the idea. All right, he thought—a boat, and with only him on it they'll all be safer. He didn't object further about going to Eva's house because he wanted to see his granddaughter, to hug her and tell her he loved her. He also wanted to figure a way to contact Cynthia in D.C. But after that—he'd go to the boat.

As the ancient Ford pickup maneuvered the narrow streets of Old Town Key West, it was followed several car lengths behind by a truck labeled "Durgan's Lawn & Garden Service." When the pickup turned into the driveway on Olivia Street and pulled into the garage, the pursuing truck parked on the south side of the cemetery. On the opposite side, another truck of identical make was already parked under the sheltering limbs of a drooping banyan tree. That one was labeled "Harry's Heating and A/C Repair Service."

No one noticed either truck as being unusual. Neither did anyone notice the old taxi cab parked near the graveyard's west gate. Nor did anyone see the man perched in the second floor front window of The Poor House Inn on Poor House Road, binoculars dangling from his neck, a Savage Arms 220 bolt-action sniper rifle mounted on a tripod base at his side, its sleek barrel poking one inch past the sill of the open window.

CHAPTER EIGHTY-SIX

Chopper fully lived up to her nickname.

She shouted, "Da-Da Tea-Tea, Da-Da Tea-Tea," as she ran to her granddad while looking like a jet-propelled cartoon character with arms churning high overhead and legs bouncing.

When the rotor-blades arrived at his knees, Teagarden ignored the pain and scooped her up, closed his eyes and clutched the small body wearing only a diaper. During the embrace, he inhaled the aromas of toddler saliva, apple purée, sweet shampoo, and cornstarch powder from her puffy baby flesh—which was also his own flesh. When he opened his eyes, his daughter, the nanny, and Pangolin were all looking on with radiating smiles. For Pangolin and the nanny, it was the outward smile of universal human kindness. His daughter's smile was deeper, with the inexpressible happiness of generational blood.

"*Ella esta muy feliz de ver a su abuelo*," said Pilar, the nanny. "She has been, you know, mucho happy for this moment."

"*Sí*," Eva agreed. "*Mi hija esta muy feliz de que todos es aquí juntos.*" Looking at her father, her eyes gave a discreet glance at Pangolin while trying not to reveal that she was equally happy that he, too, was present.

Were it not for the deadly circumstances that brought them together, it would have been the perfect Hallmark moment, a Norman Rockwell illustration in *The Saturday Evening Post*. It was the moment Eva wanted for her father. And for Teagarden, it was the moment he'd ached to feel since the ordeal began. If he was going to die, he wanted to embrace his grand-daughter, one final time.

The perfect moment was short lived.

From the living room where the television was tuned to an all-news station, came a broadcast voice that drew Teagarden's attention. He shifted Marnie to his left arm and marched to the next room as she ceased being Chopper and tightly clutched his neck along the way. The others followed.

"...and I cannot reveal full details at this time, but I can say there is increasing evidence to that effect. And because of it, we are asking all involved policing agencies to stand down until we can figure out exactly what is going on," the voice said, though it was not that particular voice that drew Teagarden's attention.

"Hey, that's the congressman from Louisiana," his daughter said. "What's his name?"

"Alderman," Pangolin answered. "He's the Speaker of the House."

"Right, Alderman. Where is he? That's not the Capitol Building."

They had spoken over the set's volume, so they all missed the question posed by the off-camera reporter.

"...well, we are not prepared to say there's a connection at this time. Let me just say that our sympathies go out to the family of Congressman Toddman Lee Gaynor. We represented different parties, but he served this nation and his district in Kentucky for longer than any person in any district in the history of this nation. And for that he deserves praise from all Americans."

The off-camera voice spoke again, "Sheriff, is this a trick by law enforcement to encourage a wanted fugitive to surrender?"

The camera panned to another man standing beside the House Speaker.

"No," the man said, "I don't do tricks in my work. After

talking with Speaker Alderman, and being summoned to the hospital for this press conference, I see there is reason to believe Teagarden could be innocent. He's wanted in my district for the murder of an eleven-year-old boy. But that's not to say he is guilty. Not by any means."

"And—that—is Sheriff Klumm of Bethel Township, New York State," said Teagarden, referring to the uniformed officer next to the House Speaker.

"The man who tried to kill you on the lake in New Jersey?" Eva asked.

"Yep. He's a smart guy. I actually voted for him."

"But if he surrenders, will you arrest him?" the reporter asked.

"I have agreed to stand down, as long has he goes into the custody of the House Speaker here and the guardianship of the Homeland committee, which is offering temporary amnesty pending full investigation. If he does that, I will not move to arrest him at this time."

"Isn't this highly unusual, Sheriff?"

"Yes, it is. But as I said, I've seen evidence I did not know existed until this morning. Evidence that shows the case has national security ramifications. So if he goes into protective custody with the federal committee, I will stand aside for the time being, pending resolution that satisfies the laws of my county and the state of New York."

"Ma'am, did Teagarden participate in any way in the murder of Danford Shackton yesterday at the Watergate?"

The camera panned from Sheriff Klumm, across House Speaker Alderman, to woman lying in the hospital bed.

"No, just the opposite," she said. "I was there. Shackton was trying to help just as House Speaker Alderman is now trying to help. The sniper was trying to kill Teagarden, but he shot me in the leg and killed Danford instead. Sam is totally innocent. And I would like to add that the evidence the House Speaker is talking about is no longer exclusively in the hands of Teagarden." She looked at Speaker Alderman, who nodded judicious approval. "It is now in the hands of every member of the House Sub-CIST Committee."

"And that is Cynthia Blair," Teagarden said. "She's the woman who saved my life by helping me escape New York City, and saved it again by helping me escape Sparta."

He sat down with Marnie still hugging his neck as he watched the television screen. "Oh, Cynthia, I am so happy to see that you're okay," he said softly, speaking in the toddler's ear. She tightened her grip on his neck.

"What is the nature of this evidence?" the reporter asked Cynthia.

"Not to be revealed," the Speaker interrupted in a stern voice. "At least, not at this time. But I assure you, in very short order the matter will be made public after investigation by the House Sub-CIST Committee and determination that the evidence is valid."

"How close are you to a determination?"

"Close."

"There's been speculation that your evidence proves the existence of domestic black ops, official hit teams with deep cover that can, and—*have*—killed Americans with covert legal impunity. Is that true?"

"No comment at this time," the Speaker repeated.

The reporter persisted, "The speculation goes on to say that among the people who've been killed are high-ranking men in government and social movements dating to the 1960s."

"As I said, no comment. Now, we need to wrap this up because attorney Blair needs rest. She's here at GW Medical Center recovering from a serious gunshot wound. We're asking Mr. Teagarden to contact my office. Once he does, we'll work together to figure a way for him to enter protective custody while all evidence is properly investigated."

The satellite interview concluded as Cynthia gave a nod and vague smile at the camera. Teagarden knew it was directed at him, that she was reassuring him that she was doing well and meeting with success in "working it" from her end as she had promised in the Watergate garage.

The camera panned to the reporter, a middle-aged, good-looking man with a slight paunch, wearing a light gray sports coat and no necktie. He maneuvered to stand in front of the House Speaker, the wounded attorney, and the sheriff, where he thanked the interviewees and handed the news back to New York. The on-set anchor thanked the reporter and noted that it was the same hospital where President Reagan was taken after the 1981 assassination attempt. When the newscast moved on to the next story, Teagarden noted it was about Iran's threat to destroy Israel and the U.S. in a full-blown preemptive nuclear attack committed in the name of Allah. It was the same news lineup he'd heard on the radio in Madison Park Euro Lodge.

"Oh brother, they're still putting me ahead of the end of Western civilization," he said.

Eva turned off the set. The room went silent. The news about Teagarden was good. In fact, it was the first good news they had had all week. Teagarden knew there were two reasons for it. First, the in-hospital interview was Cynthia's doing. She made it happen to force the hands of others on Capitol Hill, at the FBI, and elsewhere, while letting him know of progress being made. Second, it was because Danford Shackton had e-mailed those pages to every committee member—*before*—being shot and killed in his own living room. He couldn't guess at the meaning of the sudden death of elderly Congressman Toddman Gaynor, but he knew the House Speaker was now offering the same bargain that Shackton had tendered. Presumably, though in the hospital, Cynthia was already in protective custody of the House Sub-CIST Committee.

He knew that his daughter was on the verge of discussing how he should go about contacting the House speaker's office to initiate the process. Pangolin likely was thinking the same and had ideas of his own.

But no one had time to form words.

Marnie was uncomfortable with the suddenly altered room chemistry and squirmed to be released. Teagarden complied, letting his granddaughter slide from his arms to a standing position just as the doorbell rang, which instantly sent her back into Chopper-mode. She streaked for the door, arms flailing overhead.

Two seconds later, before anyone could catch her, she had both tiny hands on the brass knob and was vigorously throwing open the front door with impressive strength.

CHAPTER EIGHTY-SEVEN

McCanliss took a carefully controlled breath and focused the crosshairs.

Donnursk had moved his truck to the front of the house on Olivia Street. He left the truck and walked to the door, flyer in hand. At the front door, he rang the bell. It was stupid, but at the same time it was so stupid it could easily work. The set-up made him look legit. The lettering on the truck backed him up. He was a harmless local businessman making a cold call. What kind of killer politely rings the doorbell holding a discount coupon for tree trimming? Then, once the door was open, out comes the Glock and blam, blam, blam. Everybody dies.

Simple. No muss, no fuss.

Afterward, he would return to his satellite truck, drive back to D.C., claim mission accomplished and let the P.R. office worry about the media fallout.

Perched in the second floor window of The Poor House Inn, McCanliss considered killing Donnursk as he walked to the door. But he decided to wait. Killing him at that moment would be too easy. And anything too easy takes all the fun out of it.

The DC-3 pilot who'd taken him for a tour of the Keys and Cuban air space appeared in the open doorway. He was rushing to pull the child away. Crowded behind, McCanliss could see the mother, Eva. Behind her was the main target—Teagarden. He closely watched Donnursk's right hand. As the left hand gestured to present the flyer, underneath it, the right hand moved for the Glock.

Blam-phfft!

McCanliss intentionally put the first shot in the doorframe, which sent splinters flying, but harmed no one. Donnursk fell backward as the door slammed in his face. He dropped his circular and raced back to his truck, trying to get a fix on where the shot came from. Just for fun, McCanliss fired three more times into the sidewalk and yard ahead of Donnursk's feet.

Blam-phfft! Blam-phfft! Blam-phfft!

Dirt and concrete kicked up with each bullet.

When Donnursk reached the truck, McCanliss had a quick decision to make. Kill him now, or let him go and kill him later. He decided to split the difference.

Blam-phfft!

He put a .338 Lapua Magnum 8.6x70mm bullet squarely through the instep of Donnursk's right foot, shattering the metatarsal bones. After falling and writhing in pain, Donnursk managed to rise to one leg and reach for the door of the truck.

Blam-phfft!

This time the bullet slammed one inch from the door handle, sending the message that Donnursk would not be allowed to re-enter the truck cab.

He fell again but crawled to safety behind the truck. He was in agony, but it could have been worse. He'd taken two Adderall tablets during the drive and two more while waiting for Eva Ghent to arrive at the airport. The amphetamine induced a surge of strength and focus that should help him push through until he could get medical care. Its use had plenty of history. Berlin fed amphetamines to the Nazis for six years and the Pentagon fed it to soldiers in Iraq and Afghanistan for a decade. It was known to help suppress the natural inclination to just lie down and give up from exhaustion or pain.

Behind the protective cover of the truck's back end, he

caught his breath and wiped his face. This was no police officer shooting at him. It was, of course, McCanliss. And it was equally apparent that the old guy was toying with him. Otherwise, he'd be dead already. The shots to his foot and truck door meant McCanliss was using a finely tuned telescopic sight.

Donnursk choked through the pain of the foot wound. At least it was not a bleeder. He couldn't see the sniper, but guessed he was probably on the roof of one of the houses to the west. He looked for escape routes. The open street behind him was no option. Neither was getting into the truck and driving off. No point in charging the house where Teagarden and his family were hiding. He could wait for the cops, which should be all of two more minutes, maybe three.

Or...

CHAPTER EIGHTY-EIGHT

McCanliss couldn't believe his eyes. While "Dunno" Don-nursk was hiding behind his truck on one side of the cemetery, he caught new movement and retrained the telescopic sight to the other side.

Rose?! Really?

Of course. How could he have missed it? He should have seen it coming. It was the tenth floor's strategy for ensuring no more screw-ups, which meant everyone on the tenth floor was scared that a full blown meltdown loomed. If Operation Dear John were to blow open to public view, it had the potential to end with the complete emptying of FBI HQ at 935 Pennsylvania Avenue—furniture, wanted posters, people. Everything. They'd bring in a fumigator to spray every cubicle, then rename it the "New FBI Building" and purchase an ad in the *Washington Post* to re-staff from top to bottom.

But Thomas Rose? Mr. Good Looking straight from Central Casting? The company stud who didn't know his Glock from his cock?

Yet there he was.

He emerged from Harry's own truck on the other side of the cemetery and was stumbling through the tombstones, the visual definition of a fish out of water. The man had no idea where he was going, or what he was going to do when he got there. But, by God, he was making the effort.

At that moment, Donnursk made his move. It was a gimpy, mostly one-legged hurdle from behind his truck to the cover of the grave markers. He lunged through the south gate and dove behind the nearest stone mausoleum. It was a double-high concrete chamber, tall enough to hold two coffins stacked one atop the other.

The cemetery wasn't a great choice, but it was his only option. Among the tombstones, Donnursk hoped to take out McCanliss if he could locate his sniper's perch. Then, he'd survive until the police arrived and claim he was a civilian bystander until the home office intercepted on his behalf.

The two DFC agents made their moves, unaware they were in the same orbit, hurtling toward each other. Watching it play out, McCanliss grinned. They looked like panicked bunny rabbits: one desperately wounded, the other scared shitless.

"Wow," he said, "this is fun."

He hadn't expected to be so wonderfully entertained on his final mission. He departed his guestroom, leaving the sniper rifle mounted on the tabletop. No one challenged him in the downstairs reception area. Two guests stared out the front window, wondering what the all the racket was about. On the street, he cranked Chispa's ancient taxicab. Slowly cruising clockwise just outside the gate, he watched the gladiatorial action play out among the tombstones in the Old Town Key West Cemetery.

CHAPTER EIGHTY-NINE

The gunshots did it. They made him snap awake.

From the truck window, Rose saw Donnursk before Donnursk saw him. He ran from the truck to take advantage of his luck. If this went well, he could kill Donnursk and McCanliss before either of them knew he was on the scene.

Rose stalked the tombstones, Glock in hand, making him think he really could do the macho thing after all.

Circling east to flank Donnursk, Rose scurried across a gravel footpath, sending up a small dust storm in the subtropical heat which he thought looked cool, like a movie scene. He darted from one grave marker to another. Within fifty feet of his target, foolishly, he took a shot that missed.

Startled, Donnursk turned. He was bloody and in agonizing pain, his back pressed against the stone mausoleum, the knee of his good leg pulled to his chest, his wounded leg stretched before him on the stone path. The wound looked like a volcanic eruption below the ankle. It oozed with blood, flesh, bone, and shoe leather.

"Jesus, Rose, is that you? Did you just shoot at me?"

"Afraid so," Rose answered.

"You asshole, why did you do that?" When Rose did not immediately answer, Donnursk said, "Oh—Watergate?"

"Afraid so," Rose said, crouching behind an arching gravestone for cover.

"You using Ice Skater's truck?"

"Yep."

"Did you see him?" Donnursk asked.

"Nope."

No way Rose was going to tell Donnursk that he'd fallen asleep in Ice Skater's truck after a marathon drive and missing whatever happened before the shots roused him. "Where's Teagarden?" Rose asked.

"Daughter's house," Donnursk said. "Over there near my truck, on Olivia Street." He nodded in the general direction. "Listen, we can work on this. We can get Teagarden together. Trippler and the tenth floor will be okay with it. As long as the job gets done, they won't care. It's Teagarden and Mc-Canliss they want, not me."

"I know," Rose said.

"So, what do you say?"

Rose poked his head above his protective tombstone. He looked at Donnursk some twenty-five feet away, his back pressed against the stone mausoleum, his face pouring with sweat, blurring his vision. There was no one else around, nor was there any traffic, except a clunky old taxicab cruising outside the cemetery gate. That's when sound of the first police siren pierced the air.

"C'mon, Rose, what do you say? The local boy scouts are coming. Help me get back to my truck."

Rose let his nose rest on top of the gravestone. He looked like the old "Kilroy was here" cartoon. Behind the cover of the rectangular grave marker, he cocked the hammer on his Glock, as four Key West Police Officers arrived in three patrol cars. Unaware that the call they were answering was taking place inside the cemetery gate, they surrounded Donnursk's truck, guns drawn.

Rose raised his Glock, carefully aimed and fired. Again he missed his target. He even missed the mausoleum. The shot blitzed a bouquet of fresh tulip blossoms on a distant grave. The shattered petals fluttered to the ground like feathers.

In response, Donnursk fired one shot without carefully

aiming. The bullet struck Rose in the forehead just above the bridge of his nose. For a moment, the effect seemed benign. His head reacted as though he'd been gently pushed by an unseen hand, a barber adjusting it to clip the sides, a lover tilting the handsome face for a kiss.

And there was no blood. Not a single drop.

A moment later, the eyes in the Kilroy cartoon face atop the tombstone went blank. His cheeks scraped the stone until his knees gave way and his body twisted as he dropped with a thud to the dry grass. Above him, the tombstone read *Devoted Fan of Singer Julio Iglesias.*

Pushing through the pain, Glock in hand, Donnursk rose and stumbled in the opposite direction of the arriving KWPD. McCanliss, meanwhile, emerged from the back of what used to be his own truck, toting a heavy black satchel that he carried to his current ride, Chispa's taxicab.

On the south side, the police officers rushed into the cemetery compound. They shouted at Donnursk.

"Stop…Drop your weapon…Freeze."

Donnursk ignored them. He knew it wasn't the best strategy, but he didn't see a better one. Five minutes earlier, he believed his destiny was to be the next boss of FBI's DFC. Now, he was finished. They had told Rose to eliminate him just as they had told him to eliminate McCanliss.

"Trippler," he muttered. "She's to blame."

He limped past the tombstones, mindless of the dead Thomas Rose, the approaching KWPD, the surging foot pain.

"Drop the weapon!"

He could have done the job, but they hadn't trusted him. After McCanliss screwed up in Bethel, the tenth floor panicked.

"Last warning…Stop where you are…Put your gun on the ground!"

It was the big risk of DFC membership. They made it understood from the beginning. Being on the only team in the U.S. with supreme authority to conduct domestic, pre-emptive kills meant a risk of being killed by order of the DFC if necessary. An occupational hazard, like black lung disease for a coal miner. That's why they all enjoyed a pay scale higher than ordinary agents. But no one ever thinks it'll happen to them. No one ever thinks it'll—*really*—be necessary.

He looked over his shoulder at the four crouching uniformed cops spread out behind him, guns drawn as they maneuvered from gravestone to gravestone for cover.

That's when they fired. All of them.

Most of the bullets struck him between neck and groin. Of those that did not hit the intended target, one struck a double-wide mausoleum, three struck the exteriors of conch houses on the north side of the cemetery, and one banged the rear door of a dilapidated old taxicab with an engine that sounded like a washing machine set to the spin cycle.

Where Donnursk fell, the gravestone read *I Told You I Was Sick.*

CHAPTER NINETY

"He's still alive."

"Who?" Eva asked her father.

"Harry, the one who's trying to kill me. From Bethel. The one I told you about on the flight from Virginia Beach."

Standing in the kitchen, Teagarden thumbed through the photos his daughter had snapped with her cellphone moments after the shoot-out. The war against her father had arrived at Eva's front door, which triggered her fight or flight reflex. And she wasn't about to flee. Fleeing was not what the U.S. Navy did. Her instinct was to fight back. Having been in the Navy since she was eighteen and a Navy pilot since twenty-two, she instinctively prepared a response.

"All right, here's what we're going to do..." she said after the shootout.

At the conclusion of her instructions, her father remained in the house with Chopper and the nanny in the baby's bedroom, while she and Pangolin bicycled through the cemetery. Before departing, she connected a Bluetooth remote lens to her baseball cap next to the insignia of the U.S. Navy, and set her cellphone to snap a photo every three seconds. Rubbernecking as she pedaled, the camera received hundreds of covertly snapped photos before the KWPD set out barriers and shooed away the quickly gathered crowd of gawkers.

When they returned to the house, Teagarden flipped through the images on her phone. Several of them would have been the envy of any photojournalist in a war zone.

"I'm pretty sure I saw that man when I was hiding in the boathouse in Sparta" he said, looking at the shot of a bullet-riddled Durgan Donnursk. His was on his back, his head propped against the tombstone, eyes open, staring straight ahead. Except for the holes leaking rivulets of red, it was the casual reclining pose of a man watching football on TV.

Teagarden scrolled forward to the shot of Rose and pinched the screen to get a close-up. "I've never seen him before."

"How many hit men are assigned to this thing?" Pangolin wondered aloud.

"Two fewer than this morning," Eva pointed out. "My question is, why are they now killing each other?"

"The law of diminishing returns," Teagarden answered. "Basic mathematics. There're too many of them and they're getting in each other's way. Plus, they're panicking. Whoever's running the operation is scared past the point of reason. That's probably to my advantage, but my key problem remains. McCanliss is not one of those two dead men. He's still out there. That means the answer to Pangolin's question is—at least three hit men are targeting me, two of whom are now dead. Please believe me that this McCanliss guy is not someone any of us wants to challenge." He handed the cell-phone back to his daughter. "And that's a photo of the truck McCanliss was driving in Bethel. I guess he abandoned it. Silly, isn't it?"

"What's silly about it?" Eva asked.

"Black ops hitmen driving around in trucks called *Harry's Heating and A/C Repair* or *Durgan's Lawn & Garden*. It's absurd."

"Not really, Dad. In the military, that's what we call a pretty good cover."

Teagarden shrugged.

"I guess they can't exactly wear T-shirts reading *Covert Killer*, though that's what they are, or were. It's definitely what McCanliss still is."

"I got a good look at the inside of that truck while Pang and I were peddling around the cemetery," Eva continued. "It's loaded with high-tech equipment." She scrolled back to photos of the truck's interior. "You see that console? That looks like radar-tracking equipment straight from a carrier-based Hawkeye AWAC. The panel on the opposite side looks like a laser-guided bomb station. And, hey, look at that. That's a pair of night-vision goggles hanging overhead. These guys lack for nothing."

"Great," Teagarden moaned. "My federal tax dollars put to good use trying to kill me. That's just great."

"And there's that couple by the south gate wearing Minnesota Vikings T-shirts," she said, continuing to scroll through the shots. "They came close to being arrested."

"What'd they do?" her father asked.

"Nothing, which was exactly the problem. When police officers tell you to move along, it's best if you move along. And look at that, the driver in that old taxi was doing the same as us. He just circled the cemetery, eyeballing everything. He's in the background of a bunch of these shots. Maybe he was taking photos too."

Pangolin's ears perked up. He saw the taxicab while they were biking and wanted to pedal closer but he couldn't manage it without challenging the KWPD's comfort zone. After their audacious tour of the cemetery grounds, one cop shouted, "Get out or get arrested."

They got out.

"Let me see that," Pangolin said. He scrolled through the shots. "Sam," Pangolin said thoughtfully, "describe this man McCanliss."

Teagarden took a breath, recalling what he knew about the man he'd seen in Bethel, near Union Square Park, on security video from the lobby of the Madison Park Euro Lodge, near The Argonaut Hotel in Times Square, and most recently from the boathouse window on the lake in Sparta.

"White male, about six-foot-three, two-hundred pounds or so, about sixty-years-old, as long powerful arms and a receding hairline. His most distinctive feature is a thick scar on his upper lip to correct what must have been one hell of a cleft palate."

"That's the guy I've seen knocking around here in old town," his daughter said. Hearing that was too much for her father.

"Eva, that's it. That monster is still out there. He's alive, and he's still plotting to get me and he doesn't care who else gets killed along the way. For all we know, he killed those two in the cemetery so they wouldn't get me before—*he*—gets me. I've come to understand how crazy he is, and—*that*—is exactly how crazy he is. It's personal with him now. He wants to be the one who gets me, which makes me an ugly risk to you and Marnie. I told you I shouldn't have come here."

"Okay, okay. Easy, Dad."

She knew the conversation was adding to her father's strain. The challenges he'd faced during the past week were beyond most civilians' coping skills and she didn't want him to have another breakdown.

Pangolin, meantime, knew something else. He verged on telling them that he, too, knew McCanliss from the previous day's tourist flight onboard his DC-3. But while Eva was trying to assuage her father's fears, he changed his mind. He decided to keep it to himself, because he had a job to do. Alone. And if he told Eva about it, she wouldn't let him go.

"Try to keep it together, Dad."

She put a hand on her father's arm. The bout of crying on the DC-3 while coming back from Virginia Beach was only the second time she'd seen her father shed tears. The first was at her mother's memorial service the previous November, when he was in a wheelchair, still wearing casts on both legs.

"Listen, Dad, I know this sounds crazy at this point, but we're family. We're in this together. You, me, Marnie—" she looked at Pangolin, wondering if she should name him as well, but decided against it, "—and we're going to get through this as family."

"Eva—"

"It's no good, Dad. You've handled it until now, but you're tired. You need rest. You need sleep. And that's what you're going to get. Meantime, I'm on the job now. Got it? No more solo for you. I'm here. Cynthia Blair is in Washington. And we're going to make this thing stop."

"But Marnie—"

"Marnie is fine, and she's going to stay fine. I'll see to it. She will not leave my sight until this mess is over."

That did it. From the back room, the toddler heard the voices all along, but when she heard her name, there was no more resisting. She escaped her nanny's supervision during a game of hide-and-seek. While Pilar was hiding, Chopper strategically ceased playing. She opened the door and ran to the kitchen, rotor blades flying.

"Da-Da Tea-Tea, Da-Da Tea-Tea."

He picked her up after she threw her arms around his legs. Watching her father and daughter, Eva was ready with her plan.

"All right, Dad, here's what we're going to do…"

CHAPTER NINETY-ONE

The Tomcat, Wisteria Island, FL

It was an odd dream, disquieting yet peaceful.

He was hiding in the woods the way Billy Carney did the day he spied on the house in Bethel. His wife Kendra was standing on the small front porch of their house. She was smiling with great happiness, looking out at nothing in particular. Next to her stood Cynthia who was neither smiling nor frowning, her face totally neutral.

What did it mean? Dreams were like the mystery of numbers. They all meant something. Sometimes the meaning was obvious. Sometimes it was more mysterious than the pulsating heart of the solar system.

He awoke from the first healing sleep he'd had since Thursday in the boathouse. His body had desperately needed it. He'd been able to grab only fitful naps while on the run. When he woke, the lights of Key West some five hundred yards off the stern of Pangolin's boat were just beginning to glow in the approaching darkness.

To the starboard lay Sunset Key, a small privately owned island brimming to the edge with condos and cottages for the affluent. He was closer to another small land mass on the port side. Called Wisteria Island, it was a mid-twentieth century landfill created by the U.S. Navy, and currently only occupied by clusters of wild shrubbery. No people were allowed, though campers frequently snuck ashore for the thrill of breaking the rules, as all Conchs tend to do from time to time.

He was surrounded by scores of other boats at anchor, some small, some large. One in particular, a huge yacht, was given wide berth. No matter their size, they all held anchor at respectful distances, creating an odd sort of suburb, a floating community of boat dwellers who gave an occasional arm wave or the hoisting of a martini glass at sunset.

Teagarden was aboard one of them, *The Tomcat.* He'd teased Pangolin about the boat's name, assuming it referred to randy sexual adventures.

"Not at all," he was told. "It was my last fighter, the F-14 Tomcat. When they replaced the pilot with Robbie the Robot, I retired from the Navy. No use being a pilot if you're not piloting."

They reached the sailboat by motorized dinghy which Pangolin kept tied on the west side of Key West where tourists congregate to watch the sunset. It was there that a small army of buskers hoped to earn tips entertaining sunset watchers each night with a lineup of sword swallowers, jugglers, and acrobats.

Before leaving him alone on *The Tomcat*, Pangolin gave Teagarden a quick tour of the galley kitchen and emergency radio, pointed out the cabinet that held the .45 semi-automatic pistol and twelve-gauge shotgun. The combination code for the gun cabinet's padlock was 4-5-1-2, easy to remember because the numbers matched the two weapons. Finally, before departing on the dinghy, Pangolin left his own cellphone with Teagarden for emergency use.

Sitting under the protective awning of *The Tomcat's* open deck, Teagarden used the binoculars to scan the crowd of tourists watching the sunset on Key West. He'd changed to fresh clothes left at his daughter's house during previous visits, including a beach hat. And he hid in the back seat of her truck for Pangolin's drive to the dinghy. Teagarden hoped it all added up to mean that McCanliss couldn't possibly know where he was. Then he thought like hell. That man is the Prince of the Air. He knows everything.

He surveyed the crowd of tourists, pausing the binoculars to focus on everyone who seemed more than six feet tall. One of the jugglers twirling fire batons fit the bill.

Not McCanliss.

A guy slowly strolling the waterfront with his arm around a young woman was easily the right height, but he was African-American.

The tallest man in the crowd was a giant—ten feet tall. He was a clown walking on stilts.

Certainly not McCanliss.

He withdrew his laptop from the backpack and logged onto the internet, still using the name Dan Jones and his "yel-low4submarine," password. It had been a couple of days, so he scrolled back, reading Dan's most recent e-mails, to see how he was doing.

From: danjones@orangecircle.com
To: sandyjones@orangecircle.com
    Mom is right, it is all your fault.

From: sandyjones@orangecircle.com
To: danjones@orangecircle.com
    Dear Dan,
    I am sorry but I can no longer make excuses to your mom or Amy. I told them you've run off to liberal New York for reasons unknown to me. Your mother just looked at me and said it was all my fault, while your daughter only cried.
    And no, I am not using your e-mail to embarrass you. Are you in trouble? That's what they do, they get your e-mail, then they steal your life. I pray you really are my husband and not some trickster in that ungodly big city.
    Please, *please* come home soon.
    Love,
    Your wife, Sandy

From: danjones@orangecircle.com
To: sandyjones@orangecircle.com
So, it's been more than a day has it?

Well, even at that, not a day goes by that you don't tell me I am doing everything wrong.

And one more thing—are you trying to embarrass me by sending e-mail in my name to Hollywood movie makers and military bases in Florida?

Such foolishness will only keep me away longer.

From: sandyjones@orangecircle.com
To: danjones@orangecircle.com
Dearest Dan,

I haven't heard from you in more than a day. Please, even if you are angry at me, please let me know that you are alive.

Love,

Your wife, Sandy

From: naskeywestpublicrelations@usnavy.mil
To: danjones@orangecircle.com
Subject: Dogfight Girl Sequel
Will be happy to meet regarding sequel to *Dogfight Girl* at Navy Air Station, Boca Chica Key, Florida. Please phone the P.R. Ofc. at N.A.S. Key West at your convenience.

Ask for Raymond Bakerfield.

Best Regards

Public Relations Office

And that's where I came in.

So, Dan, I'm getting a better picture of you. You're not gay, suicidal, bankrupt or running from the law. And there is no other woman. You're just an all-American, middle-aged, married man exhausted with being relentlessly ridiculed and reprimanded by mother and wife.

"Hang in there, Dan. New York's not so bad. But she's

right about one thing. As a pilgrim from the provinces, you do need to be careful in the big city."

He trolled online news sites for the latest on his own situation. His daughter was right; Capitol Hill was boiling with anticipation. No link was made with the two deaths in Key West Cemetery, but following Friday's bizarre death of an aged rightwing congressman, reporters suddenly smelled blood from one end of Pennsylvania Avenue to the other. After that impromptu broadcast from Cynthia Blair's hospital room, global media were zealously speculating that Teagarden was completely innocent. One inside-the-Beltway reporter called him a "heroic figure" and claimed to have a Deep Throat-source code-named "Orpheus" who could prove the FBI was hiding "a big load of (—bleep—) stretching back to Prohibition." The op/ed columnists were moving into his corner, writing under headlines like: "Let Painful Truths Be Known," "Shine a Light" and "Out, Out Damn Spot." Others speculated on who this secret source named Orpheus may be. The suspect list included the CIA, FBI, NSA, teenage hackers, Russian trolls, foreign spies, the VEEP and even the man elected to the nation's highest office in 2016.

"All that's nice, but none of them knows the whereabouts of McCanliss," Teagarden muttered to himself. "I'm here alone. Whoever Orpheus is, he can't do me much good while Mr. Mental Case is still out there."

He again trained the binoculars on the Key West tourist wharf. The big attraction of the moment was a crew of acrobats flipping from each other's shoulders. He scanned the other boats at anchor, but saw little evidence of activity. One large boat had a group of cocktail drinkers, a family party on an old cabin cruiser was barbecuing dinner, and a small sloop had a sleepy-looking man with a beer in one hand and a rod-and-reel in the other, with a line that dangled over the side.

"Good luck with the fish," Teagarden mumbled.

He panned the glasses to Wisteria Island. There was nothing except the twisted shadows of jagged wild shrubbery in the twilight.

"Eva's right," he said, still talking to himself. "I need more sleep."

He returned to the *The Tomcat's* sleeping compartment and dropped into blank unconsciousness.

CHAPTER NINETY-TWO

Key West, FL

The X-47 lay in the hangar like a surgery patient, comatose under anesthesia.

The fuel line was transplanted, but the patient was not yet revived. The gray titanium underbelly remained open while engineers and technicians tested and retested their work.

The benefit of being in the civilian hanger was the team of twenty-four-hour security guards armed with M4 carbines. They were the reason Eva was present with her daughter in tow.

She hadn't lied to her father. She said Marnie wouldn't leave her sight, and she was keeping her word. As her dad said, the most dangerous member of the group—Harry Mc-Canliss—was still out there, still on the job.

And she realized that Pangolin was right about the media. The fact that reporters and cameras were not camping on her driveway was, ironically, a liability. Who would have thought the media could provide a valuable service by relentlessly gang-banging a big story like this one? Not her. She contemplated contacting local and national media. But it was another after-noon phone conversation that convinced her otherwise.

"These men answer to no one," Cynthia told her on the phone. "It's being learned that they're completely off the books. And I'm being told by House Speaker Alderman that there's speculation at least one of them has gone solo—a complete renegade. His motives are unknown, but we can assume that what's driving him has nothing to do with money, God, or country."

"Great," Eva complained. "They all went off the deep end long ago and now at least one has found a *deeper* end to dive into. Makes you wonder where the bottom is."

"Well put," Cynthia said. "A lot of people inside the beltway are wondering the same. The good news here in D.C. is that the higher-ups who managed this black ops team have been suspended and face congressional subpoena."

"Will that help stop the one who's gone solo?"

The pause at the other end of the line said it all.

"It'll help eventually," Cynthia said. "Meantime, I think you and your dad must continue to take every precaution until we can get you into federal protection."

That conversation helped Eva make up her mind by the time Pangolin returned from securing her father on the boat. She would decamp to the civilian hangar that had been temporarily claimed by the U.S. Navy pending full repairs of the X-47. She'd stay there with Marnie until Washington figured out how to police the dark ops people. Meantime, the security detail surrounding her robo-plane would be good security for her and her child.

Besides, it was her job to supervise work on the bird. Her father and daughter were her family responsibility, but that airplane was her professional duty. Turns out, that rigged-up emergency landing at Key West Airport was working in her favor in more ways than one. Unfortunately, only Marnie could make the trip to the hanger with her. The guards would challenge her father, Pangolin and Pilar, but not the kid. They took turns playing with Chopper while she caught up on loose ends. Using the Dan Jones address, Eva e-mailed her dad. She received a call from a man named Willy Baaktau in Washington, who had the deepest most melodic Dixified Cajun accent she'd ever heard. He told her, "Just hang tight till Monday.

That shooting down there in the Keys is just now starting to get play inside the Beltway. Things are beginning to go our way so just hang on."

Easy for you to say, you're in Washington.

She was trying to hang on. Her father was hiding on a sailboat, and she was hiding in an open-air hangar with her daughter, who was asleep on a blanket with her two favorite stuffed animals.

She walked around the thirty-eight-foot-long plane where it loomed over her in the semi-darkness. The wings were folded in to fit inside the hangar, which made the futuristic triangle look less like an airplane and more like a spaceship. Technical glitches had delayed approval for combat readiness of the 47-series. One of those glitches was a faulty fuel line, which, she knew would help cover her butt in the current situation. Then the whole program was mothballed, probably because pilots were threatening to do what Pangolin had done, which was—quit. But mothballed doesn't mean canceled. Meantime, she was still in charge. And when they're eventually sent into war, each of these Unmanned Combat Air Vehicles (UCAVs) would heighten America's invincibility around the world—*without*—risk to pilots. It meant there would never again be downed pilots held as POWs and paraded in front of cameras to America's shame.

It was a subject Pangolin had mentioned before he dropped her and Marnie at the airport. They'd parked behind the main civilian terminal, where the nose of the X-47 could be seen poking from its cover. From there, they could read the name in neon white lettering on the nose: *Little Bomber-Bot.*

"Tell me something," he said, looking at the tip of the spaceship. "How can a nation be invincible and have leukemia at the same time?"

"I don't follow you."

"This morning at your house, your dad gave me that decoded diary. Eva, I read the whole thing."

"Okay."

"You read it, right?"

"Yeah, in your plane, on the way back from Virginia Beach."

"Well, don't you call that cancer?"

She knew she didn't have an answer that would be good enough for him. Kasey Landrew, aka Pangolin, was the most honest man she knew, aside from her father. And it was his honesty that made him tough. Straight shooters are always tough. Unfortunately, it also made him inflexible. Instead of trying to say the right thing, she just said what came natural, what popped straight from the heart.

"Pang, both my dad—*and*—that airplane are what makes this country great."

The answer was apparently good enough for him. He leaned over in the cab of her old pickup to kiss her goodnight. After the kiss, she put her hand on the side of his face and continued to speak her mind.

"By the way, I still love you even if you are twenty years older than me and hate the X-47 program. I'm sorry I dumped you for a commercial airline pilot. I'm sorry my name is Eva Ghent instead of Eva Landrew. It was a dark mistake on my part to think it wouldn't work because of the age difference. Please forgive me. Oh, and one more thing—Marnie is your daughter."

CHAPTER NINETY-THREE

Her words erased the pain of the last three years.

Knowing Eva's feelings left Pangolin buoyant with happiness. For the first time since becoming a U.S. Navy fighter pilot, he felt appreciation for just being alive.

So...that sweet baby girl was really his. He had adored her at first sight. Now he knew why.

Early on, he'd wondered if Eva's pregnancy might actually be his child. There had been a couple of occasions that made it possible. "Mistakes," she later called those encounters. Two months after her wedding, when she learned of her husband's girlfriend and was as unhappy as he'd ever seen her, they had one final tryst. Her new husband was making the Miami-to-London run with nearly three hundred passengers in the back of his 747. Afterward, she told Pangolin that she would not see him again—ever. The decision had been firm, final, the stuff of no return. In the Navy it was called "stand down." Cease and desist. Return to carrier deck.

And she was right. It was better that way. Sneaking into the bed of another man's wife, even though he loved her, was nothing he'd ever done before or since. He still missed her, but was glad the affair was finished.

What followed was a total change of lifestyle. He took refuge in his newly adopted persona. Instead of Kasey, or Captain Landrew, U.S. Navy, Retired—he became Pangolin. It had been his pilot's nickname. Many years earlier, after getting his noggin shaved during the first stage of flight training at Pensacola, a curving patch of birthmark and brown freckles was revealed on his naked skull. It swept along the back of his head from ear to ear. After being variously described as a *demonic sleeping animal, undulating road kill,* and multiple creative descriptions of excrement, it was eventually named as a Pangolin, which stuck. He had to look it up: *exotic insect-eater, armored scales, burrowing, nocturnal.* It was found only in certain tropical corners of the world, places like Borneo and Pago Pago. After Pensacola, the affectation found its way onto his helmet and the fuselage of his F-14 Tomcat. He became Pangolin, U.S. Navy pilot.

Now he was Pangolin, the hippie pilot of a classic DC-3. During the past three years, he'd let his hair grow long enough to tie into a ponytail. He made a living giving tourists thrills by buzzing Cuban airspace, and he lived a marginal hermit's existence on a small sailboat anchored off Wisteria Island. But there was more. Since retiring from the U.S. Navy and assuming his Key West nickname, he'd gotten to know other local mavericks. Like him, they were fiercely independent old Conchs who went mostly by nicknames. Like him, for whatever reason, they didn't care to discuss their past.

One of those loners he'd come to know was an eccentric Conch named Chispa, the Key West Queen of Haul. She was physically big and brawny with an outsized personality to match. He wasn't certain whether it was her old heap of a taxicab captured in their surveillance photos after the shoot-out. It could have been. He was certain of one thing, however: that was not her behind the wheel, navigating the perimeter of the cemetery after the shooting. That was none other than McCanliss, the same man who said his father died in Vietnam and his son in Iraq.

He decided to investigate Chispa's houseboat by himself. That way there'd be no further risk to Teagarden, Eva, or Marnie—the child he now knew to be his own daughter.

He parked Eva's pickup at the edge of the swampy inlet.

Behind him lay twin lines of airport approach lights. In the far distance he could see the outline of his DC-3 safely parked at the end of the runway. In the near distance, just beyond the polluted inlet, was the open hangar. From that angle, he could see the rear end of the X-47 and the single Pratt and Whitney engine that powered it, the same turbofan that powered the F-15 and F-16. At least those two aircraft still required pilots— for now.

Chispa's taxicab was there, parked on raised landfill next to her decrepit dump truck. Her ancient wooden pleasure boat was moored to the side of a narrow, rotting pier that had once been a causeway for bird-watchers in the swamp. For better anchoring, she'd illegally tied her boat to a telephone pole on the opposite side of the road. Nothing seemed out of the ordinary, though it was difficult to be certain because he'd never been there before. They knew each other only as periodic denizens of the airport terminal, where they hustled the tourist dollar along with others handing out flyers for snorkeling, fishing, jet-skiing, paragliding, and sunset watching.

He cut the noisy engine of the old Ford pickup.

Maybe it would be best to call the police. If his instincts were right and Chispa was in trouble, it could end with more ugliness. That was the last thing he wanted, especially now that his life was set to change yet again, this time for the better.

He stepped from the truck and called out: "Hey, Chispa? You home? It's Pangolin."

When there was no answer he stepped aboard the boat.

"Chispa, it's Pangolin, the DC-3 pilot. Request permission to come aboard."

He knocked at the pilot's cabin, entered and stepped down to the lower level living compartment.

"Hello, anybody—"

The sudden stench was foul, yet held a touch of saccharine sweetness at the same time, like cheap perfume. He'd smelled that odor before, in Iraq and Afghanistan. And in Bosnia before that. After it registered in his brain, he sensed something else. He sensed he was not alone.

He lifted one foot to back away, to ease quietly from the small room. Before he could shift his weight and complete a step toward full retreat, there came a swooshing noise that concluded with a hard thud to the neck, hard enough to send him walking in space.

When he fell, he fell hard.

CHAPTER NINETY-FOUR

Sunday, July 28, 2019
The Tomcat, Wisteria Island, FL

He finally felt rested.

While waiting for sunrise, Teagarden sat in the open stern of the sailboat nursing his second mug of coffee. He'd slept through the night with blissful calm. Thankfully, that longer second bout of rest passed without more unsettling dreams. There had been no more haunting images of Kendra or Billy Carney. After waking, he found a frozen food package containing two ham-and-cheese biscuits, which he microwaved and devoured, along with a glass of milk and a fresh pot of coffee.

Now, in the very early hours, Cynthia was e-mailing him from her hospital bed through the webmail of poor Dan Jones.

From: c.blair@pathblazer.com
To: danjones@orangecircle.com
   good progress here, the spkr's asst. e-mailed during night… emgcy committee meeting set for sunday p.m.…

From: danjones@orangecircle.com
To: c.blair@pathblazer.com
   u'r up early…okay, but what's it mean?…and, more importantly, how's your leg?

From: c.blair@pathblazer.com

To: danjones@orangecircle.com

wow, u'r up early too...it means posibl amnesty & full legal standdown—as soon as TODAY!...plus i am told handwriting been confirmed as that of Clyde Anderson Tolson (CAT)...document is legit...as if we didn't know...and, leg fine, out of hosp. tomorrow, wear cast for a month...then phys thpy...looking fwd to seeing you...

From: danjones@orangecircle.com

To: c.blair@pathblazer.com

wonderful news...thank you...and...i think i forgot to tell you something impt. in that panic at watergate...

From: c.blair@pathblazer.com

To: danjones@orangecircle.com

okay?...

From: danjones@orangecircle.com

To: c.blair@pathblazer.com

i love you too...

She did not respond. But then, she didn't have to.

Sipping the coffee, he wanted to phone Eva on Pangolin's phone and wake her up, but he didn't. Her last communication of the night had not been to him. It wasn't an e-mail, but a particularly long text message sent to Pangolin's cell: *pang, hope i did not startle you...am desperately afraid f/dad... bullsht in cemetery was TOO close...anyway, marnie really is your baby...I'm yours too if u like...sorry it took so long f/me to wise up...*

Eva did not know that Pangolin gave his cellphone to her father on *The Tomcat.* Except for Dan Jones, he was not in the habit of reading communications not meant for him. This one, however, was impossible to miss.

347

So, the father of my granddaughter is not who I thought.

It took a moment to process the information, though he wasn't surprised. Nor was he upset. In fact, he was pleased. Teagarden had pegged John Ghent as a calculating opportunist and skirt chaser on first sight. The quick conclusion of his daughter's marriage confirmed it. Plus, the man had been a total no-show as a father. He didn't want the pregnancy, and after Marnie was born, he didn't want the daughter.

Captain Kasey Landrew, aka Pangolin, on the other hand, would be a wonderful dad.

Darkness on the eastern horizon emitted a thin layer of light that would soon explode into searing radiance. He watched the show in the sky slowly unfold, confident that he was safe for the first time in the last eight days and that his ordeal was nearing an end. Thanks to Danford Shackton's commitment before he was assassinated, Cynthia's work in D.C., and now his daughter and future son-in-law's protecttion on Key West, he felt a solution was near. When it was finally over, attending Sunday services to give personal thanks would be in his future.

He had seen to it that his wife's funeral was secular, as she wanted. Personally, he did believe in a supreme being, but hadn't participated in organized religion in many years.

His faith had always centered on the unknowable mystery of the universe. For him, God could be found in numbers and in science. For all he knew, instead of a being, God might actually be a mathematical formula. But losing his wife, and now the experience of the past week, had expanded his way of thinking. It had been so emotionally wrenching that a personal expression of gratitude to God for his safe deliverance felt like the right thing to do.

And who knows? If church-going expression of faith turns out to be rewarding, maybe I'll stick with it.

He wondered if Cynthia had a religious faith and whether she attended services with any regularity. They hadn't gotten far enough in their short, tumultuous relationship for that sort of conversation.

The dawn widened just as the insect-buzz arrived at the rear of the boat. Searching for the source, he looked up, and toward the east into the blazing morning light, which caught his eyes dead center, blinding him. The sound had the persistent, low-key mechanical buzz of a dragon fly, or a humming bird, or a...

Phfft!

His chest felt a momentary sting. One second later, his face felt nothing when it slammed the boat's deck.

CHAPTER NINETY-FIVE

It wasn't a dream, yet he wasn't awake. He was in some netherworld, some odd, in-between place.

The number three was where the number six should be on the boat's brass wall clock. That was strange enough. But the floor was where the wall should be, and the door to the stern was cockeyed. You had to be unnaturally bent to walk through it. To egress, you had to walk at a forty-five-degree angle.

He strained to remember a cartoon lodged deep in his memory, buried in the sand at the bottom of the ocean. It was a cartoon where all the characters wore nightgowns, had unnaturally dangling arms that dragged the ground, and walked at angles in a run-on puzzle of optical illusions.

Returning to consciousness was nothing like waking from sleep or emerging from anesthesia after knee surgery. It was more like rising from the dead.

"You back yet, Teagarden?"

The voice was so close it was startling. But it was too soon. He wasn't ready.

"Did you hear me?"

His eyes focused.

He was on the boat's narrow bed. He was in the small living quarters of *The Tomcat*. It was beached. That's why the number three was where the number six should be on the clock, why the floor was where the wall should be, why the door leading from the small living compartment could be used only by bent-over-sideways people. It was because the entire boat was leaning. It was beached on Wisteria Island and he was inside the cabin.

"Yes," Teagarden said to the voice. "I hear you."

"That's good," the voice said.

"Am I dead?"

"No, not yet."

"Not yet?" When the voice did not respond, Teagarden said, "Why not yet?" His eyes were unsteady, still not seeing clearly. His ears, however, could do their job.

"Because the K-32 drone was set to stun," said the voice. "One more click of the dial, from stun to fatal, and it would have spit epipoxilene. Very lethal stuff. One drop to the skin of that serum with one one-hundredth of the toxin triggers instant heart failure. Totally untraceable. We call it the 'mother's milk' of black ops."

Teagarden was certain now. Coconut's death was no accident. His sweet dog sensed the danger. He smelled the poison. That big, lumbering, wonderful, old, best boy knew what was going down. He intentionally leapt to take the venom so as to sacrifice his final hours and save his human.

"Why set only to stun? You want me dead, don't you?"

"Instant death would be too easy for us both. And a disgrace for someone as accomplished as you. You've come too far for that." Teagarden wondered what to say, but could think of nothing. "I'm going for a walk. You will follow me outside. We'll have our final encounter out there. In the bushes of that abandoned island. Do you hear me, Teagarden?"

"Yes, I hear you."

He could barely make out the shadowy image of a large man, bent to the side as he exited the door. He heard him scramble over the side of the boat to the narrow beach of Wisteria Island. He realized Harry McCanliss had found him.

CHAPTER NINETY-SIX

Teagarden sat up and shook his head from side to side. He tried to force all lagging brain cells to catch up. That seemed to help. His eyes focused. He stood on his creaking knees, rubbed his eyes and rolled his head around. His body felt the lingering effects of a powerful fever, as though he'd risen from a two-week bout of the Asian flu.

Try not to throw up.

He leaned across the kitchen counter. The tiny sink was under him in case he needed to heave. He looked from *The Tomcat's* port window. McCanliss stood beyond the narrow beach, at the edge of the tall shrubbery. The demon was waiting, his long arms dangling at his side, looking back at the sailboat.

Waiting for what?

He checked the starboard window. Nothing, except coarse sand and a thick layer of surf-strewn pebbles where the boat had beached to the starboard. At the stern, the sun was still rising above the other live-aboard vessels anchored peacefully at respectful distances. The nearest boat was a wooden hulk, an antiquated pleasure craft bobbing unanchored in the shoal about twenty-five yards off. He could read the name: *Beyond Bayonne*. He hadn't seen it before, but sensed it played a role in McCanliss's arrival on *The Tomcat*.

Guns. Oh my God. There are guns onboard.

As his consciousness powered up, he remembered. There were two firearms on the boat, a twelve-gauge shotgun and a military issue .45 Colt.

He stumbled to the safety cabinet and began rotating the combination dial on the padlock. It was silver and black, like the cheap lock on his locker in high school: spin twice; right to the first number, left past the first number, and so on.

1-2-4-5. No good. 5-4-2-1. No good. 4-5-1-2. That did it.

Knowing next to nothing about handguns, he withdrew the twelve-gauge. It was a standard pump action, not what he preferred as a former competitive skeet shooter. Skeet shooters use an automatic or a double barrel. They're quicker and help maintain focus. The necessary strength involved in pumping the next shell into the chamber compromises focus and aim, which is never good for competitive shooting.

The movies are to blame.

Audiences like pumps because of Hollywood. Very silly. It's sexy to pump-and-fire, pump-and-fire—especially when the hero (or sweaty heroine) holds the pump and jerks the stock, instead of holding the stock and jerking the pump. He put four shells into the magazine, then chambered one and inserted a fifth.

Five shells.

He looked again from the small portside window. Mc-Canliss was still there, still standing at the edge of the waist-high shrubbery. Still waiting. Waiting. But, waiting for what?

The cellphone.

That's it. He needed to call the police. Where was Pangolin's phone? He felt for it, but it was not in any pocket. He glanced about. Nothing.

The next chaotic instant was more than nothing. It was a volley of popping noises from the beach. They were gunshots, and each bullet struck the sailboat: bow, stern, bow, stern, bow, stern.

Teagarden instinctively dropped to the uneven floor as chips of fiberglass and teak molding flew about inside the cabin. The shots continued: bow, stern, bow, stern.

Duck and cover. It's what his parents did during the Cuban Missile Crisis. It better work now for me.

He ducked and covered.

The next volley was aimed more mid-hull and seemed to go on for an eternity. The brass clock was slammed, the coffee pot shattered, a hole opened in the kitchen cabinet, a ricochet echoed in the hatchway. Shots hit the port light, grab rail, lower hull, upper hull, keel.

God damn it!

Return fire, dummy!

Without exposing himself, Teagarden extended the twelve-gauge from the angled doorway, pointed the barrel in the general direction of McCanliss and fired. He gave a quick glance from the port window.

McCanliss was still standing. He was walking backward, nearly to the point of disappearing inside the shrubbery and reloading what appeared to be a Glock with a full clip. Just before slipping into the greenery, his arm extended, his fingers curved several times in quick succession over the top of his palm. It was yet another taunting gesture telling Teagarden to come out, to follow him. Immediately afterward, he took one additional step backward and disappeared into the heavy foliage like a specter on a haunted island.

That's what the gunshots were about.

He'd intentionally aimed high and away from the position where he knew Teagarden was cowering on the floor. It was a message. McCanliss wanted to be pursued. After a week of fox-and-hound, he wanted the final stage of the hunt to be between the two of them, alone on the small uninhabited island.

Teagarden remembered thinking that macho bravado might be the Achilles heel of this psycho. Now he knew it was true. Yet the challenge still lay in capitalizing on it. He had no idea how to make it work to his benefit.

Teagarden slowly eased through the lopsided door, stepping on Pangolin's cellphone that lay on the other side. He didn't bother picking it up; it had already been smashed. Beside it lay his laptop, also crushed.

Staying low, he slid over the starboard bow to the beach where he had the cover of the entire boat to protect him. He lumbered around the front of the hull, racing as best as his knees could carry him across the narrow beach, which wasn't very fast.

He entered the thick growth of prickly pines twenty-five yards to the east of the spot where McCanliss disappeared. Once inside the cover of greenery, he realized he'd made a stupid mistake. He'd failed to bring the box of shotgun shells. He had four shots remaining.

Four shots, compared with McCanliss's arsenal of a full clip. How many bullets did a Glock hold—seventeen? Nineteen?

Those numbers are not good!

CHAPTER NINETY-SEVEN

Ten feet into the rough, Teagarden squatted as low as he could manage.

The sand beneath his toes was thickly dotted with a residue of broken rock and fragmented shell. The shrubbery was mostly weather-beaten evergreens. They were droopy, furry variations of Christmas trees that naturally grew on the tiny island, stubbornly surviving the odds against everything nature tossed: sun, wind, salt, sea.

He too intended to stubbornly survive, though he knew he needed more of the remarkable luck that had been so generous to him over the past days.

He checked the twelve-gauge. He'd failed to pump another shell into the chamber after firing that first shot. He racked the next shell from the magazine into the chamber, then crouched lower, alert and listening in case McCanliss heard the *kah-chuck*.

Behind him, he could make out the narrow beach beyond the shrubbery, the outline of the foundered *Tomcat*, the emerald green waters, and the speckled, shadowy images of other boats bobbing at anchor. One boat in particular seemed to be advancing, drifting toward the beach. It was the old wooden pleasure craft, a houseboat named *Beyond Bayonne*. He contemplated running back to *The Tomcat*, gesturing frantically for help, yelling at other boaters like a desperate Robinson Crusoe, doing anything to sound the alarm that might convince them to summon the police or Coast Guard.

It didn't happen. As if he knew what Teagarden was thinking, McCanliss made the first move.

Pop!

The shot cut through the evergreen trees at ground level, missing Teagarden.

"I just want to say congratulations," McCanliss shouted. He was about fifty yards to the left and his voice carried on a misty early morning breeze. Teagarden instinctively dropped flat and wormed into the sand like a flounder.

"Congratulations for what?"

"You know for what," McCanliss said. "For outsmarting me. For outsmarting the DFC, the NYPD, the D.C. police. Very good. It's like you stepped out of an old movie or a comic book. I've enjoyed it."

"What's DFC?"

"C'mon, Teagarden, don't mess with me on the day of my death. It's Deep Field Command. You figured it out. Domestic black ops. Been around since the sixties. Because of you, Capitol Hill and the media are figuring it out right now. You even managed to get my face on CNN. That was damn good."

"I can't be that good. You found me on the boat. How'd you know I was there?"

"Followed you and that hippie pilot with Chispa's taxi. Then I watched you take the dinghy to Pangolin's boat. You see, Teagarden, it's not all listening devices, drones and satellites. Sometimes old fashioned shoe leather is still the best way. The newcomers don't know that."

Teagarden had no idea who Chispa was, but had no intention of asking. The voice didn't seem to be shifting. Unless the wind was doing tricky things with acoustics, McCanliss was staying put.

"Why do you say this is the day of your death?" Teagarden shouted. "You're still trying to kill me just like you did in Bethel. If you succeed, you win—you get to live."

"Oh, I *will* succeed," McCanliss said. "It's just you and me now. I *will* kill you. But I will *not* live. After you're dead, I'll do myself."

"Why?"

"Why? *You!* That's why. Because of you, the bureau tried to kill me, and the DFC will disband. That means you win. You'll be dead, too. But you win."

"I don't call being dead winning."

"Yeah, that's strange, I'll grant you. But that's the way of black ops. You're a part of it now, so you just have to accept it. Black ops is the only game where you can die and still win."

"Is that how you justify killing Billy Carney, Svetlana, Danford Shackton and the Shelbourns? You just call it the black ops game?"

"Yup. And don't forget Chispa, here in Key West."

There was that name again. Weird.

"While you're at it, don't forget Coconut. Apparently you've never heard the expression 'kill a man's dog, break a man's rules.'"

"Would you like an apology?"

"No, thanks."

He sensed the social hour had concluded and that Mc-Canliss was on the move, stalking through the bushy pines. With the 9mm Glock, he wouldn't have to get close. The shrubbery wouldn't present much of an obstacle for his weapon. But for Teagarden's twelve-gauge, the shrubbery was a problem. The hardiness of the evergreens would deflect a portion of the pellets housed in each shotgun shell. That meant he suffered yet another handicap. Unlike McCanliss, he needed a relatively close and clear line-of-sight to make his shot work.

Because it was easier on his knees, Teagarden army-crawled from the direction of McCanliss's voice, toward the center of the island. Along the way, he disturbed a nest of seagulls that took noisy flight. Fearing it would bring McCan-liss down on him, he rose to a cave-man squat and scrambled off, stepping over the nest holding three mottled brown eggs.

After a few seconds, he stopped to listen.

Nothing.

He ducked through the shrubbery toward the north side, where he stopped just short of the beach to peer from a wall of green. What he saw was astonishing.

He and McCanliss were not alone on the tiny island.

CHAPTER NINETY-EIGHT

There were two boys. Young men, really.

Tanned to a fine bronze, each had broad shoulders, narrow waists and wore only boxer style swim shorts. One struggled with a spaghetti jumble of nylon rope as he tried to hoist the brightly colored red and black sail. The other strained like a mule behind the twin hulls, pulling at a Y-shaped configuration of nylon to tug the vessel from its hiding place inside the wall of evergreen. It had been pushed three-quarters into the shrubbery. Like a car too long for the garage, only its rear end poked out, which was concealed with chopped-off pine branches for camouflage.

Teagarden understood immediately.

They were illegally camping and had been awakened by gunfire and loud conversation about death, dying, and murder. Their natural response: *get the hell off of Wisteria Island.*

Teagarden's instinct was to rush toward them.

When he stumbled from the cover of evergreen, his eyes wild with panic and shotgun in hand, the young men were paralyzed. They stared in disbelief and raised their arms in surrender.

"Don't shoot, don't shoot."

Teagarden realized he'd made a potentially costly mistake. Now there were three people in mortal danger. He thought of turning and ducking back into the thick shrubbery, but doubted that would save them. Instead, he hobbled forward, making desperate hand gestures for them to *hush, quiet down, stop shouting.* But they didn't understand. They saw only a wild-eyed man, twelve-gauge pump in hand, limping toward them.

"Don't shoot, please don't shoot."

When he got within ten feet he spoke as loudly as he dared.

"Guys—hush. I'm not going to hurt you. Please, I need to get off this island. A man is trying to kill me." He gestured to their catamaran. "Take me with you." He looked over his shoulder for any sign that McCanliss was coming up from behind. There was none. "C'mon, guys, let's go—fast!"

It worked.

Their paralysis unlocked. The two scrambled to push the catamaran off the beach. Teagarden helped as best he could. Now that he was closer, he saw how young they were, maybe eighteen, certainly no more than twenty. He guessed they were fraternity brothers, college friends working summer jobs in Key West.

"Jimmy, get the anchor lanyard," one said. "It's staked into the sand over there."

"Okay, got it."

Jimmy ran fifteen yards to the right and yanked a two-foot metal stake from the beach, freeing a nylon lanyard serving as a safety mooring. He tossed the stake to his companion.

"Scotty, tie it off or it'll drag."

They got as far as ankle deep water when the first shot rang out, hitting nothing in particular. McCanliss emerged from the green wall crouching low, pivoting like a panicky groundhog. He fired another shot in their general direction, again hitting nothing in particular before lunging back inside the greenery.

Teagarden cursed. As the others watched, he stepped away from the catamaran and lumbered toward the point where McCanliss had reentered the thick evergreens. He aimed and fired.

Blam...kah-chuck...blam...kah-chuck...blam...kah-chuck...

blam...kah-chuck...CLICK...kah-chuck...CLICK.

That was it—he'd used his four shells. The shotgun was empty. He could walk into the evergreens to see if McCanliss was dead or he could help with the catamaran. He chose the latter.

"Okay, let's hurry."

He dropped the shotgun in the sand. This time, they got as far as knee-deep water and were all about to climb aboard the catamaran when McCanliss emerged again. He was not stooping and showed no sign of caution. He walked to where they stood in the surf. At the end of his long right arm, he held the Glock.

"Almost, Sam," McCanliss said. "Good try."

Teagarden realized that his lunge from the evergreens had been a ploy. McCanliss deliberately drew his shotgun fire. It was clever. After hearing the *click, click* of the empty chamber, he knew it was safe to emerge.

"This has got to stop!" Teagarden shouted.

McCanliss nodded and rubbed his balding head with his left hand. He glanced at the two boys, the sky, the green waters of the Gulf, and back at the two boys.

"I agree," he said. "Now's the time."

He casually raised the Glock and fired twice. Each bullet struck its target. The first hit Jimmy's tan, sweaty face below his left eye, sending him reeling backward into the surf. The second struck Scotty in the teeth on an upward trajectory. He, dropped to a straddle on the left hull of the catamaran, head drooping back, a bucket with a leak in the bottom, sending a steady stream of blood into the water.

Teagarden stared at the gradually reddening surf. He too was about to die, and he had no doubt that this black ops sociopath meant it when he said he would take his own life afterward. The Key West police or the Coast Guard would have the unpleasant job of lugging four bodies from Wisteria Island. Teagarden sent a last thought to his daughter: *Don't blame yourself, Eva.*

McCanliss pointed the Glock at Teagarden.

"None of this will stop the Dear John File from going public," Teagarden said softly. It may have sounded like a final, desperate attempt to delay the inevitable, but it wasn't. It was merely what came to mind while speaking to no one in particular, except maybe to the God he planned on becoming more acquainted with.

"That's good," McCanliss said. "I decided while sitting with my best friends, the snow leopards of the Central Park Zoo, that the Dear John File—*should*—go public. The FBI has been so incompetent they deserve it."

He was going to make one last statement before shooting, but was interrupted by a mechanical buzz that drew his attention. It was a drone, about the size of a baseball, hovering ten feet overhead.

McCanliss instantly understood the danger. He raised the Glock and aimed at the K-32 a moment too late. It fired before he could squeeze off a shot.

Harry McCanliss fell backward onto the rough sand of Wisteria Island's narrow beach.

CHAPTER NINETY-NINE

No longer floundering, the *Beyond Bayonne* was laboring under its own smoky power.

Exhausted, with aching body and heart, Teagarden stood beside the catamaran in the shallow surf growing redder from the young men's gushing head wounds. He put a hand over the right side of his face to block the glare, straining to follow the arc of the small drone as it circled back, away from the island. It eased to a landing on the aft deck of the old wooden houseboat that slowly chugged closer.

Teagarden waved. The man in the pilot's cabin gave a small, quick wave in response while struggling with the stubborn, unresponsive controls of the old boat.

The huffing motor slipped to neutral, then made a grinding noise as it shifted into reverse. A whirlpool of dirty backwash churned at the stern to ease the impact when the bow of the *Beyond Bayonne* hit the island's sand bar, bringing it to an abrupt stop. A cloud of gray exhaust wafted ashore, passing over Teagarden, the catamaran, the bodies of the two young men and McCanliss. After a moment, the engine shutdown and the pilot stepped from the cockpit with a downcast look.

It was Pangolin.

They stared into each other's eyes for a prolonged time. Each felt a great sadness for the two boys that lay nearby, their young bodies limp, their wonderful energy interrupted, draining into the Gulf of Mexico.

"The Coast Guard is on the way," Pangolin called out

from the deck of the *Beyond Bayonne.*

Teagarden nodded appreciation. Gradually the red-tinted water returned to a full emerald green. Pangolin eased over the gunwale of the *Beyond Bayonne* and waded ashore. Avoiding the body of McCanliss, they both stumbled to a rocky outcropping at the surf's edge, and sat down, their bare feet bobbing in the undulating shallow surf.

"You're a fast learner," Teagarden said. Pangolin gave him a confused look. "The drones." He nodded at the prostrate body of McCanliss behind them. "You're a fast learner on those drones."

"Not fast enough, unfortunately." Pangolin nodded at the other two bodies snagged by nylon cable wrapping the catamaran. He sighed. "I'm sorry I didn't get here faster." He regarded the body of the man he'd taken up on the DC-3. The man he respected and had given extra time in the cockpit because of the story about his father and son dying in service to the U.S. He wondered why he didn't get any sense that he was a thorough sociopath at the time.

"I hear you," Teagarden said. "Still, you got—*him*. At least that job is finally done."

"I suppose so. I had no idea they were making those drones that small. The suitcase on board the houseboat held two, each not much bigger than an apple. Two video screens are built into the suitcase along with remote controls. It's a compact, portable little air force." He wiped his face with the palms of both hands. "Nasty little machines. If they keep that up, the entire U.S. Air Force will eventually be nothing more than swarms of killer mosquitoes. I'll tell you something, it's just plain ironic."

A high-powered motorboat appeared on the western horizon, rounding the slip between Sunset Key and Wisteria Island. At nearly the same time, a helicopter appeared overhead.

"Coast Guard?" Teagarden asked.

"That would definitely be the Coast Guard," Pangolin

confirmed.

They watched the boat approach. Maybe thirty feet long, it was a muscular vessel and a welcome sight because it carried what Teagarden wanted all along, had wished for from the first moment. It was the cavalry—the good guys. At last.

"What's ironic?" Teagarden asked. Pangolin appeared confused again. "You said it was ironic. How so?"

"Drones!" He shook his head from side to side while looking at the approaching powerboat. "I quit the U.S. Navy because of 'em. Now here I am, saving the grandfath—well, saving you from that devil back there by flying a remote-controlled drone."

Teagarden knew why Pangolin stopped himself. He was about say that he saved the grandfather of his own daughter with a drone. He chose different words because he did not know that Teagarden was already aware who baby Marnie's real father was. That was all right. The subject didn't need to be discussed at that moment; there would be plenty of time for that later.

They quickly related events of the morning and the previous night.

For Teagarden it was a fairly short story that could fit into a tweet: "Slept on *Tomcat*...stung by drone at sunrise...regained consciousness w/awful sickness...forced onto island for shootout with McCanliss."

For Pangolin, the story was longer: "Suspected McCanliss was driving chispa's taxi...went to check on her...discovered her murdered on board the *Beyond Bayonne*...got knocked out by blow to head...regained consciousness with awful headache...saw Teagarden and McCanliss exchanging shots... cranked houseboat motor...set up drone case...chugged toward island...sent drone aloft for aerial attack."

"You only had a headache?" Teagarden asked. "You didn't feel wretchedly ill, like feverish or drugged from the drone hit?"

366

"No," Pangolin said. "I wasn't hit with a drone. I'm not sure what he hit me with. A roundhouse karate kick, maybe. I never saw it coming in the dark. That guy had the longest arms and biggest fists I've ever seen. Whatever it was, it felt like a bowling ball. Put me out cold all night." He rubbed his neck and head. "Lord, I've still got a mighty ache."

"When you put that drone into the air just now, did you reset it to kill?" Teagarden asked. "Or did you leave it on stun?"

Pangolin cocked his head toward Teagarden. Before he could ask, "What the hell are you talking about?" the answer came from a voice behind them.

"He...left...it...on...*stun*."

CHAPTER ONE HUNDRED

They turned from their craggy seat at the surf's edge.

Behind them stood McCanliss, Glock in hand. Like some absurd Hollywood sequel, he'd risen from his own grave to threaten them yet again. Teagarden could see from his eyes that he was not yet fully conscious, but recovering from the same wretched fever he'd experienced in the boat. McCanliss was trying to focus, trying to will every cell and synapse back to health.

"And you're right," McCanliss went on slowly, "it does cause a nasty hangover." He shook his head. "Those K-32's are potent bastards, even without epipoxilene."

Pangolin spoke before Teagarden could find words, "Sir, that's the United States Coast Guard approaching the beach and circling overhead. There's no way you can escape."

BLAM!

That was McCanliss's answer. His shot at Pangolin missed, though not intentionally. His intent was to kill, just as he'd easily shot the two young men still lying where they were snagged by nylon ropes attached to their catamaran. Mc-Canliss had missed because he was teetering, likely seeing double, the result of being hit by the K-32 set to stun.

"Do I look like I give a fuck about the Coast Guard?" he said. "I enjoyed my ride in your DC-3, you commie-loving, liberal bastard, but this is my last day on Earth. Yours, too."

BLAM!

He fired again, this time at Teagarden, but missed again.

Teagarden dove from the rocky outcropping to the beach and rolled into the shallow breakers. As he did so, he remembered his failure to capitalize on Harry's biggest weakness—his own arrogance. He'd accurately diagnosed the man's Achilles heel, but had failed to fully strike at it.

BLAM! BLAM! BLAM!

McCanliss took several more shots at Teagarden's moving target, his unfocused eyes confused by the slowly rolling surf, the sun's glare, and the rapidly approaching boat whose captain laid on the foghorn.

Ah-OOOO, Ah-OOOO, Ah-OOOO.

When he saw that all shots missed, McCanliss squared his shaky legs as best he could. He stepped toward Teagarden, taking careful aim. At the same time, Pangolin reached into his hip pocket for the gun he'd taken from Chispa's bedside bureau on board the *Beyond Bayonne*. He aimed and fired, emptying the small nickel-plated weapon.

Pop, pop, pop, pop, pop, pop, pop, pop, pop, pop.

Of the ten .22 caliber bullets, four hit the devilish target: one in the shoulder, one in the abdomen and two in the left leg. The others only kicked-up sand behind the long-armed man. Incredibly, he remained standing.

McCanliss looked with drugged confusion at his bleeding wounds, then back at Teagarden and Pangolin.

"I told that dumb bitch her .22 wouldn't stop shit," he mumbled. He gave a defiant laugh, and raised the Glock again, ready to resume shooting. He knew it would be his last action before falling and bleeding out. Just before he fired, his macho, drunken swagger was momentarily distracted by yet another drone.

It was directly overhead, descending like an elevator, much larger than the other drones, the size of a basketball. Instead of a quaint buzzing sound, it made a noisy motorized whirring noise, more like a finely tuned sports car, as it descended to a point about ten feet off the ground. It came to a hovering stop, glittering with silver reflections in the sun, like a disco ball. It spun around forcefully before firing.

Vah-WOOSH-tah!

Unlike the small K-32, it did not spit venom, nor did it fire a projectile. Instead, it shot only a powerful force of concentrated air directly at McCanliss, whose torso opened-up like the sail on a clipper ship shot through with cannon ball. It turned his midsection into an open window the size of a Kindle. For the briefest moment, McCanliss looked down— *and through*—the rent in his abdomen where he could see the coarse beach sand behind him. It was stained with the remains of his own blown-out guts.

After McCanliss fell, dead at last, the drone resumed flight, returning straight to the helicopter circling high overhead.

CHAPTER ONE HUNDRED ONE

Wednesday, July 31, 2019
The Carolinas, 35,000 Feet

Sam Teagarden sipped a can of diet soda during the flight north.

"It's not too cramped in here," he said. "There's plenty of room for a pilot. But you need to put in a window."

"It's not cramped because I took out the bomb bay payload equipment," his daughter's voice said in the headset. "And there's no window because there's no need for one."

"Where am I now?"

"You just passed Charleston at thirty-five thousand feet, traveling at Mach point-nine. In one minute you'll come up on Fort Bragg's radar in Fayetteville."

"Speed it up, will you? Push it to Mach two. I want to know what that feels like."

"Can't do it, Dad," the voice said. "The X-47 is not designed for supersonic flight. Just hang in there. You'll be on the ground in Washington in about a half hour."

It was her idea. After the national news broke that her dad was not a murderer or an intentional whistleblower, but only a decoder of an encrypted, long-lost diary that would force reinterpretation of American history—everything changed. But not all of it was good. For the next three days, a far different sort of war raged. Mostly, it was a war of words in Washington and on the so-called news networks, where it was more about stomping and shouting than legitimate transfer of information via responsible journalism. And once the media found Eva's house on Olivia Street, its occupants became home-bound prisoners. The Key West P.D. was forced to partner with the Florida State Police to provide twenty-four-hour pro-tection on order from the governor, who was acting on request from the president.

Violence broke out more than once in Old Town. It was initiated by crazed Americans, otherwise patriotic, who wanted Teagarden in prison, or worse, because they wanted the past to stay where it was—*in the past*. More importantly, they wanted the past to stay—*what*—it was, which for them was conveniently tidy. It was the past they knew, and they didn't want to become acquainted with a different history.

When shots were fired at the Conch House on Olivia Street, the governor summoned the National Guard, which set up a three-block security perimeter around the house. Only year-round residents were allowed to pass what was quickly nicknamed in Key West fashion, "Checkpoint Closet Case," in honor of J. Edgar Hoover.

But the discord was not limited to Key West.

There were news reports of fights, marches, demonstra-tions and disorderly behavior across the country. The politics fell on both sides of the aisle. About forty or perhaps forty-five percent supported the idea of amnesty should any actual crime be determined on Teagarden's part, in exchange for knowing the truth. A slight majority of about forty-seven-percent wanted him arrested and prosecuted for high treason, crimes against the state and generally being a no-good, un-American SOB. Those who wanted him prosecuted faced crit-icism for having no knowledge of what information he actual-ly bore. Truthfully, no one did. People knew only what was leaked to the media, which merely hinted that Teagarden was purported to have proof that John Edgar Hoover led a secret life as a closet queen while simultaneously—allegedly—running a national police agency both racist and homophobic, and that he—allegedly—ran a secret domestic black-ops program whose crimes—allegedly—ranged from spying, blackmail, and murder, to assassination of a president, a presidential candidate and a beloved civil rights leader.

What a word, "allegedly." The media loved it. Every report used it a dozen times. Some on-air commentators said it four or five times a minute.

The national madness and the continuing danger to her father led Eva to the idea. She proposed it to Cynthia, who proposed it to House Speaker Alderman, who liked it for security reasons and for its sheer drama. The commander of the Naval Air Station at Boca Chica, however, did—*not*—like it. In fact, he walked to the gaggle of microphones at the air station's main entrance gate to say no and publicly scorned the proposal. But when he received an unexpected call from the Speaker of the House, he issued the order that was released to the media.

"Upon request of the Democratic House Speaker of the United States Congress, U.S. Navy Captain Eva Ghent will be allowed to remotely pilot an X-47 currently stationed at Key West civilian airport, to Washington, D.C., with her father on board.

"It being for the purpose of guaranteeing his safe delivery to the hearing of the House Homeland Security Subcommittee on Cybersecurity, Infrastructure and Security Technologies that convenes Wednesday on Capitol Hill."

"May I have another soda?"

"Sorry, Dad," his daughter's voice told him in the headset. "The X-47 doesn't have galley service. I'm sure they'll have lunch for you in Washington. Maybe a nice buffet."

"Lunch? I'll be lucky if they give me a bottle of water. Please just concentrate on your joystick, or game control or whatever you call it."

"Actually, you're already fully programmed. I haven't

touched any controls since you took off from Key West."

He didn't like the sound of that.

"Well, just keep looking at the computer screen or what-ever it is you normally look at."

"Will do, Dad. By the way, since you've been in the air, we've had a change of plans."

"Oh?"

"Yes. Instead of landing at Reagan National, you're going to land somewhere else. Somewhere safer because it's closer to Capitol Hill. It's what I wanted from the beginning. They just approved it."

Teagarden racked his brain, but could think of nothing.

"Dulles, Andrews and Baltimore are all *farther* from Capitol Hill than Reagan National," he said.

"Right, and you're not going to land at any of them either. Hang on, I've got to plot new coordinates. Give me a minute. I'll get right back to you."

CHAPTER ONE HUNDRED TWO

Washington, D.C.

The news flew as fast as the X-47.

It wasn't just broadcast and social media that spread the news, but rapid-fire word of mouth caused a crowd to quickly gather around Washington and along the National Mall. Offices emptied. Traffic stopped. From the Kennedy Center to RFK Memorial Stadium, people looked to the skies.

From her remote control station at Boca Chica Key, Captain Eva Ghent saw the gathered masses and opted to give them a show for her dad's arrival as a latter day Prometheus. She maneuvered the X-47 in a series of concentric circles that tightened with each subsequent loop. She circled the city, the Northwest quadrant, the Washington Monument. Finally, as arranged, she lined up for approach to land on East Capitol Street, the urban avenue leading to the front door of America's seat of government.

The crowd grew quiet as the sleek, triangular ship descended. The pavement had been rapidly closed to traffic. And it was plenty long, longer than the landing deck of the U.S.S. Ronald Reagan where this remotely piloted jet would be stationed when tapped for service in service to the U.S. Navy. As for width, that was no problem. The X-47 could be programmed to land in Times Square if need be.

It eased from the sky, nose toward the west, looking like a true spaceship bearing strange tidings for the people of Earth.

The wheels first touched down at the intersection of East Capitol and Third Street. Thousands of heads pivoted to watch it roll past Second Street, past the Supreme Court Building and the Library of Congress, past First Street and onto the Capitol grounds. Just beyond the visitor's center, its nose labeled *Little Bomber-Bot* turned ninety degrees to point due south and came to an easy stop at the east steps, the main entrance to the U.S. Capitol Rotunda.

Teagarden thought of making some sort of joke, perhaps asking, "Are we there yet?" But he didn't have time.

"There you go, Dad," his daughter said, as the gull wing doorway swooshed open. "Good luck at the House hearing."

"Thanks, sweetheart."

Outside, a rollaway ladder not being available, Capitol Hill police arranged for a power truck with a cherry picker bucket to help him egress from the X-47. Next to the truck was a limo, and next to the limo stood Cynthia, Sheriff Klumm and House Speaker Henry Wayne Alderman of Louisiana. Beyond them, long lines of Metro police officers stood at attention. A few days earlier, they wanted to shoot him down in the street. Now, he was the object of their protection.

He gently kissed Cynthia, who was on crutches, as she whispered, "I love you," into his ear. He shook hands with Sheriff Klumm, who said, "I apologize, sir." He shook hands with House Speaker Alderman, who gestured to the limo and said, "Here's our ride to the House hearing room in the Rayburn Office Building."

CHAPTER ONE HUNDRED THREE

Saturday, August 17, 2019
Bethel, NY

Classic rock blasted all week from just about everywhere.

It pulsated in earbuds, roared from old-fashioned boom boxes and speakers inside cars, houses, pitched tents and hundreds of camper trailers. Those who couldn't get a parking spot on or near hallowed ground settled for parking along Route 17B, the narrow highway that cut through the village of Bethel. It was a nationally watched event. And everywhere there were camera crews recording the three-day celebration of the fiftieth anniversary of the great Woodstock Music Festival. The TV anchors gave a blow-by-blow account of the past, cutting away to half-century-old film clips of the real event.

"Fifty years ago at this hour Arlo Guthrie was playing *Coming into Los Angeles....*" and, "Fifty years ago at—*this*—hour, Santana was playing *Soul Sacrifice...*"

Knowing her father was tiring of it, Eva turned off the television set at mid-morning, the third day of the golden anniversary. She also knew he'd turn it back on for the afternoon ballgame.

It was a great joy for Teagarden to have all the people he loved safely gathered under one roof, including Pangolin and Cynthia. The day was his fiftieth birthday and Marnie's third. Eva worked to make certain it was a happy one, starting with

377

breakfast where Marnie's granddad and her real dad showered her with pre-party presents and kisses before the real party, set for later in the evening.

Part of the day was set aside for tying up loose ends. He wrote letters of condolence to "the lost list." There was the Carney Family in Bethel; the Gelayeva family in Chechnya; Ms. Myrna Shelbourn in Arlington; the brother of Danford Shackton in D.C.; and finally to the Sloan family in Dayton, Ohio, where first cousins Scotty and Jimmy lived and attended college. It wasn't much, but until something better or more meaningful came along, it would have to do. He was bombarded with book and movie offers to tell the story of his ten days on the run. One respected publisher wanted to call it *American Prometheus*. A TV show suggested *Ten Days that Shook America's Soul*.

If he did eventually accept a book offer, he planned to share proceeds with the families who lost loved ones because of the national tragedy that exploded like a cancer decades after the behavior that caused the disease.

On the sundeck, he logged on to Dan Jones' e-mail, using the password "yellow4submarine" one last time:

From: sandyjones@orangecircle.com
To: danjones@orangecircle.com
Oh Dan, that's wonderful. We are so excited to hear the news. And I promise not to make judgments about your need to flee your home obligations.

May I make an appointment with Dr. Landman after your return, just to make certain everything is fine?

From: danjones@orangecircle.com
To: sandyjones@orangecircle.com
I have decided to make a trial reconciliation. But NO guilt about NYC, which I love and will return to in a heartbeat. Am arriving on Amtrak at Quincy Station on Saturday.

Surrounded by those he loved, Teagarden silently saluted Dan for going home to his family. He'd contemplated sending a full explanation for the mysterious piggy-back e-mail about Hollywood, German beer halls, drinking, smoking, Washington committee hearings, and all the rest. He changed his mind after seeing their effort to reconcile. Tendering the whole story could make things worse. Best to let them kiss and make up without tempting them to cash in on their fifteen minutes of fame.

Next up was Camp Summer Shevat.

His daughter and future son-in-law didn't want to fight the crowds, so they stayed home with Chopper to listen to the rock-and-roll celebration from the sundeck while Cynthia and Teagarden waded into the masses and neighboring woods. They walked toward the compound on Zabłudów Boulevard where he secretly downloaded the Dear John File on that second day of his "odyssey," as many in the news media were calling it. He knocked on the bungalow door.

"I don't think anyone's home," Cynthia said.

"What shall I do with this?" he asked, Torah in one hand, a clothes hanger dangling over the other shoulder. Inside the zipper bag was a new suit of Hasidic clothing, complete with tzitzit vest and prayer strings of the same large size as the one he'd stolen.

"The resident may not have returned since your visit," she said. "You could just leave it in the closet."

He checked the door. Unlocked.

She stayed on the rickety porch while he entered and hung the clothing bag inside the small wardrobe cabinet and put the replacement Torah on the bedside table. Cynthia may have been right about the occupant. He clearly hadn't returned. The two-room space had been ransacked. The furniture was upside down, the mattress ripped open. The old computer had been dismantled and the hard drive was missing.

It was like stumbling upon archeological evidence of Mc-

Canliss's work during a previous era. If the Coast Guard hadn't finally killed him with a drone, he'd now be facing criminal charges, along with his old boss Paula Trippler and two dozen others nobody ever heard of. It was happening primarily because of damaging testimony from Clyde Anderson Tolson's diary, and a man named Walter Natujay, recently retired from the FBI, who *The New York Times* identified as the whistle-blower code named Orpheus. Once he received full amnesty, Natujay confirmed every aspect of Teagarden's story.

"Okay, only one more thing to do," he said to Cynthia back on the porch of the bungalow.

On the way home, they stopped at the office of Sheriff Curt O. Klumm. He was out, maintaining order during the Woodstock anniversary celebration, as were all his deputies. His secretary, however, was in. So was a black Labrador named Missy, a ward of the sheriff's office who had a litter of six puppies just turned eight weeks old. They were confined to a big box in the back room beside the ancient Xerox machine.

Teagarden picked out two puppies, a blond and a chocolate, paying the secretary three hundred dollars for each with his newly issued MasterCard which, the secretary assured him, would be passed on to the local SPCA.

"What are you going to call them?" Cynthia asked as they walked home along hills celebrated as hallowed American ground, each carrying one of the squirming pups.

"Well, I plan to call the blond Coco-Too," he said. "He's my fiftieth birthday present to myself. But the name of this other little fellow will be up to Chopper, since he's going to be a present for her third birthday."

Halfway home, they stopped for Teagarden to point out the approximate location on the hillside where he was born in a makeshift tent while Country Joe called out his Fish Cheer and played "I Feel Like I'm Fixin' to Die Rag," for an audience of four hundred thousand.

"I was a preemie," he said. "Mom thought it was safe to go to the concert. Ha, little did she know that I'd be coming along during the show."

"Kind of like me," Cynthia said.

"How so?"

"Well, little did I know that you'd be coming into my life, too." She took his arm and leaned to him for a kiss. "Sam, my instincts about you were right. From the start, I knew you were a good and smart man. Now I know you're as honorable as they come."

He responded to her lips with tenderness.

During their embrace, rock music of the American past vibrated around the countryside. The words were mostly about love and sex, but occasionally there were lyrics about war, peace and truth.

ACKNOWLEDGMENTS

I am indebted to a number of people who assisted in reading and critiquing the manuscript as it evolved. They include Carol Pettis, my friend since fourth grade; Graham Smith, whose encouragement was particularly gratifying as he is a connoisseur of the genre; Penelope Ghartey; Jessica Broome; Stephen Weiss; Lisa Weiss, who read it a dozen times; and Barbara Shapiro who provided masterful copyediting guidance.

Many thanks to Eric Campbell and Lance Wright of Down & Out Books for shepherding the manuscript into print and ebook form.

Finally, to the Coen Brothers—call me.

Gray Basnight worked for almost three decades in New York City as a radio and television news producer, writer, editor, reporter, and newscaster. He lives in New York with his wife and a golden retriever, where he is now dedicated to writing fiction.

ww.GrayBasnight.com

On the following pages are a few
more great titles from the
Down & Out Books publishing family.

For a complete list of books and to
sign up for our newsletter,
go to DownAndOutBooks.com.

Tushhog
A Scotland Ross Novel
Jeffery Hess

Down & Out Books
May 2018
978-1-946502-60-5

It's 1981 in Fort Myers, Florida, where Scotland Ross squares off with a redneck clan, a Cuban gang, a connected crew from New York, and one friend who does him wrong.

Crimes of violence, drugs, and theft pale in comparison to the failure of self-restraint.

Tushhog is a story of compulsion, the types of people who take what isn't theirs, and the repercussions that follow.

Abnormal Man
Grant Jerkins

ABC Group Documentation,
an imprint of Down & Out Books
978-1-943402-39-7

Chaos? Or fate? What brought you here? Were the choices yours, or did something outside of you conspire to bring you to this place? Because out in the woods, in a box buried in the ground, there is a little girl who has no hope of seeing the moon tonight. The moon has forsaken her. Because of you.

Dead Guy in the Bathtub
Stories by Paul Greenberg

All Due Respect, an imprint of
Down & Out Books
March 2018
978-1-946502-87-2

Crime stories with a dark sense of humor and irony. These characters are on the edge and spiraling out of control. Bad situations become serious circumstances that double down on worst-case scenarios. A Lou Reed fan gets himself caught on the wild side. A couple goes on a short and deadly crime spree. A collector of debts collecting a little too much for himself. A vintage Elvis collection to lose your head over. A local high school legend with a well-endowed reputation comes home.

This debut collection is nothing but quick shots of crime fiction.

The Place of Refuge
Albert Tucher

Shotgun Honey, an imprint of
Down & Out Books
978-1-943402-61-8

Detective Errol Coutinho of the Hawaii County Police has a serial killer of prostitutes to catch and a shortage of leads to pursue. Office Jessie Hokoana of the Honolulu P.D. has an undercover assignment that tests her loyalties and takes her to the brink of death.

When their cases collide in the rainforest of the Big Island, family ties turn deadly, and there may be no *pu'uhonua*—no place of refuge—for anyone.

Made in the USA
Columbia, SC
02 April 2018